"I have no e~~~~ ~~~~ your virginal body."

Julia was not sure why his words filled her with such cold. "Then you are speaking of a marriage in appearance only?"

"Certainly. What else could possibly be between us?" Deverel asked.

"Nothing, of course," she answered. "Is that what you want—to tie yourself to a loveless marriage?"

"It's not a question of what I want. Or of what you want. It is a question of what we have to do. Or do you not believe that you have a certain duty to your family?"

"Of course I believe I have a duty to them."

She had sworn she could not marry the man who had ruined her brother—but had he really been responsible for that? Everything inside her quailed at the idea of facing a lifetime in a loveless, even antagonistic, marriage. Yet, she knew that to refuse to do it would be the act of a coward.

Julia looked Deverel squarely in the eyes. "All right," she said. "I will marry you."

"A smart, fun-filled romp."
　　　　　　　—*Publishers Weekly* on *Impetuous*

CANDACE CAMP

SWEPT AWAY

MIRA

ISBN 1-55166-508-5

SWEPT AWAY

Copyright © 1999 by Candace Camp.

Look us up on-line at: http://www.mirabooks.com

Printed in U.S.A.

Prologue

Julia pulled the cap low on her head, hiding her face in the shadow of the brim, and edged closer to the horse whose head she held. Every muscle in her body tensed, and her eyes were glued to the man strolling down the opposite side of the street. *It was Lord Stonehaven, all right.* She would recognize that arrogant, muscular stride anywhere.

The horse shifted nervously as her hand unconsciously tightened on the bridle. Julia ran a soothing hand down his neck. The last thing she wanted was to alert Stonehaven. *In just a few more steps they would have him.* Her eyes went involuntarily to the darkened doorway beyond her quarry. She could see no sign of Nunnelly or Jasper, even knowing that they were there. It was a well-recessed doorway; that was why they had chosen this particular spot for their ambush.

She waited, scarcely daring to breathe. In another moment they would have the man responsible for her brother's downfall. Lord Stonehaven took one step, then another. Suddenly, without a break in his stride, he stepped out into the street, bypassing the doorway. Julia clenched her teeth against the shriek of frustration that rose in her throat. *Damn the man! How did he always manage to thwart them?*

She knew it was over, the attempt failed like the other two times, even as the two men bolted out of the black doorway toward their quarry. Lord Stonehaven was simply too good a fighter for them to subdue him without the element of surprise. Nunnelly still had a welt across his forehead from their last attempt to prove it.

Stonehaven whirled as Nunnelly and Jasper charged, and he slammed his walking stick into Jasper's midsection. The young man doubled over, and Lord Stonehaven neatly sidestepped him and drove a fierce right uppercut into Nunnelly's jaw. The burly Nunnelly staggered back, dropping the sack that they had intended to pull over Lord Stonehaven's head. Nunnelly's feet got tangled up in the sack, and he fell to the street. Stonehaven reached down and grasped the man's jacket, hauling him up.

"All right, you!" Stonehaven's crisp voice carried clearly across the street. "I want some answers—now! What the devil do you mean, attacking me? This isn't the first time, either."

For an answer, Nunnelly swung at him, but Stonehaven stepped sharply back to avoid it, releasing Nunnelly. Jasper, still bent over from the earlier blow to his midsection, charged the man, but Stonehaven turned and brought his hand down hard on the young man's neck, sending him sprawling to the ground.

Julia knew she had to do something to help. But she was also aware of how little good she would do her men in a brawl with Stonehaven. If he could deck Nunnelly like that, he would send her flying. So she scrambled up the coach onto the driver's box, taking the reins in her hands. She slapped the reins noisily, then cracked the whip. Startled, the horses surged toward the men.

Even Lord Stonehaven jumped back at the sight of the coach and four barreling toward them. Nunnelly and Jasper scrambled to their feet and came running. Julia jerked the horses to a stop, knowing that Nunnelly would have a few choice things to say to her about her handling of his prize team, and the two men jumped inside. She slapped the reins again, and the carriage took off. To her surprise, Stonehaven ran after them, reaching up to grab hold of the bar the coachman used to climb up into the high seat. He jumped up onto the step. With his free hand, he reached toward the driver's box to pull himself up. Panicked, Julia whirled and kicked him hard in the chest. It was enough to break his grip. Stonehaven fell heavily to the street.

Julia risked a look back as the horses charged forward. Stonehaven was slowly rising to his feet, dusting himself off and cursing. She turned back around and devoted herself to controlling four spooked horses. It was not an easy task. Even planting her feet firmly on the floor and standing up to haul back on the reins, she had an uneasy moment when she thought that the horses were not going to respond. It felt as if her arms would be torn from their sockets. Then the lead horses shook their heads and slowed and gradually came to a halt.

Nunnelly erupted from the carriage below. "Jaysus, Mary and Joseph!" he exclaimed, his Irish accent thick in his excitement. "Now what did ye think ye were doin', Miss Julie?"

He ran to inspect his horses, running a calming hand over them and talking to them in the special low voice he reserved for his animals.

"I was saving your ungrateful skin, is what I was doing," Julia replied crisply, accustomed to the man's rough way of talking. She turned and looked behind her.

The street stretched emptily into darkness. They had left Lord Stonehaven far behind in the mad rush to escape.

"Sure, now, and it's glad I am you did," Nunnelly allowed. "But did ye have to spook the horses while ye were doin' it? Here, Jasper!" He swung toward his hapless assistant. "Come make yourself useful and take their heads whilst I get up atop. It's little enough you've done tonight so far."

The young man bristled at the words. "I didn't see you do aught better!"

"Hush, you two," Julia sighed. "We *all* failed."

"It's right ye are about that, miss," the coachman agreed glumly as he swung up into the seat beside her and took the reins. He nodded to Jasper, and the lad let go of the horses and ran to jump up on the step at the back of the carriage.

Nunnelly looked over at Julia in her lad's trousers, rough shirt and cap. "Thank the Lord he didn't make it up here, miss, or that would have been the end of all of us."

"Stonehaven wouldn't have recognized me," Julia replied confidently. "He's never seen me. That time he came to see Selby in the country was when Mama was so dreadfully sick, and I never ventured downstairs."

"That may be, miss, but your disguise wouldn't ha' lasted ten seconds, and he'd 'a' known ye were a colleen." He shook his head. "'Tis too dangerous, yer comin' with us like this."

"Where would you two have been tonight if I hadn't come?" Julia retorted. "Besides, it's my plan. I have to be here."

This was an argument they had had many times before, and Nunnelly knew he had no chance of winning it. Julia had always been the most headstrong person he'd ever known—man or woman—and she had been able to twist him around her little finger since she was a mere slip of a girl.

Nunnelly sighed and shook his head. "The truth of it is, Miss Julie, it don't look to be workin'."

Julia sighed. "I know, Nunnelly. You're right."

This was the third time they had attempted to seize Lord Stonehaven, and he had been too quick and too good for them every time.

"He's a fighter, miss, and a good one. I've heard he works out with the Gentleman himself." His voice deepened in awe as he mentioned the most renowned pugilist of the day, Gentleman Jackson. "It's strong, he is, and quick. Some of the gentlemen can box, ye see, but in a real fight, they're more useless than Jasper there. But this one—filthy poltroon though he is—he cuts a fine figure in a fight." He paused, then added thoughtfully, "There are some men I could get to help. Even he couldn't take on four or five of us and win."

"No," Julia responded quickly. "I don't want too many people to know about this. You and Jasper are different." Both Nunnelly and the groom had worked for her family for years. They couldn't have been more loyal if they had been actual members of the family. "But strangers…it would never do for word of this to leak out."

"No, miss," the coachman agreed fervently. He was silent for a moment as they drove through the dark streets of London. They were almost home when he cast a speculative look at Julia and began tentatively, "Maybe we should forget it, miss.…"

Julia whirled around, her eyes shooting fire. "What? Forget about Selby? Do you not care anymore about him? Do you not care if his name is cleared or if Gilbert has to live under the shadow of scandal all his life? Don't you care about getting the man who did it to him? Or are you scared?''

Stung, the coachman replied, ''There's no man alive can call Mike Nunnelly a coward, miss, and get away with it. And there's no call to be tellin' me I don't care about yer brother. It's jist that I'm thinkin' of you, Miss Julia. Maybe it's time ye did something else, time ye got on with your life, thought of marrying and babies and such....''

A lesser man would have quailed before the fierce light in Julia's eyes. ''Marriage? Babies?'' she replied scornfully. ''Are you saying that I should tend to my knitting and let men do the work? Besides, how do you think I shall get a husband with the world thinking my brother was a...a thief!'' Her eyes filled with angry tears.

''Now, don't ye go tryin' to change the subject on me. It's this plan we're talkin' about, not your brother, God rest his soul.'' The coachman crossed himself and continued. ''The fact is, we did our best, miss, and it didn't work. We've been here three weeks now, followin' him around, watchin' him go in and out, chasin' women and playin' cards and goin' to that club of his. Why, it's a miracle to catch the man alone. Always with friends or some fancy piece on his arms—which, beggin' your pardon, miss, you shouldn't even be seein'.''

''I know.'' Julia's expression turned thoughtful.

''Three times we've managed to take him by surprise and alone, and he's got clean away, every one. If we don't be usin' more men, then what're we to do? I ask you. It's suspicious he is now—did ye hear what he said to me? He knows it was us before, maybe not the first time—but some stranger tryin' to knock ye over the head

three times, it can't be jist bad luck. There's no sneakin'
up on him again.''

''I realize that. You are right. Obviously this plan isn't
going to work. But I am not going to give up. Not after
what he did to Selby.''

Three years earlier Julia's brother, Selby, had been
accused of stealing money from a trust fund of which
he was a trustee. The man who had accused him, and
who had proven to the world that Selby was guilty, was
Deverel Grey, Lord Stonehaven. Though Selby had insisted he was innocent, public opinion had been hard
against him. Indeed, the evidence had been compelling,
convincing almost everyone except Selby's wife and sister. In the end, Selby had shot himself while he was
alone at his hunting box. People had called it suicide
and taken it as further proof of his guilt. Even Phoebe,
his wife, thought he had killed himself, driven to it by
despair over his inability to make anyone believe him.
Only Julia had clung to the belief that the shooting had
been an accident, but she had placed the blame for his
carelessness on the despair and frustration he had felt.
The ultimate blame, she believed, lay with the man who
had hounded Selby to his death, Lord Stonehaven.

Julia turned to Nunnelly, her chin jutting out in the
stubborn way he knew so well. ''We will simply have
to come up with another plan.''

''Another plan?'' The coachman frowned. ''Have ye
hatched another one, then?'' The workings of Julia's
mind awed—and often alarmed—the stolid Irishman.

''Yes, one just came to me.''

''What is it, then?''

Julia glanced at the loyal servant. There was no way
that she could tell him the truth. ''Let's wait and see.''

Nunnelly grumbled at her answer, but Julia ignored

him, settling back in the high coachman's seat and contemplating the dark houses around them. It was a daring plan. But it was, she thought with swelling hope, a plan that could work.

They had been studying Lord Stonehaven for weeks now, and she knew his weaknesses. She would use those weaknesses against him, and this time she would succeed.

She would bring Lord Stonehaven down—by seducing him.

1

"Julia, no! Absolutely not!" Phoebe, Julia's petite blond sister-in-law, jumped to her feet at Julia's words, her hand flying to her chest as if to keep her heart from leaping right out of it. "You cannot. You must not. You don't know what you are saying!"

Julia sighed. She had known that Phoebe would react like this to the announcement of her new plan. Seduction was simply not something a well-bred young lady of 1811 set out to accomplish. "I *do* know what I'm saying. And I don't intend to actually sleep with the man."

Phoebe let out a strangled cry and sank back into her chair. "Julia!"

"I should think that would please you," Julia stated practically.

"Well, of course I don't want you to—to—you know—but, Julia, dear, you show such a want of propriety! To even speak of such a thing!" Her cheeks flamed at the thought.

"How else can I explain it to you?" Julia had little use for many of the conventions of Society. Because of her mother's long illness, she had not made her debut when she should have, and then there had been the tre-

mendous scandal around her brother, after which she and
Phoebe had been ostracized by the ton. So she had never
lived through a stifling London Season, her every word
and action examined and criticized by the leading lights
of the fashionable world. That, Phoebe was sure, was to
blame for Julia's lack of conventionality.

Julia knew that it went much further back. Her
mother, like Phoebe, had tried to instill ladylike behavior
in her daughter, but her sweet nature had never had the
iron necessary to win in a battle of wills with Julia. Both
her father and brother had doted on Julia, and they had
found her bright wit amusing and her courageous spirit
admirable. She had been allowed to express herself
freely, to study where her curious mind led her, and to
attempt whatever physical feat intrigued her. As a result,
she had a quick mind and an even quicker tongue, could
ride as if one with her horse, could hit a bull's-eye with
both firearm and arrow, and brimmed with a confidence
that few women of her age had. The best that her mother
had managed to do was to teach her manners, dancing
and the obligations of a lady. In public she had learned
to curb her tongue and control her actions, primarily so
that she would not cause her mother or Phoebe distress.

Phoebe moaned and sank her head in her hands. "Julia, you cannot do this. Selby would be furious with me
if he knew! I shouldn't have let you come to London. I
shouldn't have agreed to any of this. Your first plan was
bad enough—kidnapping Stonehaven and forcing him to
confess! But this…!''

"Phoebe, don't fail me now." Julia crossed the room
and knelt in front of the other woman's chair, taking
Phoebe's hands in hers. Phoebe was as dear and sweet
as a woman could be, and Julia understood why her
brother had loved her so much, but there were times

when Julia wished that her timid sister-in-law had a little more fire in her. "You mentioned the first plan. Remember how you worried and fretted over it? You were afraid that I would get hurt if I went along with Nunnelly and Jasper. You were afraid my reputation would be ruined."

Phoebe nodded. "Yes. I was cast into despair every time you went out!"

"But nothing happened, did it?" Julia continued. "I came back safely every time, even tonight, and Lord Stonehaven never had the least clue that the lad atop the coach was I."

"I know, and I thank the Lord for it."

"Then believe me when I tell you that nothing bad will come of this, either. I told you, I'm not about to let the man have his way with me. I'm simply talking about meeting him, flirting with him, leading him on a little. Encouraging him to talk about what he's done."

Phoebe gazed at her doubtfully. "Do you think that will work on a man like Lord Stonehaven?"

"I am certain of it. Look—" she sat down on the floor beside Phoebe's chair and eagerly explained "—there are two things I learned from following Lord Stonehaven these past three weeks. One was that taking him by force simply will not work. I did not know the man. I assumed that someone who did as foul a thing as he did to Selby would be too cowardly to even resist us. But physically he is strong and, I must admit, quite brave. He did not run from two men, instead he stayed and defeated them!" She could not keep a tinge of admiration from seeping into her voice. "Even tonight, when we were in the carriage and running away, he came after us—knowing that there were three of us. *But*—" she paused significantly "—the other thing that

I discovered about him is that Lord Stonehaven is very fond of women.''

''A roué?''

Julia shrugged. ''I don't know that I would go as far as that. He doesn't seem to pursue innocent maidens. I have only seen him with sophisticated ladies and, uh, well, women of a certain sort.''

''Oh, Julia…'' Phoebe moaned.

''But don't you see? That will work to our advantage!'' Julia cried. ''The man has a weakness, and it is women. That is why I realized that if I could get close to him, talk to him, I could worm the truth out of him. Why, you yourself have told me that it is when a man is pursuing a woman that he is most vulnerable, the most eager to please. Doesn't it follow that that is when he will be the most likely to tell me what I want to know?''

''I don't know.'' Phoebe looked uncertain. It seemed to her that Selby had been at his most vulnerable after they had made love, but she certainly could not reveal something like that to his sister!

''I have found with my suitors that they are amazingly eager to talk, especially about themselves and how clever they are and what great things they have done. They want to impress me. I suspect that Lord Stonehaven is the same way.''

''Perhaps so, but, Julia, I think that you are getting in over your head. You haven't even made your debut, and Lord Stonehaven is a wealthy man who has been on the town for some years. I am sure he is in his thirties.''

Julia raised her eyebrows and stood up, putting a hurt look on her face. ''Are you saying that you do not think I can attract a sophisticated man like Lord Stonehaven? That only those who live in a little town like Whitley are drawn to me?''

Her gentle sister-in-law looked horrified, as Julia had known she would, and she forgot her questions for a moment in a storm of anxiety. "Oh, no, I did not mean that! Dearest Julia, you must know that I would never think you could not attract any man you wish. You are the most beautiful woman I know. Not just in Kent—I am sure that if you had had a Season in London, you would have outshone all the other debutantes."

Julia smiled. She had not really had any qualms about her ability to attract a man, sophisticated or not. She had merely wanted to distract Phoebe from her worries. Julia Armiger had been assured that she was a beauty from the time she was old enough to toddle. The eager pursuit of her since she was sixteen by every gentleman within the vicinity of their country house had done nothing to disabuse her of the notion. Indeed, looking in the mirror each day was reassurance enough of that. Her figure was tall, slender and high-breasted, the perfect body for the high-waisted, soft, flowing styles that were currently popular. Her hair was a rich auburn, thick and inviting, and her eyes were a vibrant blue, accented by thick lashes. Everything about her face, from her creamy white complexion to the narrow arch of her dark brown brows to the sweet curve of her full lower lip, all combined to create a perfection that would perhaps have been cold if it had not been for the warmth of her smile and the pert little dimple that often creased her cheek.

Julia was not vain about her beauty. She accepted it as a fact, just as she accepted that she could handle a horse or read a book. Her beauty, she had found, meant a great deal more to others than it did to her. Indeed, there had been times when it had been a trial, when she had wished when conversing with a man that he could talk to her about something more interesting than the quality of her skin or the brightness of her eyes. It seemed to her that, in choosing a wife, it would be more important to find a pleasing personality such as Phoebe had than great beauty.

"Do you forgive me, dear Julia?" Phoebe asked with some anxiety, and Julia bent to give her a reassuring hug.

"Of course. I was merely teasing you. You have paid me compliments often enough to turn my head, I assure you."

Phoebe smiled and relaxed. "Good. What I meant to say was that Lord Stonehaven has had far more experience than you. I am sure that he will admire you the moment he sees you, but it is what he might do that worries me. You intend only to tease him, but he is a dangerous man. An unscrupulous one! Think what he did to Selby, who had been his friend for years. What if you arouse him, and he—he does not behave like a gentleman? What if he—" She lowered her voice. "What if he forces you?"

"I may not have made my Season, but I have had some experience with men. I do not think the ones in Kent are that different from other men. I have always been able to handle my suitors, including the one or two who made less-than-gentlemanly overtures to me."

Phoebe's eyes widened. "No! They did? Who?"

Julia chuckled. "Squire Buntwell, for one."

"Squire Buntwell! That old pudding!" Phoebe exclaimed indignantly. "What would he think a woman like you would want with him? Why, he's fifty if he's a day, and married, besides."

"I don't think he was overly concerned with what *I* wanted, only with what *he* wanted. Anyway, I made it clear to him that he should look elsewhere for his satisfaction.'' Julia's eyes twinkled with laughter as she recalled the incident.

"What did you do?"

"I stamped hard on his instep and punched him in that fat stomach. And while he was doubled over, trying to catch his breath, I told him that if he ever tried it again, I would tell his wife, the pastor and all the gossips in the county. He would be a laughingstock. I think he saw my point.''

Phoebe giggled. "I am sure he did. But I don't think that would necessarily work with a man like Stonehaven.''

"Perhaps not. However, I can carry Selby's detonator with me,'' Julia said, naming the small pocket-size pistol in her brother's collection. "I would think that a man's ardor decreases dramatically when he's staring down the barrel of a firearm.''

"Julia!'' Phoebe looked shocked, but could not keep from bursting into laughter.

At that moment they were interrupted by the tumultuous entrance of a six-year-old boy.

"Mama! Mama! Oh, Auntie, there you are. I was looking everywhere for you. Look what I got!'' He held out one grubby hand, palm up, to reveal a prize he knew would be far more appreciated by his aunt than his loving, but strangely squeamish, mother.

"A caterpillar!'' Julia cried, echoed somewhat less enthusiastically by Phoebe, and bent down to look at the prize in the boy's hand. "Wonderful, Gilbert! You didn't squash it a bit, either.''

Gilbert nodded proudly. "I know. I 'membered what you said, how the green juice was like blood to him, so I didn't squeeze him.''

"Good lad.''

"Could I keep him?" He looked over at his mother. "Please?"

Phoebe smiled at the boy. Sturdily built, he had an angelic face, with her own light blue eyes and sweet smile, but Selby's strong chin and jaw. A cloud of bright red-gold curls added to the illusion of a cherub. Phoebe, while she might not share her son's fondness for worms, snakes and caterpillars, rarely could deny him anything.

"Of course you can, sweetheart. Just make sure to put him in a container, though, or he might frighten the maids."

"Get Nurse to find a jar for you," Julia instructed. "And remember, put holes in the top, and a twig and some leaves inside for him."

Gilbert nodded and bounced out of the room to show his prize to his nurse. Phoebe looked after him with a sigh, her eyes filling with tears. Gilbert, only three years old when his father died, could not even remember Selby. "If only Selby had lived to see him grow up."

Her wistful words hardened Julia's resolve. "And he would have lived to see him—if Stonehaven had not hounded him to death. Phoebe, I have to make Stonehaven reveal the truth, don't you see?"

Phoebe nodded. "I know."

"If I do nothing, Gilbert will always have to live under the shadow of the scandal. He'll hear the whispers. People will turn away from him, refuse to meet him or issue him an invitation." She paused, not adding, "The way they have us." But Phoebe knew that truth as well as she.

The scandal surrounding Selby and his death had sealed Julia and Phoebe off from "polite society." Phoebe no longer went to London for the Season. Julia, who had not yet made her debut, had accepted that she never would. The blot on the family name was too great. Even in the small circle of their country acquaintances, there had been those who had cut them. Wherever they went, even church, they saw people whispering and staring. When they had moved to the Armiger London house a few weeks ago, more than one Society matron had looked the other way when she saw them. The memory of the ton was very long.

"No," Phoebe whispered fiercely. Normally sweet-tempered, a threat to her beloved child was enough to turn her into a fiery avenger. "That cannot happen to Gilbert. We must not let it." She looked up into her sister-in-law's vivid blue eyes, and her jaw hardened with determination. "You are right. I was being weak. Of course we must continue to try to prove Selby's innocence. You do what you must. Whatever it takes."

Julia grinned. "I knew you would stand firm, Phoebe." For all her gentle nature and her worries about impropriety, Phoebe alone out of everyone they knew had believed as firmly as Julia herself that Selby was innocent of the accusations and had been as determined to prove it.

Phoebe gave her a quick smile and picked up her sewing again. Then she stopped and looked up questioningly. "But, Julie, dear…how are you going to meet Lord Stonehaven? We don't go out in Society. Indeed, I am sure that we would not be received even if we tried."

"No. That is a problem." Julia did not deem it necessary to tell Phoebe that the kind of woman that she planned to be for Lord Stonehaven would not be one he would meet at Society fetes. It was better if Phoebe did not know quite *all* the details. "But I've been thinking— I believe I can get help from Cousin Geoffrey."

"Geoffrey Pemberton?" Phoebe's face cleared, and she smiled. "That's good. He is a most elegant gentleman, so courteous. I am sure he will know just what to do."

"No doubt." Julia did not tell her that she was not seeking her cousin's advice in the matter, merely his aid in executing her own scheme. She knew exactly how she intended to meet and interest Stonehaven. It was unfortunate that it required the help of some willing male. She was sure that Phoebe would have been alarmed to know that she was seeking out her cousin's help because he was the least shockable gentleman she knew, and also the laziest. If she kept after him long enough, Geoffrey would eventually give in rather than expend the effort of arguing.

"But, Julia, don't you think that Lord Stonehaven will be suspicious of your motives, no matter how he meets you? I mean, your being Selby's sister."

Julia smiled in a way that Phoebe found a little blood-chilling and said, "Ah, but, you see, I am not going to be me."

Julia found her cousin alone in his apartments later that afternoon. She had wisely waited until after three to give him time to awaken, eat and get properly dressed for the day, all three occupations that required a great deal of time. When his man ushered Julia into the drawing room, bowing and intoning her name, Cousin Geoffrey looked up at her with a startled stare that reminded her forcibly of a doe spotting a hunter.

"Cousin Julia!" he exclaimed, rising politely and casting a quick, nervous glance around. "What are you doing here?"

"No way to escape, Cuz," Julia responded cheerfully,

coming forward to offer her hand. "Please, sit down. Surely we needn't stand on ceremony."

"No. No, of course not. Escape, indeed!" He offered a faint laugh. "As if I did not enjoy your visits to the utmost."

Julia chuckled. "Don't lie to me, Cousin. I remember quite well when you told me that you found my visits wearing in the extreme."

Her cousin smiled languidly. He was a nice-looking man—a trifle plumpish around the waist, but he hid it well with waistcoats, and he boasted a nice turn of leg. Being related to them on their mother's side, he had escaped the red hair that plagued the Armigers. Selby had often despaired of his bright carrottop hair and easily burned white skin, but Geoffrey's hair was brown, as were his eyes, and he had a most charming smile. He dressed in the height of fashion, but never to the extremes, for he said that he found keeping up with the latest fads much too taxing. His taste was elegant, as Phoebe had said. His furnishings, like his clothes, were exquisite; his wines were always the best; and if there was a cook better than his, he would not rest until he had hunted him down—in his own lazy fashion, of course—and lured him away from his present employer. Being endowed with enough money to satisfy his expensive tastes and to ensure that he would never have to exert himself, he was a content man.

"My dearest Julia, you know that I am quite fond of you...."

"In your own way," she interjected, smiling.

"Yes, of course. While it is true that I am a little—shall we say, wary?—of these odd paroxysms of energy that seize you at times, in general you are one of my preferred relatives."

"Given the way you feel about most of your relatives, I am not sure how much of a compliment that is."

"I was taken aback, though, to find you visiting me here. For one thing, it isn't exactly *done,* you know, calling on a man in his bachelor quarters."

"What else should I do?" Julia replied pragmatically. "I wanted to see you."

"A little note dropped by to let me know you were in the city—that's the ticket. I was quite unaware of your presence, or I would have called."

Julia dismissed the niceties of proper behavior with a shrug. "Phoebe and I came up a few weeks ago."

"Ah, the fair Phoebe." Another smile creased his face. "How is that lovely creature?"

"As kind and sweet and motherly as ever. Not as sad, however. Time tempers all grief, I suppose."

"Yes. It is only kind, you know. Otherwise, I am sure that we would not be able to live."

"But neither she nor I have forgotten Selby."

"Of course not. It's not to be expected." He was watching her more warily now, sensing that they were arriving at the meat of Julia's quest.

"Nor have we forgiven those who drove him to his grave."

"My dear, you sound positively Greek. Whatever are you talking about?"

"I am talking about clearing my brother's name. I need your help to do it."

If she had not been so intent on her mission, Julia would have laughed at the horrified widening of Geoffrey's brown eyes.

"But, my dear cousin, you know I am not much good at this sort of thing."

"What sort of thing? You haven't even heard what I'm going to ask."

"I mean revenge and all that. Ferreting out clues, finding the guilty party."

"You won't have to do much," Julia assured him. "I just need you to get me inside one of the nicer gaming establishments. Madame Beauclaire's, to be exact."

Geoffrey's eyes now looked as if they might pop right out of his head. "Have you gone mad! A lady at a gambling hell!"

"I wouldn't call it a hell, would you? I know Selby used to go there, and he said it was quite a genteel establishment. He said that there were even ladies who attended."

"There are females there," Geoffrey admitted. "There are even sometimes a woman or two of the ton—but never one who is young and unmarried. Most of the women you would find there are, well, uh…"

"Loose?" Julia suggested.

"Really, Julia, you must stop these frank ways of yours if you are ever to get anywhere in Society."

"And *that*, dear cousin, is something we both know will never occur. Not after what happened to Selby."

He sighed. "I know. It's a terrible thing. I wish there were something I could do about it…." He shrugged eloquently.

"There is. You can escort me to Madame Beauclaire's. One cannot get in without an invitation, I've heard. I am sure that *you* would always have an invitation."

"Of course." He looked slightly offended that there could be any doubt about the matter. "However, I rarely go. Gambling is so taxing, I find. All that tension—the fear of losing, the excitement of winning. Just watching some of those poor devils is enough to tire me.'' When Julia said nothing, merely continued to watch him, he sighed and continued, ''What good will it do, anyway? How can your going to Madame Beauclaire's clear Selby's name?''

''Lord Stonehaven goes there—so I have heard.'' Julia refrained from mentioning that she had observed him entering the small, elegant house on three different occasions—twice with a beautiful woman on his arm. ''I need to speak with him.''

Geoffrey groaned. ''You're not going to confront Stonehaven in the middle of Madame Beauclaire's, are you? It wouldn't be at all the thing, you know.''

''I'm not that dead to propriety, Geoffrey. I don't intend to confront the man at all. I simply want to talk to him.''

''If you hope to persuade him that Selby didn't do it, I must warn you that I think it's a lost cause. The evidence was overwhelming—those letters Selby wrote, his using that name....''

The trust that Selby had been accused of stealing from had been set up for Thomas St. Leger, the son of one of Selby's friends. Walter St. Leger, the father, had died when he was only twenty-nine, leaving behind a widow, Pamela, and a young son. While the mother, of course, had the guardianship and care of the boy, the estate had been put into a trust until Thomas reached his majority, and Walter had named as trustees four of his friends: Sir Selby Armiger; Deverel Grey, Lord Stonehaven; Varian St. Leger, who was also his cousin; and Major Gordon Fitzmaurice. The fund was actually administered by an agent in London, who took care of the investments of the trust. The trustees' job was to oversee the boy's needs and to direct the agent to remit money to his mother as needed. In theory, any of the four trustees could order the disposition of the money, as long as the request was in writing and was co-signed by another of the trustees. In practice, it had been Selby who most often had made requests for the money, because his estate lay near Thomas's lands, and it was he who frequently saw the boy and who had the closest relationship with him.

Lord Stonehaven had grown suspicious when he learned that four large sums of money had been withdrawn from the trust within the space of a year, and that each of them had been sent not to Thomas St. Leger or his mother, but to a person named Jack Fletcher at a London address. A search had turned up no such person and no reason for money to be sent to him. The money had simply disappeared. All four letters requesting the transfer of funds had been written in Selby's hand and signed by him. They had been countersigned, of course: once by Varian St. Leger and three times by Major Fitzmaurice, but neither of the two men could recall the letters. The most damning thing had been the name Jack Fletcher. All the trustees had known that Jack Fletcher was a false name made up by Selby when they were all young men first sowing their wild oats. Upon being caught in some scrape or other at the university, Selby had always blamed it on Jack Fletcher. The name had become something of a joke with him; thereafter, whenever anything happened—an accident or a prank gone awry—he would laughingly say that Jack Fletcher must have done it. He had even gone so far as to invent a family history for the fictitious man and endow him with all sorts of bizarre characteristics and peculiar looks. The fact that the money had been sent to that name seemed an egregiously arrogant act on Selby's part, a mental thumbing of his nose at the world, and it was taken as proof positive that he had committed the crime.

"I know how damning it looked," Julia admitted. "It shows you how far the real thief went to make it look as if Selby were the one who had done it."

"But Selby's suicide..." Geoffrey said delicately. "Why would he have killed himself if he had not—"

"He didn't kill himself!" Julia snapped, whirling around to face him. Her eyes blazed, and she set her fists pugnaciously on her hips. "Selby had too much courage for that. He wouldn't have abandoned Phoebe and Gilbert to the scandal. Phoebe—well, I'm afraid Phoebe thinks that he did kill himself, that he was so upset over the fact that no one believed him that he put an end to it. But I am certain it was an accident. He was at his hunting lodge. He was probably cleaning his gun or—or loading it to go out and shoot, and it went off somehow. No doubt he was so distracted by worry and the feeling of being under suspicion that he was careless in a way he would not have been normally. His death was a direct result of Stonehaven's hounding him." She narrowed her eyes at her cousin. "Don't tell me that you are one of the ones who thought he was guilty."

"I don't know what to believe," her cousin replied honestly. "I would have said he was one of the most honest and trustworthy men I know. It seems inconceivable that he could have betrayed a trust like that. But the evidence—"

"Was faked!" Julia said flatly. "Someone very carefully set out to make sure that Selby was the one blamed for the disappearance of the money. That someone, I am convinced, was Deverel Grey."

"Lord Stonehaven?" Geoffrey goggled even more. "Really, Julia, if there's anyone more unlikely than

Selby to do such a thing, it is Stonehaven. I never met anyone who was such a stickler about honor and duty.''

"Lip service," Julia told him with an airy wave of her hand. "Phoebe and I have been thinking and talking about this for a long time. The culprit has to be Stonehaven. He discovered it, and he pursued it diligently.''

"Wait. I've lost the scent. If he had done it, surely he would have wanted to keep it secret.''

"Not when he had put so much time and effort into making it appear that another man had done the deed. He probably realized that someone, the agent or one of the other trustees, would soon begin to question the large expenditures. He had carefully established my brother as the criminal. So he exposed him to the world and whipped up public opinion against him. Selby didn't stand a chance after that of getting anyone to listen to him. The vigor with which Stonehaven pursued him fairly reeks of malice. Why would he have been so intent on destroying Selby if not for the fact that he was desperately trying to hide the fact that he was the real thief?'' Julia gave a decisive nod of her head to underscore her point.

"It does make a certain sense," Geoffrey agreed slowly.

"Of course it does! It had to be someone who knew a great deal about Selby and about the trust. It had to be someone with the opportunity to do those things. Since Phoebe and I *know* that it was not Selby, then it is obvious that the real culprit must be the one who worked so hard to lay the blame on Selby—Stonehaven.''

"But how? Why? Stonehaven is a very wealthy man, you know. He wouldn't need to steal money from St. Leger's trust.''

"So everyone thinks," Julia replied darkly. "Who really knows about another man's finances? Don't you see? That is precisely why I need to talk to Lord Stonehaven. I need to discover the reasons, the means."

"Do you think he will simply tell you?" Geoffrey assumed a falsetto voice. "'Oh, Lord Stonehaven, do tell, did you embezzle forty thousand pounds from young Thomas's trust?'" He lowered his voice to a gravelly pitch. "'Why, yes, dear lady, I did. I'm so sorry that you asked, for of course I could not lie.'"

Julia grimaced. "You know I'm capable of being much more deceptive than that. Maybe I won't be able to get him to confess, but surely I can get enough information out of him that I will be able to figure it out."

"How can you possibly deceive him when everyone knows you are Selby's sister?"

"Ah, but very few people in London know who I am. And, of course, I shall give Lord Stonehaven a false name."

"Of course," Geoffrey murmured. "I should have realized...."

"Please, Geoffrey..." Julia put on her most winsome expression. "Tell me that you will help me. Say you'll escort me to Madame Beauclaire's. That's all you will have to do. You don't have to stay with me or see me home or anything. I'll take care of all the rest."

"I can't just abandon you there. I shall have to escort you home."

"That's not much," Julia noted.

Geoffrey sighed. "You always make things sound so reasonable. So simple. Then they wind up an utter wasps' nest."

"It won't. Even if it does, I promise that I will not

involve you in it. I will never reveal that you were the one who got me inside.''

Geoffrey cocked one eyebrow at her. ''If I refuse, how long are you going to keep after me to do it?''

Julia gave him a dimpling smile and tilted her head to one side, pretending to weigh the thought. ''I'd say until the day I die.''

''I thought as much.'' He shook his head. ''I know I shall regret this. I shall probably end up either in gaol or fighting a duel. But I shall do it.''

Julia let out a little shriek and impulsively hugged him.

''Cousin, please,'' he protested. ''You'll wrinkle my cravat!''

''Sorry.'' She stepped back, still smiling. ''Tonight, then?''

''Tonight!'' He looked thunderstruck. ''My dear, at least give me a chance to prepare myself.''

''Pooh. There's no preparation necessary. It's better to strike while the iron's hot.'' She knew from following Stonehaven that it had been several days since he had gone to Madame Beauclaire's, so this evening seemed an opportune moment. However, she could hardly tell Geoffrey her reasoning.

''Where do you get such vulgar expressions?'' Geoffrey drawled. ''All right. You win. Tonight it will be.''

It took all Julia's and Phoebe's combined efforts to get her ready in time. She had decided to wear one of Phoebe's dresses, since a married woman's wardrobe allowed for a more flamboyant selection of color than the pastels and whites to which maidens were relegated. Though Phoebe's blond looks were not enhanced by some of the jewellike colors that flattered Julia's vivid

coloring, there were a few gowns of suitable appearance
and style, primarily one of a vivid peacock blue satin
that made Julia's blue eyes bright pools of color and also
was a perfect complement to her auburn hair and creamy
skin.

Since Phoebe was both shorter and rounder, the dress
required some creative work on the seams and hem. But
Phoebe was a fair hand with the needle, and the dress,
fortunately, was stylishly narrow, so there was not much
hem to lengthen. After Phoebe was through with it, Julia
took the dress to her room and quickly pulled out the
threads that held the ruffles of lace in place at the neckline, thereby lowering the neck of the dress to a level
that would have horrified Phoebe. An upswept hairdo
with artfully arranged wisps of curls gave her a stylish
but somewhat tousled look, which she thought would
surely make a man think of running his hands through
her hair. The newly redone dress, when she pulled it on
and fastened it, fit her like a glove. The high waist and
low neckline combined to cup and reveal her full breasts
to their best advantage, and the long, narrow skirt em-
phasized the slender length of her legs. Her cheeks were
flushed with excitement, and her eyes blazed. She had
not, she thought, ever looked better.

Julia suffered a brief qualm as she thought of the acting job that lay before her. She must convince a man
whom she despised that she was attracted to him. She
must also make him believe she was an experienced
woman of the world, fully capable not only of arousing
a man's desire, but also of fulfilling it, for if he thought
she was the well-bred young lady fresh from the country
that she really was, he would doubtless keep his passions
leashed, and that was the last thing she wanted. His desire must well up hot and strong, the kind of feeling that

could sweep a man into revealing far more than he normally would. Whatever she had told her cousin and Phoebe about merely talking to Lord Stonehaven, her real intention was to bring him so quiveringly close to the brink of mindless passion that he would reveal anything.

Prudently, she wrapped her cloak around her before she descended the stairs to meet Geoffrey. It would not do for either him or Phoebe to get a glimpse of how her dress actually looked. Geoffrey would probably not be as shocked as Phoebe would, but he was all too likely to pronounce that her attire was "not the thing" and refuse to take her until she changed. When she entered the drawing room, Phoebe, who had been chatting with Geoffrey, sprang to her feet.

"Julia! You look beautiful!"

"Egad, Cuz," Geoffrey added. "Indeed you do. I shall be the most envied man in the room tonight."

Julia favored him with a dazzling smile. Phoebe came forward to hug her and whisper a wish for good luck to her. Then Julia took Geoffrey's arm, and they left.

The carriage drive was not long, for which Julia was grateful. She could not keep her mind on the languid chitchat in which Geoffrey engaged. The knot of nerves in her stomach grew as they drew closer to the gaming house, and by the time they pulled up in front of the small, elegant structure, she was afraid she might disgrace herself and ruin everything by being sick.

She took Geoffrey's arm with an icy hand and walked up the steps to the house, hoping that she looked calm rather than terrified. Geoffrey was greeted with courteous familiarity at the door and quickly ushered inside. She felt the eyes of more than one occupant of the house turn toward her as they strolled in, but she was too busy gazing all around her at the strange atmosphere to pay attention to anything else.

It was a house like many others, decorated with no lack of taste or expense, with the difference that instead of couches and chairs and the usual things that filled the drawing room and dining room, the rooms opening off the entry were furnished with tables and chairs, all filled by men playing cards. There were only two women among the fifteen or twenty men she could see. One was a silver-haired woman with a fortune in jewelry around her neck and at her ears. Her eyes were fixed intently on the cards in her hand, and a feverish spot of red colored each cheek. The other female was a petite woman with improbably blond hair and an overly voluptuous figure stuffed into a gown designed for a sylph. Julia's first thought was that the woman looked vulgar, but she quickly reminded herself that she, too, was dressed in less-than-ladylike attire.

A servant came up to take her gloves and cloak. Julia dawdled over the tasks, reluctant to reveal her attire to Geoffrey, but fortunately, before she had to draw off her cloak, a friend of Geoffrey's hallooed at him from the next room. Geoffrey lifted his hand in a wave and smiled. He was as convivial as he was lazy, and Julia knew that he would spend the evening drinking and conversing with his friends in endless rounds of cards, and therefore, in his careless way, would probably lose all track of her.

"Ah, there is Cornbliss. I suppose I must go to him." He looked back at Julia. "Shall I introduce you? What is your name, by the by, or I shall make a shocking slip, I'm sure."

"Jessica," Julia answered quickly, having spent a good part of the afternoon cogitating on names and other matters of deception. ''That way, if either of us slips and starts to say my name, we can change it quickly.''

''Clever girl.''

''Jessica Murrow,'' she added. ''As for who I am, it doesn't matter.''

''I shall maintain an air of mystery, that's always handy when one doesn't know what one's doing.''

Julia smiled. ''Go join your friends. I shan't mind, and I don't need to be introduced.''

''If you are sure?''

Julia nodded. She had counted on Geoffrey's laziness and general unconcern to keep him out of her hair, and she was happy to see that she had been right. With a brief salute of his lips against the back of Julia's hand, he strolled away to join his compatriots. Relieved, she shrugged out of her cloak and handed it to the long-suffering footman who still stood waiting for her. Quickly she stepped into the room opposite the one her cousin had entered and moved out of sight of the wide doorway. Thus established, she took stock of her surroundings.

She had never before been in such an intensely masculine atmosphere. It must be, she thought, similar to a gentleman's club, that inner sanctum of masculinity from which all women were excluded. Smoke rose lazily from cigars and pipes without regard to feminine sensibilities. Snifters of brandy and glasses of port or wine sat on the tables beside them. The rumble of male voices filled the air, punctuated now and then by a bark of loud laughter. Julia suspected that she would hear things tonight that would make her blush.

She wandered through the room, then out the connecting doors into the larger room beyond. This, she realized, must be a small ballroom. Here, in addition to

the tables of cardplayers, were two tables centered by
the popular wheels of chance and another long table
where a game of dice had drawn the attention of a large
number of men. A woman in her forties stood beside
one of the players, seemingly observing the play, but
Julia noticed that her eyes were rarely fixed on the table.
Her gaze roamed the room with calm efficiency, taking
in everything without seeming sharp or inquisitive. She
smiled and nodded at one person or another who raised
a hand in greeting, and after a moment she moved away
from that table to another one. This woman, Julia decided, must be Madame Beauclaire herself, for she definitely had the air of someone in charge. Julia studied
her covertly, a little amazed to find that the mistress of
a gaming house moved and spoke with such an air of
gentility. Her dress of olive green crepe was less revealing than Julia's own, very much the sort of thing a
middle-aged Society matron would wear to a party, and
only a simple strand of pearls encircled her throat. She
wore only one or two rings, including a simple gold
wedding band, and a set of small diamond-and-pearl ear-
bobs danced in her earlobes.

Her gaze turned to Julia, and Julia knew that she was
summing up her clothes and manner in the first steps to
determining exactly who and what this stranger was.
When she looked straight at Julia, Julia favored her with
a small smile, then turned away—without haste—and
moved back out into the entry hall. A visit to the music
room across the hall, where a woman vainly battled the
noise with a number on the pianoforte, established that
Lord Stonehaven was not in the house.

Julia took out her nerves on the lace handkerchief she
carried, wringing it between her hands. What was she to
do if the man did not come tonight? Even if he came,

how would she occupy herself until that moment? She had felt the gazes of more than one interested man on her during her stroll through the rooms, and she felt sure that it would not be long before she began receiving invitations of a decidedly improper sort. The best thing, she thought, was to keep moving, and with that in mind, she turned and started across the hall back to the larger room. Just as she did, the front door opened, and she turned. The footman who had answered the door stepped aside with an obsequious bow.

Lord Stonehaven stepped into the hall.

Julia stopped short. Suddenly she could not breathe. Nor could she tear her eyes away from the figure standing at the other end of the hall. He was tall, with the wide shoulders and long, muscled legs of a sportsman. Elegantly attired in black evening wear, a starched cravat tied perfectly at his neck, he was the picture of a well-to-do gentleman. Diamond studs winked at his cuffs.

He looked up, and his eyes met hers. For a moment they were frozen in time, staring at each other. Stonehaven was, Julia had to admit, the most handsome man she had ever seen. Thick black hair, cut fashionably short, framed a square-jawed face of perfect proportions. His mouth was wide and mobile, his nose straight, and two black slashes of brows accented eyes as dark as his hair and sinfully long-lashed. A stubborn chin with a deep cleft and a small slash of a scar on his cheekbone gave his face a firmly masculine set.

Hate spurted up in Julia, hot and tasting of bile, and her heart pounded crazily. She detested this man with a fury that threatened to swamp her. And tonight she had to make him want her more than he had ever wanted any other woman.

2

Julia broke her paralysis and looked away from Stonehaven. Slowly, affecting an air of unconcern, she continued on her path into the large gaming room. Her heart was pounding like a drum, and it was all she could do to keep herself from turning to glance back at him. Was he still watching her? Would he follow?

She knew that she could not look, could not seem interested in him. Ever since she had come up with the idea of luring Lord Stonehaven into her feminine web, she had thought carefully about how to do it. He had been a friend of her brother's for years, albeit not one of his closest, and Selby had spoken of him now and then, usually in the context of some sort of sport—hunting, boxing, marksmanship. He was, she knew, a man who thrived on competition, who liked a challenge. So she had determined that the best way to attract his interest was to appear disinterested herself. Let him be the hunter. Let him come to her and try to win her favors—that was the way to fix his desire on her.

Still, it took all her willpower to refrain from looking. She strolled into the gaming room and down the length of it, moving as far from him as she could get. She paused behind a table of players and idly observed them for a few moments. She could not have said what they were playing, and she did not even notice the inviting smile that one of the men sent her way. All her attention, all her thoughts, were on the room behind her and the question of whether or not Lord Stonehaven had entered it. She was about to turn away toward another table when a masculine voice spoke behind her.

"Are you fond of piquet?"

A thrill shot down her nerves, but she made herself turn casually to look at the speaker. Lord Stonehaven was standing only a foot away from her, a smile that she could classify only as supercilious touching his mouth. He was watching her, his dark eyes faintly amused. He was even more handsome up close, she thought, the sort of man who would set young women to giggling and smirking. Julia, however, had no desire to do either one; the urge she felt rushing up inside her was a strong desire to launch into him, fists flying. *This man had ruined her brother!* Her anger was so deep and bitter, she could almost taste it. It was going to require all her self-possession, she realized, to pretend to calm indifference.

"Were you addressing me, sir?" she asked in as cool a voice as she could muster.

"Why, yes, I was." The amusement in his eyes deepened. "Sorry—I realize that we are not acquainted, but I presumed upon a common interest." He made a vague gesture toward the room.

"Indeed." Julia gave him a small smile, letting a hint of the dimple appear in her cheek. She had, after all, to give him some encouragement even as she pretended to elude him.

He returned the smile, and Julia felt her stomach turn a little flip. Who would have thought that a man such as he could have so much warmth in his eyes? She glanced away quickly, then worried that she had been too demure for the part she was playing.

"Have you played here before?" he asked, and she turned her attention back to him. "I have not seen you."

"No. This is my first evening here. I came with a friend."

"A good friend?" he asked in a slow, rich voice, and she realized that he was subtly asking if she was some other man's mistress.

"No," she replied, hoping that her cheeks did not betray her by reddening. "Not a *good* friend."

"How nice for me. Then I am hopeful he will not mind if I get you a glass of punch."

"It does not matter. You see, it is *I* you must ask about such things, not any man."

He grinned, his eyes twinkling. "Ah. An independent woman, I see."

"Indeed I am."

"Then may I escort you to the refreshment tables?" He offered her his arm.

She slipped her hand into the crook of his elbow. "That would be very nice."

There was something quite freeing about acting this way, Julia thought as she walked with him into the hall. She had never before in her life been in a place like this, where there were no matrons watching, no expectations on everyone's part of how a young woman should act and what she should say. Though Julia considered herself a free thinker, she had been raised to act as a young lady should, and she had always been aware of the need to act in such a way as not to bring any embarrassment to her family.

Like any other young woman, she was careful not to

dance more than twice with the same man and not to flirt too much with any one man, lest she be said to be forward. She had always to pay her respects to the old ladies who lined the walls at the county cotillions, looking like a group of well-fed buzzards in their invariably black dresses, and to be careful not to say something to offend them. If a man wanted to escort her down to dine at a ball, he had first to request permission of her chaperon. These were the sorts of restrictions that chafed at her, but which she knew she could not flout without bringing down local censure not only on herself but on poor Phoebe, and before that her mother, for their perceived laxity in training her.

But here there were no duennas, no women who could enumerate her family lineage back to Queen Elizabeth, if not beyond. There was no one to gossip or to care how she acted, no conventions to flout. No one even knew who she was, so her family name could not be called into shame. There was not the least likelihood that anyone would be shocked by her behavior, unless perhaps she decided to take it into her head to get up on a table and remove all her clothes—and from what she had seen of many of the avid cardplayers here tonight, most of them would be concerned only because she was wasting one of their card tables. She could, she thought, say exactly what she wanted and act precisely how she pleased, and no one would give it a second thought.

''I hope your thoughts concern me,'' her companion said, and Julia turned to look at him, startled.

''What?''

''Your smile was one of such happiness, I was hopeful that I figured in your thoughts.''

''Oh.'' Julia chuckled. ''Now you have me, sir, for if

I say they were of you, then I am over bold, and if I say they were not, I am insulting.''

''I suspect that you are a woman who does not care particularly if either is said of you.''

Julia gave him an enigmatic smile. ''I would say that would depend on who was speaking.''

''Ah. Well, I am not so foolishly brave as to ask whether I would be one whose opinion would matter to you.'' They had reached the rear-most room of the first floor, where a long sideboard held not only a punch bowl but a number of platters of cheeses, meats, breads and cakes. ''No, pray, do not answer. Tell me instead what to put on your plate.''

He picked up a glass plate and began to fill it with various delicacies, though Julia doubted that her nerves would allow her to eat much, if any, of them. She would have protested that she did not want to eat, but she knew that being alone with him in the dining area was far better for her purposes than returning to the card rooms. Once he had filled two plates and added cups of punch to them, Stonehaven led her back into the entryway and up the stairs to the second floor. Julia followed him, surprised.

''But where are we going?''

''Only a quieter place to talk and eat.'' He gestured toward a low velvet sofa against the wall at the side of the stairs. A potted palm shielded it partially from view, and it offered a comfortable, quiet place to sit.

Julia sat down, taking her plate, and he sat down beside her, much closer than was proper. It was odd to have a strange man this close to her. She was very aware of the heat of his body, the breadth of his shoulders, the faint scent of his masculine cologne. She had never thought about his *smelling* this good, she thought. Impatiently, she called back her errant thoughts; she had to concentrate on her purpose.

"Are there gaming rooms up here?" she asked, more to keep her thoughts on track than to satisfy any real curiosity.

"Yes, these rooms are where you find those who like to dip deep." He gestured toward the two closed doors that lay in front of the stairs. "That room over there, where the door is open, is simply a sort of sitting room, where one can pause to collect oneself between games. I don't believe that I have ever seen anyone in it."

"The gamesters here do seem preoccupied with their cards," Julia admitted, taking a bit of cheese on a cracker and finding it quite tasty. Perhaps she was hungrier than she had thought.

"Mmm-hmm."

Julia glanced at him. He was watching her eat, his own food untouched on the plate, and the heat in his eyes sent a shiver straight through her. His gaze slid down from her mouth, taking in the long curve of her white throat, and came to rest upon the swell of her breasts above the dress. Julia resisted the impulse to tug the dress higher. She had more than once surprised a hot, secret look on the face of one of her admirers, but none of them had ever looked at her like this—as if they had a right to do so, as if they were picturing her without any clothes on at all. And certainly none of their love-struck gazes had ever made her feel this strange combination of shivers and heat inside.

She swallowed hard, unsure how to respond. She tried to think what a woman of the sort she was playing would do, but her mind was curiously sluggish. He reached over and ran his forefinger down her cheek and across her jawline to her chin.

"You are a beautiful woman."

"Th-thank you." His skin felt like fire upon hers, and Julia had the sudden, awful feeling that she was in over her head.

"I noticed you as soon as I walked in."

"Indeed?" Now his finger was tracing the line of her throat down to the ridge of her collarbone.

"Indeed. I believe you noticed me, too. Am I right?"

"I saw you, yes." Julia struggled to pull her thoughts together. She could not let herself be distracted. She had achieved her goal of catching Lord Stonehaven's interest. Now she had to use it to her advantage. She could not sit here like a mannequin, saying only yes and no.

What would a woman such as she was supposed to be do? A crafty, experienced sort. The first thing, she thought, was that she had to be in control. It would never do to let a man like Stonehaven think that he could win this easily, that he could disturb her thoughts or monopolize her time or expect her to give in to him. For one thing, she suspected that he would lose interest more quickly. For another, it was essential for her purposes that she retain control of the situation.

Accordingly, she slid as far to the side of the sofa as she could, moving away from his hand, and whipped open the furled fan she carried. She wafted it a time or two in front of her, looking at him across the top.

"Or, at least," she continued in as bored a voice as she could muster, "I believe that it was you. I barely glanced at the door, you see."

"I see." Oddly enough, he seemed amused by her answer. Julia decided that she had made the right move. He must be pleased that she was planning to provide him with something of a chase. No doubt, with his looks and wealth, women fell all too easily at his feet.

She stood up. "Thank you for showing me about a little and for getting me a plate of food. I confess I was feeling a trifle peckish. Now I am ready to return to the tables."

"Of course." He rose, too and, taking her half-finished plate from her, set both their dishes down on the small occasional table nearby. "Allow me to escort you to a table. What is your game? I believe you were observing a table of piquet."

"Actually, I am most fond of loo," she replied. "Do you play, Mr.— I am sorry, I am afraid that I don't know your name. Most improper, I'm sure, to be conversing with you, not even knowing your name." She cast up a twinkling sideways glance at him, as though to say that improper behavior was not unknown to her.

"Deverel Grey, ma'am. And yours?"

She was so startled at his calling himself by his name and not his title that she forgot for an instant what name she had chosen for herself. "What? Oh, excuse me..." She affected a little chuckle. "I fear my mind was wandering." She hoped he would be piqued by her inattention, not suspicious that she was making up a name. "Jessica Nunnelly." She knew that she had said the wrong last name, but it had been the only thing she could think of. A moment afterward she remembered that she had told her cousin that she would use Murrow. Ah, well, hopefully Geoffrey and Lord Stonehaven would never discuss the matter.

She took his arm, and they went downstairs. She was somewhat uncertain of his interest when he left her and chose to play at a game in the smaller connecting room, but she was reassured when she saw that he had taken a seat from which he had a direct line of sight of her. More than once, as she played, she felt his gaze upon her. It was a little difficult to keep her mind on her cards. She had never in her life played with a table of only men, let alone for stakes as high as these. Nor was she accustomed to hearing men talk with little regard for her presence. She lost, but, then, she had expected to do so; she had brought an ample amount of money with her. It was more of a problem dealing with one or two of the men, who behaved with a freedom and familiarity that she was not accustomed to. In retrospect, she was faintly surprised to realize that Lord Stonehaven had acted with a great deal more gentility.

Why had he not used his title? Was he afraid that it would make her chase him for his money? It was possible, she supposed, that he was displaying a certain modesty, even courtesy, so that a low-born sort such as she must appear to be would not be intimidated by his stature—but that seemed unlikely. He was far too arrogant a man for something like that.

She grew tired of playing cards, and her nerves were beginning to fray. Julia decided that it was time for her to leave. It was a gamble, for once she was gone, he might forget her, but she was hoping that her departure would, instead, leave him wanting more. If nothing else, it should demonstrate to him that she was not overly interested in him, that she did not care to stay to see if he would talk to her again. She scribbled a note to Cousin Geoffrey, saying that she was taking a hackney home and not to worry about her, and gave it to one of the waiters to take to him in the other room.

Then she rose to her feet, saying, "I am sorry, gentlemen, I fear I am somewhat tired. I believe I will call it a night."

It had not occurred to her that one of the other players, a man who had directed several overly warm comments to her tonight, would rise, also. "Allow me to escort you home, ma'am."

Julia shook her head quickly. "No, thank you. That won't be necessary, although it was most kind of you to offer."

She turned away dismissively and started toward the door, but her admirer did not take the hint. He followed her, saying, "You must allow me to. It is not safe for a woman alone on the streets this late."

"I shall take a hackney," Julia countered. "Please stay and enjoy your game."

"There is other game that I find much more interesting," he said with a wolfish grin.

Julia did not reply, merely turned away coolly and asked the footman to fetch her cloak and gloves. She had to wait for the footman to return from the cloakroom with her things, and her suitor waited with her. Would this importunate fellow follow her into the street?

When the footman returned with her cloak and held it out for her, the man seized it and held it up for her. Julia cast him a freezing look. There was a movement behind her, and as she turned to see what it was, a male voice said, "Sorry, sir, the lady is already committed to me for escort home."

She looked up into Stonehaven's face. He was gazing at the other man with a cold stare, his hands outstretched to take the cloak. For a moment her swain did not move, his face set in obdurate lines. Then, with ill grace, he handed over the cloak to his rival.

"Of course, Lord Stonehaven," he said with a trace of bitterness. "I did not realize that this bird of paradise belonged to you."

Julia could not suppress a gasp of astonished anger. Stonehaven's jaw tightened.

"Since she is a woman," Stonehaven said, "not a cat or a piece of jewelry, I would hardly say that she 'belongs' to me. However, Miss Nunnelly has favored me by allowing me to take her home this evening."

"Of course. Women of her sort always prefer a greater income."

"I shall choose to ignore that insult this time," Stonehaven said in clipped tones. "However, if you offer another to me or to Miss Nunnelly, you shall find that I am not so lenient."

Stonehaven turned without waiting for a reply and draped the cloak around Julia's shoulders.

"Thank you." Julia kept her voice cool and calm. She was not about to let it show that the man's insult had jolted her. Instead she turned toward the persistent suitor and said, "I think you will find that what women of any station prefer is *courtesy*."

She swung around, taking her gloves from the footman, and walked out the door, which the footman jumped to open for her. She heard Lord Stonehaven's chuckle behind her as he followed her, pulling on his own gloves.

"A wicked riposte, Miss Nunnelly."

"And quite true, my lord." She was glad that the obnoxious fellow, for all his other faults, had at least spoken Stonehaven's title. Now she would not have to worry about slipping up. "I wonder how it was that the plain Mr. Grey became Lord Stonehaven."

"I was Mr. Grey a number of years before I was Stonehaven," he replied easily, coming up beside her and taking her elbow in his hand. "Though I do hope that no one referred to me as *plain* Mr. Grey."

Julia could not hold back a smile at his words. "I am sure that they did not, my lord."

"It was precisely for that reason that I said nothing about Stonehaven—to avoid all this 'my lord'-ing. My friends call me Deverel, or Dev."

"I would not think we have known each other long enough to count as friends."

"But surely rescuing you from that fellow should make you deem me a friend."

Julia glanced up to find him smiling down at her. It had never occurred to her that her nemesis would possess a charming manner or a smile that made her feel a trifle weak in the knees. He was dangerous in more ways than one, she realized with a start. She would have to watch out for him.

"Still, it seems presumptuous for a woman like me to call a lord by his Christian name."

"Even if I give you permission? Perhaps we could exchange the favor, and I could call you Jessica."

"Ah, but then, I fear, you would find me bold."

"Some men appreciate boldness."

"Are you such a man?" She gave him a challenging, provocative look, feeling once again the curious elation at the freedom she was experiencing as a "shady" woman.

"I think it would depend upon who the woman was." The look in his eyes clearly indicated that she was one of those women whom he would appreciate.

Again Julia felt a strange lurch in her stomach, and she quickly glanced away. Looking around the quiet street, she said, "No hackneys. I had hoped to find one."

"You must allow me to take you home."

"Oh, no," Julia answered hastily. That would never do. He might not know that her house had been the home of the Armiger family for the past hundred and fifty years, but he would certainly know that it was not the sort of house in which a woman of her supposed type lived. "It's not necessary."

"I insist."

Julia stopped dead still and gave him a pugnacious look. "And I refuse."

He stared at her for a moment, nonplussed, then laughed. "My dear Miss Nunnelly, you are one of a kind. And to think I almost did not come tonight—it is enough to give one the shivers! A hackney it shall be. But I think we will have better luck if we turn up and go over a street or two." He steered her across the street and up a narrow side lane.

Julia strolled along beside him, uncertain as to exactly what she should do to make things go as she wished. There was something quite unnerving about his physical presence—the nearness of his body and its latent strength, the warmth and firmness of his fingers upon her arm—yet at the same time it was exciting. She supposed it was the excitement of the game: pitting her wits against his, the lure of winning, the fear of exposure. Whatever it was, she had been unprepared for the exhilaration she felt.

Stonehaven's steps slowed as they neared the next, busier street, and Julia glanced up at him questioningly. He came to a halt, turning to face her. His hands went to her waist and pulled her closer. Julia's breath caught in her throat; suddenly her heart was thundering. Reflexively, she brought her hands up to his chest as though to hold him off, but there was no strength in her hands. She could feel the heat of his body even through his clothes, the steady thrum of his heart.

"I think you are the most beautiful woman I have ever seen," he said in a low voice.

She wanted to return a quip, but the words stuck in

her throat. His face loomed closer, filling her vision. Then his lips were on hers, hot and soft, pressing against her, opening her mouth. Julia stiffened in surprise as his tongue swept inside her mouth. None of her suitors' kisses had prepared her for anything like this. Fire sizzled along her nerves and slammed into her abdomen. Her muscles suddenly turned to wax. His arms went around her tightly, pulling her into him. His body was amazingly hard against her own softness, all bone and sinew, and the difference was thrilling. His mouth possessed her, taking ownership; his hand cupped her bottom and pressed her into him. She could feel him throbbing against her and the insistent pressure of his fingertips digging into the soft flesh of her buttocks.

Julia's whole body trembled under the storm of sensation, and all she could do was curl her fingers into his lapels and hold on for dear life. He made a sound of male satisfaction deep in his throat as he felt the heat surge through her body.

Finally he lifted his head and looked down at her, his dark eyes glittering fiercely. "Jessica..."

Desire slammed through Stonehaven like a fist at the sight of her face, soft and glowing. She had the dazed look of a woman who had just discovered passion, and though his mind knew that it must be artifice, for she was obviously a woman accustomed to men, his body responded to the lure. She was, indeed, incredibly beautiful, and he had wanted her from the moment he saw her, but now the need to have her was fierce, undeniable. He would not be at ease again, he knew, until this bewitching creature was in his bed, turning into fire beneath his hands and mouth.

Julia saw the heavy passion in his face, the sudden, unmistakable determination to have her. It was what she had wanted to arouse in him, but the reality of it sent a thrill of unease through her. For the first time doubt assailed her: What if she could not control this situation? What if she could not leash and use the need that raged in him?

The sudden trepidation was enough to cut through the fog that had seemed to possess her mind. She stepped back abruptly, one hand going to her stomach as if to still the tumult inside her.

"No." He reached for her, but she quickly moved another step, and he stopped. "Don't go. Stay with me."

"I cannot." She glanced wildly up the street and saw, like a gift of fate, a hackney rolling slowly along the cross street. She lifted her hand and waved, calling out.

The driver on his high perch peered down the street toward them and obligingly stopped. Julia started toward it, but Stonehaven laid a hand on her arm, stopping her.

"No, do not go yet."

"I must."

"Let us just walk a little longer."

She arched her brows. "I know where your 'walking' leads, my lord."

"Is that so bad a thing?" he countered softly. "You did not seem to think so a moment ago."

"I am not a prize so easily won," she responded. "I fear you will find me cheap."

"Never."

She shook her head and started to pull away. His fingers tightened.

"At least give me your address, so that I may—"

"I cannot."

"Why? Have you a husband at home?" Anger roughened his voice.

"No. Please, just let it be."

"But how will I find you? When will I see you again?"

She looked up at him. His face was hard and fierce, as if the hunger in him had peeled back the layer of easy charm and exposed the powerful reality beneath. His words were not so much a question as a demand.

Julia willed a saucy smile onto her face. She felt as if she were baiting a bear. "I am quite partial to gaming, as you know."

Then she tugged away and, lifting her skirts to her ankles, ran toward the waiting carriage.

3

"Weren't you scared?" Phoebe asked, leaning forward to peer into Julia's face as they walked. They were taking their usual morning constitutional through Hyde Park, and Julia had given her sister-in-law a carefully expurgated account of what had happened the night before when she met Lord Stonehaven. "I can't imagine talking to him. Was he purely evil?"

"Well, no," Julia admitted. "He was rather charming, actually. It makes sense, of course, when you think about it. If he were obviously wicked, people would have realized that he was lying about Selby. But because he seems gentlemanly and engaging, one assumes he is telling the truth, that he has pure motives."

"Mmm. I suppose so." Phoebe looked disappointed. "I guess I had begun to picture him wearing horns and a tail."

Julia smiled. "Me, too. But you have met him, have you not?"

"A few times. He and Selby were not close friends, not as Selby was with Varian, say, or Fitz," she said, naming the other two men who had been trustees of Thomas St. Leger's trust, along with Selby and Lord

Stonehaven. "They had been friends when they were younger, and, of course, they met at their club and parties. But those last few years, Selby spent most of his time at home, you know."

That fact, Julia knew, had been because of Phoebe. Selby had been a little wild in his youth—not only playing pranks such as the ones he had attributed to Jack Fletcher, but also gambling and drinking too much. But after he fell in love with Phoebe, his life had changed. He had settled down at home in Kent, and had become much more serious and attentive to the business matters of the estate. Selby would travel to London sometimes on his own, and occasionally he and Phoebe would go up for a round of parties and such, but, especially after the birth of their son, they lived a quiet country life. Unfortunately, it had been Selby's wilder, younger times that people had remembered when Stonehaven had accused him of thievery.

"Stonehaven was pleasant enough," Phoebe continued, her brow wrinkling. "A little remote and stiff, I thought. We never talked long. I always thought he found me boring."

"Nonsense," Julia replied stoutly, although she could understand, deep inside, how some could find Phoebe's sweet personality a trifle insipid. "If he did, then it was he who was to blame, not you."

"I was always glad when he moved on to talk to someone else. He made me a trifle...uncomfortable."

Stonehaven had made *her* a trifle uncomfortable, too, Julia thought, but not, she suspected, in the way he had affected Phoebe. He had unsettled her, brought out strange responses that both puzzled and surprised her. No one had ever kissed her the way Lord Stonehaven had last night—one of the things she had been careful to not tell Phoebe—and the way she had felt when he did so shocked her. Her body had raged with all sorts of wild sensations, and she had wanted, shockingly, to feel more of them. Julia wondered if that made her a wicked person. Was that how "loose" women felt? And was it those feelings that made them abandon all propriety?

What was most disturbing to her was that she had felt those things with Lord Stonehaven. *She hated him!* Yet when he kissed her, when he crushed her body against his and his mouth consumed her, she had melted. How could a man she despised have made her feel that way?

The only answer she could find was that it was the kiss, not the man, that had made her react so strangely. She had not felt such a kiss before; gentlemen didn't kiss that way, or at least they did not kiss ladies like that. No doubt it was part of the licentious life Lord Stonehaven lived, sinful knowledge that he had gained with women of dubious repute. It was probably the very sinfulness of the kiss that had rocked her. Their vicar, in his sermons, often warned of the temptations of sin, of the lure that evil held for humans. Julia had not really understood it before, but now she did. That kiss had tempted her, had made her feel and act in a way she would never have dreamed she could, had overridden, at least for a moment, her thorough dislike of Lord Stonehaven. She supposed that if any other man had kissed her in that way, she would have felt the same. She had a tendency toward lewd behavior, apparently.

Well, she knew now what she had to watch out for, Julia thought. Next time she would be prepared for that kiss, and she would stand firm against it. She would not let herself be swept into such a maelstrom of pleasure.

"Will you see him again?" Phoebe asked now.

"Oh, yes," Julia responded quickly. "I mean, well, I shall have to, of course. Last night was just the beginning. I wanted to catch his interest, that was all. I didn't expect to gain any knowledge. It will take a little while to get my hooks firmly into him, and then I will begin to reel him in."

Phoebe giggled. "Honestly, Julia, you do say the funniest things. You make him sound as if he were a fish."

"Well, and so he is," Julia responded. "A prize fish, whom I intend to hang on our wall."

"Are you—will you go back to that place?"

"I shall have to. I have no other way to meet him. Naturally I couldn't tell him where we live."

"Oh, no," Phoebe agreed with a little gasp of horror. "When will you go back? Tonight?"

"No," Julia replied reluctantly. She wanted very much to return to Madame Beauclaire's tonight—only because she was filled with eagerness to get the truth out of Stonehaven, she told herself—but she knew that to do so would ultimately work against her. "I cannot let him think that I am eager to see him again. Men like a chase, I understand, and Stonehaven seems to me to be a man who likes it particularly. I have to build up his anticipation, make him begin to worry that he will not see me again. Then, when he does see me, he will be much more enthusiastic."

Phoebe nodded. "I'm sure you are right. I am merely impatient. I want so much to hear his confession."

"I think I shall return on Friday. That will give him two days to stew and wonder. How does that sound?"

"I don't know. I was never much good at that sort of game. The only man I cared about was Selby, and I wanted to see him so much that I could not pretend otherwise."

Julia smiled at Phoebe's slightly guilty expression and reached out to link her arm through hers. "'Tis just that you are too honest and good a person to prevaricate, my love. It rather makes you wonder about me, doesn't it— that I find it so easy to do so?"

"Julia! Don't say such things!" Phoebe would never allow any negative words about one of those she loved, even from the loved one herself.

"Lady Armiger!" A man's delighted voice came from the left of them. Phoebe and Julia turned to see a man and woman walking toward them. The man was smiling delightedly. The woman looked frozen in stone. "Miss Armiger," the man continued. "How wonderful to see you. I had no idea that you were in town."

"Varian." Phoebe smiled, holding out her hand. "How good it is to see you. But how can it be that we have become Lady Armiger and Miss Armiger, when before we were Phoebe and Julia with you?"

Varian St. Leger had been a good friend of her husband's, and he had visited many times at their home. At the time of the scandal, Varian had been one of the few who had not been immediately convinced of Selby's guilt. "I cannot believe it of Sel," he had often said. "I know the evidence looks black, but, damme, it just seems impossible." They had seen little of Varian the past three years, though he had stopped in once or twice when he had been by to see young Thomas. Being Thomas's cousin, he had taken on the responsibility of visiting with Thomas and his mother as Selby had formerly done.

"Phoebe, then." Varian took her hand, smiling down warmly at her. "I did not wish to presume. And Julia." He took her proffered hand next, smiling. "I have been lax this year, I am afraid. I haven't visited Thomas even once. It is fortunate that he and his mother are in London this summer.''

"Yes, of course.'' Phoebe cast a rather timid glance at the woman who was standing stiffly beside Varian, not saying a word. "How do you do, Mrs. St. Leger?''

Pamela St. Leger did not speak, merely gave Phoebe a short nod, her face not softening even slightly. Pamela, Thomas's mother, had been long and loud in her condemnations of Selby. Julia had heard that she had wanted to sue Selby's estate for the monies that had been removed from the trust. However, the decision had not been up to her, of course, but to the trustees, and they had not done so—due primarily, Julia felt sure, to Varian St. Leger's influence. All Pamela had been able to do was cut them socially, and that she had proceeded to do with a vengeance. She had refused to attend any gathering where Phoebe or Julia were in attendance, and had been heard to declare at the slightest provocation that she was sure she did not know how either woman dared to show her face anywhere. She had even gone so far as to move her patronage each Sunday from St. Michael's in Whitley, the local village, to St. Edward's in Marshburrow, on the other side of the St. Leger estate. Julia suspected that her move had been at least in part influenced by the fact that the vicar's wife, Mrs. Fairmont, had refused to knuckle under to Pamela's social edict to shun the Armigers.

"Good morning, Mrs. St. Leger,'' Julia spoke up, favoring Pamela with a blazing smile.

Pamela turned and nodded briefly toward her, as well, her nostrils flaring slightly. Julia knew that Pamela had disliked her long before the scandal, and Julia thought that she had seized the opportunity of the scandal to avoid being in Julia's company. A raven-haired woman who had been considered a beauty in her day, Pamela did not like to be in the same room with Julia. She could perhaps fool herself into thinking that she was more attractive than the quiet Phoebe, but she could not compete against Julia's vivid looks. Personally, Julia found life much more pleasant without Pamela's presence, and she and Phoebe had not wanted to socialize the past few years, anyway, but she did resent the fact that Pamela had forbidden her son Thomas ever to fraternize with them. Thomas was quite fond of all the Armigers and had frequently visited Selby. Julia had come to regard him as something of a younger brother. Thomas was the only other person besides Phoebe and Julia and their servants who was convinced that Selby had not stolen the money from the trust. Julia found it cruel that Thomas's mother had denied him the company of the other people who shared his love and his mourning for Selby.

Of course, Thomas disobeyed his mother, sneaking over to visit Julia and Phoebe whenever he got the chance. He had joined with them in deciding that Lord Stonehaven must have been the real thief and the engineer of Selby's downfall. Stonehaven had visited him the least of his trustees and was, in Thomas's opinion, a "cold fish." It was Thomas who had first suggested that they capture Stonehaven and force him to reveal his criminal behavior, and he had wanted badly to play a part in the seizure. It had seemed a stroke of good luck when his mother had decided to go to London for the Season, and he had begged and pleaded and cajoled until finally Pamela had broken down and agreed to let him accompany her.

He had thought he would be easily able to join Julia in the escapade, but he had found out, much to his chagrin, that he was far more imprisoned in the house in London than he had been in the country. He was under the constant careful eye of the London tutor his mother had hired, and there were no afternoon rides, since he had had to leave his horse in the country. As a result, Julia had seen him only twice since they had come to London. Of course, she was glad now, considering the turn her plans had taken. Thomas, though only fourteen, would probably have gotten terribly male and disapproving about it all.

Her eyes twinkling devilishly, Julia went on speaking to the stony Mrs. St. Leger. "Odd, isn't it, that we should run into one another here in London, when we never see each other in Kent, even though we live only miles apart?" When Pamela said nothing, merely raised her eyebrows, Julia pressed, "Don't you think so, Mrs. St. Leger?"

Pamela stirred uneasily, glancing at Varian, who was watching her. "Indeed," she said through tight lips.

"Phoebe and I were remarking only the other day that we rarely see you anymore. We hoped that you were not eschewing social life, as some matrons do in widowhood. Phoebe thought it was probably that you, as she is, are still in mourning for your husband, but I told her I thought that could not be the reason, for you were frequently at parties after he died, and I was sure that you had put off mourning—oh, within a few months after Walter's funeral."

Bright spots of color leaped into Pamela's cheeks at Julia's words, delivered with a wide-eyed innocence that did not fool the other woman for a minute. She knew as well as Julia that there had been a great deal of talk about the brevity of her mourning for Walter St. Leger, which

Phoebe's presence in her black widow's weeds three years after Selby's death seemed to underscore.

"Yes. Walter never liked black on a woman," she said in a clipped voice, driven out of her disdainful silence by the need to justify herself.

"Ah, of course." Julia smiled with understanding. "I'm sure Walter would have been very pleased to see you. I told Phoebe I did not think it was mourning that kept you away from the small social pleasures of Whitley. I was sure it was probably some physical infirmity. I hope not lumbago—that can be a terribly painful thing, I understand."

Pamela's eyes shot fire. "No, I assure you it was not 'physical infirmity' that kept me away. Indeed, I attend many soirees and balls, Miss Armiger."

"Indeed? Why is it that we never see you, then?" Julia wrinkled her brow in puzzlement.

"Are you determined, then, to hear it?" Pamela snapped. Julia wondered if she realized how unattractive she looked like this, her features sharp and hawklike, her eyes narrowed, and her lips, never full, reduced to a mere line. "I do not go where you are received, as you no doubt know. No woman of any standing would."

Varian's expression of shock and distaste as he looked at Pamela was precisely what Julia would have wished for. But all her satisfaction was wiped out when she heard Phoebe's sharp intake of breath and turned to see the hurt on her face at Pamela's verbal slap.

"Phoebe, I'm sorry," Julia said softly, curling her arm around her sister-in-law's waist.

"Mrs. St. Leger!" Varian snapped. "Really! I am quite sure you did not mean that." He glared at her significantly.

"Everyone knows it!" Pamela retorted defiantly, still

too caught up in her anger to care that she looked mean and spiteful in front of her son's trustee.

"Phoebe, please, accept my apology," Varian went on, turning abruptly from Pamela toward Phoebe. "I assure you that most people do not feel that way."

Phoebe smiled at him. "You are most kind, Varian. I know that *you* do not."

"Indeed not. I hope you will allow me the honor of calling upon you while you are in London."

"Of course."

He turned to Julia and made his apologies and goodbyes, adding that he trusted her to "take care of Lady Armiger." Then he hustled Pamela away.

Julia turned to Phoebe. "Oh, Fee, I'm sorry. I should never have goaded her like that. I was so intent on forcing her to admit what a witch she is that I didn't even think about you. I should have known it would hurt you. It is simply that I am so thick-skinned, you see. No, please, don't cry."

Phoebe shook her head, giving Julia a shaky little smile. Her eyes sparkled with sudden unshed tears. "No. It isn't that. It was your calling me 'Fee.' Selby always used to call me that. Remember? He was so fond of pet names."

"Yes, I remember." Julia felt tears clogging up her own throat at the memory. Even Julia he had shortened to Julie, and he had almost never called Phoebe by her full name. "He called you 'Fee' and 'Delight.'"

A little noise escaped Phoebe at her words. "Oh, Julia! How can it still hurt after all this time?"

"I don't know." Julia hugged the other woman tightly. "Sometimes I think that it will always hurt, at least a little."

"I want to prove that Selby didn't do it," Phoebe said

in a fiercer voice than Julia had ever heard from her. "I want to prove that it was all Stonehaven's doing and make that dreadful woman eat every nasty word she's ever said about Selby or you or me!"

"We will," Julia promised, setting her jaw. "We will."

Julia was in the sitting room the next day, her fingers busy letting down the hem on another one of Phoebe's dresses so that she could wear it. Her mind was occupied with her plan to manipulate Lord Stonehaven into confessing to his crime. She knew that she could not allow herself to be distracted again, as she had been last time by his kiss. She had to be firm and in control, and she had decided that the best way to do that was to plan the things she would say and do to lead him to talk, down to every last word and gesture.

The housekeeper, a fussy, plump woman in a white mob cap and an equally snowy apron, was standing beside Phoebe while Phoebe went over the menus for the rest of the week. Phoebe was engaged in another of a seemingly unending series of struggles over what should be served.

"You see, Mrs. Willett," Phoebe was saying now, "I don't really *like* duck."

"But, my lady, duck was always one of the master's favorites." Mrs. Willett had been used to ruling the London house largely unchecked for over thirty years. The butler might go back and forth from the country house in Kent to London with the family, but the housekeeper stayed in charge in London over the long months—and even years, lately—when the family was not there, running a skeleton staff to keep the house in shape. Her guiding rule in any situation was to do exactly as she had always done.

Julia glanced over at Phoebe, who was biting her lip and looking worried, and Julia knew that Phoebe was, as Mrs. Willett had intended, feeling like an unloving, ungrieving widow for not wanting to eat one of her dead husband's favorite dishes.

"Nonsense, Mrs. Willett," Julia stuck in crisply. "You and I both know that duck was our *father's* favorite dish, and that is why you served it all Selby's life. Besides, it doesn't really matter whether Selby liked it or not. The point is that *Lady Armiger* does *not* like it. She does not want it on the menu, and I see no reason why it should be there, when your employer does not wish it. Do you?"

A look of hurt that would have crumpled Phoebe's opposition settled on the older woman's face. She pushed her spectacles back up her nose and said in a resigned voice, "Very well, Miss Julia—if you want it that way. I do work for your family, have done so for over thirty years."

"Yes, I know, and an excellent housekeeper you are," Julia agreed to soothe the woman's wounded feelings.

"My, yes," Phoebe agreed eagerly, a tiny frown of concern creasing her forehead. "I did not mean to imply that there was anything wrong with the way you perform your duties."

"Of course you didn't." Julia jumped in before Phoebe could get carried away with her assurances and wind up telling the woman to leave the duck on the list. "I am sure Mrs. Willett understands that you merely want a change in the menu. It is the sort of problem at which she is quite adept, isn't it, Mrs. Willett?"

"Of course," Mrs. Willett agreed, smiling. Julia knew

that in a few more minutes the menu change would have become her own idea, and woe to any of the kitchen staff who objected to it.

At that moment, there was the rumble of carriage wheels coming to a stop in front of the house. Julia and Phoebe glanced at each other in surprise. A visitor to their house was a rare occurrence—they had had no callers since they came to London three weeks ago, except for young Thomas every now and then when he could sneak away from his tutor. Julia stood up and crossed over to the windows. A sporty curricle had stopped on the pavement, and as she watched, a lad in livery hopped down from the back and hurried forward to take the horse's head. A man, dressed elegantly and severely in black and white, was climbing down from the open vehicle. Julia's mouth opened in horror.

"Oh, my God!" she exclaimed, her hand flying to her throat. She stepped back quickly.

Phoebe was on her feet in an instant, hurrying toward her in concern. "What's wrong? Who is it?"

"Lord Stonehaven," Julia croaked. "He's found out."

"What?" Phoebe whirled and looked out the window, then turned back to Julia. "Oh, no! What shall we do?"

The sound of the front door knocker resounded through the house. Julia started toward the sitting room door, the only thought on her mind to tell the footman not to answer the door. But that efficient servant was already swinging open the front door, and Julia ducked back inside the room.

"Miss Julia, what is it?" the housekeeper asked, concerned by the look of fear on Julia's face.

"A visitor. Tell him we aren't home, Mrs. Willett," Phoebe suggested, her face pleading.

How could he have found out who she was? There had been no one at Madame Beauclaire's who knew her, except Geoffrey, and Geoffrey would never have told Stonehaven who she really was.

"He must—he must be coming to pay a call," Julia stated, reason overcoming her initial spurt of fear. "Somehow he's found out that we are here. That's all, I'm sure." But it would still be disaster if he saw her here!

She could hear the footman walking toward the door, Stonehaven's steps right behind him. In another few seconds he would be here. She glanced around wildly. There was no other way out of the room. Aside from slamming the door in his face, there was no way to avoid his seeing her. Julia's mind raced.

"Pardon me, Mrs. Willett," she murmured as she reached over and pulled the woman's spectacles from her face, followed by her large mob cap. Grabbing her own shawl from the back of her chair, Julia dived behind the chair just as the footman stepped into the room.

"Lord Stonehaven, my lady," he droned.

4

Phoebe numbly turned toward the door, where Lord Stonehaven stood right behind the footman.

"My lord," she said through bloodless lips, struggling not to look toward the chair where Julia had disappeared nor at her astonished housekeeper, who stood clutching at her disarranged hair and blinking.

At that moment Julia popped up from behind the chair like a jack-in-the-box. Phoebe let out a gasp, quickly smothered. Julia had wrapped the long shawl loosely around her, effectively hiding her figure. Atop her head she wore the housekeeper's outmoded mob cap, covering up every last strand of her distinctive red hair. The older woman's glasses were perched on her nose, turning her lovely blue eyes strangely large and swimming. To add to the disguise, she was frowning, her jaw set and her mouth narrowed into a thin line.

Stonehaven's brows rose slightly at the sudden appearance of this apparition, and he faltered in the midst of saying Phoebe's name. He added tentatively, "And, uh, Miss Armiger?"

"Yes!" Julia barked in a hoarse voice. "That is who I am—not that it's any concern of yours."

"Julia…" Phoebe protested weakly. She disliked the man fully as much as Julia, but she could no more bring herself to be rude than she could jump off the top of the house.

"Well, 'tis true," Julia snapped. Her heart was thundering inside her chest so loudly that she thought the others must hear it. She wished she could see Stonehaven's face, so that she could tell whether he recognized her in her disguise or not. But with Mrs. Willett's spectacles on, the entire room was a blur. Lord Stonehaven looked like nothing except a large smudge of black and white.

"Mrs. Willett, you may go now," Julia said, turning in the woman's general direction. It was not really her place, but Phoebe's, to dismiss the servant, but Julia suspected that Phoebe was too stunned at the moment to remember to do so, and she wanted the housekeeper out of the room before she could make any remarks about her cap and glasses.

"Yes, miss." The housekeeper, looking confused, sidled past Lord Stonehaven, feeling her way along the wall and out the door.

Julia, equally blind, edged around the chair, thinking that if she could just get around it and sit down, she would be all right despite the sorry state of her eyesight. However, she had forgotten the footstool sitting beside the chair, and she stumbled over it, sending the stool flying. She let out a cry as pain shot up her foot, and she staggered, bumping into the arm of a chair. That was all it took: the bump, combined with her swimming vision and the fact that she instinctively hopped off her hurt foot, made her lose her balance, and she tumbled ungracefully into the chair.

Phoebe let out a gasp, and both she and Lord Stonehaven started toward her. Julia quickly waved them away, blushing a fiery red.

"No!" She swung her legs down off the arm of the chair and sat up straight. In her embarrassment, her voice had slipped back into its normal register, but now she brought it back down to a gravelly growl. "I'm fine. Just fine. Sit down."

Phoebe turned toward their visitor and tried to smile. It was not a successful effort. "Why—why don't you sit there on the sofa, my lord?" she said, her voice quavering a little, and gestured toward the low velvet sofa, which lay at some distance from where Julia sat.

Julia glared in the general direction of Stonehaven. Disconcertingly, her gaze lit somewhere in the general vicinity of his shoulder.

"What are you doing here?" Julia asked abruptly.

Stonehaven raised his eyebrows slightly at her rudeness, but said only, "I met St. Leger at my club yesterday evening, and he told me that you were in town. I came to pay a call."

"I realize that," Julia retorted, increasing her scowl. She wanted to get rid of this man before he could see past her disguise and realize who she was. Otherwise, their whole plan was ruined. She could think of no better way to do that than to drive him off with rudeness. Besides, she thought, it was quite refreshing to be rude to him, especially after having to hide her true feelings toward him the other night. "What I meant was, why would you come to call on us? We cannot benefit you in any way. I think that you have done the worst that you can do to my family. Surely you cannot think that we would wish to see you. So what purpose does your visit serve?"

"You are certainly a forthright young woman, Miss Armiger."

"Yes, unlike some people."

"Julia…" Phoebe blushed at her sister-in-law's bluntness.

"Why try to hide how we feel, Phoebe?" Julia asked. "I am sure that Lord Stonehaven must not be surprised to learn that we dislike him."

"It does not surprise me, no," he said, "though I must tell you that it does distress me. I hope you realize that I never meant either of you any ill."

Anger blazed across Julia's face as she said acidly, "You certainly did us ill enough by accident, then."

There was a long, uncomfortable pause. Finally Lord Stonehaven said, "Miss Armiger, I am not the one who brought dishonor to your family. Selby did that. I know that you loved your brother, but—"

"You're right. I did. I still do. And I don't know how you can have the nerve to come here today and force Phoebe and me to look at you, the man who ruined him!" She realized that the growl was slipping again in her agitation, and she stopped, clearing her throat.

"Please, Miss Armiger, do not distress yourself so much."

"It is not *I* who is causing my distress!"

Lord Stonehaven sighed. "I am sorry. Obviously I should not have come. Please believe me when I say that I have no desire to cause either you or Lady Armiger pain. I—I had hoped to heal some of the rift that lies between us."

"That will never happen." Julia shot to her feet, glaring at him, her arms stiff at her sides. "Do you think that you can ruin my brother and then be forgiven?"

Stonehaven sighed, rising to his feet also. "No. I can

see that that is too much to expect." He turned toward Phoebe. "Lady Armiger, please accept my regards. I want you to know that if I can be of service to you in any way, you have only to call on me."

Julia let out an inelegant snort. "She would as soon call on a snake for help."

"I'm sorry, Lord Stonehaven." Phoebe cast a nervous glance toward Julia. "But I think it would be best if you left now."

"Yes, of course." He bowed over Phoebe's hand formally, but, after a wary glance in Julia's direction, was wise enough not to approach her. "Good day, ladies."

He turned and left the room. Phoebe and Julia stood frozen, listening to his receding footsteps upon the Carrera marble floor. There came the sound of the footman opening the massive front door, and a moment later it closed.

Julia ripped the mob cap off her head and slammed it down on the chair, following it with the spectacles. "Oh! I cannot believe the nerve of that man! How could he come here? How did he dare! Did he think that we would welcome him? That he could just waltz in and charm us into forgetting that he is the man responsible for Selby's—"

Phoebe let out a little inarticulate noise of distress, and Julia was instantly contrite, "I'm sorry, Phoebe. I should not have said that. It was upsetting enough for you to have to meet that man. I should not have added to your distress. It just makes me so angry." She slammed one fist into the other hand. "Lord Stonehaven is utterly without feeling."

Timidly Phoebe offered, "It was rather nice of him, I suppose, to call on us. No one else does. Most people just snub us. It would have been far easier for him not to come, and no one would have thought badly of him.''

''Nice!'' Julia sneered. ''There was nothing nice about it. Trust me. He merely came here to gloat. Or perhaps it suited him to appear to be magnanimous. No doubt he thought we would grovel in gratitude at his being so kind as to notice us. Well! He'd better think again!''

''I am sure he has—now,'' Phoebe replied dryly.

Julia glanced at her sister-in-law in some surprise, then chuckled, much of her anger draining out. Julia let out an explosive gust of air and sank back into the chair, picking up the cap and spectacles and holding them in her lap. Now that it was all over and she was no longer consumed with rage, her legs were suddenly trembling, unable to hold her up any longer.

''Oh, my,'' Phoebe said, also sitting down with a plop. ''I cannot imagine how you pulled that off. I was terrified when he walked into the room.''

''Do you think he knew me?'' Julia asked anxiously. ''I couldn't see him. Did any expression of recognition cross his face?''

''No. He seemed only—well, appalled—whenever he looked at you. Oh, Julia!'' Hysterical laughter bubbled up from Phoebe's throat. ''Julia, you cannot imagine how you looked! Your eyes so huge and blurred, like a frog's.''

''Well, thank you very much,'' Julia tried for an indignant tone, but laughter broke through.

''And that cap!'' Phoebe let out a peal of laughter. ''How did you ever think of it so quickly? I am sure he didn't know whether you were a housemaid or a—a—''

''Giant frog in a dress?'' Julia suggested.

They both laughed, unable to restrain themselves, relief from the last few minutes' strain making them giddy. Phoebe described each expression that had chased across Lord Stonehaven's face at Julia's words, her imitations making Julia howl with laughter. It took some time before their hysteria died down into chuckles and then into sighs and, finally, silence.

"Well…" Julia said at last, rising. "I suppose I had better return these to Mrs. Willett and try to make amends with her."

"I am sure the poor woman thinks you have gone quite mad."

"No doubt. Ah, well, hopefully I will be able to think up an adequate story." She stood up and started toward the door, but then stopped as a new thought hit her. "Oh, no! I daren't see him tonight, as I had planned. Not so soon after this."

"No. You'd best give him a few days to forget Miss Armiger's features," Phoebe agreed.

Julia sighed, a little surprised at how disappointed she felt. But then, she reminded herself, it was only natural—merely an indication of how eager she was to bring Lord Stonehaven to justice.

Julia let three days pass before she went again to Madame Beauclaire's, but she found it difficult to wait. By the time the evening came around, she was fairly champing at the bit, eager to go.

She was wearing another one of Phoebe's dresses tonight, again with a let-out hem and the modest fichu of lace at the neckline ripped out. It was a gauzy dress in a color the modiste had termed "sea foam green." Though it did not have the tighter-fitting skirt of the dress she had worn the last time, its flowing lines clung to Julia's slender form, and the low neckline was enough, she thought, to spark any man's interest. Besides, it was a color that looked perfect with her auburn hair.

Tonight she returned to Madame Beauclaire's without her cousin's company. Geoffrey would balk, she knew, at escorting her a second time and would probably ask all sorts of awkward questions. Besides, having been there before, she did not need him now. As few women as she had seen there, she felt relatively sure that the doorman would recognize her as a customer.

Nor did she take her own carriage. It would have been handy, of course, to have Nunnelly waiting outside to take her home, but it might also interfere with her plans. Last week it had turned out very well when Lord Stonehaven had walked her out to find her a hackney. And there was always the danger that Nunnelly might balk at her going into a gaming house. Loyal as he was, he had known her since she was a toddler and had no hesitation about speaking his mind to her. He was also much too likely to give her orders, having grown accustomed to it, she thought, when he taught her to ride when she was a child. He was quite willing to break the law for her sake—he had never quailed at the thought of abducting Stonehaven—but she felt sure that he would refuse to let her put herself into a situation that might damage her reputation.

So she went to Madame Beauclaire's in a hackney, the nerves in her stomach tying themselves into an ever-expanding knot. As she had expected, the footman at the door let her in after one quick glance, bowing deeply. She suspected that he could have said with whom she had left the other night, as well. Plying her fan to hide her nerves, she strolled along the hall, glancing into the rooms on either side.

Lord Stonehaven was not there.

Disappointed, she strolled desultorily through the tables, stopping to observe a game now and then. At one of the tables, the name Stonehaven caught her ear, and she stopped short, every nerve alert.

"What?" one of the men at the table was saying, glancing toward one of his companions. "Oh, Stonehaven, yes—no, I haven't seen him tonight. Odd, he's been here every night this week, it seems."

"Yes. I've never known him to be so gambling mad."

Julia turned away, smiling to herself. *Gambling mad, was he?* She, too, knew that it was not his custom to attend Madame Beauclaire's or any other establishment that frequently. If he had been coming in every night, she could not help but believe that it had been because he was hoping to find her there. She had, after all, hinted that he could find her there when she had refused to give him her address.

Buoyed by this knowledge, she was able to sit down at one of the gaming tables with a suitably casual air and enter into play. He would come, she knew. Lord Stonehaven was not the sort of man to give up.

It was thirty minutes later that a masculine voice said behind her, "I see you have switched your allegiance. Not dipping too deeply, I hope."

Julia turned, a smile blazing across her face. *He had come!*

"Lord Stonehaven." She realized that she had probably looked too eager to see him. It never did to let a man realize that one was interested in him, and of course he would be bound to think that her broad smile was from pleasure at seeing him, not triumph that he had walked into her web. She schooled her voice to something slightly warmer than indifference. "So you are here again. I had wondered if I would see you tonight."

"I came in the hopes of finding you here, Miss Nunnelly."

He flashed his charming smile at her, and Julia's eyes were drawn to his lips, full and wide against strong white teeth. She had forgotten exactly how handsome he was up close. She moved toward him.

"I hope I am not taking you away from a lucky streak," he said. "Would you like to stay?"

"What? Oh." She glanced back at the table, a little surprised to find that she had stepped away from it. "No. I was about to leave. My luck has been uniformly bad this evening."

"I hope it was not bad luck to run into me again."

She cast him a sparkling look. "No. I would not say it was bad."

He looked down at her, and his eyes narrowed briefly. Fear slammed through Julia. His look was...almost suspicious.

"What?" she asked in a falsely light tone. "Why are you looking at me like that?"

"Oh." He looked abashed. "I don't know. I had the oddest sensation for an instant—as if I had seen you before."

Julia forced herself to smile impishly, although her mouth had gone suddenly dry. "Indeed, sir, I do believe you *have* seen me before. We met here five nights ago, if I remember correctly."

He chuckled. "Believe me, I am quite aware of that. No, I meant that you reminded me of someone else. A certain look, the way you tilted your head—but that, of course, is absurd. There is no other woman as beautiful as you."

His words made her feel as if a tight band were encircling her chest, squeezing hard, but she managed to say, "A pretty compliment, my lord."

"But heartfelt." He seemed to dismiss the matter as they strolled out into the hallway. There he stopped and glanced around, then looked back at her. "I find I do not wish to stay here. Would you care to—go somewhere else?"

"I—what do you mean, my lord?" *Was he suggesting that they go to his house?*

Julia felt suddenly panicky. She realized that in all her thinking about how to lead him on, what to do or say in order to get him to confess, she had not really given any thought as to where it would be accomplished. She had hazily imagined them sitting in a garden or strolling along the street or something of the sort. *Where did one go on assignations?* She could see that her education was woefully lacking in this area. Going to a gentleman's house would be unthinkable for a lady, but, of course, it would be entirely different for a woman of loose morals, such as she was pretending to be. That was exactly the sort of compromising position a woman such as that would get into. Still, it seemed to her that things were moving much too fast. She really did not want to be alone with Lord Stonehaven in his home.

"I thought we had agreed to cease all this 'my lord'-ing," he told her. "My name is Deverel."

"Yes, of course…Deverel."

"I hadn't really thought of where we would go. I simply realized that I would like very much not to play cards tonight. I would much rather spend the evening talking with you."

"I have no objection to that," Julia replied a little breathlessly.

"I have a friend whose house is always open to visitors. Actually, it is the house of a...woman of his acquaintance."

"His mistress," Julia replied knowledgeably. There were few ladies who did not know that gentlemen frequently made such arrangements.

Stonehaven's mouth quirked up in a smile. "You are dangerously blunt. Yes. It is the house of his mistress, but he is nearly always there, and many of his friends, as well as her friends, of course."

"I see." It was not exactly a bawdy house where women of the night plied their trade, Julia thought, but it must be just a step above that—the house where a man kept his light-o'-love, and he and his friends went to drink and talk and flirt with other women who were equally free with their favors. Julia supposed she ought to be appalled at the thought of going to such a place, but instead she found herself filled with curiosity. She had never actually met a kept woman, let alone been in one's house.

"Yes," she continued, flashing him what she hoped was a beckoning look. "That sounds much better than staying here."

"I am glad you agree." He was already steering her toward the front door.

The footman fetched her cloak, and Lord Stonehaven draped it around her shoulders, his fingers brushing lightly across her skin. Julia swallowed, trying to ignore the shivery sensation his touch created in her.

They walked out into the quiet night air, and Stonehaven turned to the left. "Shall we walk? It isn't far."

"Yes, of course."

They strolled along, her hand hooked in the bend of his arm. Julia struggled to think of something to say.

She had spent all day, it seemed, thinking of things to say and questions to ask to lead him where she wanted to go, but now, none of those carefully planned remarks seemed to fit.

"I had hoped to find you here one of the past few nights," Stonehaven commented, interrupting her jumbled thoughts.

"I am not quite *that* eager a gambler."

"Neither am I. I came each night in the hopes of finding you."

"Flatterer." Julia flashed him an arch glance.

"No. 'Tis true. I am quite shameless."

"A shocking flirt is more like it."

"You wound me." He put on an air of mock hurt.

"As if you did not know..."

"'Tis no flirtation to say I have been searching for you every night since we met. Ask any of my friends. They will tell you that I have shirked my social obligations dreadfully. I cried off from going to the opera two nights ago, and yesterday I stayed only fifteen minutes at Lady Abersham's soiree."

"All because of me?" She arched a brow. "I suppose it had nothing to do with boredom."

He chuckled. "Perhaps that did motivate my departure somewhat."

"Deceiver. I am, in short, a handy excuse."

"Never that, I assure you. Rather, I think, your absence is the cause of my boredom."

Julia laughed. "You are a clever man with words, Lord Sto—I mean, Deverel."

"No cleverer than you," he returned.

"Oh, dear." Julia made a face. "No fate worse than being termed a 'clever' woman."

"Indeed?"

"Yes. I find there is little that cools a man's ardor faster than discovering that a woman has a mind."

"Perhaps some men." He looked down into her face with a light in his eyes that sent tendrils of heat curling through Julia. He stopped, pulling her to a halt, with him. Lifting his hand, he stroked his knuckles lightly down her cheek. "Personally, I find that wit makes a beautiful face twice as alluring."

"Indeed," Julia answered breathlessly. She discovered that her vaunted wits had deserted her. She could only stare up into his dark eyes, every nerve in her body alive.

Softly, with his forefinger, he traced the curve of her bottom lip. "I would like to kiss you right here on the street, but I am afraid that, if I do, I will not be able to stop."

The sound of his husky voice, the touch of his finger, faintly rough against her tender flesh, were enough to make Julia weak in the knees. She tried to pull her thoughts back together, but for a moment the best she could manage, it seemed, was to keep breathing.

"I wouldn't mind," she said honestly, then stopped, appalled, as she realized what had slipped out of her mouth. She shook her head, stepping back.

To her surprise, Stonehaven chuckled. "Good gad, my girl, a little more of that sort of response and we shall find ourselves in a hell of a predicament."

Julia was sure that she was blushing up to her hairline, and she was grateful for the dark. "I—I'm sorry. I didn't mean that."

"I sincerely hope that you did," he replied, his eyes gleaming. "Unfortunately, however, I cannot act upon it now. Shall we continue on our way?"

He held out his arm, and Julia took it self-consciously.

She could not believe that she had said something so bold. It had apparently pleased him, which was good for her campaign, of course, but she found it most upsetting, because it was not anything she had planned. Why had she said that? Surely she could not really have meant it! There was something about this man that brought out the most outrageous things in her.

They continued to a brick cottage, small but attractive, where Stonehaven's knock was immediately answered by a maid. She greeted Stonehaven with a curtsy and a friendly smile. ''The master's in the music room,'' she told them, somewhat unnecessarily, as the laughter and the sound of a piano flowing from that room betrayed the location of the occupants of the house.

Stonehaven handed the maid their outer things and led Julia toward the sound of merriment. Julia stepped into the room, staring with some astonishment and awe at the scene in front of her. A man clad in a hussar's uniform was sitting before the piano, his fingers nimbly running over the keys. A woman stood beside the piano, holding, to Julia's amazement, a long, thin cigar in one hand. As Julia stared, she took a puff from it and let the smoke trail lazily out her mouth. There were several other men and women in the room, some standing, some sitting, and on one side of the room, in a small area cleared of furniture, there was even a couple doing some sort of jig. The room buzzed with noise; people were talking in at least two or three different conversations, and one man was trying to sing along with the music. Cigar smoke made the room hazy, and glasses with varying amounts of brown liquid were scattered across every available table.

But what attracted Julia's attention the most, after her first hasty glance, was the fact that in a chair close to the window sat a man with a woman perched on his lap. The woman's dress was sheer enough that one could see through it, and when she turned toward the new arrivals, Julia could plainly see the dark brown circles of her nipples. After a brief, disinterested glance, the woman turned back to her companion, and they resumed the long kiss in which they had been engaged when Julia and Stonehaven entered. Julia was sure that her own cheeks were flame red. She glanced hastily away, only to see that in another part of the room another woman sat on another man's lap. These two were not kissing, as they were both engaged in a boisterous conversation with a man standing beside their chair. However, the man on whose lap the woman sat had one arm looped around her waist, and as Julia watched, he casually slid his hand up the woman's body and inside the bodice of her low-cut dress, cupping her breast.

Julia swallowed, feeling acutely embarrassed. *Was this how she was supposed to act?* Her own dress seemed almost prim compared to the attire of the other ladies, whose bosoms seemed ready to pop out of the low necks of their dresses. All of the women were rouged and powdered, and Julia was relatively sure that the guinea gold ringlets of one of them were definitely not her own. Julia realized that her own vision of what a bird of paradise wore was far more conservative than the actuality. She could not look away from the scene, which held a certain bizarre fascination.

One of the women was running her fingers up and down the arm of her companion, who had removed his jacket and was clad only in a shirt. Now and then her fingers strayed to the front of his shirt and even inside the opening at the top to his chest underneath. He seemed to have no objection to this action at all, only paused every now and then to give her a lingering pat on her derriere. The woman whose male companion had cupped her breast showed no inclination to move his hand. Rather, she wiggled on his lap, giggling.

"Stoney!" A man hopped up from a seat near the piano, his face wreathed in smiles. "I say, old man, didn't expect to see you here tonight. Callie, look! Here's Stonehaven, come to pay us a call."

His last words were directed toward the cigar-smoking woman beside the piano, who turned at his words, smiling. When she saw Julia, her eyebrows went up a trifle, and she gave her a quick, assessing look up and down. "Hallo, Dev," she called across the room and the noise. "It's about time you thought of your friends. And who is your guest?"

"Allow me to introduce you." Stonehaven guided Julia across the room to the man and woman. "Miss Nunnelly, I'd like you to meet my good friends. This is the Honorable Alfred Brooks. And Miss Callandra Cooper." He turned toward Julia. "Miss Jessica Nunnelly."

The honorable Alfred bowed to Julia, murmuring, "Ravishing. How do you always manage to find the most beautiful females in the city, Dev?"

"Not *all* the most beautiful ones." Stonehaven made a polite demurral, bowing toward Alfred's companion. "You have captured one of the loveliest yourself."

Callandra simpered at the compliment. Stonehaven chatted for a moment with his friend, then moved with Julia toward the edge of the room. Julia's gaze kept returning to the woman and man on the chair by the window. They were still kissing, and now his hand was sliding up her leg, shoving aside the flimsy skirt. She looked hastily away, her heart hammering inside her chest. *Was this what Stonehaven would expect of her?* Doubts assailed her. She looked down at her hands, unable to meet Stonehaven's eyes.

"Gad, it's noisy in here," Stonehaven said. He bent down to Julia's ear and said softly, "Shall we go outside? There is a nice garden in the rear, and a bench where we can sit and talk."

"Oh, yes," Julia agreed quickly, smiling up at him. "That sounds most agreeable."

Stonehaven took her by the hand and led her down the hallway and out a door. They entered a small side garden that smelled richly of herbs and followed a path around the house to where the garden widened out into a large array of flowers. A tinkling fountain stood in the center of the small yard, and in front of it was a stone bench.

Julia strolled with Lord Stonehaven along the path to the bench. The soft summer breeze caressed her skin, and the scent of roses hung thickly in the air. It was blessedly quiet. They sat down on the bench, and Julia noticed that Stonehaven had not let go of her hand. She tried to pull her scattered thoughts together, to recall herself to her duty and to the plans she had made. She could not let her brother down, she reminded herself, just because her sensibilities had been shocked by the scene inside. It might not be easy, but she had dedicated herself to worming the truth out of Lord Stonehaven, and she could not hesitate now. She had to go forward with her plan.

"Your friend seemed most happy to see you," she began tentatively.

Stonehaven smiled faintly. "Alfred is a good fellow. Openhanded to a fault. It sometimes gets him in trouble, I'm afraid."

"Oh?" she asked encouragingly, thinking that friends in trouble was a good path to be following.

He shrugged. "Just the usual. He is often taken advantage of." He shook his head and smiled at her. "Please, let us not talk of Alfred. A dull subject, I'm afraid."

"How unkind!" Julia's eyes sparkled at him. "Then let us talk of something more interesting. You, for instance."

"Me! No, I am afraid that you have hit upon another dull topic."

"I doubt that." In her somewhat limited experience, Julia had found that most men's favorite topic of discourse was themselves, so she did not take him at his word. "At least, *I* do not find it dull. I know nothing about you."

"There is little to tell. What would you like to know?"

What you did with that money, she thought—and how you made it look as if my brother had taken it. But those were scarcely things she could say, so Julia merely smiled and said, "Why, everything. I hardly know where to begin." She paused. "Are cards your passion? Is that how you spend your days?"

"I usually reserve it for the nights. But, no, I would not say that gambling is a *passion* with me." The look in his eyes gave her little doubt as to what he did regard as a passion. "'Tis merely a pastime."

"I see. And what do you do the rest of the time?" She hoped that he might mention the trust in his activities; she was beginning to see that it was not so easy as she had thought to direct their conversation along the path she wished.

He shrugged. "The sorts of things one does. I go to

my club when I'm in London. Pay calls. I've been known to race my curricle or to spar a few rounds at Jackson's. Even attend to some business affairs." He grinned. "You see? I told you it was deadly dull." He lifted her hand, idly stroking down the back of her hand and each finger to the tip. "I am sure it would be much more fun to talk about you. Where are you from? London?"

"No, Kent," she replied automatically, then worried that she had been too truthful. But then, she reminded herself, thousands of people lived in Kent; he wouldn't necessarily think of Thomas St. Leger or his nearby neighbors, the Armigers.

"Indeed? I come into Kent now and then."

"Really?" she murmured vaguely. She was finding the way he was caressing her hand quite distracting.

"Yes. I have a ward who lives there, and I visit him sometimes."

"A ward? You mean you are someone's guardian? Is he a relative?"

"No. I'm not his guardian, merely a trustee of his money." He made a dismissive gesture. "I am afraid it's not very interesting."

"Oh, no, it sounds quite interesting. So you invest his money and such?"

"We direct it. There are two other gentlemen who are trustees, also. But let's not talk about that." He brought her hand up to his lips. "I would much rather talk about you. Or not talk at all."

Julia raised a coquettish brow. "Indeed? Do you find talking with me so boring?"

"Never." He began to kiss each individual finger, his eyes gazing into hers all the while. "It is just that there are so many other interesting things about you."

The warmth of his lips against her fingers sent tingles running through Julia. She did not understand how something so small could set up such a strong reaction within her. "My lord..."

"Deverel," he murmured, turning her hand over and planting a lingering kiss on the inside of her wrist.

"Deverel..."

"What?" He was kissing his way slowly up her bare arm, his lips hot and velvety on her skin, stirring her senses.

"I don't think we should be doing this."

"Why not?" She could feel his smile upon her skin.

"Uh, well, anyone could walk out here at any moment and see us."

"That's true. But unlikely." He had reached the point of her shoulder and now began to trail kisses across her collarbone to her neck.

Heat welled up in Julia so quickly and explosively that it almost frightened her. "Deverel, stop."

There was a touch of panic in her voice, and Stonehaven lifted his head, looking at her in a puzzled way.

"Why? What's the matter?"

"I—" Julia was embarrassed by her moment of fear. She looked up at Deverel. His eyes were dark and smoldering in a way that made her insides quiver. Her eyes dropped to his mouth. She thought about their kiss a few nights earlier, and warmth blossomed in her loins.

She could not stop now, she told herself. She was not about to act the coward. She had to lead him along until she got him to talk. It was a delicate line to walk—to give just enough to keep him interested without giving in entirely. She had known that from the start. She had also known that Lord Stonehaven was no schoolboy to fall easily into her trap.

Julia drew a steadying breath and smiled at him. "Nothing. Nothing's the matter," she said, putting her hand behind his neck and pulling his head down.

5

Though she had experienced it before, Julia was not quite prepared for the torrent of sensations that flooded her at his kiss. She trembled beneath the onslaught, and her fingers tightened against his neck, as if to help her hold on. She had never touched a man so boldly before, and she was very aware of the warmth of his skin and the way his hair brushed her fingers.

He kissed her long and deeply, as if he could reach her very soul, and his arms wrapped around her, pulling her into him until she could scarcely breathe. Their bodies strained together, a little awkwardly because of their seated positions on the bench, until finally Deverel pulled Julia onto his lap. She leaned back against his supporting arm, giving herself up to the pleasure of his kiss.

When at last he broke their contact, it was only to trail kisses across her cheek to her ear and take the fleshy lobe between his teeth, teasing it gently. She could hear the harsh rasp of his breath, and the sound was somehow exciting, too. Little shivers of delight radiated through her. She knew she must get a grip on herself, must control what was happening, but everything was too new and startling.

He began to kiss his way down the side of her neck, and as he did so, his hand slid up from her waist until it cupped her breast. Julia jumped in surprise, drawing in her breath in a gasp. ''Deverel!''

''Mmm?'' He continued to make his way down her neck to her shoulder.

''I—uh—'' She didn't know what to say. Her whole body was throbbing, and there was a restless ache between her legs. This was not working. She was getting in deeper and deeper without discovering anything. She gestured vaguely back toward the cottage. ''The house…your friends…''

He raised his head and looked at her. His eyes glittered ferally, and his chest moved up and down in harsh, rapid pants. He glanced back toward the house where she pointed, then cast a long look at her.

''You're right,'' he said finally. ''This place is hardly private enough.''

He closed his eyes as if fighting to gain control of himself. His arms loosened around her, and Julia made herself hop off his lap, a little surprised at how reluctant she was to do so.

''Wait…Jessica…'' He reached toward her, but Julia took another step backward.

''Ah, no,'' she said, pleased at the flirtatious tone that she forced into her voice. ''I don't know what sort of women you are used to, but *I* am not the kind to fall so easily into dalliance.''

Irritation flashed across his face, and for a moment Julia thought that he was about to flare up in anger, but then he sighed and leaned back against the bench, looking up at her and saying in a bantering voice, "Oh, and what kind of woman are you, then?"

"The sort who places a high value on herself," Julia retorted coolly.

He chuckled. "Indeed. I would say that you are one whose value is higher than most."

He stood and came to her, his lazy smile telling her that he understood her game. No doubt it was not uncommon for a bird of paradise to play a waiting game, trying to raise the stakes.

"What next, then?" he asked.

Julia hesitated. This was exactly what she wanted—to have everything in her control. But she was not sure exactly what to do. She knew that she must arrange things differently. This evening everything had been too vague, and she had left him too much in control. She should arrange their rendezvous in some private place where she could ply him with alcohol to loosen his tongue while she allowed him a few kisses and caresses. But where could such a thing take place? She obviously could not have him come to her home, and everything engrained in her by her upbringing rebelled at the thought of going with him alone to his house.

Suddenly a thought struck her, and she grinned. "Well...I must confess that I have a great desire to visit Vauxhall Gardens to view the fireworks."

While Vauxhall Gardens was the sort of place where a lady might go, as long as she was in a well-chaperoned party, it was also a public entertainment that anyone could attend, and Julia had heard rumors that it was a favorite spot for dallying among gentlemen and ladies of the night. There were private boxes to be had, where one could have a supper catered, and if one left one's box, there were all sorts of secluded walkways where a couple could stroll alone in the dark—or pause in the shadows for a few stolen kisses. Moreover, people often went to it in masquerade, which meant that one could keep one's identity a secret. All these things combined to make it a perfect site for their rendezvous.

"Do you?" he responded, the glitter in his eyes telling her that he was well aware of the suitability of Vauxhall Gardens. "Certainly you must see them. Shall we say tomorrow evening?"

"No, I am afraid I could not do it tomorrow." She must, after all, keep him dangling for a while in order to whet his appetite. "What about the day after that?"

"As you wish," he replied graciously, inclining his head toward her.

They took their leave of their host—Julia glanced around but could not find the couple who had been so busily engaged on the chair by the window—and quit the house. Once again Julia turned down his offer to escort her home. He pressed his case for a while, but finally gave in and hailed a hackney for her. He did not try to kiss her again, but let her go with a brief, courteous brush of his lips upon the back of her hand. Julia climbed into the vehicle, and it started off.

Deverel watched the hackney until it turned the corner. Then, with a sigh, he started toward his own home. It was, in truth, an earlier hour than he generally kept when he was in the city, but he found that he had little interest in any of the pursuits with which he could pass the remainder of the night. Without Jessica Nunnelly, the evening was suddenly flat.

It was strange that it should be so, he knew. He was a man quite familiar with women, both of his own class and of the demimonde, and he enjoyed their company.

However, he was well past the age of tumbling head over heels for any of them. He was quite capable of finding a new woman attractive and desirable without feeling that he could not rest until she was in his bed. It had been many years since any woman had kept him awake or sent him chasing night after night to the same place in the hope of running into her again. But that was precisely what had happened with this woman. The instant he had seen Jessica Nunnelly across the hallway in Madame Beauclaire's, desire had surged through him. He had wanted, immediately and fervently, to sweep her up in his arms and carry her home to his bed. Amazingly enough, when he talked to her, he found that the fire in his loins continued unabated—even grew.

She was a trifle cool, yet when he kissed her, she had flamed to life. Her dress stamped her as a bird of paradise, yet her carriage and speech would have been worthy of a duchess. She had wit; she was mysterious; she stirred his blood. And he had been consumed since the moment he met her with a deep and lustful desire to make her his.

He could imagine her in his bed, naked and languid with lovemaking, that glorious auburn hair spread out upon his pillow, her blue eyes smiling up at him. Indeed, it was an image that had been plaguing him day and night for days. Now, the thought of being alone with her at Vauxhall Gardens two nights from now filled him with an impatient lust.

He didn't know why she had insisted on meeting him there rather than letting him escort her to the Gardens any more than he could figure out why she had twice refused to allow him to escort her home. He wondered if she had a husband or another wealthy "protector." The thought filled him with an unaccustomed jealousy.

Or it could be something she did to add to her air of mystery—he had to admit that, if that was the case, it certainly worked. He was almost as consumed with curiosity as he was with lust. Where had she come from? Why had he never seen her before? Or at least heard of her!

It seemed extremely unlikely that a diamond of the first water could have been inhabiting the demimonde of London for any length of time and he had not heard of her. On the other hand, she certainly did not seem like a green lass fresh from the country. She was too sophisticated, too poised. She spoke and acted like a woman of gentility. Had he met her anywhere else in more ladylike attire, he would have assumed she was a member of the ton. There had been moments when he was kissing her when her reaction had seemed naive and inexperienced. She had even looked embarrassed when she had glanced around at the free-and-easy scene at Alfred's house. Yet no lady would have appeared in that dress, let alone showed up unaccompanied at Madame Beauclaire's gambling house. He told himself that she must have pretended those inexperienced reactions in an effort to increase his desire; certainly her seemingly artless responses had quickened his pulse.

It occurred to him that unraveling the mystery of Jessica Nunnelly would be a delightful way to occupy his time, and he smiled to himself. He must procure a private box and supper at Vauxhall first thing tomorrow.

Julia and Phoebe were in the drawing room conversing with Geoffrey Pemberton the following afternoon when one of the footmen announced the arrival of the Honorable Varian St. Leger and Major Gordon Fitzmaurice.

"Of course," Phoebe said with a smile. "Show them in."

Geoffrey let out a groan as the footman left. "I think that I recall some urgent business."

"Now, Geoffrey…Major Fitzmaurice is very nice," Julia admonished her cousin.

"The man has the brains of a muffin."

Even the kindhearted Phoebe had to smile at the description. "Perhaps. But he has always been most kind to me."

"In that case," Geoffrey said, nodding graciously toward her, "I suppose we must endure him." He sighed and looked toward the door, muttering, "Too late to leave now, anyway."

Two men entered the drawing room. One was Varian St. Leger. Beside him was a squarely built man of military bearing. His hair was brown, his eyes gray, and his countenance was blankly pleasant.

"Varian. Fitz," Phoebe greeted them with the warmth of old friends. "It is so kind of you to call."

"Kind?" Varian replied with a smile at the delicate blond woman. "Indeed, it is nothing of the kind. It was purely selfish pleasure that made us come here today, not kindness."

Geoffrey made a noise deep in his throat, and Varian turned toward him. "Excuse me, Pemberton. Did you say something?"

Geoffrey returned the look blandly. "Indeed, no. I was simply moved to think that you denied yourself pleasure for so long."

Varian blushed, and Fitzmaurice looked confused.

"Denied yourself what pleasure?" Fitzmaurice asked. "You haven't gone pious on me, have you, Vare?"

"Now, Geoffrey…" Julia began warningly. "How

was Varian to know that we were in town? We told no one."

"I was speaking more about the past three years than the past three weeks." He raised a languid eyebrow at St. Leger.

"Pemberton is right, Julia. Do not scold him. I have been neglectful of you and Lady Armiger. I should have come to visit more often at Greenwood. I was a coward. I rode over more than once when I was visiting young Thomas, but when I crested that hill above Greenwood, I would begin to think about Selby and—"

"Oh, no, pray do not distress yourself," Phoebe cried softly. "I understand. Greenwood is full of memories. People are different. The memories, you see, give me comfort, so I am well content to live with them. And Julia and I had each other."

Phoebe quickly turned the conversation to other channels—a discussion of the London weather, the Season, the latest on-dits. Julia glanced at her cousin after a few minutes and saw that his eyelids were perilously close to shutting.

"What have you ladies been doing in town?" Varian asked after a while.

"Very little, actually," Phoebe replied. "Shopping. We've taken Gilbert to some of the amusements."

"Actually," Julia interjected, "we're here to investigate the embezzlement."

The room fell into a dead silence. Geoffrey's eyes popped open, and he regarded his cousin with some trepidation.

Finally Varian spoke. "What did you say?"

"The crime Selby was accused of. We are going to prove that he did not do it."

The two men stared at her blankly.

Fitzmaurice looked confused. "But, I say…didn't he do it?"

Varian sent him an admonishing glance, then turned to Julia. "I am afraid I don't understand. Certainly I could never quite credit that Selby would have done anything wrong, but the evidence—"

"The evidence was made up," Julia said crisply. "I am sure of it. It is the only explanation. Phoebe and I know that Selby did not do it, which gives us an advantage over everyone else because, you see, we know that for the evidence against Selby to be so strong, it must have been manufactured deliberately to make it seem that Selby did it."

"I don't understand," the major complained.

"I am astonished," Geoffrey said dryly.

"But, Julia…" Varian frowned with concern.

"Don't you see? It's the only logical explanation. You yourself said that you could not imagine Selby doing it."

"Yes, I own that it was hard to believe, but it's hard to imagine someone laying such a detailed plan to get Selby. And why Selby? Everyone liked him."

"Apparently not everyone. But I doubt that it was any particular spite directed at Selby. I think it was rather that he was the most logical candidate, since he handled most of Thomas's affairs. Such a letter coming from one of the rest of you might have aroused suspicion in the agent, don't you think?"

"I suppose."

"Are you saying that some other chap stole young Thomas's money?" Fitzmaurice asked, understanding beginning to dawn on his face.

"You are exactly right, Major," Phoebe assured him.

"And he made it look as if Selby had done it?" Fitzmaurice looked indignant. "Well, I say! That was a damned shabby thing to do. Beg your pardon, ladies."

"It's perfectly all right, Major," Julia said graciously. "That is precisely what I think, too."

"I'm not saying that you aren't right," Varian said slowly. "No one could be happier than I would be if it turned out that it was not Selby. But I'm afraid I don't see how you could *prove* that it was not he."

Julia was aware of her cousin stirring anxiously, but she ignored him. "Oh," she said with a vague wave of her hand, "that is my secret. We wouldn't want word to get out."

Geoffrey relaxed with a faint sigh.

"But if you are right," Varian persisted, "and it was the work of some other person, don't you think that it is rather dangerous for you and Lady Armiger to be trying to find out his identity? If he was unscrupulous enough to not only steal the money but ruin a man in the process, I'd say he was a dangerous person."

"That's right," Fitzmaurice chimed in. "Wouldn't be a gentleman."

Geoffrey let out a choked sound and suddenly found something of great interest to look at on the floor.

"I daresay you are right," Julia allowed, suppressing her own smile. "He is no gentleman. But I doubt that there is any danger. The man must be a coward. Look at his actions! No bold and daring thievery there, but a sneaking sort of stealing, involving no real danger to himself. And to lay the blame on someone else—it's the act of a coward."

"But even a coward, if cornered, can turn on you," Varian warned.

"I'm no milk-and-water miss. If that happens, I will be able to take care of myself."

These words only served to make Varian look even more worried, but he said nothing more on the subject.

Major Fitzmaurice spoke up unexpectedly. "I remember once when we had a thief in the regiment. Bad business, that."

"Indeed?" Phoebe asked with polite interest. "And did you manage to catch him?"

"Oh, yes. Well, I mean, not I. I didn't know he'd been stealing until after it was all over. Been stealing out of other men's kits, you see. Joseph Bollinger was the one who caught him—always a canny one, he was. Not good ton, of course. Wouldn't present him to your sister, say, but a lot in his brain box." He frowned, remembering. "Never could understand him."

"How edifying," Geoffrey said with awful irony and stood up. "I am sorry, ladies, but I am afraid that I must take my leave now. Arranged to meet someone at my club."

"Of course." Julia smiled at him. "I quite understand."

"Going to Brooks's?" Fitzmaurice asked. "Wait, and I'll walk with you. I've been meaning to talk to you. Came around to your house the other day, but you wasn't there. In need of a little advice—it's my valet, you see."

"Of course it is."

Julia suppressed a smile at her cousin's frozen expression as the two men left the room. Varian St. Leger stayed a few minutes longer, once again entreating her to reconsider the idea of catching the embezzler. Phoebe seemed pleased by his solicitude, but Julia grew impatient after a time, and when he finally took his leave, she let out a gusty sigh of relief.

"Thank heavens they're gone. I would never have

told them if I had known that Varian would be so old-maidish about the whole thing.''

''I thought it was very kind of him to be so concerned about us,'' Phoebe protested gently.

Julia looked at her sister-in-law closely. She wondered if perhaps Phoebe had a special feeling for her husband's old friend. Varian would, Julia supposed, make a good match for Phoebe. He was invariably kind and solicitous, and his breeding was impeccable. If he was a trifle dull compared to Selby, well, she had to admit that it would be difficult to find another such as her brother had been—particularly among their rustic neighbors. And, much as Phoebe had loved and mourned Selby, she was not the sort of woman who would be happy living a single life. She was a sweet creature who needed someone to fuss over and admire as much as she needed someone to lean on. Still, Julia could not but feel a little pang of sorrow at the thought that someday in the not too distant future she would probably lose the company of her sister-in-law and nephew, if not to Varian St. Leger, then to some other man.

It was a lowering thought. Julia was a warm and affectionate creature, used to loving relationships with both her parents and her brother. She knew that it would be difficult for her to live a life alone, but she saw little chance for anything else. She had been cut off from Society during the past few years, when she had been of an age when most young girls made eligible marriages. Even if she was able to get Stonehaven to confess and thus save her family name from dishonor, she was old enough, at twenty-four, that she would probably be considered a spinster. Certainly she would be past the age of making her come-out in London, and, besides, she had no older female relative to act as her chaperon, anyway.

There were certainly no men among her limited acquaintance in Kent whom she could bear the thought of marrying, and, besides, she was beginning to feel that perhaps she was too independent to marry any man. Kind though Varian St. Leger might be, his warnings and disapproval irritated her. Even her cousin had been doubtful and questioning about her scheme. And she was not even a dependent of either one of them! She could well imagine what life with a husband must be like, always full of strictures, warnings and rules.

Nor could she think of a single man who could live up to her ideal of what a man should be. She supposed that having a brother like Selby had spoiled her. He had been so fun and full of life, always ready with a quip or a story. But he had by no means been a lightweight. He had been a man of courage and principle, the sort of man who was a bruising rider to the hounds but was also a concerned and dutiful landlord to the tenants of his estate. She could not imagine marrying a lesser man, could not tie herself to someone with whom she could not share laughter and problems and intelligent conversations.

Lord Stonehaven's image popped into her mind, startling her, and she immediately pushed it away. *How absurd!* Handsome he might be, and clever, as well as possessed of a certain charm, but she could not imagine anyone whom she would be less likely to marry. Not only was he a man of low character, he was her enemy, her nemesis!

"Julia? Julia?" Phoebe's voice cut through her thoughts.

Julia looked at her and realized from the other

woman's puzzled expression that she must have said Julia's name several times. "What?"

"Is something the matter?" Phoebe asked in concern. "You had the fiercest look on your face."

"No, I—my mind was just wandering. I'm sorry. You are right. Varian was simply being kind. No doubt my nerves are stretched, waiting for tomorrow night." She had not told Phoebe where she was going, knowing that she would be horrified to think that Julia would be alone in a box at Vauxhall Gardens with Lord Stonehaven. However, she had let her know that she thought that the next evening might bring what they had wished for.

"I know. Poor dear...aren't you frightened?"

"Frightened? No. At least, only of failing at my task. No harm is going to come to me."

Phoebe frowned. "I cannot help but worry. What if he were to find out who you are? Or what you are up to? He is *not* a gentleman—I mean, not in the true sense of the word."

"It won't happen. I won't let the truth slip out. I don't think he would hurt me, anyway." She didn't know exactly why she was so sure of this fact, but she was. "The worst that could happen would be that he would tell everyone how I was masquerading at Madame Beauclaire's, but I don't think he would relish the world knowing that he had been so gullible that I had been able to take him in."

"If you are sure, dear..."

"I'm positive. Now, let's talk of something else. What do you say we steal Master Gilbert away from Nurse and take him for a romp in the park?"

This idea pleased Phoebe immensely, and so they spent the rest of the day with Gilbert, playing games and chasing butterflies, returning so tired that they were happy to dine and go to bed at an unfashionably early hour.

Julia fell asleep almost as soon as her head hit the pillow and was deep in slumber some hours later when an unaccustomed noise brought her awake. She opened her eyes, confused and not knowing what had awakened her. Her room looked much the same as always. She turned her head toward the other side of the room, where the two long windows stood open to let in the cool night air. There, in front of one of the windows, silhouetted by the pale light from outside, stood the dark figure of a man.

6

It took a moment for it to register in Julia's sleep-numbed brain that there was an intruder in her room. She lay frozen, gazing at him. His face was a dark blank, devoid of features. Then the dark form started across the room toward her in a rush. The movement released Julia from her paralysis, and she screamed at the top of her lungs, throwing back the covers and leaping out of bed. Instinctively she reached out and grasped the first thing she could find on her bedstand.

It was a book, and she brought it up and swung it with all her might. The heavy tome crashed into the side of the man's head, and he let out a yelp of surprise and pain. Julia screamed again and pulled back for another swipe with her weapon. The man backed away hastily.

At that moment Phoebe's voice sounded in the hall, calling Julia's name, and in the next instant the door crashed open and Phoebe ran in, brandishing a large metal candleholder. Her appearance broke the attacker's nerve. He turned and dashed back to the window. Julia pursued him, with Phoebe right behind her, and the man barely managed to make it out the window before Julia reached it.

He grasped a branch and swung recklessly out, moving hand over hand across it until he reached a branch on which to put his feet.

"Blast!" Julia cried. "He's getting away."

Phoebe joined her at the window, and they stood looking down at the man who descended the tree like a monkey. Out in the hall there was the sound of running feet and several voices. Then Sidle, the butler, rushed into the room clad in a nightshirt, his nightcap tilted over one ear and perilously hanging, and one of Selby's dueling pistols in his hand. Right behind him came Mrs. Willett, her stout form encased in a bright yellow wrapper, carrying a rolling pin. Bringing up the train were two footmen and a pair of maids, all wide-eyed.

Julia had to hide a smile at the sight of them. "It's all right," she reassured them. "He's gotten away."

"What happened, miss?" Sidle asked, hurrying to the window and looking down in time to see the dark figure scale the wall to the street and disappear. "Burglar?"

"Yes, it must have been, I suppose," Julia said, amazed to find that her knees were suddenly weak. She sat down on the window seat, and Phoebe joined her, curling a comforting arm around Julia's shoulders.

"How awful for you!"

"Did he take anything, miss?" This came from the housekeeper, who was pragmatically engaged in lighting a candle.

"No. He hadn't time. It must have awakened me when he came in the window. I screamed and he ran at me—to stop me screaming, I guess. Then I hit him, and Phoebe came in, and he ran."

"A fine thing we're coming to," Mrs. Willett went on indignantly, "when robbers are climbing into respectable houses and scaring the wits out of everyone."

"Yes, I daresay."

The housekeeper went on in this fashion for several more minutes, bemoaning the state of the city these days and the morals of its people, until finally Julia managed to stem her tide of words and shoo all the servants out of the room. Sidle was somewhat reluctant to leave, fearing for Julia's safety, but he finally cleared his mind by decreeing that the two footmen must take turns standing guard in the garden for the rest of the night. Neither of the footmen looked entirely happy about this decree, but they left without grumbling, along with the others. Julia closed the door behind them and turned back to Phoebe.

"Oh, Julia! Was it horrible?" Phoebe asked sympathetically. "Were you terribly scared?"

"Shocked, is more like it," Julia said. "I wasn't frightened until afterward. It all happened so quickly— I just did the first thing that came into my mind."

"Yes, whacked him over the head." Phoebe giggled. "He must have been astonished to find you awake and attacking *him!*"

Julia smiled. "I imagine he was. He seems a singularly incompetent thief. Why did he go to the trouble to climb that tree? He could have broken in downstairs with much less effort—and not awakened anyone, either. Besides, the silver and expensive things are downstairs."

"No doubt he was looking for jewels. How was he to know he was climbing into the room of a young woman who would have nothing but a string of pearls in her jewelry box?"

"I suppose." Julia sighed and looked at the open window. "I shall have to close and lock my windows now. I do hate sleeping in a stuffy room."

Phoebe patted her hand sympathetically. "This will

be over soon, and we can go back to Greenwood. To tell you the truth, I will be glad to leave London.''

Julia nodded. ''It can't have been much fun for you.'' There had been, of course, none of the parties and entertainments that Phoebe and Selby had enjoyed in the past when they visited the city. Phoebe had not even had the excitement of trying to trap Lord Stonehaven. She had merely been stuck in a smaller house than she was used to with a six-year-old boy deprived of his normal country pursuits.

Phoebe smiled. ''It was fun to shop and, oh, just to see the sights again. I had forgotten what a bustle there always is here. I like the city—although I have to admit I can't help but feel a little jealous when I think of how we used to go to the opera and the theater and all those parties. Am I very wicked? I do hate so being snubbed.''

''Of course you're not wicked! It is the ones who snub us who are. *You* are the sweetest and kindest woman I know. It's only natural to like parties and such. I would think you very odd if you did not miss them. I miss them, too, and I have never even been to a London party.''

''They do rather throw the rector's wife's dinner parties into the shade,'' Phoebe agreed with a dimpling grin.

She began to talk about some of the more elegant parties she and Selby had attended during their Seasons in London, and they pleasantly wiled away a half hour in this manner. By that time their nerves were restored, and Phoebe picked up her heavy candlestick and went back to her own bedchamber. Julia closed both her windows and locked them and, on a sudden impulse, even turned the key in the lock of her door. Then, blowing out the candle, she climbed into bed.

It was some time, however, before she was able to go

to sleep—although she was not sure whether this fact was caused by nerves over the attacker or over her upcoming dealings with Lord Stonehaven. Whatever the cause, as a result she slept very late the next morning.

She spent much of the afternoon in her room, altering one of her mother's old gowns. Being several years old, it was not quite à la mode and required fairly extensive renovations. The dress was dark royal blue and consisted of a silk underdress covered by a layer of very sheer silk decorated with lace. Julia had had the idea for converting the dress the other night when she had seen the boldly dressed woman at Alfred's house. She redid the bodice, carefully taking out the thicker silk layer beneath the lace on the bodice. She also narrowed the skirt, as it was fuller than was fashionable now.

The result, when she put it on, made her blush. She was not as exposed as the woman the other night had been. The lace was thick enough that one could not actually see her nipples, but enough of her skin showed through to make it extremely titillating. The neckline was a trifle high, not the low, square-cut neck that was popular nowadays, but given the tantalizing glimpses of bare flesh beneath, Julia thought that it was rather more alluring with a high neckline. Thank God for her light cloak, she thought, for Phoebe would never have let her out of the house looking like this.

She took a long, soaking bath in water perfumed with attar of roses, letting the hot water soothe her jangled nerves. Her abigail then put up her hair in a simple style with only a small knot of ribbons for decoration, for Julia thought it best not to do anything that would distract one's eye from her scandalous dress. After that, the girl helped her dress, for it was impossible to button up the frock in the back without help. Delicate sandals completed the outfit. She would have liked to add a touch of color to her cheeks and lips, but as she had no pots of rouge, she had to content herself with pinching her cheeks and pressing her lips together to deepen their rosiness.

She was ready to go, but a glance at the clock on her mantel told her that she was almost an hour too early. She waited, pacing the floor, her nerves growing by the moment. Phoebe came to visit her, and Julia hastily grabbed a shawl and wrapped it around her to conceal the revealing bodice. Phoebe, not seeing the bodice, approved of the dress and assured Julia that she looked wonderful. The deep blue color, she told her, turned her eyes a wonderful color.

Finally Julia left, wrapped in her light cloak and with a pale blue, lace-trimmed half mask upon her face. She had thought, trying it on earlier, that she looked rather good in the mask. It gave her a certain air of mystery, while emphasizing the blueness of her eyes. She was still a trifle early, but she could not bear to wait any longer. Once again she hailed a hackney and took it to the entrance of the Gardens. As Vauxhall lay on the other side of the Thames, she found the trip more unnerving than the others she had taken alone in a hackney. However, her driver acted with complete propriety, even asking her if she was certain that she wished to go there and warning her that it was no place for a young miss alone. She assured him that she was being met, and though he still seemed unsatisfied, he drove her there.

She was relieved when the conveyance drew up in front of the entrance and she saw Stonehaven's tall form waiting for her. She recognized him in an instant, even though he, too, wore the half mask that most of the revelers at Vauxhall Gardens masquerades wore. His was a very plain black silk, but it lent a certain piratical look to his lean face. She noticed that two lone women walking by cast eyes of interest over him.

Julia had been worried about what she would do if Stonehaven had not arrived yet. She had heard tales of the young bucks who frequented the gardens, openly ogling and even making advances toward unaccompanied females, which was the sort of thing she had never had to deal with. She jumped down from the carriage, smiling broadly in her relief. Stonehaven's face, which had looked stern, lightened when he saw her, and he strode toward her.

"There you are." He reached out to take her hands, smiling, and his eyes glowed in a way that started her pulse pounding. "I was afraid you might have changed your mind."

"I'm not late, am I?"

He chuckled. "No. 'Tis the other way around. I am early."

There was a discreet cough from the driver of the hackney, reminding them that he had not yet been paid. Julia reached into her reticule, but before she could bring out her money, Stonehaven had already done so, giving the man a sum that made him grin hugely and tip his hat in appreciation.

"You needn't have done that," Julia protested. "Besides, I am certain that you must have paid him too much."

"Nonsense. A poor thing I should be if I let you pay for your own hackney. It's galling enough that you would not let me escort you."

"I am well able to take care of myself. I am not, after all, a delicate flower of a maiden," Julia commented dryly.

He leaned closer, breathing in her scent. "You smell like a delicate flower." He brushed his knuckles lightly down her cheek. "And your skin is as soft as any rose petal."

"You, sir, are an inveterate flatterer."

"Nay. Ask anyone, and they will tell you I am fatally blunt."

As they continued their light banter, he took her arm and was leading her into the center of the entertainment park, where the private boxes were lined up facing the central mall. He opened the door in the rear of one of the boxes and stepped back to allow her in.

It was a pleasant enough room, with a small table and a few chairs, as well as a sofa against the back wall. The front consisted of a waist-high wall, with the area above that open to the Gardens, but Julia noticed that at either end hung dark velvet curtains that could be drawn to avoid the stares of the vulgar crowd, if one wished to. An oil lamp glowed on a stand against the far wall, casting a low, warm light over the room, and a candelabra waited in readiness on the table. A covered supper had been laid out for them on the table, several bottles of wine already uncorked and "breathing" in readiness.

"I dispensed with the servant," Stonehaven said, indicating the table. "I thought we could fend for ourselves tonight."

"Yes, of course," Julia answered a little breathlessly. Even as inexperienced as she was, she recognized that it was a scene set for seduction, from the plush curtains to the golden lamplight to the padded brocade couch.

"Here. Let me take your cloak." He came forward, reaching out to take the wrap from her, but when Julia pulled it off, revealing for the first time the provocative dress, he stopped dead still. His words died in his throat, and he simply stared at her, his eyes traveling slowly down over her bosom, teasingly cupped by the array of lace, revealing and concealing her flesh in a manner designed to arouse.

His eyes flared with an unholy light, but he controlled himself enough to take her cloak, though there was the slightest tremor in his hand as he did so.

"You are very beautiful," Stonehaven said, his voice husky.

A thrill ran through Julia at the sound of his charged voice, and it was all she could do to say, "Thank you."

She thought that he was going to take her in his arms and kiss her, but instead he turned away and hung her cloak on a hook. Julia stripped off her gloves, reminding herself sternly that she had to be in firm control tonight. This was her best chance to catch the man, and she could not get rattled. By the time he turned back, she thought she had herself well in hand.

"Shall we dine?" he asked, gesturing toward the table.

"I think I would rather watch the passing parade for a moment, if you don't mind. It is such an interesting lot of people, don't you think?" She gestured vaguely toward the bottles of wine on the table. "Perhaps we might have a little drink?"

"Of course." Stonehaven went to the table. "Would you care for a glass of wine? Sherry? Ratafia?" He mentioned two drinks commonly drunk by ladies.

"Sherry would be nice." Julia smiled at him and strolled over to the half wall that looked out on the middle area of the gardens. She had not taken off her mask, and she was glad of it, for the stares of several of the young men passing by were far too bold. She felt safer

behind the mask; at least no one would know her face
if they should ever meet her again.

Stonehaven came up beside her, handing her a glass
of golden liquid. It took only one hard look from him
to discourage a young man who had started to walk over
to their box.

They sipped at their drinks as they watched the people
stroll along. Julia thought that she would indeed have
enjoyed seeing them if it had not been for the nerves
knotted in her stomach. She took a sip or two of the
sherry in the hope of relaxing, but she had no intention
of drinking much tonight. She was unaccustomed to
drinking liquor except for a glass of wine at dinner—
and usually not even that. She certainly did not want to
become inebriated herself in the attempt to loosen Lord
Stonehaven's tongue. Tonight she needed, more than
ever before, to be in full possession of her senses.

Stonehaven made a joking comment about a sprig of
fashion who was walking past their box now. Dressed
in the tightest of pantaloons in a pale shade of lavender,
with a coat of bright blue, quite padded in the shoulders
to make up for the defects of his figure, he obviously
considered himself up to the mark. The points of his
collar were alarmingly stiff and high, making it almost
impossible for him to turn his head, and his snowy white
cravat was tied in an intricate manner. Across the figured
waistcoat that showed between the lapels of his coat
stretched a gold watch chain from which hung such a
number of fobs and seals that they clattered together as
he walked. He strolled along slowly, giving everyone the
opportunity to admire him. When he saw Julia and
Stonehaven watching him from their box, he bowed toward them, no doubt sure that they were staring because
they were so entranced with his attire. Since he had to

turn the whole upper half of his body in order to do so, Julia had to clap her hand over her mouth to hide the fit of giggles that threatened to engulf her.

"Atrocious girl," Stonehaven told her, smiling lazily. "You nearly made me choke—I'd just taken a drink."

"Nonsense. 'Twas not *I* who made you laugh. It was that popinjay."

"The Tulip of Fashion? Oh, no, laughable though he is. What nearly caused me to lose control was the way your mouth dropped open. You looked like a landed fish."

"How unkind of you to say so!" Julia protested, spoiling her appearance of indignation by chuckling. "You show a lamentable lack of conduct."

"*I?*" He cocked an eyebrow at her. "What is that old expression? Something about the pot calling the kettle black?"

They passed some time in this bantering way. Julia asked him who this person was or that. One very grand-looking woman, whom she supposed must be a member of the peerage, was, he informed her, one of the most famous madames in town, while a plain white-haired woman in an outmoded black dress was, he said, a duchess.

"No!" Julia protested. "I can't believe it." She glanced at the empty glass in his hand. "You must be foxed."

He laughed. "I'm not. I tell you, that is the Duchess of Denwater. They live in a grand, decaying pile up in Yorkshire, and both she and the duke are the most amazing skinflints one ever saw. It's said she pinches every penny and pays such miserable wages that she can't keep a full staff. She comes down to London once a year and drives her son and his wife mad. The duke stays at home, despising to travel. The son has to beg for every cent he gets from them. It's fortunate his wife has a small legacy or the Lord only knows what they'd do. He has to borrow on his expectations as it is.''

Julia shook her head as she reached out for his glass. "Let me refill your glass," she offered.

He shook his head. "I thought you were sure I was foxed.''

"I should have known you would cast that back up at me." Julia took the glass from his hand despite what he had said and went to the table to pour him another drink.

"Are you trying to get me drunk?" he teased, following her to the table and pushing his mask back off his head.

Julia looked up into his twinkling eyes, holding out his glass, and said provocatively, "Why, of course. How else could I 'have my way' with you?''

His fingers curled around the glass, touching hers, and he gazed down at her warmly. "Indeed, my dear Jessica, there is no need for you to do anything to achieve that. I am already yours.''

Julia's mouth went dry, and her heart began to knock wildly in her chest. She gazed at him, unable to think of anything to say. He set his glass of wine down on the table with one hand, and with the other he pushed up her mask and laid it aside.

"I dislike any part of your face being covered," he murmured.

He bent to kiss her.

Julia braced herself. She had prepared herself to hold out against this first kiss. She knew that she must not allow it to rock her off her feet as she had been the other two times. But he surprised her by not kissing her deeply or fervently, but with the lightest of touches, his lips brushing hers like butterfly wings. His mouth returned again and again, gently taking first her upper lip, then her lower, between his lips. It was teasing, distracting and thoroughly arousing to her senses.

Stonehaven raised his head and looked down at her with a faintly questioning look. Julia stared back at him. She didn't know what he wanted her to say, but she was afraid that if she opened her mouth, it would be to ask him to kiss her again.

With the greatest exercise of self-will, Julia made herself step back. "Perhaps—perhaps we should have that supper now."

He stepped aside, saying, "Of course," and held out a chair for her.

He removed the covers and solicitously helped Julia to a portion of everything laid out before them. Julia took a sip of wine to steady her nerves and began to push the food around on her plate. She had never felt less like eating.

"Tell me about this ward of yours," she said, hoping that it would sound only as if she were groping for a topic of conversation. She had tried her best to come up with some less obvious way of bringing it up, but she had not been able. She only hoped that the three glasses of wine he had drunk would already have made his reasoning less clear.

He looked faintly surprised, but said only, "Young Thomas, do you mean? I had forgotten that I'd mentioned him."

"Not by name. You merely said that you visited him in Kent. I beg your pardon, I forgot—you said you were not really his guardian, but only his trustee." She frowned and speared a green pea. "I am afraid that I do not entirely understand the difference."

"I have no guardianship of his person. He lives with his mother. I merely administer a trust fund that his father set up for him. His father, Walter, and I were good friends."

"Ah, I see. How sad that he should have died so young." She thought it best not to concentrate entirely on the trust for fear of rousing his suspicions.

"Yes. A riding accident. Most unexpected and unfortunate. Especially for Thomas. He has no father, and neither I nor the other trustees live nearby. Only one did and he—well, he is dead now, too."

Julia's stomach knotted at the mention of her brother's demise, but she managed to say in a normal voice, "How tragic. This seems an ill-fated story."

"Yes, it *was* tragic. On all counts."

"What happened to him?"

Stonehaven shook his head. "No, let's not talk about such sad things tonight." He lifted her hand and kissed it. "I would much prefer to concentrate on something pleasant, like you."

Julia could have screamed with frustration, but she forced herself to smile. "Indeed, you are right. This is not a night of gloom." She picked up the wine bottle and refilled his almost empty glass. "We should be merry."

He lifted his drink toward her in a toast, and she responded, clinking her glass against his. She took a sip. She had avoided drinking as much as she could, but in her nervousness, she had already downed two glasses. Since she had managed to eat almost nothing, she was beginning to feel woozy. She forced herself to eat a little, trying to think of a way to bring Stonehaven to talk about what she wanted him to. It did not seem wise to return directly to the subject of the trust for fear he would grow suspicious.

After they finished eating, they, too, took a turn through the gardens. "I suppose it is only fair to allow everyone to criticize us the way we did them," Julia said, mask and cloak once again in place, as they strolled along the grassy thoroughfare between the boxes.

"I protest! We did other things than criticize. As I remember, there was a dress you coveted."

"Ah, yes, the pink one. It was lovely. It would never do, however, for one with my color hair. That is a color that Ph—uh, that *few* people but blondes can wear." She smiled at him, hoping that he hadn't noticed her stumble.

How could she have slipped and almost said Phoebe! It was, she thought, that she was beginning to feel so used to Lord Stonehaven, so familiar with her role, that she was forgetting that she was playing a part. In fact, there were times when she found herself relaxing and being herself instead of trying to get information out of Stonehaven. Earlier this evening, for instance, when they had been watching the passing parade of people, she had enjoyed their banter and had been, for a brief period, just what she appeared to be: a young woman flirting with a man and taking pleasure in his company. The thought of it horrified her. How could she have forgotten, even for a few minutes, about Selby and what this man had done to him?

They reached the end of the promenade and took one of the small paths branching off from it. As they drew into the more secluded parts, it was brought home to Julia quite forcibly why Vauxhall Gardens was not a place a maiden went unless escorted by some responsible male. She saw a young woman being chased by an obviously inebriated man, but her shrieks were so playful, and she was laughing with such glee, that it was obvious she intended to be caught. In the shadow of a tree she saw another couple in a fervent embrace. It was clear that even without a private box one could find an ample number of places to be intimately alone here.

When two young blades reeking of alcohol made their swaying way past them, one of them almost bumping into Julia, Stonehaven decided that it was time to return to the box. "It is almost time for the fireworks, anyway."

Back in their box, Stonehaven poured himself a brandy, offering Julia one, which she declined, and they sat down before the open wall to watch the fireworks display. Julia could not help but enjoy the fireworks, oohing and aahing and clapping her hands whenever one was especially spectacular.

"That was beautiful!" she exclaimed, eyes sparkling and cheeks flushed with pleasure, when the display was finally through.

Stonehaven looked down at her, smiling. "No, it is *you* who are beautiful."

He reached over and pulled the curtains closed. Julia's heart began to race, and her stomach was a knot of nerves again. The time had arrived, she realized, and she wasn't sure whether she was more scared or excited. Stonehaven took off his mask and tossed it onto the table, then reached up to remove hers, as well. Surprising her, he reached into an inner pocket of his jacket and pulled out a small box.

"Here," he said, extending it to her. "A token of my esteem."

Startled, Julia took the box and opened it. Inside, on a velvet cushion, lay a delicate bracelet of sapphires and diamonds. Julia drew a quick, awed breath. "It's beautiful!"

"I am glad you like it."

"But I can't take this!" she said instinctively, thrusting the box back toward him.

"What?" He looked stunned. "What are you talking about? Do you not like it?"

"Of course I like it! But—" Julia came to a flustered halt. She could hardly give him the response ingrained in her: that a lady could not accept such a gift from a man who was neither her fiancé nor her husband. From a man who was no such relation one could take nothing but flowers or candy or perhaps some small, impersonal thing—never a bracelet, especially such an obviously expensive one. "I, uh, it is far too expensive. I couldn't possibly."

He chuckled. "Now that is a refreshingly different opinion." He folded her hand over the box, holding it in his own. "Take it. Please. When I saw it, I was reminded of your eyes, and I knew that it would do for no one but you."

Julia knew that she should take it if she wanted to remain in character. But she could not. It would make her feel...dirty, as if she had been bought. It was silly, of course, to quibble over it, since she was pretending to be exactly the sort of woman who was paid for her favors. If she had no qualms over that, why should she balk at accepting a gift? But Julia simply could not accept the gift. Somehow it hurt that he should think she was the sort of woman who would.

"No, please, do not ask me to. I cannot," she said in a low voice, pulling her hand away. She walked away from him. She felt strangely like crying.

"I'm sorry. I have offended you." He sounded both

puzzled and remorseful. He followed her, grasping her arms from behind. He bent closer, his breath ruffling her hair. "If I have been clumsy, please accept my apology. It was never my intent to upset you or to offend you in any way. I merely wanted to express my feelings for you. I wanted only to give you something. Now I've made a muddle of it."

He bent down lower and laid a kiss upon the bare skin overlying her collarbone. Julia sucked in her breath at the frisson of pleasure. "Please say you will forgive me," Stonehaven murmured.

His lips trailed across her shoulder, touching her with fire. Julia tilted her head away, unconsciously offering her long white neck to his marauding lips. He seized the opportunity she offered, kissing his way slowly up her neck to her ear, where he nibbled gently at the lobe. Julia released a breathy little sigh. His lips were creating all sorts of sensations in her. She knew dimly that she should stop him, but her mind was cloudy, and she could not seem to find the words she wanted. Wherever his lips touched, her skin immediately turned to fire.

Finally, exerting great effort, she stepped away, bringing a shaky hand to her face. "Lord Stonehaven... Deverel. I—I—you will find me silly, I am sure, but I am not ready for this."

"My dear girl, there is nothing you need do to prepare," he assured her quickly, moving to her. He put his hands at her waist, pulling her gently back against him.

"But, I mean, I—think you believe me to be a—more of a sophisticate than I am. But I am not even from London, and I am afraid that I—"

He let out a low chuckle, and his mouth went to work on the other side of her neck. "What has London to do with it?"

"I'm not sure," Julia answered honestly, thinking that she must sound like an idiot. *Where had all her wits gone?* She closed her eyes, concentrating on blocking out the warmth of his mouth on her skin, the velvety feel of his lips, the occasional light nip of his teeth. "Uh, what I mean is, I think perhaps this is wrong for me to do."

She turned, breaking his hold, to look up into his face. She realized instantly that that had been a mistake. The heat in his dark eyes was almost tangible, affecting her in much the same way as his kisses. She pressed her lips together, and his eyes fell to her mouth. The dark, slumbrous look that came into them set off an explosion of heat in her abdomen.

She swallowed hard and said, "Doing something wicked can haunt one the rest of one's life, don't you think? Haven't you ever done anything wicked? Did you long to talk about it, but you couldn't? Did it fester inside you?"

Stonehaven looked at her oddly. "Wicked? Improper, perhaps, but surely this is not wicked."

He bent and brushed his lips against hers playfully, then raised his head and regarded her, one eyebrow lifted. "Did that seem wicked?"

The touch of his mouth distracted her, but Julia felt she had found a good line of questioning, and she followed it doggedly. "No, of course not, but you know how one thing leads to another. Sometimes we can want something so much that we do something wrong, but then we—we excuse it. And gradually we go on to more and more wrong things, until we are in so deep that there is no way out. Haven't you ever felt that? Done that?"

He blinked, then shrugged his shoulders. "I—I'm not

sure. I suppose I have, but at the moment I am not thinking clearly. My mind is too befogged by you."

He bent again and kissed her, this time more lingeringly. The taste of brandy on his tongue was heady. Julia felt her knees weakening, and she grabbed hold of his coat to steady her. When at last his mouth left hers, she blinked up at him, dazed, for a moment.

"Um, I—have you ever done anything wicked?" she asked a little desperately.

He laughed. "Jessica…whatever is amiss? Do you think that I don't care for you? That what I feel is fleeting? I can promise you that it is not. If you are asking if I will treat you in an honorable manner, I can assure you that I will. I am not the sort of man to play fast and loose with a woman."

She almost groaned. Why would he not cooperate?

He drew her closer and rested his head against hers. "I give you my word. I will provide for you. I will treat you well." He kissed her hair, then the side of her face. "Has another man treated you badly? I promise you, I am not like that."

He wrapped his arms around her tightly, pressing her into his hard body. He kissed her closed eyes, then her cheek, and finally his mouth came to rest upon hers again. His kiss was deep and heated. His breath seared her cheek.

Julia trembled as heat washed over her. She knew she ought to protest, ought to move away from him. *This was going all wrong!* He was not saying what he was supposed to. She had been completely unable to draw him out; all he wanted to do was kiss her. Yet she could not even summon up irritation with him. All she could feel was this wonderful, tingling, amazing fire that was spreading through her body as he kissed her again and again.

Finally he lifted his mouth from hers, but only to explore her neck. He moved down to the bare skin of her chest above her dress. His hand came up to cup her breast through the thin lace covering. His thumb circled her nipple, making her jerk in surprise. The movement of his skin on her nipple seemed to send a direct signal to her loins, which were suddenly throbbing urgently. She could feel her nipple hardening, pressing against the lace.

He groaned and in a quick movement bent to sweep her up in his arms, then turned and carried her to the couch at the back of the room.

7

Panic spurted up in Julia, and she moved in his arms. "No. Pray…"

"Shh." His voice was soft and soothing, and she realized that he took her protest for some kind of last-minute nerves that he could soothe away.

He laid her down on the couch and knelt beside her, his arms still around her. He began to kiss her again while his hand roamed over her front, caressing her breasts through the lace. Julia brought her hands up to his chest to push him away, but, strangely, she found them sliding up around his neck, holding on to him. His kiss was drugging, far more intoxicating than the sherry.

His mouth left hers and began a trek down her throat. Kissing, nipping, sucking, he feasted on her soft skin, and when his lips came to the lace, he edged his tongue beneath it, tracing the line of the lace across the tops of her breasts. His tongue touched her nipple through the lace, and Julia gasped, stunned by the unexpected action and by the explosion of pleasure within her. She had never felt this way, had never even known that such a feeling was possible. She trembled under the onslaught of sensations as he circled her nipple with his tongue, causing it to harden and thrust against the lace. Her pleasure was heightened by the faint friction of the material upon her delicate flesh. His mouth closed around the hard bud, softly suckling it. Julia moaned as a tremor shook her, and her breath came fast and hard.

The strangest things were happening inside her. Suddenly moisture was flooding between her legs, and the tender flesh there was throbbing with each quick beat of her pulse. She squeezed her legs together, trying to ease the pleasurable ache, but it seemed only to grow.

"Deverel," she whispered.

His only answer was a groan, and his hand moved slowly down her body, sliding over her abdomen and into the crevice between her legs. She realized instantly that it was this touch that she craved, this heat and firmness, and she could not keep from arching up against his hand. She could feel even more heat surge through him, and he began to move his hand against her, somehow both satisfying and intensifying the longing there.

He reached down and slid his hand up her leg, shoving up her skirts. "You are so beautiful," he murmured.

He moved down the couch to touch his lips to her ankle, then her calf, then her knee. When his warm mouth reached her thigh, Julia jerked upright, startled out of her daze of pleasure. "No! Deverel, wait...."

She glanced around distractedly, trying to pull herself together. *She could not do this!* She saw now how foolish, how blind, she had been about this whole thing. It had been naive to think that she could seduce him only a little bit, that she could hold a man like Stonehaven off with a few kisses and caresses. Even plying him with drink had not helped. Instead of his telling her what she wanted to know, he was pulling her into a dark pit of desire from which she had the awful feeling that there was no escape. She had not guessed what strong sensual desires had lain hidden within her. Even less had she guessed that Stonehaven would have such an effect on her. But she knew that she was rapidly losing all willpower, and if she remained here much longer, she would be giving herself to her worst enemy!

The horror of the thought gave her the strength to sit up, swinging her legs off the couch. Stonehaven sat back on his heels, looking confused. "Jessica? What is it? What's wrong?"

"I can't! I just can't!" Julia pushed herself to her feet.

"But, my dear…did I do something? Say something?"

"No! I can't explain!" Her words came out on a little sob.

She turned and ran to the door. Snatching her cloak off the hook, she flung open the door and ran out into the night. Behind her she heard him call her name, but she did not check or look back, simply ran like a mad thing through the people milling around the grounds. She was a country girl and used to physical exercise, but she knew that she was no match for him. He would have caught up to her, she was sure, but that an inebriated gentleman, seeing him chasing her, quixotically stepped in front of him, saying, "I say, there, I don't think she wishes to see you."

Stonehaven, of course, shoved him aside easily, but the incident had slowed him down enough that Julia was able to reach the line of hackney coaches outside the gardens before he caught up with her. The driver of the hackney, taking in the situation at a glance, slapped his reins over the horse's back as soon as Julia flung herself into the carriage, and they took off just as Stonehaven put out his hand to take the door handle. For an instant

Julia thought that he would grab hold of the carriage and climb in even though it had started moving, but he did not. She had one last glimpse of his frowning face, and then they were past him and moving at a spanking pace.

It was over. She had failed! Sorrow welled in her chest, and suddenly Julia could not hold back the tears. She put her face in her hands and sobbed. She would never see Deverel again—and Selby's name would never be cleared.

Julia spent the next day sunk in gloom. When Phoebe asked her concernedly what was wrong, she could say only that she had failed Selby.

"Oh, no!" Phoebe protested, reaching out to take Julia's hand. "I am sure that Selby would not feel so."

"*I* do." Julia sighed. "When it came to it, I was weak."

A frown of worry creased Phoebe's forehead. "What happened? Did he—*harm* you?"

"No. Oh, no. Only my pride was wounded. I saw what a fool I had been."

"No, don't say that."

"I was no match for Stonehaven."

"But only consider. He is a man steeped in evil. It only stands to reason that in that sort of contest, he would win."

"I suppose. But it does not help Selby any—or Gilbert. He will have to live with the blot upon his name."

"Perhaps we will be able to think of some other way," Phoebe suggested soothingly.

"Perhaps," Julia agreed, but she was not convinced, and her spirits remained low all day.

The next morning she was surprised by an early visit from Thomas St. Leger. Thomas was fourteen years old, and over the last year had suddenly spurted upward. He was absurdly thin, with matchstick arms and legs, and hands and feet that seemed far too large for him. His fair hair was thin and flyaway, and his face was dominated by a nose that he had not yet grown into. But he was a lad of great enthusiasm and warmth, and his smile made one instantly forget his ungainly appearance.

Though Thomas was the young man whose trust had been embezzled, he had loved Selby dearly, taking him as a kind of father after his own father had died, and he was as convinced as Phoebe and Julia that Selby had been falsely accused. Always having been a trifle scared of the brusque Lord Stonehaven, he had readily agreed with them that it must have been he who had embezzled the money and set it up to look as if Selby had done it. He had been in on their plot from the first, but Julia had not informed him of the change in direction she had taken in the scheme, for she had found that males, even at a young age, tended to take a dim view of women behaving as she had done. Fortunately, in London they had seen little of the lad. Today was only the third time that he had managed to elude his watchful tutor and make his way to the Armiger house.

The butler informed Julia and Phoebe, still at breakfast, of his arrival.

"Thomas?" Julia asked, her spirits brightening. "Send him in, of course. And set a place for him. I am sure he will be feeling a mite peckish."

Indeed, being an adolescent boy, Thomas was hungry even though he had already eaten an early breakfast at home. He piled his plate with eggs, ham and bacon from the sideboard and dug into it with gusto.

"That was delicious," he said, after bolting down a great quantity of food in the time it had taken Julia to eat a square of toast and finish her tea. Then he looked all around the room for lingering servants before continuing. "Sorry. I can't stay long. I just came to tell you that we are returning to Farrow tomorrow."

"Really? This is rather sudden, isn't it? The Season isn't over yet."

"Mama has her skirts in a swirl," Thomas said inelegantly. "She's been in a taking ever since she found out you two were in town. I can't think why she dislikes Julia so."

Both Phoebe and Julia had a fair idea why, knowing that Pamela St. Leger was jealous of Julia's beauty, but they refrained from saying so to her son.

"Anyway, she had a row yesterday with Cousin Varian. I think it was about his calling on you. He left, looking stiff as a board and not even saying goodbye to me, which ain't like him at all, I can tell you. I suppose Mama must have put his back up. So this morning she says that we're leaving for home immediately."

"Today?" Julia asked in amazement.

"She'll try. Once she gets in a pet, there's no stopping her. She has all the servants flying around trying to get everything packed. That's how I was able to slip away without anyone seeing me. But by the time the post chaise is packed, it will probably be too late to leave, because Mama refuses to travel after dark. She's terrified of highwaymen." He shrugged, accustomed to his mother's erratic behavior. "So we'll wind up going tomorrow anyway. Probably at the crack of dawn, because she's going to get Fitz to escort us, and you know how he is, being a military man."

"I'm sorry that your visit is being cut short," Phoebe said sympathetically.

But Thomas dismissed the thought with a wave of his

hand. "It's all right. London's been a dead bore—stuck all the time with that tutor, doing nothing but visit stuffy old museums, and no riding except once or twice on a hired hack, and *that* was practically as bad as not riding at all." Thomas, ungainly as he might be on foot, was a skillful rider, seemingly at one with his horse. Going without his daily rides had galled him considerably.

"You will be much happier at home."

Thomas nodded. "I daresay. I have to admit, I've been fair sick for Farrow. And Mama never tells me anything that she gets in letters. At least, nothing interesting. Just stuff about that insipid Beasley woman—and what do I care about her silly card parties?"

Phoebe nodded sympathetically. "I am sure you would be much more interested in hearing about Theo Huntington's breaking his leg trying to take a fence on his new hunter."

"I should say so!" Thomas exclaimed, leaning forward. "That cawker. He always fancies he's bang up to the nines, but he always rushes his fences. I hope the hunter wasn't injured."

Phoebe smiled. "No. He came trotting home sweet as you please. That's how they knew that something had happened to Theo, so they went out to search for him. But the vicar's wife wrote that he's mad as hops about it and wants to sell the horse now."

"Does he?" Thomas appeared much struck by this idea. "By gad, I'd like to take him up on that. I wonder if I can persuade Varian to spring for it. Perhaps I'd better dash him off a note before I leave. I shall talk to Fitz about it on the way home. If he and Varian agree, then I shan't even need to approach *him.*" He spoke the last word in accents of disgust.

His words seemed to remind Thomas of his other reason for coming, and he turned toward Julia. "What of our plan? Have you seized Stonehaven yet?"

"No." Julia stirred uncomfortably. She hated admitting to her young friend that she had failed. "We couldn't get him. Nunnelly tried several times, but De— I mean, Lord Stonehaven—always escaped. He gave Nunnelly a black eye once, too. So I—I devised another scheme."

"Another one! What? Did it work?"

"No. Nothing's worked," Julia said disgustedly.

"Well, what did you try?"

"I thought…he seemed to be fond of female company, so I—oh, I pretended to be someone else and—"

"What? You tried to get it out of him by flirting?" Thomas let out a rude crack of laughter. "What a corkbrained notion. I could have told you that that wouldn't fly. I don't think he's in the petticoat line. Mama don't like him above half because she threw out a lure for him—more than once, truth be known—and he never bit at all."

Julia's temper flared at his contemptuous dismissal of her idea. "You are fair and far off. He *does* like women, and he liked me. But I couldn't get him to talk about the scandal. And I, well, finally I couldn't go through with it."

Thomas frowned. "Go through with what? *Julia!*" His voice turned stern. "Exactly what did you *do?* What couldn't you go through with?"

"Nothing reprehensible." She paused, then added honestly, "At least, not horribly so. I didn't…" Her voice trailed off.

"By Jove! I should think not!" His voice cracked boyishly, detracting from his male outrage. "Whatever made you decide to do that? Can you imagine what kind of tale he's going to spread about you now?''

"He didn't even know who I was. I will remain a mystery woman.''

"Unless you happen to run into him sometime—or unless he thinks to connect that carrottop of yours with Selby's hair.''

"My hair is not carrot-colored!'' Julia protested. "He won't connect us, anyway. There's no reason to. And I will never meet him. He doesn't come to Greenwood, and I doubt that I shall ever travel to Buckinghamshire or even to London again. That's not important, anyway. I wouldn't care if he knew I had behaved scandalously if it had cleared Selby's name. The thing is that I failed, and I don't know how we're going to prove that Stonehaven did it, not Selby.''

All three of them fell silent, thinking their own thoughts. After a moment, Thomas said, "You could still kidnap him, you know. A few days without food or water ought to encourage him to talk.''

"I told you—we tried three times, and we failed. He is too good a fighter. Nunnelly would have to hire some other men to help overcome him, and I don't want any outsiders in on it. It's too dangerous.''

"The whole thing is dangerous,'' Phoebe agreed. "Even if you could force him to confess, he could still accuse you of kidnapping him.''

Both Julia and Thomas waved aside this poor-spirited statement.

"He would be too proud to admit that a woman had bested him,'' Julia said with assurance. "Anyway, once I had a signed confession and the world knew what he'd done to Selby, as well as to Thomas, he would be in utter disgrace. Who would believe him? Or care?''

"The problem is getting him," Thomas agreed. "Once he's in that hut we fixed up, he'll talk, all right. A man who would do what he did to Selby has to be a coward, down deep."

Julia felt a twinge of unease at this statement. She had always believed, like Thomas, that the sneaky nature of the man's crimes indicated that he had no real heart or courage, but after being around him the past few days, she was not as sure now.

However, at that moment Phoebe said something that sent all other thoughts flying out of her head. "Perhaps if we can't force him physically, we could trick him."

Julia sat bolt upright, staring at her sister-in-law. "Fee! That's it! You've struck it right on the head. We shall trick him into going to the hut!"

"How?" Thomas asked bluntly.

Julia smiled like a cat who'd got into the cream. "Don't worry your head about that. I have my ways."

Julia pulled aside the curtain and peered out of the carriage. There still was no sign of Deverel. She sighed, her stomach knotting. What if he was so angry with her that he would not come?

She had refused to tell Thomas the exact nature of her plans and had sent him home, saying that it would never do for his mother to discover at this late date that he was sneaking out to visit the Armigers. When he had protested that it wasn't fair, she assured him that he would be the first to know—after Phoebe, of course— what transpired with Lord Stonehaven. After he left, she had explained the rudiments of her plan to Phoebe, and though of course Phoebe fretted about the uncertainty and the danger to Julia if something went wrong, she had finally had to agree with her that what Julia was suggesting was probably the only way of salvaging their scheme.

Then Julia had sat down to pen a brief note to Lord Stonehaven. It took her some time and several start-overs before she got it precisely as she wanted it. Then she had found a likely-looking street urchin to deliver it for her. After that, there was nothing to do but wait until seven o'clock, when she had asked him to meet her in front of Madame Beauclaire's.

It was now five minutes until seven. Julia had had Nunnelly pull the carriage up across the street from the house ten minutes before the appointed time. She did not want to miss Stonehaven if he came early. She flicked aside the curtain again and was rewarded by see-ing a familiar figure coming down the street toward her.

Julia closed her eyes in relief, sending up a quick prayer of gratitude, and opened the door of the carriage. He saw her at once and started across the street to her. She remained standing, leaning out of the carriage in the hopes that it would draw Stonehaven's eye away from the top of the coach, where Nunnelly sat, holding the reins. Even though Nunnelly had his coat collar up and a hat pulled low on his head, it was still possible that Deverel might recognize him as the man who had as-saulted him on three other occasions.

However, Deverel did not even glance toward the coachman as he went to Julia and bowed over her hand. "Jessica." He straightened, looking at her in a quizzical way.

"Come into the carriage," Julia said and sat back down.

He followed her suggestion, closing the door after him. The carriage began to roll immediately. Nunnelly had his instructions.

For a moment Julia and Deverel simply looked at each other. Finally Julia looked away. "I am sorry. I hardly know where to begin."

"Nor do I. I am confused. Did I offend you the other night? Or were you merely playing games with me? I confess that I scarcely know whether to be angry with you or apologetic."

"No. It was neither, rest assured. Please believe that. I know I must have seemed absurd. Rude, even."

"I was concerned. I went after you. I can't understand why you ran from me."

"I—I was scared."

"Of me?"

"No. Of course not. Well, perhaps a little. I am not as...well, experienced as you think. Indeed, my lord, you make me lose my head a little. It frightens me." She paused and cast an inquiring glance across at him. "I hope that does not make you angry."

He smiled faintly. "I cannot think how it would displease a man to hear that he has such an effect on you. But I fail to see how that is any cause for running away."

"I—I went there thinking that I could handle the situation, but then, as it went along, I realized that I could not. You were much more sophisticated than I, and I was being swept along."

He leaned forward, taking her hand. "Are you saying that you did not wish to make love to me?"

She nodded. "Not there. Not that night. I could not bear for it to happen on a sofa in a box at Vauxhall Gardens."

"Dear girl! I had no intention of making love to you there, either. I did not realize you thought that. I meant to remove to my house, where we could be private and uninterrupted all night long. You must think me a very harum-scarum sort to believe that I would take you there.''

"I am not entirely used to London ways. I told you that I was from the country."

"You should have told me your fears. I could have relieved your mind."

"I didn't think. I panicked. Can you forgive me?''

"My dear Jessica…of course I can. There is nothing to forgive. I have merely been worried that I had offended you. That I had done something *you* would not forgive. I have been thinking about you ever since that night, racking my brain for what went wrong and how I could fix it. You cannot imagine my relief when I got your note this afternoon." He did not feel it necessary to tell her of the alternating fury, hurt and worry that had plagued him for the past two days—nor of how infuriating it had been that he had been unable to put her out of his mind.

"Really?" Julia was sincerely surprised. She had thought it would take a good deal of persuasion to charm him out of being miffed. What she had done, after all, had been an insult.

"Really." He smiled and lifted her hand to his lips. "Now I must ask whether you will permit me to see you again. Whether I may hope for more from you."

Julia smiled at him. "I should not be so bold, I am sure. But I cannot lie. You may hope for more." She looked away, saying, "In fact, I had hoped that tonight…"

"I have no plans," he assured her. "Let me tell your driver my address."

"No," Julia said hurriedly. "No, I cannot go there. It, well, it just wouldn't seem right." He looked puzzled.

Julia's words sounded lame, even to her ears, so she hurried on. "I know of a place. A secluded spot. It's in Kent."

"Your home?" he asked, surprised.

"Nearby. It is small, but quite cozy—and we can be alone there, unbeknownst to anyone...." She let her voice trail off invitingly. "Do say that you will come."

"Right now? But wouldn't it be better if I stopped and got a few things from my house? I mean, if it is out of town—I am hardly prepared."

"Oh, no," Julia said teasingly, leaning back negligently in the corner and casting him a seductive smile. "I don't think we can do that at all. I am abducting you, you know."

"Are you?" He cocked an eyebrow, falling in with her joke. "For what purpose are you abducting me? I promise, no one would pay to get me back."

"I care nothing for that. My purpose, you see, is to make you my slave."

Even in the dimness of the carriage, she could see the subtle shift of his face at her words, the heat that suffused his features. "Indeed?" he replied a little hoarsely. "In what way shall I serve you?"

"In any way I choose," she responded archly.

"Lord, but you are a teasing little wench. Already you have me hard as stone, and I have not even touched you."

Heat flooded Julia's cheeks at his words, and she hoped that he could not see it. He reached across the carriage and pulled her out of her seat and onto his lap. "I trust," he said thickly, "that this is a long journey." He bent to kiss her.

Julia had expected that she would have to indulge in some kisses and caresses to keep Stonehaven interested and unsuspicious for the three-hour trip to the Armiger estate. If she was honest with herself, she had to admit that she had even looked forward to it a little bit, at least deep down inside, knowing that it would not end in his taking her maidenhood. That, surely, he would put off until they reached their destination—and then, of course, it would be too late.

So she gave in easily to his kiss. She wondered if he would caress her as he had the other night, touching her in those wild, intimate places and taking her breast in his mouth. When he cupped her breast in his hand, she let out a little sigh of satisfaction. It was reprehensible of her, she knew. But it felt so good!

He kissed her over and over again, until her lips felt tender and swollen and very well used. Julia kissed him back, giving in to her baser impulses and telling herself that it was all in a good cause—as well as probably the only chance she would ever have of experiencing such kisses, unless and until she married. She twined her tongue around his and even boldly invaded his mouth. He did not seem to mind the boldness, for his breath grew more heated and heavy, and now and again he groaned as if he were caught somewhere between pain and pleasure.

One of his arms was around her back, supporting her, but the other roamed her body insistently, cupping her breasts and teasing her nipples to hardness, then moving lower to caress her abdomen and legs, and finally sliding up under her skirt to explore her legs, coming to rest at last upon the hot, moist center of her desire. Julia gasped, clenching her legs tightly around his hand. She could feel the shudder that ran through his body at her action. He buried his face in her neck.

"Oh, God, I must stop or I shall go further than I intend," he muttered hoarsely against her skin.

Julia nodded assent, too lost in her desire to form coherent words. He was right. It would be disastrous if they went any further...but everything inside her wanted to.

Deverel let out a long sigh and set her away from him, pulling down her skirts. They removed to opposite corners of the coach, looking at each other, neither of them saying a word. It seemed as if they rode that way for hours. Julia's whole body was still aflame, and she noticed how the rocking and swaying of the coach seemed to heighten the fire between her legs. She tried to ignore it. She looked everywhere but at Deverel. She reminded herself of what an awful man he was and what he had done to her brother. She rolled up the curtain beside her and gazed out at the moon-washed landscape. Nothing eased the hunger within her.

"Take down your hair," he said huskily from across the coach.

Julia glanced at Deverel, startled. "What?"

"I want to see your hair down."

"Oh. Uh—I—" She wasn't sure she ought to, but it seemed a far smaller thing than what they had been doing earlier. She reached up and began to unpin her hair. The luxuriant curls uncoiled and fell one by one, until at last her rich, fiery hair lay in a tumble all around her face and down her shoulders.

She glanced over at Deverel. He was watching her, and in the moonlight that streamed through the window, she could see that his face was heavy and slack with hunger, his eyes dark, unreadable pits.

"Come here," he said hoarsely.

She could not resist either his voice or his look. She

moved across the coach, and his hand guided her into the seat beside him. She was surprised when he turned her a little sideways, so that her back was to him. But then he began to undo the myriad buttons that marched down the back of her frock, and she understood.

"No," she breathed, but she did not move away, even as she felt the sides of the material begin to part and fall open against her back.

"Shh," he murmured. "I will not do anything you mislike."

She knew, miserably, that her misliking it was not the problem. "But I—"

She stopped, the words dying in her throat, as he placed his lips upon her back. Gently, tenderly, he began to lay hot kisses over the smooth skin of her back. His hands came up in front to cup her breasts, and he kneaded and caressed them as his mouth explored the expanse of her back. Julia let out a noise, half sob, half moan.

"No," she whispered. "I cannot bear it."

"Nor I," he replied, pulling her onto his lap so that she could feel the hard, insistent throbbing of his desire for her. "But I cannot stop, either."

"You must."

She could hear the rasp of his breath as he pulled down the front of her dress. It fell easily, and he pulled the sleeves off at her wrists, leaving her torso exposed to his gaze. He looked at her hungrily, his eyes glittering. His hand moved slowly over her breasts, caressing her naked skin. The night air touched her nipples, making them point saucily, and Deverel began to trace first one, then the other, with his forefinger, making them thrust out even more pointedly. Her breasts felt full and almost aching, and she knew that she wanted to feel his mouth on them again, as he had done the other night.

Finally he satisfied her desire, bending down and running his tongue around one nipple. She jerked involuntarily at the sizzle that ran through her. He teased each nipple until Julia was panting and moaning; then he pulled one of them into his mouth and began to work on it with his whole mouth, sucking and rubbing and lashing it. Julia let out a little sob and squirmed on his lap. She was pleased to note that her action brought a response from him equal to her own.

Roughly he shoved up her skirts, caressing the insides of her legs as he laved her breasts with his mouth. His hand came to rest at last on her femininity, separated from him by the cloth of her undergarment, hot and wet from the strength of her desire. He moaned against her skin, and his fingers began to move rhythmically, gently rubbing the damp cloth against Julia's tender skin.

Deverel raised his head and looked down at her. Her bare skin was palely washed with moonlight. Her luxuriant hair tumbled down, curls falling over her chest and separating across her breasts. Her nipples were swollen and ruby red from his ministrations, thrusting up invitingly at him. She moved her hips inexpertly against his hand, urging him on. He thought that he had never beheld a lovelier picture nor wanted a woman more than he did at that moment.

But he also knew that he must wait. He did not want to take her like this, hastily and clumsily in the seat of a coach. He drew a deep breath and pulled his hand away, leaning his head back against the squabs of the seat.

"Deverel?" Julia asked in a dazed voice, the tremor of desire evident in it.

He swallowed hard and ignored the unspoken plea. After a time he opened his eyes and looked at her. The sight of her was as lovely as ever. He picked up one of her curls and idly stroked it across her nipple, watching as it pebbled erotically. The sight sent a tendril of pure heat curling through his loins.

"We must stop," he said regretfully.

That was the last thing Julia wanted at that moment. She felt as if she were made entirely of fire. Everywhere he touched her, the heat had flamed higher and higher, until she thought she might fly apart. Indeed, there was something churning in her loins already that felt perilously close to exploding.

However, she knew that he was right, and she closed her lips against the whimpers of protest that threatened to rise from her throat. He let out a groan and pulled her up against his chest, holding her so tightly she could scarcely breathe.

"Don't look at me that way, or you shall unman me," he murmured against her hair, his voice trembling with desire. "You are the most enchanting woman I have ever seen. I have never wanted anyone as I want you."

"Nor have I," Julia admitted candidly, her voice coming out so hoarse and low that she scarcely knew it.

After a long moment he released her, and she turned away from him, pulling her bodice back on. He buttoned it up the back, his fingers shaking a little and getting the buttons wrong in places. Julia tumbled back onto the opposite seat and huddled into the corner, closing her eyes. She could not even look at him for fear of the desire in her leaping out again.

She had never felt so jumbled and confused in all her life. How could she have acted like such a wanton with this man? And how, having felt like this in his arms, could she now tie him up and coerce him into confessing? It was all the most horrid, muddled mess, and she did not understand how it had turned out so wrong. Her body throbbed with passion for Deverel Grey—the one man she hated above all others. Her mind seemed unable to function, for she *felt* more than thought her confusion and distress.

The coach rolled inexorably on toward home, and she wondered how in the world she was going to carry off her scheme. She was afraid that she could not. But she did not know what she would do instead. How could she tell Nunnelly to forget their plan? How could she face Phoebe and say that she had let their enemy escape solely because her own body betrayed her? And what would she say to Deverel—that it had been a mistake? That she had dragged him out here to knock him over the head, not to bed him? She wanted to burst into tears—and at the same time she wanted to throw herself across the coach into his arms and tell him to forget his sensibilities about taking her here and now.

She felt the carriage slow and turn down a lane, and before long their way became rougher and slower. They were nearing the hut. Julia sat up, swallowing hard. She glanced at Deverel, her stomach knotting. His eyes were open, and he was watching her, but she could not read his face. She wondered what he would say if he had any idea what was in her head.

She would have to abandon her plan. She called herself a coward and a fool, but she knew that she could not go through with it. As soon as the carriage stopped, she would tell Nunnelly to forget her instructions. Then she would somehow convince Deverel to get back in the carriage and return to London. She would stay here at home, for she could not face Phoebe or anyone else.

The carriage rocked and bounced to a halt. Deverel immediately reached out and whipped open the door. He jumped down from the coach and turned to help Julia. She followed more slowly, trying to think what to say to both him and Nunnelly. She leaned out of the doorway, reaching down to take his hand. Suddenly a dark figure loomed up behind Deverel. Julia gasped, crying out, "No!"

But at that moment Nunnelly swung down hard with a cudgel, cracking it into the back of Stonehaven's head. Deverel crumpled to the ground.

8

Julia let out a shriek and jumped down out of the carriage. "Nunnelly! You weren't supposed to! Not yet!" She knelt worriedly beside Deverel's prone body. "Oh, dear—he's so still. Is he breathing?"

"Faith, now, of course he is. 'Twas only a tap I gave him. I'm thinking 'tis easier to hit him here and drag him to the door, don't ye see, than to be followin' you two up to the door to crack him."

"Oh…" Julia let out a moan. She turned Deverel's head and delicately probed with her fingers. "I think he's bleeding."

She pulled her handkerchief out of her pocket and pressed it to the raw lump on Deverel's head.

"Don't get in a taking, Miss Julie. Ye can't be losin' yer nerve now. 'Tis too late. The deed's been done. I'll be taking him up to the hut. Ye stay with the horses."

He bent and grasped Stonehaven under the arms and lifted his torso, then began to walk backward, dragging the lower half of Stonehaven's body. He made his slow way along the little path leading to the old shepherd's hut, which Julia and Thomas had fixed up and reinforced for the purpose of imprisoning Lord Stonehaven. Julia turned and went over to the horses. She took the lead's bridle and stroked his nose, talking soothingly to him, more for herself, she thought, than for him.

Nunnelly was right, she told herself. She was being a coward. Where was her vaunted courage? Where was her loyalty to her beloved brother? Was she going to give up on clearing his name simply because his enemy had seduced her in her carriage? She felt horribly low and guilty, but she was not sure which she was feeling worse about: capturing Stonehaven or wanting to abandon her plan.

She let out a low moan and rested her head against the horse's neck. Things had seemed so much easier and clearer when they had planned this.

"All right, miss." Nunnelly's voice came behind her. "The devil's tied up, all right and tight. He'll be comin' around any minute now." He looked at her, concerned. "Is it squeamish ye're feelin', miss?"

Julia nodded a little shamefacedly. "I suppose I am. Oh, Nunnelly, all of a sudden, there at the end, I didn't feel as if I could do it! Am I wrong? What should I do?"

"It's not for me to say, miss. What changed your mind?"

"I don't know." She could hardly tell him that she had been demoralized by the man's lovemaking. And now that she thought about it, she saw that that was all it was. She still believed that Lord Stonehaven had embezzled the money and purposely implicated her brother. She still believed that he was responsible for the destruction of their lives. The only thing that had changed was that she had weakened. She had let her own vagrant desire make her irresolute.

Julia stiffened her back. "I'm sorry. For a moment I

lost my courage." She raised her chin. "I will be all right now."

Nunnelly looked relieved. Julia felt sure that he must have been disconcerted to see her act so oddly. "I'll go in with you, miss, to see if he's awake."

"You needn't. I shan't turn back again. You should probably stay with the horses."

He cast an eye at the docile animals. "They'll be all right. I'm thinking yer fellow won't be in a mood to talk. Ye'd best ride back to Greenwood with me and let him stew for a night."

"You may be right. I'll see if he's awakened yet."

She marched resolutely up the path to the door, not arguing when Nunnelly followed. Drawing a sustaining breath, she pushed open the door and stepped inside.

Deverel was seated in a sturdy wooden chair, his legs tied to the front two legs of the chair. A rope was wrapped around his chest and the back of the chair, lashing him to it. His head was up, and his eyes open, and he was looking dazedly around the room. Julia could see the muscles bunch in his legs and arms as he moved against his bonds, testing their strength. He turned his head at their entrance. His expression was frowning and confused.

When he saw Julia, his face fell into grim lines, and his eyes narrowed. "Why, you cunning little jade!"

Julia flinched inwardly. She had expected him to be furious, had known that he would revile her, but she had been unprepared for it to feel as if his words had stabbed her in the heart.

"Here, now, there's no need to be talking that way." Nunnelly stepped forward, his meaty fists clenching. "'Twas me that put that knot on yer head, not Miss Julie."

"Ah, so it's Julie now, is it?" Deverel said scornfully, his eyes boring into Julia. "What happened to the other lass, the *compliant* one? The one so timid and sensitive that she ran away rather than—"

"Are ye deaf? Shut up, I said!" Nunnelly roared. "Ye're not in charge now, me fine lad, and ye better keep a civil tongue in yer head when ye're speakin' to the mistress."

"She's not *my* mistress."

His tone gave the words an ironic stress.

"You'd better go, Nunnelly," Julia said hastily. If her loyal servant stayed here, she had little doubt that Stonehaven would goad Nunnelly into punching him, even tied to the chair as he was.

"Nunnelly?" Deverel asked, brows rising. "Your father? Or your husband?"

Nunnelly's eyes narrowed, and Julia hastily waved him away. "I can handle this myself. As you can see, you tied him up perfectly well, and he shan't be able to harm me. I am sure he will be calmer and less obstructive with only me here." What she thought, but did not add, was that the men's male posturing would only serve to make matters worse.

Nunnelly cast a last reluctant look toward Stonehaven. "As ye wish, miss. I'll be right outside," he added significantly.

"Why, you're the footpad!" Lord Stonehaven exclaimed suddenly, peering at Nunnelly. "Of course. I was stupid not to realize that it was all connected. Three attempts on me, and when they failed, the temptress was sent in."

Nunnelly's eyes flared with fire again, but Julia hastily put her hand on his arm and urged him out of the room. She closed the door behind the coachman and turned to face Deverel, her insides knotting. He kept a hard, steady glare on Julia as she moved across the dirt floor of the one-room shack until she stood a few feet away from him.

"What a fool I was!" His face was cold and white with fury, his dark eyes glittering wildly. "Like a stallion after a mare in heat—too blind to see that your gorgeous flesh was a trap!"

"I am sure that you will feel more like talking later," Julia told him coldly, struggling to maintain her poise. She refused to let him see that his insults had hit any mark with her.

"Talking!" he exclaimed. "Is that what you want of me? I'm willing to talk right now—though I daresay you'll care little for what I have to say."

"Perhaps after spending a night here you will be more amenable!" Julia flared.

He let out a laugh of scorn. "If you think that, then you don't know me. You stupid little strumpet! Did you honestly think that you could bend me to your will this way? Do you think that I will pay you to release me? What are you planning to do? Shoot me if I don't give you money? Starve me to death? You'll hardly get any payment if you do. Or are you fool enough to think that I will cave in at the thought of being hungry or of being stuck in this uncomfortable place? Let me save you the time and trouble. I will not give in to you. You can hold me here forever, and you will never get one shilling from me."

He shook his head, looking disgusted. "You made the wrong choice, my girl. I would have offered you a carte blanche. You could have been sitting pretty in your own house, lots of jewelry and fashionable clothes, a nice allowance—if only you had stuck to what you are good at—seduction. As it is, you will be sitting in Newgate. You and your ape of a friend out there and whoever else is in on this with you.''

''There is no one else in on this. I am the only one responsible.''

He rolled his eyes expressively. ''Of course. I should have realized that. One so commonly finds a whore masterminding an extortion plot.''

''I am not a whore!'' Julia's hand itched to slap him.

''That rankles, does it?'' He smiled smugly. ''What is it they say about the truth hurting? But then, perhaps *whore* is the wrong term. You didn't exactly sell your body, did you? Just used it to betray me. I suppose that makes you more a Judas than a whore, doesn't it?''

''I did not betray you. It was your own lust that did that,'' Julia retorted. ''If your brain commanded your body rather than the other way around, you wouldn't be here, would you?'' She raised her hand. ''No. No need to speak. The answer is obvious.''

''As obvious as the way *your* body responded in the carriage?''

Julia raised an eyebrow. ''Indeed? You were the man who just pointed out how I *deceived* you.''

She could tell from the glint of renewed fury in his eyes that she had scored a hit. His lip curled, and he said, ''Get out of my sight. You'll never get anything from me.''

''Fine.'' Julia started toward the door. She paused, her hand on the doorknob, and turned back to him. ''We shall see if you are singing the same tune tomorrow morning.''

He smiled evilly. ''Yes, we shall. Go try to sleep now. Think about how much you've lost. Consider your dilemma—threats are worthless unless you can carry them out.''

Julia cast him a look of intense dislike and swung out of the door. She slammed it shut behind her and locked it, sticking the key back in her pocket. Then she stalked out to the carriage, scowling.

She was glad for her anger. It kept at bay the dismay she had felt when she first walked in and saw Deverel trussed up like that. It held back the shame she had felt each time he had looked at her with disgust and contempt, the hurt when he had labeled her a whore.

She huddled in the corner of the carriage all the way from the shepherd's hut to the graceful manor house that was her home, clutching her anger around her like a cloak. She raged at the names he had called her. *How had he dared, when it was he who was the scoundrel?* She fumed at his defiant attitude and smiled with bitter satisfaction at the change of face that would doubtless occur in Lord Stonehaven when he had been alone in the hut for a few hours.

But she could not sustain her fury for long, and by the time they reached the house, the hot pitch of rage was gone, leaving her feeling sick and lost. The house was dark, and her bed had not been made up for her, for, of course, the servants had not expected her home. Julia slipped in the back door, unlocked as was often the case in the country, and made her way with only a candle up to her room. It was a cheerless scene—dark, the bed covered with a coverlet and no sheets beneath, no welcoming fire burning in the grate to take off the evening chill.

Looking around at the room brought her spirits even lower. Julia sank down in the overstuffed chair by the fireplace and rested her head on her hands, elbows propped on her knees.

She had blundered. Julia saw it now and wondered why the thought had never occurred to her before, when she was rushing down this path with headlong determination. Deverel Grey was not going to give in to intimidation and threats. He was far too strong, too powerful. She had told herself that he was a coward because of the nature of his crimes. It had made sense, and perhaps it was true in some ways, but after she had gotten to know him better, it had been stupid of her to believe that he would cave in to her threats. She had been foolish and pigheaded not to realize that this was no man who would confess because one pressed him to.

She had the awful, sickening feeling that everything he had said about himself just now was true. He would not give in. He would not tell her the truth, would not confess to his crimes just because she imprisoned him. He was a strong man, and stubborn, and his rage at her only strengthened his determination. She had seen it in his eyes tonight—he would rather die than give in to her. When he did not talk, what was she to do? Starve him? Beat him? Leave him to waste away in that hut? It was absurd, of course; she could not do any of those things. The man was right: threats accomplished nothing if one was unprepared to back them up.

She thought back on her vague plans. She and Thomas and Phoebe had never discussed what they would do if Lord Stonehaven did not confess. It had not occurred to any of them that he would not. She saw now that they had believed what they wanted to believe. They had talked and talked about what they would do, but in each of their scenarios, Stonehaven had acted just as they wanted him to. They had made no allowance for his refusing to confess.

Julia sank her head into her hands with a groan. She did not even want to think about the other things he had said, the names he had called her, the vicious shredding of her honor. But she could not keep from it. It did not matter what *he* thought of her, of course. It *did* matter, however, that she was beginning to feel a sick shame herself. She had thought that any means would justify her ends. In her desperate desire to salvage Selby's reputation, she had let herself sink to her enemy's level. She had told herself that it was all right to pretend to be a shady woman, since she was not going to actually sleep with him. But she wondered now if it wasn't just a matter of degrees. By pretending to be a whore, by dressing and acting like one, hadn't she been selling herself? Hadn't she, by letting him kiss and caress her, been giving him her body in return for the hope of getting information? She had always been willful; she was quite ready to admit it. But she had never before let her headstrong nature lead her into doing something wicked. Now she was afraid that she had.

Tears gathered in her eyes as she realized despairingly that she must let Lord Stonehaven go. It meant that she would probably never be able to prove that Selby had not embezzled the money. It galled her to think that Lord Stonehaven would be able to continue to live free from scandal or retribution. But what purpose would it serve to keep him in the hut any longer? He would not give in, and she would only increase her sins if she made him suffer hunger and thirst.

Julia indulged in a brief cry, and afterward she felt better. There was one good thing, at least, about this whole affair, she told herself: Lord Stonehaven did not know who she was. He had assumed that she had kidnapped him in an attempt to get money from him, and she had fortunately not mentioned anything about Selby yet. He knew her as Jessica Nunnelly, and, though he had heard Nunnelly call her ''Julie,'' she doubted that he would remember—or even know—that Selby had a sister named Julia. Since she and Phoebe did not go out into Society, he would never meet her. Nor was it likely that he would connect her with the odd-mannered, bespectacled creature whom he thought of as Miss Armiger. At least he would not be able to tell the world what she had done and bring ruin down on the Armiger family a second time.

She got up and made her quiet way back down the stairs and out the side door. She hurried across the yard to the stables and there took a bridle and saddle from the tack room and slipped along the stall doors until she came to that belonging to her own mare, Clover. Clover greeted her with a pleased whinny and nudged her head against Julia's chest. Julia stroked her nose and whispered that she was sorry that she had not brought her a carrot this time. Quickly and efficiently, she slid the bridle over the mare's head and fastened the straps, then led her out of the stable. She was afraid at any moment that one of the grooms, who lived upstairs, might be awakened by the small noises she was making and come downstairs to see what was going on. Of course, once he saw who she was, he would not stop her, but he would exclaim about it, and Nunnelly would doubtlessly awaken and demand an explanation, too. Julia did not feel up to telling him that she was letting Stonehaven go, that all his efforts had been for nothing.

She led the horse out of the yard and over to a tree stump that would allow her to mount. There she stopped and put the saddle on Clover, pausing now and then to stroke her and tell her how much she had missed her the past few weeks. When she was done saddling the mare, she climbed onto the stump and mounted, and they set off toward the shepherd's hut. She rode slowly, letting her trusty mare pick her way in the pale light, and as she rode, she tried to decide exactly how to let Stonehaven go.

She had not really thought about the details of it when she left the house, but she could see now that there would be problems. She had intended merely to cut his bonds, then ride off, leaving him to find his way from the hut to the road. But it occurred to her that if he left the hut and sought help at the nearest cottage, he would soon learn that he was on Farrow land, quite close to the Armiger house, and she feared that he would become suspicious that the kidnapping had had to do with Selby. That would never do. She could, of course, run off, leaving him the horse, for then he might very well ride until he found the highway back to London, might even go back to London without really realizing how close the Armiger house lay. But she could not do that, either, because that would mean giving up her favorite horse. She could see that she had acted rashly once again. She should probably have roused Nunnelly and had him carry the man back to London and leave him there, no matter how incensed Nunnelly might have been about her giving up.

For a moment she considered turning back and doing that, but then she thought that Nunnelly would not do it until the horses had been given a chance to rest, and she did not want to wait any longer. She would feel far too guilty about leaving Deverel there in that uncomfortable position with nothing to eat or drink for several more hours. Besides, she did not want him to get a good look at her in the daylight. Finally she decided that the thing to do was to tie his hands but release him from the chair. His muscles were bound to be cramped from being tied in that position, so she did not think she had to fear his attacking her while she did those things. She would blindfold him and make him get on the horse, hands tied, and lead him to the highway to London. There she would release him and ride home, hoping that he would grab a ride to London without inquiring about who lived in the area.

After some time she caught a glimpse of the hut, nestled in the trees ahead. She rode on, her nerves tightening, and stopped in front of the shack. Dismounting, she tied her mare to a nearby sapling, then strode toward the cottage.

Through the cracks in the shutters she could see the dim glow of the oil lamp, which she had left burning. It made her feel a trifle better to think that at least she had not left him sitting bound in utter darkness. She reached the door and paused, drawing a steadying breath, then reached out to turn the knob.

A faint movement to her right caught her attention, but before she could even flinch, an arm like iron wrapped around her, clamping her own arms to her sides, and a hand came up to cover her mouth.

Fear paralyzed Julia for an instant, but then she began to struggle and scream. Her cries were muffled by the hand on her mouth, and her struggles were utterly futile, given the strength of the arm around her, but she refused to go down without a fight.

How had he gotten loose? She had no doubt that it was Stonehaven. It would stagger the imagination to think that there happened to be some other man lurking around the hut in which he had been held, waiting to attack her. But it had seemed impossible for him to get free. Nunnelly had bound him, almost too tightly, she had thought, and though they had not gagged him, there wasn't a soul for miles around to have heard him yelling.

Julia kicked backward, connecting once or twice with his legs, but with her arms immobilized, she had little chance against him. He bore her to the ground, turning her around so that she lay facing him, and effectively pinned her there by straddling her. His strong thighs clamped her legs together, and she was very aware of the intimacy of their positions. His hand had left her mouth so that he could grasp both her hands and bring them together in front of her. She screamed, knowing that no one could hear her, but having to make the attempt, anyway. It took him only a moment to wrap one large hand around both her wrists, holding her arms helplessly together. Then he reached into the pocket of his jacket and pulled out his elegant handkerchief and stuffed it into her mouth, effectively muffling her cries.

Next he picked up a length of rope from the ground and lashed her wrists together. By the time he had done that, Julia had managed to spit the kerchief out, and she began to shriek again, but with her hands tied, Deverel could devote his efforts to gagging her, which he did again, taking the handkerchief and shoving it between her lips, tying the ends tightly behind her head. Julia glared at him impotently, and he raised a sardonic eyebrow.

"How does it feel, my dear, to be on the receiving end?"

He slid down her legs and off her, taking her ankles in his hand and holding them firm while he tied them together, as well. Then he stood and gazed down at her, surveying his handiwork in the dim light. Apparently satisfied, he reached down and pulled her to her feet. When she was standing, he wrapped her cloak, which had gotten twisted and pushed behind her, around her once more and retied the ribbons at the top tightly. Then he pulled the hood of the cloak forward as far as it would go, effectively hiding her face from any observer who did not come right up and peer into her face.

Julia swallowed, trying to push down her fear. What was he doing? After he had gotten free, why had he waited to ambush her? Why had he not simply fled? Her hopes of escaping a scandal were quickly fading. Indeed, at the moment she was in fear not only for her reputation, but for her very life. She could think of no reason for him to have waited as he had unless he meant to exact revenge upon her for what she had done. She shuddered to think what form that revenge might take. It seemed all too likely that he would take from her what she had teased and trapped him with—the pleasures of her body.

She closed her eyes, trying to still her trembling. She refused to let him see that he had terrified her. He might strip her of her virginity tonight, but she would be damned if she would let him see that he had beaten her.

Expecting him to drag her back into the hut now and rape her, she was surprised when he bent and picked her up in his arms, then carried her not toward the shack but to her horse. He tossed her up onto the mare so that she lay facedown upon it, head dangling down on one side and her feet on the other. It half knocked the air from her, and she lay there ignominiously, the blood rushing to her head, while he adjusted the stirrups to suit his long legs. Then he untied the mare, talking softly to her, and climbed up into the saddle. She thought she felt his hand brush over her bottom, and she stiffened, but he pulled her none too gently over and up, so that she sat sideways on the horse in front of him, his arms around her, forcing her against his chest. He clicked to the horse and tapped her with his heels, and they started forward.

Julia saw with some relief that he started along the faint track in the opposite direction of her home, moving instead toward Farrow. But long before they reached Thomas's home, they came upon a better-marked path and took it instead. They rode for some time and finally came out upon a road that led to the village of Whitley. Julia sat passively as the ground stretched out beneath them. She knew that, bound and gagged as she was, there was no point in struggling. When they reached their destination, whatever it might be, there might be an opportunity to get away, and she would take it. She did not let herself think about the difficulty of escaping with her ankles bound together.

Finally, they reached the village, and Stonehaven turned the mare into the yard of the inn. Julia stiffened. A new fear swept over her. *Was he going to turn her over to the authorities for kidnapping?* The local constable would recognize her in an instant.

It was the dead of night, and the inn was dark and quiet. Stonehaven, however, did not hesitate to set up a shout for the innkeeper. He dismounted and pulled Julia off. Making sure her hood was still far forward, he picked her up, cradling her against his chest, so that one could see nothing of her except a feminine shape. Her cloak effectively hid her bound hands and feet, as well as her face.

He carried her to the door and pounded upon it. "Innkeeper! Open up. I need a room!"

From inside came a muffled roar to keep it down, and

a few moments later the rotund innkeeper, still in his nightcap and nightshirt, his trousers hastily pulled on beneath, opened the door.

"What the devil do ye mean—" he began wrathfully, but stopped when the light of his candle revealed to him a man whose clothes and bearing proclaimed him instantly to belong to the world of quality. He lifted his candle, peering more closely at the bundle in the gentleman's arms.

"My wife is sick. I have need of a room immediately."

Julia began to squirm and make noises around her gag, for at his words, the prospect of rape had again raised its ugly head, shoving the threat of discovery back into the more remote regions of terror. However, Stonehaven's arms merely tightened around her, stilling all motion, and his hand pressed her head into his chest.

"As you can see," he said smoothly, "she cannot even speak, she is so weak."

"Oh, aye, come in, come in, sir." The innkeeper stepped back, holding the door to let him enter. "What be wrong with her, sir? Do ye be needing a doctor?"

"No, I think not. Traveling often lays her out like this. She is of a delicate constitution." When the landlord peered out into the yard, empty save for Julia's horse, Stonehaven went on, "Our chaise broke down some distance back. Our coachman is repairing it, but my wife was feeling so sickly that I decided to take her ahead on my horse and get us a room for the night."

"Of course, sir. The best thing for her." The innkeeper, always happy to make a profit, turned and led them through the public room and up the stairs. "I'll give ye the room at the back. It's the quietest we got, only the garden behind it and no one staying in the room next to ye.''

His words made fear squeeze Julia's heart, but Stonehaven said with satisfaction, ''Sounds like just the thing.''

The landlord opened the door to the room, asking if he would like to have a warming pan brought to warm up the sheets or perhaps a hot brick for the lady's feet.

''No. We'll be fine. I know my girl, and all she needs is a night's sleep.''

The landlord lit the candle on the small table by the door and bowed out of the room. Stonehaven bent and turned the key in the lock. Then he carried Julia across the room and tossed her onto the bed. She landed with a thump, the hood of her cloak falling back and the sides opening. Julia was very aware of the picture she made, utterly helpless, bound and gagged, her skirts rucked up to the knees, showing her stocking-clad legs.

He loomed over her, his eyes traveling slowly down the length of her body, and a wicked grin lit his features. ''Well,'' he said, ''I think we might say that you are completely in my power.''

9

Deverel sat down beside her on the bed, and the mattress sagged beneath his weight, sending Julia sliding into him. She did her best to wriggle away, and he smiled. Casually he slid his hand down her front, touching her breasts and abdomen through her dress in a way that was devoid of feeling, demonstrating only his power. She squirmed, blushing hot with humiliation, feeling far more shame than she had in the carriage, when he had touched her so intimately and looked upon her naked chest.

"Oh, yes, I could take you if I wished," he told her conversationally. "I could claim that prize with which you teased me." Her nipples stood out against the material of her dress, and he took one bud between his forefinger and thumb and rolled it a little. Julia was horrified to feel it harden beneath his contemptuous touch. "Does the thought frighten you? I cannot imagine why. Given the way you make a living, I would think you are quite used to a stranger's touch."

Julia made a strangled noise of rage and glared at him.

"Well, you needn't worry," Stonehaven continued, taking his hand away and standing up. "I have no interest in sharing the questionable pleasures of your body. Frankly, the sight of you fills me with disgust. I would as soon bed a snake.''

His words stung, but Julia went limp in relief. She could see that his pride had been too much wounded to permit him to admit that he desired her. The source of his anger, she thought, was not so much that he thought she had meant to swindle him, nor even that she had made him look foolish. He was furious, she thought, because she had deceived him, had pretended that she felt passion for him. Well, she was certainly not about to admit to him that her passion had been anything but feigned.

''I shall take the gag out now. I want to talk to you. But if you scream, I shall tell our landlord the whole story and send for the authorities. I don't think you wish to end your days at Newgate, do you?''

Julia shook her head. He looked at her for a moment, seeming to judge her, then reached down and untied the handkerchief and pulled it from her mouth.

Julia's mouth was as dry as cotton. She felt sure she could not have yelled even if she had wanted to. But she was not about to draw a crowd. The last thing she wanted was to attract attention, to have the innkeeper in here and then the constable. She didn't know what Stonehaven wanted, but her only goal at the moment was to get away from him without his finding out who she was or dumping her in the gaol.

She tried to speak, but it came out only as a croak. She cleared her throat, wet her lips and tried again. ''What do you want from me, then?''

''Something quite simple, I assure you. I want the names of your accomplices. I want the person who thought this up, who decided to use me.''

"I told you earlier. That is I."

He grimaced. "Do you take me for a fool? I know that there were at least two others in on it with you—the man who drove the coach and one other, at least on the occasions when they tried to take me on the street, before they conceived of the idea of sending you in as bait. Is two the total number? Neither of them seemed like a leader of the gang to me. I would have said flunkies both. Someone paid all of you, and I want to know who that is."

Julia gazed back at him, setting her chin. There was nothing she could tell him. He obviously refused to believe that a mere woman could have come up with a scheme such as this.

"It is bound to be someone who knows me somewhat," he continued in a musing voice. "Enough that they know my movements, where I live, how to—" he cast a hard glance at Julia "—how to intrigue me."

"It doesn't take much intelligence to know that a woman is the best way to topple any man," Julia said coolly.

"A sharp, maybe," he suggested, ignoring her comment. "Someone who has seen me in places like Madame Beauclaire's. Someone who mingles with the ton to some extent. Perhaps it was he who taught you how to speak and act so that you seem almost a lady. What is he to you? Your lover? Your procurer?"

It took a moment for Julia to realize what he meant, that he was suggesting that this imaginary man provided her with prostitution clients. Fury flared in her, erasing her fear for the moment. She sat up, eyes flaming. "You bastard! How dare you?"

He made a derisive noise. "My, aren't we the fine lady now? I'm beginning to change my mind. Perhaps you are an actress. It would seem to fit your skills, as well as your morals. Is that it? Are you and your lover in the theater?''

"You are a fine one to condemn my morals!" Julia snapped. "What were you doing in that carriage or at Vauxhall Gardens? Holding off my rapacious advances like the saint you are?'' Her mouth curled in contempt. ''That's just like a man, to try his best to seduce you and then blame *you* because he was tempted. You would not have been so vulnerable, would you, if you had not been a libertine!''

"There is some difference, madam, between being swept away by desire and cold-bloodedly plotting to ensnare someone. The latter person has no heart.''

"But you do? What a bald-faced lie. You have no compassion, no feeling, no *heart*. You are the sort of person who would coolly stand on the bank and watch a person drown rather than get your clothes wet.''

His eyebrows lifted at the venom in her voice. ''Indeed? And how did you, who know me not at all, manage to come up with that assessment of my character?''

Julia stopped, nonplussed. She had been so carried away by her anger that she had almost been to the point of revealing who she was and why she had done what she did. That, she was sure, would have been a mistake, perhaps even a fatal one. She had kept her mouth shut about her identity because she did not want to embroil her family in another scandal. It occurred to her now that it was probably safest in other ways, too, not to let on who she was. Stonehaven would not be pleased to learn that anyone suspected him of committing the crime he had blamed on Selby. He might even decide that he had better make sure she didn't go around spreading her suspicions to others.

"I know men of your type," she said sullenly, and lapsed into silence again.

"Let us return to the subject at hand—your accomplices. Since you seem to have such difficulty in talking about them, why don't we start with the easiest one, the man who knocked me over the head. Who is he? You called him Nunnelly—a relation? Or is your name false, as well?"

"He is no relation. And neither of us is named Nunnelly. 'Twas a name that, uh, we came up with to hide our identities."

"What is his true name?"

"I don't know."

"Come, come, you don't know your own accomplices' names?"

"Only his first name—'tis Fred. I never heard him called anything else."

"And the other?"

"What other?"

"There were two of them the times they tried to kidnap me before."

"Oh. That was Will. He cried off after that last attempt—no stomach for hitting people, you see."

"And your leader?"

Julia rolled her eyes and was silent.

"You might as well tell me, you know. I am a patient man. I'm quite willing to stay here until you tell me the truth—or until you tell the constable."

"You won't turn me over to any constable," Julia said with more confidence than she felt. "Then you would never find out about that other man—and I think you would be very interested."

"Indeed? Why is that?" His face remained cool and blank, but Julia could see the flare of interest in his eyes.

She shrugged and slipped into the accent of one of the upstairs maids. "Well, sir, it might be because the one what 'ired me—aye, and taught me to talk fancy, too—is one of your own."

"My own?"

"That's right. I was just a poor girl, working in a tavern, I was, when this gentry sort, a lot like you, come in. After I got off work, he said to me, 'Jessie, me lass, 'ow would you like to come with me and make a lot of money?' 'Course I was willing. 'Oo wouldn't be, I ask you. So he takes me up in his fancy curricle and drives me back to this grand 'ouse. There's a woman there, see, 'oo teaches me 'ow to talk like gentry." Julia abandoned her accent for the moment, asking in a grande dame manner, "She did a splendid job, don't you think?"

"Splendid," Stonehaven agreed dryly.

"And 'e bought me lots of byootiful clothes, like the dresses I been wearin', and she taught me 'ow to walk and sit and all, without slouchin' or lettin' me back touch the chair. Was proper exhausting, it was."

"No doubt. What was the object of all this tiresome education?"

"Why, to trap you, of course. What else? 'E says, 'I'll get that'—well, 'e called you a word me dad would 'a switched me proper if I'd said. That gentry fellow 'as a powerful dislike for you."

"What is this gentry fellow's name?"

"I don't know. 'E told me to call him Andrew, so that's wot I did, but I don't think it was 'is real name. She, the lady wot taught me, she always called 'im 'my lord.'"

"Why did he hold such a 'powerful dislike' for me?"

"Well, 'e didn't say, exactly, but once he said that you was a thief." Julia watched him closely.

"A thief!" He raised one eyebrow. "And what was I supposed to have stolen?"

"I'm not rightly sure," Julia said, then added pertly, "'Ave you stolen so much that you don't know which thing 'e's talkin' about?"

Stonehaven sighed. "You are a most dedicated liar, and you're talking a bag of moonshine, as we both know. I have never stolen anything from anyone, and I doubt sincerely that there is any gentleman who harbors such ill will toward me that he would spend the time and the ready grooming you to seduce me. The accent, the walk, the demeanor—those were not things learned in a few weeks' study in some mystery lord's house. I daresay it took you years to acquire them. In fact, I am rather inclined to believe that you were raised speaking and acting that way. My surmise is that you are some well-bred girl who was wild from the time she was young and who probably disgraced her family by running away with her dance tutor—or perhaps a traveling troupe of actors."

"You have a fascination with actors, haven't you?" Julia asked. "Why is that, I wonder?"

"Dammit!" He turned away, slamming his hand down on the small table beside the bed so hard that the oil lamp on it wobbled. "You are the coolest bit of muslin I ever saw! Nothing rattles you, does it? Seduction, kidnapping, being caught red-handed—certainly not lying! That, it seems, is what you do best."

"Oh, I do many things well," Julia responded calmly. She was not sure exactly why she had such an urge to goad Stonehaven, when all sense told her that it would be better to try to calm his seething rage. All she knew was that it was her last weapon against him, and she was not going to go down without a fight.

He snorted. "I am sure you do, no doubt most of them in bed. However, I have no interest in sampling your wares tonight. If you think to seduce me into letting you go, you are fair and far off."

"I wouldn't think of it. The thought of your touch sickens me, quite frankly. Indeed, it was all I could do to stand to let you embrace me, no matter how much money I was going to get."

"Then you are indeed a marvelous actress, my girl," he snapped, jaw tightening. "I have never before met a woman who could flush with heat on cue or cause her nipples to pebble or soak her pantalets with—"

Julia vaulted off the bed with an inarticulate cry of rage. Had she not been tied up, she would have flown at him, biting and clawing. As it was, with her ankles bound, she could not maintain her balance after her impetuous jump off the bed, and she fell heavily.

He let out an oath and strode over to her, bending down to pick her up. "Are you mad? Whatever possessed you to do such a thing?"

Julia had knocked the wind from herself in the fall, as well as hurting one arm and hip and getting a crack on her head that had made her eyes water, so it took her a moment to speak. By that time the fury had subsided, and she was able to say coldly, "I wanted to kill you."

"The truth hurts, doesn't it?"

She turned a flat gaze upon him. "Is it the truth? You speak of physical reactions caused by certain actions, sir. Any person could doubtless cause them. I spoke of emotions. If you were so sure that I enjoyed your kisses and caresses, then I doubt you would be quite so enraged by the thought of my 'using' them to trap you. Now would you?"

She was rewarded by the tiny flare of anger in his

eyes, quickly suppressed. He did not reply to her, merely picked her up once again and set her on the bed.

He untied her cloak and removed it, hanging it on a hook by the door. Then he squatted down in front of her and took her feet in his, removing each of her shoes.

A shiver ran through Julia at the touch of his hands on her feet, and she snapped, "What are you doing?"

"Taking off your shoes…unless you prefer to sleep in them?"

"What are you talking about?"

"It is obvious that we are getting nowhere. Hopefully, if you sleep on it, you will be more cooperative in the morning. I can assure you that I, at least, will be in a better humor for a night's sleep."

"You expect me to sleep like this?" Julia held out her bound hands.

"I don't remember your worrying excessively over whether I could sleep—or even sit comfortably—with my arms and legs bound to that chair."

Julia could not mask the guilt that touched her face at his words, and he said, faintly surprised, "Ah, so that arrow went home, did it?"

"I—I did not want to hurt you." She thought that she must sound as if she were begging his pardon, which she *would* not do, so she lifted her chin and looked him defiantly in the eye. "But I did not shrink from it. Your comfort was not a consideration."

"Obviously. However, I find I haven't as hard a heart as you."

To her astonishment, he began to undo the knot that bound her ankles. "I trust," he said, "that you will not take it into your head to flee for the door. It is locked, and I would easily catch you. Then I would have to tie your ankles up again, forgetting all about mercy."

He took the rope that had bound her ankles and tied it to one of her wrists, just above the rope that held her hands together.

"What are you doing?"

"Allowing you a bit of movement—without letting you have the freedom to get into trouble, as you no doubt would, being the most troublesome female I have ever met." He led her to the foot of the bed and tied the other end of the rope to the bedpost closest to the wall. "Now I shall untie your hands, with the same warning. If you start to fight or try to untie yourself, I shall bind you up again in a trice, and I think you will find it infinitely more awkward."

Julia nodded her understanding. She refused to thank him.

He untied her hands, and Julia could not hold back a sigh of relief. Unconsciously she rubbed the red marks on each wrist. Stonehaven looked down at her wrists. His jaw clenched, and he turned away abruptly.

"There are the conveniences," he said, gesturing toward the wall, where a washbasin and pitcher stood ready on a table, towels hanging on the lyre-shaped chair back. Next to it was a plain brown wooden commode, in which was hidden, Julia knew, a chamber pot.

She could not help but feel a rush of gratitude toward Stonehaven, and she remembered with even more guilt that she had shown him none of the same consideration.

He walked toward the door, saying, "I shall go outside for a few moments. Since I am quite good at tying knots, I shouldn't waste my time, if I were you, trying to undo the one that binds you to the bedpost."

"I shall not endeavor to flee," Julia said. "Not now, I mean, though I won't guarantee for the future."

He turned and shot her a quizzical look, brows raised.

Julia gazed back at him pugnaciously, hands on hips. "There's no need to look like that. I give you my word!"

"Ah, and I am sure I consider your word a bond," he replied ironically.

The gratitude Julia had been feeling toward him disappeared, and she glared at him. "Go on, then! Think whatever you like!"

He bowed toward her in a sardonic way and left the room. She noticed that he took the key with him and locked the door. She grimaced toward the blank door and stuck her tongue out. Then she turned to avail herself of the opportunity he had offered.

She felt much better once she had used the facilities, awkward though it had been with one hand tied to the bedpost. It was not quite as uncomfortable to wash her hands and face, and she felt much relieved afterward. If only she had a brush, she thought, she would be able to feel almost satisfied. However, she did not have one, so she had to content herself with running her fingers through her hair to comb it. She had not put her hair back up after Deverel had had her take it down in the carriage, and it was, as a result, rather tangled.

With a sigh, she sat down on the end of the bed to await Stonehaven's return. She occupied herself by examining the rope around her wrist and the knot that kept it there, as well as the knot around the post of the bed. She had promised not to undo them at this time, but, she reasoned, she had not said she would not look at them for future reference. Depressingly, however, she could see that he was right in his assessment of his knot-tying ability. It would take her ages to undo the thing, if she was able to at all. The best recourse was a knife, but unfortunately, she did not happen to have one of those handy.

It occurred to her to wonder how Lord Stonehaven had gotten out of his bonds back at the hut. She would have sworn that Nunnelly tied a sturdy knot. He must have used something to cut his way free—had he had a knife secreted about him that he had somehow managed to get to? She could not imagine how. He had probably used something there in the hut to cut it. She glanced around the room, wondering what object in here she might use. The only things she could find within reach were the washbasin and pitcher. Perhaps, if she broke one of them, the shards would be sharp enough that she could use one of them to cut through the rope. Tomorrow morning, she thought, she would not give any promise not to run, and she would see what she could do with broken pottery. She craned her neck to look out the nearest window, hoping that there might be a tree handy for climbing down. Unfortunately, it was too light inside to allow her to see anything out there.

The door opened behind her, and she jumped guiltily and whirled around. She had been so busy looking that she had not listened for his footsteps in the hall.

"No hope there," Deverel told her with annoying good cheer. "I looked when I was outside. There are no trees or trellises or even a useful drainpipe. I fear it is a sheer drop straight down."

She gave him a quelling look and sat down on the bed, looking, she hoped, as indifferent and disdainful as a duchess. Stonehaven turned the key in the door, locking it. Julia noticed with some hope that he had left the key in the lock. She would be able to unlock the door—if only she could get free from this rope that bound her to the bed. He took off his jacket and hung it carefully over the back of the chair. Next he yanked off his cravat, much rumpled and disordered, and pulled his shirt out of his breeches. Julia wondered with a certain amount of horror if he planned to undress in front of her, but he removed nothing else except his shoes and stockings.

He strolled over to the washstand and, rolling up his sleeves, began to wash his hands. Julia, seeing his wrists for the first time, let out a gasp. There were several streaks of dried blood on his wrists, particularly the left one. She saw now, too, that there were streaks of blood on his shirtsleeves.

"What?" He looked up at the noise she made.

"Your arms." She pointed. "What happened? Why are they bloody?"

He glanced down at them as if a little surprised to see the blood there. "That's where I cut free of the rope. That's why I had only those short lengths of rope. I couldn't untie them, the way your friend bound me, so I had to cut them loose."

"But with what?" Julia felt a little sick, looking at the jagged cuts that decorated his flesh.

"The chimney of the lamp you left. I worked the chair over to it, pulled off the chimney and broke it."

Julia turned away, feeling guilty. But she hadn't expected him to go to such lengths to free himself! How could she have known that he would be so stubborn and recalcitrant? After all, she had not set out to hurt him, she reasoned, shoving aside the thought that she had intended to hit him over the head from the very start. Anyway, he was the enemy, she reminded herself; she could not allow herself to be softhearted about his hurts.

Stonehaven looked at her consideringly for a moment, then returned to washing his face and hands. When he was through, he went to the bed and turned down the covers. Julia, watching him, said with some asperity, "Do you plan to leave me standing here all night?"

"I might point out that it is no worse than you deserve. However, that is not my intention."

He came around to the end of the bed and, to her surprise, began to work at the knot that tied the rope to the bedpost. She assumed that he intended to bind her hands together again, and she sighed at the thought of trying to sleep that way. However, to her surprise, he did not wrap the rope around her other wrist, but tied it instead to one of his own wrists. She gaped at him.

"What are you doing?"

"Ensuring that you do not try to escape during the night. I assume you realize that even a heavy sleeper would awaken if you tried to untie this rope. Since I am not accounted a heavy sleeper..."

"But that means that you and I—" She glanced toward the bed, then back at him, and a blush started in her cheeks.

"Yes, we shall have to sleep together. Don't worry about your precious virtue." He gave the words a sarcastic emphasis that reminded her of how little he regarded her virtue as a precious commodity. "I believe I already made it clear that I lost all desire to bed you once I discovered what you were." He executed a little bow, saying, "Like you, I shall give you my word that I will not molest you."

Julia sniffed. "Then I must say that, like *you,* I place little credence in your word. It seems to me that honesty deserts a man when it comes to getting a woman into bed."

He raised a brow. "I assure you that at this point I am interested in nothing but sleep. However, if you care to sleep on the floor, I am sure that I could rebind your hands and attach them to the bedpost.''

''No!'' Julia looked at the dusty floor with revulsion. ''I will sleep in the bed,'' she agreed, somewhat sulkily.

He made a gesture toward the bed, inviting her to climb in first, and she did so, sliding beneath the covers and moving as far away from Deverel as the rope would stretch. She turned her back on him, lying as stiff as a board, every sense alert. She felt the mattress sag beneath his weight, then heard the gust of air as he blew out the candle. The room was plunged into darkness. He moved around a bit and then—impossibly quickly, it seemed to Julia—she heard his breathing grow slower and more even. He was, she thought with some resentment, already asleep. Of course, she was glad that he had not tried to have his way with her, she told herself, but it seemed a trifle insulting that he was able to go to sleep with so little disturbance—especially since she was lying wide-awake, every nerve stretched to the utmost.

She sighed and turned over, twisting and moving around in an attempt to get comfortable. After a time she slid her hand noiselessly across the sheets, following the rope until she found the knot which tied it to his arm.

''I believe I pointed out the futility of trying to undo that while I slept.'' His voice came out of the darkness, causing her to start. ''I am, as I told you, a very light sleeper.''

Julia made no reply but merely turned over again. Exhaustion finally won out, and she fell asleep.

Though the curtains of the inn were not heavy, allowing the sun to light their bedchamber as soon as it dawned, the light streaming through the window was not enough to waken the exhausted sleepers, who had been up until something close to dawn themselves. It was nearing noon before Julia was finally dragged from her sleep.

It was the heat that did it. She was burning up, in the midst of a dream in which she was tramping through a sunny meadow on a glaringly hot day. No matter how far she walked, she could not seem to reach the trees in the distance. Her throat was parched, and she was sweating, and her skin felt as if it were on fire. She came slowly out of the dream, blinking.

She was indeed wrapped in heat. She pushed against the weight draped over her, and finally it dawned on her where she was. She was in the inn, and the weight that lay across her was Deverel's arm. Her eyes flew open in alarm, and her brain started to work again.

She and Stonehaven were lying in the middle of the bed, cuddled together, with her back to his front, fitted together like spoons in a drawer. She could feel the hard length of his desire against her buttocks, prodding against her insistently. The arm that was bound to hers lay behind her, but his free arm was draped across her body, just as one of his legs was thrown over hers. Most disturbing of all, his hand was cupped familiarly around her breast.

His body was like a furnace. She felt as if she could scarcely breathe. Making it all worse was the fact that her skin was tingling and her loins were heavy and aching. Her breasts were swollen and the nipples taut. She was, in effect, thoroughly aroused by him without any effort on his part. What was the matter with her? Why did the man she hated cause such a reaction in her?

Deverel let out a small groan and snuggled his body closer to her, if that was possible. Julia was aware of an insane desire to push her hips back against him, but she controlled herself. He murmured something incomprehensible and nuzzled into her hair. She felt his breath on her neck, then the warm, velvety touch of his lips to her skin.

Julia let out a low shriek and rolled over, shoving against him with all her might. She managed to push him out of bed, and he landed with a thud on the floor, his eyes flying open in confusion, but her satisfaction was spoiled by the fact that their bound arms pulled her off, too. She landed a second later on top of him.

He let out a lurid oath. "Are you trying to kill me? Or simply wake up the whole inn?"

"You were touching me. You said you would not!" She tried to scramble off him but was hampered by their bound hands and the bed on one side of them. She wound up wallowing on him, and her face flamed bright red when she felt the inevitable response of his body beneath her.

He saw her look and chuckled. "'Tis you who are causing it, my girl. I have done nothing."

"Oh!" She managed to roll off on the far side of him, and they lay awkwardly, arms joined on top of them. "Get up. I think I would rather go to gaol than have to spend another moment with you."

She struggled to her feet, and he, too, rose, reaching out to steady her when her heel caught in her hem and she almost tumbled down again. Julia straightened her skirt and jerked her arm away from him, shooting him a glare.

"I think you must have an odd notion of gaol, then," he replied mildly.

Julia ignored him, shaking out her dress and reflecting that it would never be the same. She looked across the room into the mirror and let out a heartfelt groan. "I look as if I've been sleeping in a ditch!"

"No. How can you say that? There's not a speck of dirt on you."

She narrowed her eyes. "Are you always this annoying in the mornings?"

"I am, I fear, instantly alert when I wake up." He smiled wickedly. "Especially when I awake from so pleasant a dream."

The look in his eyes left her little doubt what that dream had involved. Julia curled her lip and stalked across the room toward the mirror. "I have no brush," she moaned. "Look at my hair."

He gazed, as instructed, upon the mass of tangled curls. She looked, he thought, like a woman who had passed a night of heated lovemaking, and the image sent a curl of hunger through his loins. The strangely good humor in which he had awakened vanished. It galled him that he could still desire this woman after the way she had betrayed him. His whole body was throbbing, and the dream he had had of making love to her was, now that he thought about it, most irritating. She was a trollop, and though he had never deluded himself that she was anything but a woman of easy virtue, he had thought that she returned his liking and passion, that she wanted him and not just the things he could give her. The way she had rejected the bracelet he had tried to give her had strengthened that belief. After all, there were any number of men, he was sure, who would be more than happy to be her protector—but she had chosen him.

Now, of course, he saw what folly that idea had been. She had played him for a fool. She had never had the least intention of giving herself to him. She had merely

been stringing him along so that her cohorts could kidnap him.

He cast her a dark look, forcing himself not to say
any of the things he was thinking. That would make him
too vulnerable. Instead, he addressed her complaint
about the lack of a brush. "Here. I have a comb."

He walked over to the chair, pulling her with him, and
took the comb from the inner pocket of his jacket. Julia
took the comb and began to try to pull it through her
hair, but her right hand was bound to his left one, and
she jerked his hand awkwardly. She cast him a look of
dislike, and he answered by snatching the comb from
her hand.

"Here. I'll do it."

He grabbed a hank of her luxuriant hair and began to
comb through the ends, carefully removing the tangles.
He could smell the sweet scent of roses that still clung
to the strands. He remembered the way they had felt in
his hands last night, and the pulse in his loins grew faster
and heavier. He combed his way through her tresses,
section by section. Her wayward curls twined around his
fingers, soft as silk. His throat closed, and his mouth
turned dry. He suspected that she could hear the rasp of
his breath.

She could, and the sound of it shook her. He was not
nearly as immune to her as he had claimed, even awake,
and she could not deny a certain spurt of triumph at the
knowledge. She was intensely aware of his closeness, of
the heat of his body, the sound of his breathing, the way
her hair caught on the faint roughness of his skin. Heat
flooded her abdomen.

She jerked her head away from him. "That—that's
fine."

She shoved the thick mass of her hair back behind her

shoulders. Deverel stopped, his hand arrested in midair, then tossed the comb onto the chest of drawers. He turned and walked across the room to the washbasin, and she, of course, was compelled to go with him. He had to dump the old water out of the basin, which meant going to the window and raising it, then picking up the basin and carrying it to it. With each movement, his hand jerked at Julia's irritatingly, and she had to follow him. They bumped into each other twice. He poured some water from the pitcher into the basin and reached down to scoop it up, carrying her hand and arm with it.

He made a noise of exasperation and reached over to the knot at his wrist to untie it. Julia went still. Escape suddenly beckoned. Stonehaven was looking down at the knot and did not see her other hand ease out to grasp the handle of the pitcher. It was not easy to untie the knot with only one hand, and Deverel frowned down at it in concentration. At last he pulled it free.

''There!'' he said, as the rope uncoiled from his wrist.

As it fell free, Julia swung the pitcher up at him with all her might. She intended to hit him on the head, but he moved reflexively backward, so that it struck a glancing blow on his chest and shoulder. She turned the pitcher upside down in her swing, and water splashed out on both of them. Deverel staggered back a little, and, fortunately for Julia, his heel slipped in the spilled water and he tumbled down.

In a flash Julia was across the room and turning the key in the door. He surged to his feet, cursing, and started after her just as she flung open the door and bounded out.

10

Julia fairly flew across the hall and down the stairs, but she could hear the thud of Deverel's bare feet right behind her. He was faster than she, taking the steps two at a time, and he caught her at the bottom of the stairs. He grabbed her arm and swung her around.

"You little wretch!" His eyes flashed, and his face was stamped with fury.

"Let go of me!" Julia tried to twist away, lashing out with her free hand and her feet. She landed a kick on his shin, and he let out an oath.

"Dammit! Stand still!" He grappled with her, and they staggered across the floor, coming up with a thud against the wall.

By this time Deverel had his arms tightly around her, immobilizing her arms at her sides, and now he pressed his full weight against her, pinning her legs to the wall.

"Stop it! Let go of me. I can hardly breathe!"

"If you couldn't breathe, you wouldn't be chattering," he retorted, looking down into her face. Her cheeks were flushed, and her eyes sparkled with anger as she glared at him. Her hair, tumbling freely around her shoulders, was a thick auburn curtain. Her beauty struck him all over again.

He was very aware of the softness of her body against his. He tried to ignore the sensations that were sizzling through him, but it was difficult. He had been in a fever of desire for this woman for days, and the disillusionment of last night seemed not to have reduced that fever one bit. He had lied to her the evening before when he said he had no desire to bed her. He had desired it very much, and it had taken a great exercise of his self-control to lie down beside her without touching her. Then, this morning, when he had been awakened so abruptly by hitting the floor, her curvaceous body atop his, he had been jerked out of a decidedly lascivious dream featuring her, unclothed, in his bed. He had been as hard as a rock, and combing through her luxuriant hair had not helped matters.

Now, pressed against her, remembering the way her body had rubbed against his in their struggle, he was pulsing with desire again, and the fact that his passion so overwhelmed his reason made him even more furious with her. He wanted to shout, to shake her, to sink into her and make love to her until she cried out with longing, too. He tried to shove the vision from his mind. His eyes dropped down to her mouth, then lower. The bodice of her dress had been splashed with water. The muslin, always sheer, and the thin cotton chemise beneath were soaked, turning them almost transparent. The rosy brown buds of her nipples showed clearly, pressing saucily against the cloth. He took a ragged breath.

Julia, as aware as he of the intimacy of their position, was also finding it difficult to breathe. She told herself it was because he was pushing her into the wall, but she knew that it sprang more from the feel of his body

against hers all the way up and down. She could feel the
hard throb of his desire against her abdomen.

"Let go of me!" she snapped, pushing back at him
with her own body. It was that, the sudden thrust of her
pelvis against him, that made him snap.

A savage light flared in Deverel's eyes, and he let out
a groan. His mouth found hers hungrily. Julia sagged
against him, suddenly too weak to stand on her own. His
mouth consumed hers, taking her with teeth and tongue
and lips. Julia, in whom all thought of resistance had
fled as soon as his mouth touched hers, strained up
against him, frustrated that his arms clamped hers down
so that she could not wrap them around his neck.

Heat scorched them. It was only the barest remnant
of good sense that kept Deverel from shoving up her
skirts and taking her right there against the wall. He had
never felt so beyond reason, so desperate to have a
woman. It seemed, strangely, as if her betrayal of him
only made him want her more. He ground his pelvis into
hers and was further aroused by the whimper of pleasure
that rose in her throat. His arms went beneath her buttocks, and he lifted her from the floor, his mouth still
ravaging hers. His brain was aflame, registering nothing
but a vague intent to carry her up the stairs and back
into their room.

Neither of them noticed the sounds of the front door
of the inn opening, followed by voices, then footsteps
into the public room. In fact, they did not hear the col-
lective gasp of the small group that had entered the inn.

Then a male voice rang out across the room. "Good
God! Stonehaven!"

Deverel and Julia froze, the voice affecting them like
a bucket of cold water thrown over them. Deverel's arms
loosened around her, and they turned. Three people

stood about seven feet away, staring at them in horrified astonishment—a man, a woman and a teenage boy. They could not have been anyone either Julia or Deverel would less like to have seen.

"Fitzmaurice," Deverel croaked out.

"Julia!" Pamela St. Leger, beside Major Fitzmaurice, exclaimed, for once seemingly at a loss for words.

Thomas, standing beside his mother, said nothing, merely stared, his jaw dropping.

Julia turned bright red. Deverel cursed under his breath.

"Julia, what are you doing here? And—and like that!" Pamela spluttered. "Whatever are you thinking?"

Julia let out a heartfelt groan and huddled against Deverel, much to his surprise, turning her face into his chest.

"As if what your brother did wasn't bad enough!" Pamela continued, heedless of Julia's humiliation. "Here you are, carrying on like a hussy in a public inn!" Her eyes went expressively to their dishabille—their shoes off, his shirt hanging out, Julia's hair a mess. "Poor Phoebe." She sighed. "Poor Gilbert. I don't know how the Armigers will manage to hold up their heads now."

"Julia?" Deverel murmured, stiffening as the names Pamela said began to sink in on him. "Bloody hell!"

He put his fingers beneath Julia's chin and forced her head up so that she had to look at him. He read the misery and humiliation on her face, a confirmation of Pamela's words. Understanding dawned in his face. "Sweet Lord!" he breathed. "That's why…"

He broke off as Thomas spoke up for the first time. "You're wrong, Mother. Sir Selby didn't do anything bad! And," he added staunchly, "I'm sure that Julia did not, either."

"To be sure," Fitzmaurice added without conviction.

"Don't be foolish, Thomas," Pamela said with a little titter. "It is rather obvious what your dear Julia has been doing. But it really doesn't matter whether she has done anything wrong. What matters is that she is here at this inn, in the morning, with Lord Stonehaven, both of them, um, dressed as they are and locked in an embrace that would make even a widow like myself blush. Once she has been discovered in such a compromising position, her reputation is ruined. Isn't that right, Julia?"

Julia turned her head and regarded the other woman with a stony expression. She knew as well as Pamela did that her reputation was in shreds, for Pamela would delight in spreading the information around. However, she knew that it was even worse than what Pamela thought. Now Deverel knew exactly who she was, and the stunned look in his eyes told her that he also had a very good guess as to why she had kidnapped him. If he had hated her before, he would hate her doubly now. He would realize that she suspected him of embezzling the money and ruining Selby. Even though it would cost him something in terms of reputation, he would make sure that everyone knew of her being compromised—as if Pamela would not hurry to make sure of that herself! He would not rest until her reputation was utterly ruined, as Selby's had been, for then no one would believe her if she accused him of stealing the money.

She had failed, utterly and miserably. Not only had she not cleared Selby's name, she had made everything worse for Gilbert and Phoebe by embroiling the family name in another scandal.

"Well, darling," Stonehaven said lightly, "it looks like we must tell them."

Julia's head snapped back to him. *What was he talking*

about? She thought for one wild instant that perhaps he had run mad. Instead of the thunderous expression she had expected, he was gazing down at her with a smile on his face. Had she seen this expression on any other man's face, she would have said that he was looking at her with affection. But that, she knew, was impossible.

"What?" she croaked out.

"Oh, I know we were planning to tell Mother first, but given the situation, I think we must let Major Fitzmaurice and Mrs. St. Leger in on our surprise." He turned toward the others, one arm still around Julia's shoulders, holding her tightly against him so that her arm, with the piece of rope still dangling from it, was hidden from them.

"Sorry," he continued. "We had not informed anyone. We had wanted to wait until we had told Lady Stonehaven. That's where we are going now."

"To Stonehaven?" Fitzmaurice looked confused. "But isn't your estate in Buckinghamshire?" His intelligence was not great, but even he knew that Buckinghamshire lay in exactly the opposite direction.

"Of course," Deverel replied smoothly. "But we had to come to Julia's home first, of course."

"Eh?" Fitzmaurice continued to gaze at him blankly, but Pamela's face was stamped with suspicion.

Deverel made a gesture of dismissal. "But that doesn't matter. What is important is what you just saw. I admit that Julia and I were guilty of a shocking breach of conduct," Deverel said, smiling, "but it was not sinful. I hope that you will not hold it too much against us. One must make allowances, you know, for newlyweds. Julia and I were just married yesterday by special license."

His statement was followed by a profound silence.

Major Fitzmaurice's natural thinking processes were slow. Everyone else was too stunned to speak. Fitzmaurice's face was the first to clear.

"Well!" he said heartily. "That explains it, then. Congratulations, old boy." He strode forward to shake Deverel's hand. "Never thought I'd see the day. And Julia, my dear." She offered him a wan smile as he went on. "I wish you very happy, Lady Stonehaven."

Julia paled. "Oh, no! You mustn't call me that!"

"It's still Julia, of course, to you, Fitz," Deverel explained easily. "That won't change, I assure you." He turned toward St. Leger. "Well, Thomas, aren't you going to congratulate us? I know you are quite fond of Julia."

"Y-yes, yes, of course," Thomas stammered, looking questioningly at Julia. She frowned at him, hoping that he realized that it was all a hoax. However, she could hardly say so in front of his mother. "Congratulations, sir. Julia."

"How...remarkable," Pamela said with ironic emphasis. Julia felt sure that she did not believe a word of what Stonehaven had said, but she could hardly dispute it, at least, not to his face.

"Yes, isn't it?" Stonehaven smiled at her. "I could hardly believe my good fortune when Julia accepted me."

"Join us for breakfast," Fitzmaurice suggested heartily. "That's why we stopped—going back to Farrow, you see, and we figured they wouldn't have any victuals set out for us. Fortunate circumstance, wasn't it, running into you?"

"Yes. Most fortunate," Deverel replied dryly. "However, I am afraid that we must beg off this time. We really need to get on our way if we are to make it to

Stonehaven this evening." He bowed toward them. "If you will excuse us."

Without waiting for a reply, he turned toward his "bride." "Come, my love, we must finish getting ready."

Julia hesitated, feeling guiltily that she should tell them that Deverel was lying. But then Deverel gripped her arm, turning her around, and propelled her up the stairs with him, carefully keeping her arm with the telltale rope in front of them. He whisked her into their room and closed the door after them, carefully turning the key. He turned to face her.

Julia stared at him for a moment. Her knees suddenly began to tremble with the aftermath of excitement, and she sat down shakily in the chair. "Oh, no! What are we to do now? Of all the terrible luck!"

"I must say, it was, rather. But there's no time for moans and recriminations now. We have to get out of here quickly, before they think to ask some difficult questions—like why we spent the night in an inn instead of at your home."

"Why did you tell them we were married?" Julia cried, jumping back up and beginning to pace the room.

"I should think that would be obvious. It was the only possible thing that could save your reputation. God knows *you* seem to have no problem playing fast and loose with it, but I'll be damned if I'll be known as the sort of cad who would compromise a genteel young lady."

"But it makes it all worse! Don't you see? They'll find out the truth soon enough, and then it will just add to the scandal!"

"They won't find out the truth," he said, tucking in his shirt and sitting down to put on his stockings and shoes. ''It won't be a fantastic tale.'' He gestured toward her. ''Get on your shoes, girl, we need to leave.''

''But how can it not be?'' Julia felt like screaming, but she sat down obediently and put on her shoes. ''We aren't married. We can hardly—''

''We shall remedy that soon enough,'' he replied grimly.

Julia stared at him. Slowly she rose to her feet. ''Are you suggesting that you and I get married?''

''Of course. What other course is there?''

''But we despise one another!''

''In my experience, that is quite common among married couples,'' he replied lightly, shrugging into his jacket. ''The only difference with us is that we know it at the beginning instead of finding out later.''

''This is no time for jests!''

''Excuse me. It seemed to me a very good time. I find that disagreeable medicine goes down somewhat better if one smiles.''

Julia glared at him, making an exasperated noise.

''Now, if you are ready, I think that the best thing to do is to hire a horse for me from our landlord and travel to the next town, where we can hire a post chaise. We'll take your horse with us, I presume. I had thought about sending it back to your home, but then I realized that you would probably want it when we reached Stonehaven.''

''I am not going to your country house,'' Julia stated flatly.

''We shall discuss that at a more appropriate time.''

''No! We will discuss it right now, before we go any further. This whole thing is ridiculous. We are not getting married. You cannot want to marry me, and I certainly have no desire to marry you.''

"I am quite aware of your feelings toward me, and I cannot pretend that my feelings toward you are particularly civil. But we are not talking about doing what we want. We are talking about doing our duty." He fixed her with a piercing gaze. "Don't you understand what a predicament you are in? We were just discovered in a supremely compromising position by two people who will probably blab it over half of England. Fitzmaurice hasn't enough sense to keep his mouth shut, and Pamela is the sort who loves nothing so much as causing other people misery. Your reputation will be ruined, and the only thing that can save you is to marry me."

"I realize that. I'm not stupid," Julia retorted. "But there is no reason for you to make such a sacrifice. We dislike each other, and it would only be a burden to tie your family name to mine. The Armigers are in disgrace."

"So you are saying I should save myself and leave you to sink or swim? What a nice opinion you have of me, I must say."

"What does it matter if my reputation is ruined?" Julia asked a trifle forlornly. "It is extremely unlikely that I shall ever marry. I shall live out my days at Greenwood with Phoebe, anyway. I am ostracized because of what Selby—because of what you did to Selby!"

"What *I* did to Selby! Good Lord, with all your disagreeable qualities, at least up 'til now you hadn't seemed idiotic. I did nothing to Selby. Selby did it all to himself. He was foolish and weak, and he disgraced his name. He hadn't even the courage to face it like a man, but left the three of you to cope with it."

"How dare you say that about Selby!" Julia clenched her fists, glaring at him. "He was the best man that ever lived! He was wonderful and kind, and he had far more courage than a snake like you.''

''No doubt he was a paragon,'' Stonehaven remarked dryly. ''I am sure embezzlers often are.'' He held up his hand to ward off her furious retort. ''Now, let's stick to the subject of you, if we may. It is true that Selby disgraced the family, but if you create a scandal, too, it will only make matters worse. Can't you see that? There will be a storm of gossip about you, and all the old gossip about Selby, dormant for the past couple of years, will arise all over again. If you don't care about yourself, think about your sister-in-law. Think about your nephew. They were innocent parties in both instances, but they have been made to suffer and will be made to suffer again. Lady Armiger is a trifle young, I think, to be immured in Kent, but at least she has had something of a life. What about poor Gilbert? How do you think his life will be, growing up with two such scandals hanging over his head? It will be hard enough, I assure you, trying to live down what his father did, without also having an aunt who is known throughout Society as a wanton!''

Julia could not keep tears from springing into her eyes, though she struggled valiantly not to let them fall. ''I know! I know! You need not tell me. I knew what might happen if I failed.''

''But you went ahead anyway, didn't you?'' He shook his head in exasperation. ''You are very like Selby—emotional and impetuous to a fault. You wanted revenge on me because I was the one who caught Selby, so you concocted this mad scheme, knowing full well that it might all blow up in your face.''

''I thought it was worth the risk.''

''All very well for you, but what about your family?

I know," he continued sarcastically, "that considering the consequences and doing one's duty are not family traits of the Armigers. However, I think that this is one time when you are going to have to buckle down and do the right thing. For the sake of your nephew, if nothing else."

"How dare you—" Julia began hotly.

"Please. Let us not have a fit of histrionics. You may shout at me all you wish while we are riding. But now it behooves us to leave the inn."

He cast a last glance around the room, then opened the door cautiously and peered about. He stepped out into the hall, motioning Julia to follow him, which she did, stonily silent. He took her arm, and they climbed softly down the stairs. Motioning to Julia to wait for him outside, he went into the taproom, seeking the innkeeper.

Julia went outside and sat down huffily on a bench to wait for Deverel. A moment later the front door opened, and Thomas came hurrying out.

"Julia! I saw you come out."

Julia looked toward the door in alarm. "Did anyone else see me? I cannot talk to Pamela."

"No. You're safe. Mother and the major are still eating. I was watching for you, you see, and I just slipped out. I wanted to talk to you." He looked at her, distress written on his face. "It's not true, is it? You're not married to *him,* are you?"

"No, of course not. Oh, Thomas, it's the most awful mess. De—Lord Stonehaven only said that because you caught us in a compromising position. But we aren't married. You know I could never marry him."

"Thank God! But how did you end up here? Why were you kissing him?"

"Uh, well, that wasn't, you see, he—oh, Thomas, it is very long and complicated. I can't explain it now."

"But did you find out anything?" he pressed. "Did he confess after you locked him up?"

"Bloody hell!"

The two of them jumped and whirled around at the sound of Stonehaven's furious voice behind them. They had been so involved in their conversation that they had not heard him come out the front door. They gaped at him.

"So that was it, eh?" he thundered. "It wasn't just to exact your revenge on me for discovering Selby's crime, was it? You seduced me into going to that hut so that you could force me into some sort of confession!"

Julia swallowed hard, frightened by the red-hot anger in Stonehaven's face. She forced her chin up a little and said, "Yes. Of course. What purpose would it serve to stick you in a hut otherwise?"

"I thought you wanted to pay me back for the way you were hurt by Selby's scandal. To make me suffer a little—start a hunger for something I could not have, even spend a miserable night tied to a chair. It doesn't make much sense, I'll admit, but, then, when people are angry and hurt, they often don't make sense. They lash out at the nearest target." He paused, looking at her consideringly. "Just what was it you wanted to make me confess to?"

"To stealing my money yourself!" Thomas said hotly, facing the older man, his fists clenched at his sides.

"What!" Stonehaven stared at him in amazement. "Are you mad?"

"No, just smarter than you gave me credit for."

Stonehaven let out a sharp bark of laughter. "Not if

you believe that I was the one who embezzled your money. I never heard of anything so ridiculous in my life."

"It's not ridiculous, and you know it," Julia retorted. "You stole the money and made it look as if Selby did it. You ruined him and my entire family for your own selfish ends."

Stonehaven went white around his mouth. "You actually believe that I—that I took young Thomas's money—that I betrayed my honor and family, not to mention the sacred trust that Walter placed in me? And not content with that, I purposely did it in such a way that it would ruin a man with whom I had been friends for years? Ruin not only him, but his family's name, as well?"

Julia quailed before the look in his eyes, but she stiffened her spine and replied flatly, "Yes. That is what I believe."

Deverel let out an odd little breath. "I see." He glanced away. "I had thought that nothing could appall me more than discovering that my cunning little seductress was, in fact, a woman of quality and that her scheme came from personal ill will toward me. But I am learning that you have a bottomless capacity to shock me." He looked at Thomas. "And you, young man— you believe this, too?"

Thomas nodded, looking a trifle frightened, but holding his ground.

"I am overwhelmed by the esteem in which you hold me." Deverel paused. "I am afraid that Miss Armiger and I must leave now, Thomas. We have a great many things to do in the next few days. But let me assure you that Miss Armiger *is* going to marry me, and I would ask you to keep quiet about her incautious disclosure to you a few moments ago. I realize that you bear no regard for me, but for the sake of whatever affection you have for Julia, I pray you will be silent.''

''I wouldn't hurt Julia for the world!'' Thomas exclaimed.

''Good. You will not if you do not tell your mother and Fitz the truth.''

''Oh, no, my lord, I know better than that,'' Thomas assured him earnestly.

''Furthermore, I promise you that Miss Armiger and I will investigate this matter of the embezzlement most thoroughly. I warrant you that before much longer she will know exactly who stole the money.'' He turned to Julia, his eyes challenging.

Julia returned his gaze defiantly. ''If you think that you can bully me into believing it was Selby, I can tell you right now that it won't work.''

''Of course not. However, I am hoping that reason and logic will get through to you eventually.'' He paused. ''Now, I think it is time that we left, Miss Armiger. Don't you?''

''Yes.'' Julia bit off the word. She turned to Thomas and gave him a hug, whispering, ''I will be all right. And I swear to you that I will somehow get the truth out of him.''

Stonehaven led her across the yard toward the stables. ''The innkeeper consented to let me hire his gig rather than another horse. It is slower, of course, but more appropriate for a woman in a day dress. Don't you agree?''

Julia gave a little sigh of relief. Although she would not have told Stonehaven so for the world, she had not been looking forward to making a spectacle of herself by riding a horse in a muslin day dress rather than a riding habit. Last night in the dark, hurrying on her mission to the shepherd's hut, she had not given a thought to hiking up her skirt and riding astride her mare, but in the daytime it would, she knew, look quite odd, if not shocking, not to wear a habit.

"Thank you," she said, avoiding his eyes.

"You are welcome," he replied with equal stiffness.

When the ostler brought out the gig, Julia's mare tied to it in back, Stonehaven handed her up into it, then climbed up himself and took the reins. They rolled off at a snail's pace.

"The landlord said that Swanley is the nearest town with a post house. From there, we will go on to Buckinghamshire."

"And I, I collect, will have nothing to say in the matter?" Julia challenged him. "I am sorry to ruin your plans, but you will be going on to Buckinghamshire by yourself. We will pass through London, and I intend to get off there."

He glanced at her. "What maggot have you got into your head now?"

"I am not marrying you. The very thought is absurd."

"That has sometimes been my opinion of marriage, also," he replied easily. "However, it is the accepted manner of living, I'm afraid."

"Would you pray stop talking nonsense. I am speaking of *our* marriage. There is no reason for it."

He sighed loudly. "I thought we had laid this argument to rest."

"No. Not at all. There is no reason for you to marry me. You have no obligation. It can only be an embarrassment to you and your family to be attached to the Armigers, and to me in particular, after Pamela St. Leger gets through carrying this tale to everyone."

"I was involved in the same tale she will be telling," he reminded her mildly.

"But it isn't the same for a man. You know it isn't. People will cluck their tongues and shake their heads, and perhaps a few matrons will decide you are too much of a rake to invite you to their parties, but that will be it. You shan't be ostracized by the entire Society."

"No, and neither will you be, when everyone knows that we are married."

"There is no reason for you to make such a sacrifice for me," Julia said stubbornly, glaring at him. Why was he insisting on acting so nobly, when she knew that he was anything but noble? "You cannot wish to tie yourself to a—a 'cunning jade.' A 'doxy.'"

He lifted an amused eyebrow. "Ah, so that rankled, did it?"

"You despise me," Julia added, ignoring his comment. "And you must realize that I despise you. What kind of a marriage would we have?"

"A long and rancorous one, if the past day is any indication," he replied. He turned, fixing her with a steely gaze. "Listen to me. It is my intention to marry you. It does not matter how I feel about you. I told you before—it is a question of honor. Of duty. I was caught in the same compromising position as you. It is true that my punishment by Society would not be as severe. But ever afterward, there would be a certain taint to my name. I would be known as the scoundrel who seduced you, then did not marry you, who left you carrying the burden for our indiscretion."

"But I was to blame!" Julia protested. "I knew what I was doing. You did not even know who I was or that I was of good birth. I pretended to be a woman of loose morals. I am prepared to face the consequences of those actions—whatever you might say about us Armigers.''

"No," he agreed with sarcastic inflection, "I certainly did not know who you were or what you were about. I hope to God that if I had I would have behaved with more sense. However, whatever the circumstances, I was also in the wrong. I acted rashly. I could have—I should have—left when I cut my bonds. Instead, I stayed and seized you because I was furious. It was my fault that you were at that inn and my fault as well that we were caught in—uh—the manner we were caught.''

His eyes dropped to her mouth, and Julia was forcibly reminded of the passionate kiss in which they had been discovered. She remembered the taste of his lips, the texture, the searing heat, and she could not suppress a tremor.

"Besides," he continued in a flat voice, turning back to look at the road, "even if we had not been caught, I was involved with you in, uh, intimate ways that only a husband should be privy to. Having seen you, touched you—" His voice grew hoarse.

Heat surged up in Julia, and she turned her face away. How could merely his words arouse her this way? "No. Please. We did not—I mean, in the most important way, we were not—''

"No, we did not make love," he responded harshly. "I did not take your virginity. At least that sin cannot be laid at my door. However, I knew you in ways that are a husband's prerogative. It is my obvious duty, my obligation, to make that morally and legally right.''

"But I don't want to marry you!" Julia burst out, goaded past endurance. "The most important thing in the world to you may be what people think of you, but it is not to me. I cannot live in a sham of a marriage. I would rather live all the rest of my days in shame than tie myself to the man who ruined my brother!''

"I did not ruin Selby!" His dark eyes glittered with rage. "Are you mad? How can you possibly think I stole that money? Or used it to ruin Selby? Selby was my friend."

Julia rolled her eyes. "Heaven save me from friends like you."

"This makes no sense. What makes you think that I took Thomas's money?"

Julia cast him a contemptuous look. "You, of all people, should know that."

"Humor me."

"Well, I don't know how to prove it, if that is what you are trying to find out. That's why I was hoping to get you to confess."

"By seducing me?" He frowned in thought. "I do remember you asking some odd questions that night in the box at Vauxhall Gardens." A sardonic smile touched his lips. "What were you planning to do? At the peak of passion say, 'Oh, by the way, did you embezzle money from Thomas's trust?' It would have been a trifle dampening to the moment, don't you think?"

"It didn't work. Obviously." She scowled at him. "It became clear to me that I wasn't good enough at it."

"Oh, you were quite good," he assured her, and his eyes lit for an instant with an unholy fire.

"Not at getting the information I wanted."

"So you decided to kidnap me instead."

"Yes. Well, that had been our plan from the first, but it proved rather difficult in the actuality. Nunnelly said you must work out at Jackson's."

"On occasion. Who, by the way, is this Nunnelly chap to whom I owe the knot on my head?"

"You mustn't blame him," Julia said earnestly. "It was all my idea. He is so loyal to me that he would do anything for me. But he would never have done it if I had not told him to."

"A servant, then, rather than a hired assassin."

"He wasn't going to kill you!" Julia retorted, aghast.

"I beg your pardon, but, you see, I had no way of knowing that he meant only to knock me over the head and tie me up, not kill me. What if I had been carrying a gun one of those times when he accosted me? I could have shot him. It was a caper-witted scheme."

"Thank you very much. Obviously I am not as expert at criminal activities as you."

"Ah, yes, back to the subject at hand. You were going to tell me why you decided I am a thief."

"When you start with the knowledge that Selby did not do it, as Phoebe and Thomas and I did, it is much easier."

"And that knowledge is based on...?" His voice lifted inquiringly.

"On our knowledge of Selby," Julia retorted.

"I see. Then you have no evidence that would prove that he did not do it."

"Of course I do not. If I had, we would have made it known long ago. But I know my brother, and he would never have done such a thing. If, by any stretch of the imagination, he would have considered stealing money, he would certainly not have taken it from Thomas, who was like a younger brother to him."

"Very admirable sentiments from a sister. But a man will do things that are against his nature if he is subject to an overwhelming urge. Sometimes the very nicest of men can have a hidden vice, and that vice can lead them to steal and—"

"Are you talking about Selby?"

"Yes. Selby was an inveterate gambler. He lost a great deal of money. No doubt he needed to pay his gambling debts, and he seized on the idea of taking it from the trust. Perhaps he even intended to give it back when he was in luck again, but, of course, that never happens."

"That was when he was young." Julia dismissed the idea with a wave of her hand. "I know he gambled too much then. He told me so himself. Where do you think I had heard of Madame Beauclaire's? But not after he met Phoebe. Marrying her and having Gilbert changed that. He had been quite settled those last four years. He was never so bad that he endangered the estate or anything like that. But after he married Phoebe, he took an interest in the estate, and he was doing quite well at his death. I am certain of it, because Phoebe hates to go over the books with the estate manager, and she always makes me come along with her to discuss business. I know how well he left her and Gilbert provided for. Selby had no need for the money."

"Sometimes a need can be hidden."

"You are saying that Selby had a need for money which no one could discern. What piffle! The truth of it is that Selby had no reason to take money from Thomas, and certainly no inclination. And even if he had had both, he had far too much honor ever to do it. The three of us knew Selby. That is how we know that he did not do it. Therefore we were able to look at the incident without being distracted by all the—" She made a vague, encompassing gesture.

"Facts?" Deverel suggested.

"By all the false clues," Julia corrected.

"You mean as I was."

"No. I mean as you intended everyone else to be."
She clutched her hands together tightly, a little scared at
speaking so boldly to Stonehaven.

He regarded her stonily. "Go on."

"Well, since we knew that Selby was not guilty, it
was obvious that someone must have set it up to make
it appear that he was. It had to have been someone who
was familiar with the trust and the people involved and
who knew my brother well enough to have heard about
his use of the name Jack Fletcher. Who would have
thought that his playing such a silly little game would
result in such tragedy?"

"So, of course, you assumed that out of all the people
who knew Selby and knew the trust, *I* was the only
candidate."

Julia refused to shrink before the acid tone of his
words. She gazed back at him steadily. "The most logical one, certainly. There were only three other trustees.
Fitz isn't intelligent enough to think up something like
this, and Varian was a better friend of Selby's than you.
And you were the one who brought up the whole thing.
You showed everyone the letters and bruited it about
that Selby had stolen from the trust. It was clear to me—
and to Phoebe and Thomas, too—that the person who
had actually done the thievery and who had laid the trap
for Selby would be the one to spring it."

"So because I found Selby's thievery and did not hide
it, I am now the culprit?"

"Who better to show everyone the evidence than the
one who invented it?" Julia returned hotly. "No one
could miss all the clues you so carefully planted if you
made sure they saw them. Why else were you so quick
to tell? So loud in your complaints?"

"What would you have me do?" he exclaimed, his

eyes flashing. "Stand around when I found that someone had stolen from Thomas's trust? Not say anything because the man who had stolen it was someone I had known since he first came on the town? Is that your idea of honor? Because it is not mine. Walter had been my very dear friend for years, and I could not have betrayed him by overlooking malfeasance, even when it was done by a friend. Do you think it was easy for me to accuse Selby? Do you think that I did not hope and pray that he would have some reason, some explanation, for what happened? But he did not. He could not answer for any of the letters. He had no reason for the expenditures. All he did was deny and deny, without any evidence to back him up. It was clear that Selby had done it. Obvious to everyone. There were four letters in his handwriting, with his signature, requesting money from the trust. That money went to a false name which Selby was known to have used for years and years. It hardly matters whether it had been a joke or not. It was Selby's alter ego. Everyone knew it. And Selby could not give any reason for writing the letters, could not show that the money had gone to something to benefit Thomas St. Leger."

"Of course he could not!" Julia retorted. "Because he did not do it. How can one refute evidence that is false? How could he tell why he wrote the letters when he did not write them? He denied it because it was the truth, but you had constructed the web so cleverly that he could not get out of it. His denials only made him seem more guilty."

"He seemed guilty because he *was* guilty," Deverel snapped. He drew a deep breath and forced himself to speak more calmly. "He was your brother, and you loved him deeply. I know that it was very hard for you to accept that he could have done such a thing. It was hard for me to believe it, too. But once I saw the evidence, it was impossible to believe anything else. My God, Julia, he committed suicide. Isn't that a clear enough indication of his guilt?''

''He did not commit suicide!''

''What else can you call it when a man puts a gun to his head and pulls the trigger?'' Deverel retorted harshly.

''A hunting accident. That kind of thing happens all the time. He was probably cleaning it, and it went off. He had gone there to hunt, after all.''

''No. I talked to the caretaker of his hunting lodge. He said that Selby had not hunted at all. He went there, and he shot himself, and that was all.''

''He would not have committed suicide,'' Julia repeated stubbornly. ''I know that Phoebe fears that that is what happened. I think she believes that he was driven to it by the way everyone turned against him. But he was too strong. He would not have left us that way.''

''My God, woman! What will it take to convince you? The man killed himself. He left a note saying so and confessing to the embezzlement!''

There was a moment of shattering silence.

''What? What did you say?''

Stonehaven sighed. ''Selby left a note saying that he was taking his own life because he could not bear the shame anymore, because he was so guilty over what he had done. He admitted that he had taken the money.''

''I don't believe it.'' Julia's voice quavered on the words. ''I don't believe you.''

''Ask Varian St. Leger. He was at my house when I got the note from Selby, asking me to meet him at his hunting lodge. It was not far from my house, you see. I didn't want to go. I presumed he had come to beg and plead, or to argue with me again. But, of course, I did go, and Varian rode along with me. We found him in his study, dead. There was a note on the desk beside him. In it he begged everyone's pardon and admitted his guilt.''

"But how—I—I knew you and Varian found his body, but I—no one said anything about a note.''

"No. It was…Varian and I agreed that it would not help anyone to give Lady Armiger the note. There were things in it that a grieving family should not see.''

"How dare you!'' Julia clenched her fists. She would have liked to punch him. "How dare you keep that from us? We had a right to know. Phoebe should have been able to read her husband's last words. What made you think you had the right to keep them from us?''

"We did what we thought was best.''

"What *you* thought was best!'' Julia repeated scornfully, her cheeks blazing with color. "It would have been best to tell us the truth! Neither Phoebe nor I is a child. If we could handle Selby's death, I think we could have handled a suicide note, as well. I want to see it.''

"It was a very…blunt telling of what happened. You don't know what pain it will cause you and Lady Armiger.''

"No, I don't know, because I don't know what's in it, since you and Varian saw fit to treat us like children!''

"Not like children! Like a sister and a wife who loved a man very much. We did it to protect you.''

"I did not ask for your protection. And I never shall. I want to see that note.'' She looked at him with narrowed eyes. "Or are you hiding it because you are afraid that Phoebe and I will not accept that note as uncritically as Varian? Is it because Phoebe or I would easily see how false it is?''

Stonehaven's fingers clenched, and he set his jaw

tightly. For a moment Julia thought that he would start yelling. But when he spoke, his voice was low, controlled and grim. "Very well! You shall see the note. It is in my office at Stonehaven. Perhaps then you will finally admit the truth."

"I already know the truth." Nerves danced in Julia's stomach. She felt almost sick. There was no possibility now, she knew, of her getting off in London. There was now no place she wanted to go more than Stonehaven.

11

They spoke little on the rest of their journey. When they reached Swanley, Stonehaven rented a post chaise, and, while they sat down to a hearty breakfast in a private parlor at the posting house, he sent a maid down the street to purchase hairpins and a brush for Julia. Julia was surprised by the thoughtfulness of the gesture, but she was heartily glad. She had been aware of the odd looks she had received on their short trip and in the yard of the posting house. No woman went about in public with her hair loose and hanging, and Julia was very aware that hers was also wild and tangled into the bargain.

It took several minutes to brush her hair into any sort of manageable shape. She glanced up once in the mirror she was using for the job and saw that Stonehaven was standing across the room, arms folded, watching her. Her breath caught in her throat. Quickly she swept her hair up and arranged it in a simple knot from which several thick strands still dangled. These she curled around her finger until she had a cluster of three long lustrous curls. It was not the most stunning hairdo she had ever achieved, due in large part to not having the services of her maid, who was quite clever at such things. However, at least she looked presentable—as long as one did not look at the sadly crumpled state of her dress.

Stonehaven had been occupied during much of the time with writing something down on a piece of paper, which he now sealed.

"Do you wish to write a note to Lady Armiger?" he asked with the same formal courtesy with which they had addressed their infrequent remarks to one another. "I have written some instructions to my business manager, and I plan to have them delivered when we pass through London. I thought perhaps you might want to let your sister-in-law know of your plans."

"Yes, thank you," Julia replied with equal courtesy.

Dipping the pen in the ink, she scribbled a brief note to Phoebe.

Dearest Phoebe,

I have no time to write an explanation, though I know that this letter will leave you amazed. I want you to know that I am unharmed. I am traveling to Stonehaven, Lord S's estate in Buckinghamshire. He is insisting that I marry him, and he is taking me to meet his mother. Of course, I will not. (Marry him, I mean.) But he has *important information* there, and I must see it.

Love, Julia

P.S. Please pack a trunk of my clothes and send it.

She knew that Phoebe would be thrown into confusion by the note, but she had no time to write more. The chaise was already waiting for them in the yard. She promised herself that she would write a full explanation of what had happened when she reached Deverel's home. After shaking sand over the ink to dry it, she then tapped it off and folded the paper, sealing it with a wafer of wax.

Lord Stonehaven took her note, and they hurried out to get into the carriage. The chaise rumbled out of the yard, the postilion in his bright red jacket on the lead horse. One of the ostlers accompanied them as an out-rider on Julia's mare. Deverel sat across from Julia, po-litely riding on the backward side, and on the opposite end of the seat.

After a few minutes of stony silence, Deverel closed his eyes and leaned back against the squabs. Julia was not sure if he was actually going to sleep or merely removing himself from her company in the only way possible. Whatever it was, she found the situation more comfortable this way, and she was able to relax and watch the countryside go by, and even think. As a result, she thought of something to add to her note to Phoebe, and when they arrived at the post house in London, she insisted on jotting an extra line on the back of the note. Deverel then sent one of the ostlers off with both her message and his, and a few minutes later, with a fresh team of horses, they started out of London.

This time it was Julia who closed her eyes, and she soon found herself asleep. Sleeping helped wile away some of the time, and they stopped in midafternoon for a light nuncheon. After that, they rode on, too tired now of riding to much care about the awkwardness of being in the carriage together. Julia looked at the scenery, no-ticing that it was becoming like that around Selby's hunting lodge. That fact was enough to make her heart squeeze in her chest.

Phoebe—or, rather, their estate manager—had sold the hunting lodge last year, advising that it was not feasible for Phoebe to keep up a home which she never used. She had understood, but it had taken her two years to bring herself to get rid of something of which Selby had been so fond.

It was after dark, and Julia was growing sore and weary from sitting so long in the carriage, when they at last turned up a long driveway lined by magnificent trees and pulled up in front of a gracious house of honey-colored stone. The front door opened wide at their approach, and a footman bowed.

"My lord! What a surprise."

"Not an unpleasant one, I hope."

"Oh, no, my lord, indeed not. Lady Stonehaven will be so pleased. I believe that Carruthers has gone to inform her ladyship of your arrival."

"Very good. Is she in her sitting room?"

"I daresay, my lord."

"Jennings, this is Miss Julia Armiger, my fiancée."

"Your—" The man choked back his surprised exclamation, goggling at Julia. "Indeed, sir. Congratulations, my lord. Welcome to Stonehaven, Miss Armiger."

"We have no luggage. Pay off the postilion, will you? Miss Armiger and I are going up to see Mother."

They had barely reached the top of the staircase before they met that good woman hurrying down the hall. She smiled broadly when she saw Deverel and held out both her hands to him.

"Deverel! If this isn't just like you—putting us all at sixes and sevens! Why didn't you let me know you were coming?" Her welcoming smile belied any harshness in her words.

"I relied on your good nature," he replied, taking her hands and squeezing them, then pulling her close for a hug. "And the fact that I pay my servants very well.

Frankly, I didn't decide to come until this morning, and I thought it would be better to explain in person than to try to put it all in a letter that would, at best, arrive only a couple of hours before we did.''

He turned toward Julia, and his mother followed suit, her dark eyes bright with curiosity. Julia could see that Deverel had inherited his coloring from his mother, for her eyes were black, as was her hair, except for a single distinctive streak of white that ran back from her right temple. However, unlike her son, she was short and a little plump, with a smiling, pleasant face. She was dressed quite fashionably in a dove gray dress of elegant lines and expensive material that proclaimed the work of a major modiste.

''Mother, I would like to introduce my fiancée, Miss Julia Armiger. Julia, this is my mother, Lady Teresa Stonehaven.''

There was a moment of frozen silence. Lady Stonehaven looked blankly at Julia, then at her son. ''Fiancée?'' she repeated in a small voice. ''Armiger?''

''Yes.''

''Well—ah, this is certainly a surprise.'' She turned to Julia. ''Excuse me. I don't know where my manners are. How do you do, Miss Armiger? I am most happy to meet you.''

She extended a hand to Julia to shake, and Julia noticed that the older woman's fingers were strangely discolored in varying degrees of brown, yellow and green. Lady Stonehaven saw the direction of her eyes and chuckled softly. ''Don't worry. It's not dirt. I assure you, they are quite clean. It is just that I cannot seem to ever completely remove the stains.''

Julia looked up at her, blushing. ''I'm sorry.''

''Oh, no need. It startles everyone who doesn't know

me. I know you are far too well-bred to inquire, so I shall tell you. I paint. Oils, mostly. Lately I've been most interested in murals."

"Painting on the walls again, Mother?"

"Only two," she promised. "And not in your bedroom."

"Thank you."

She looked offended. "One would think that you disliked my painting, Dev."

"No, madam. I think you are aware of my opinion of your talent. However, I have no desire to awaken at night and see a group of Greeks standing across the room from me."

She sighed. "I never thought a son of mine would turn out so hidebound."

"No, ma'am. Just lily-livered."

As they had been talking, Deverel had taken the two women's arms and steered them down the hall into a small, tastefully appointed sitting room.

"What a lovely room!" Julia exclaimed. None of the furniture in the room was new, nor was it coordinated, but it was a cheerful, homey blend of comfort, practicality and beauty.

"Do you like it?" Lady Stonehaven asked, smiling. "Thank you. It is my favorite room in the house. And where I spend most of my time—when I'm not in my workroom, of course." She gestured them toward chairs, asking, "Are you hungry? Would you like some supper?"

"That would be wonderful," Deverel replied. "We had only a small nuncheon on the road and, I am afraid, missed tea altogether."

"I fear that we have already had dinner, but I am sure

that Cook can throw a reasonable meal together quickly.''

"The leftovers will be more than adequate."

Lady Stonehaven rang for a maid and was answered by the butler himself, a dignified individual who greeted Deverel gravely and assured Lady Stonehaven that a quick meal for the travelers had been set in motion as soon as they arrived and would shortly be brought up to them on trays.

"Wait, Carruthers, I must introduce you to Miss Julia Armiger. She is shortly to be my wife."

The older man was so startled that he dropped his usual carefully controlled expression. "My Lord!" He recovered himself enough to continue smoothly, "May I offer my congratulations?" The butler turned toward Julia and bowed. "Miss Armiger. What a wonderful surprise. I wish you all the best."

As soon as the door closed behind him, Julia swung on Deverel. "Why must you keep telling everyone that? You are going to look most foolish when we don't marry."

Lady Stonehaven's eyebrows rose. "Are you not going to marry? But I thought you were engaged."

"We are," Deverel responded.

"We are not," Julia said at the same time.

They glared at each other.

"Oh, dear," Lady Stonehaven said. "I must confess, I am a trifle confused."

"Perfectly natural, Mother. I am still in somewhat of a daze myself."

"I am very sorry, Lady Stonehaven," Julia said earnestly. "I know you must think we are quite mad."

"No. No—only a little."

"The truth is that, well, certain circumstances arose

that made Lord Stonehaven feel that it is necessary for him to marry me. But I assured him that it is not."

"Pamela St. Leger discovered us in a compromising position, Mother," Deverel explained. "Being a friend to neither of us, she will, I am persuaded, see to it that everyone in the ton knows about it."

"Oh, my," Lady Stonehaven said, somewhat inadequately.

"It wasn't what it seemed," Julia assured her, miserably aware that this very nice-seeming woman must now despise her.

"Of course not," Deverel agreed.

"I'm sure not," Lady Stonehaven agreed. "Deverel is certainly too much of a stickler to have done anything indecorous."

"You make me sound like a prig."

"No. Merely a man who always thinks before he acts."

Deverel arched an eyebrow and murmured, "If only you knew…"

"What, dear?"

"Nothing. At any rate, it was obvious that our only recourse was to marry. In fact, I told Pamela that Julia and I already were married."

"You seem to have an uncontrollable urge to tell everyone," Julia told him bitingly. "I cannot think why you cannot keep it to yourself."

"Oh, no, dear," Lady Stonehaven assured her earnestly. "You mustn't worry. Our servants will not reveal that you were married *here,* later than when Deverel told Pamela. They are most loyal to us."

"No. I am not worried about servants' gossip. I mean that I do not intend to marry him!"

Lady Stonehaven looked shocked. "But, my dear, I thought that it was so compromising that you have to."

"It was," Deverel confirmed. "Julia is simply too naive to understand that. Or perhaps too stubborn to accept it. Or both."

"I am not naive! As for stubborn, you are ten times worse than I am. You keep insisting that I marry you, and I have told you time after time that I will not. I don't care about the scandal. I do not want to marry you!"

It occurred to Julia that her statement would be bound to offend the man's mother, and she turned to her with a belated apology. "I am sorry, my lady. I know he is your son, but I simply cannot marry him."

"I perfectly understand." Lady Stonehaven stood up. "You know what I think we should do? I should show you to your room, Miss Armiger. No doubt you are very tired, and you would like to freshen up a little, eat and go to bed. I shall tell the servants to bring the tray to your room. How does that sound?"

"Very nice," Julia admitted, rather amazed that Lady Stonehaven was being so pleasant to her—and that she was taking everything so calmly. She must know from Julia's last name that her family was under a cloud of scandal. Not only that, Julia had been plumped down in the woman's house completely out of the blue and announced as the woman's future daughter-in-law, with the explanation that her son had to marry her because they had been caught in an indelicate situation. Then, to top it off, Julia had made it clear that she was repelled by the idea of marrying him.

But Lady Stonehaven was quite kind and acted as if nothing was out of the ordinary. She smiled at Julia and whisked her down the hall to a large, elegant bedchamber.

"This is the rose room," she explained. "It is the chamber we keep ready for guests. This isn't the first time that Deverel has dropped in on me with unexpected guests—although it is the first time that that guest was a female."

"I am so sorry, Lady Stonehaven."

"Don't think a thing of it." The woman waved away her apology. "As I said, we keep the room in readiness. I merely had one of the maids run a warming pan between the sheets. Even though it's May, I feel that the sheets are a trifle cool at night. Do you find it so?" she continued without waiting for an answer, carrying a candle to an oil lamp on the dresser and lighting it. A warm glow suffused the room. "There. That's better."

Julia looked around the spacious chamber. It was furnished with dark furniture, more elegant and more remote than that in Lady Stonehaven's sitting room. The dark green brocade bedspread matched the brocade seats of the two chairs, and both went nicely with the heavy green velvet curtains at the windows. The walls were a warm cream color, and a thick woven rug in tones of green, cream and rose softened the floor. But what Julia noticed first was that the wall around one of the windows had been painted with twisting vines of leaves, interspersed with fat pink roses. Julia had never seen anything like it on a wall before, and the depiction was so well-painted that it looked almost as if real roses grew there.

"How lovely!" she cried, going over to the window. She turned back toward her hostess. "Is this your work?"

Lady Stonehaven nodded. "Yes. I'm glad you like it.

My brother-in-law stayed in this room a few weeks ago, and he found it decidedly odd. But Stewart has always been a dreadfully stuffy person." She came over to stand beside Julia and looked at her art. "This is the first thing I painted on a wall. One day this overpowering urge came over me. It just took my mind that I should paint roses in the rose room. We had always called it that, you see, because this window looks down on the rose garden. It's a lovely sight during the day. Well, it just ate and ate at me that I should frame the window with roses, too, so finally I did. I think the servants decided I was mad. No doubt I've convinced them of it the past few weeks, for I painted a mural of Greek gods on one wall of my studio, and I have been considering doing another mural along the gallery."

She paused, considering. "Of course, the house is really Deverel's now. I suppose I should ask his permission."

"I am sure he would give it. He seems very fond of you."

"He is. The boy can be a dear—though I have no doubt that he has not been showing much of that side of himself to you today. Poor thing. Has he ridden over you roughshod?"

She took Julia's arm and led her over to one of the chairs. Julia sat down, and Lady Stonehaven took the other chair, turning toward Julia and leaning forward in a way that encouraged confidences.

"He is obviously used to getting his way," Julia admitted. She smiled and shook her head. "I should not talk this way to his mother. I am sure you must find me excessively rude."

"Not at all. Merely honest, which, frankly, I find a refreshing change to so many of the young women I meet, who cannot seem to call up an opinion of their own." She smiled, but then she said seriously, "And I know my son. After all, I've raised him from the cradle. I'm quite aware of how terribly overbearing he can be. He is so sure he is right about things—and it is quite maddening that he nearly always *is*—that he just goes ahead and decides what should be done. Even when it doesn't suit the other people involved. His father was much the same way, God rest his soul, but such a good man that I could never stay mad at him for long."

"Lady Stonehaven..." Julia leaned forward on impulse, taking the older woman's hand in hers. "Do you think you could talk to him? Persuade him that this is the wrong thing to do? He will listen to you."

Lady Stonehaven gave her hand a squeeze. "But, my dear, I'm not sure that it *is* wrong. Oh, I have no doubt that Deverel has gone about it in a draconian way that fairly raised your hackles, and I *quite* understand that you don't wish to give in to his high-handedness. It's only natural. But I fear that Deverel is usually right when it comes to points of honor. If he says that this is the only way to save your reputation, it is probably true."

"I fear that is a hopeless task!" Julia cried, releasing Lady Stonehaven's hand and jumping to her feet. "Surely you know that my family is already in disgrace. You must have recognized my name."

"Yes, I thought you must be related to that poor boy Selby. I always thought him such a lively young man. He and Dev were not really close, as Dev was with Walter, but Sir Selby came here to visit a few times. Usually when he was staying at his hunting lodge. He was well-mannered, but very entertaining, as well. The house was never dull when he was around."

Julia smiled, tears suddenly burning at her eyes. "No.

I'm sure it was not. It was that way wherever Selby went.''

"I am sure you must miss him.''

"I do. Terribly.'' She sighed and sat back down in her chair. "But you can see, can't you, that I am already in disgrace? Selby's widow and I rarely go out, and then only in our country society. So my situation would be little worse than it is now. It's hardly fair to your family to burden you with the scandal that hangs over us. I cannot think that you would wish to be allied with an Armiger.''

"Well, no, dear, of course it would not be my first choice in a wife for Deverel. But I must own, I find you excessively likable. And I would not wish for Dev to shirk his duty, in any case.''

"But it is so wrong that he should have to! We didn't do anything.''

"I am sure not. But appearances—'' She gave a little shrug and added, "And, given the scandal that has already beset your family, I am afraid that everyone will judge you more harshly. It is unfair, of course, but unfortunately, that is the way the world works. You, like Caesar's wife, must be above suspicion.''

"I don't need him to rescue me! I don't *want* him to.''

"Of course not.''

"And I don't want to marry him! I can't!''

"Because of what happened to your brother?''

"Yes,'' Julia replied, flopping back down into her chair, relieved that Deverel's mother was so understanding.

"You held Dev responsible for Selby's death, for exposing the embezzlement to the world. Of course you did. I would have done the same. I am sure Deverel was impatient with your reasoning. He has such a strong sense of duty and honor that I am afraid he is sometimes lacking in—oh, not compassion, for I know he felt quite sad and sorry about Selby—but lacking in empathy, I suppose. I fear he does not understand why people sometimes do the things they do.''

''You understand, though, don't you, why I cannot marry Deverel?'' Julia hoped that what she had said would be enough for Lady Stonehaven. She could not possibly tell her that she believed that the woman's son was actually a coldhearted embezzler.

''Of course,'' his mother replied with a sweet smile. ''The problem is, I'm not sure how you can escape it.'' She reached over and patted Julia's hand. ''Don't worry. You eat your dinner and rest now. I'm sure that tomorrow everything will seem better. We will think about it and see if we can come up with a better solution.''

''Thank you.'' Julia felt immensely grateful to Lady Stonehaven. She had expected the woman to be horrified by her son's bringing Julia home and abruptly announcing that she was his fiancée. She had been sure that Lady Stonehaven would dislike her intensely. But she had turned out to be gracious, kind and understanding. It made Julia feel strangely like crying. She thought of what would happen to Lady Stonehaven and how she would feel if Julia was able to prove that Deverel was responsible for the embezzlement, and the idea made her quail a little.

Lady Stonehaven started toward the door. When she reached it, she cast Julia a look back over her shoulder and said, ''Are you certain that you have no feelings for Deverel at all?''

Julia felt herself blushing. She could not answer. She could scarcely deny that she had feelings for Deverel.

Of course, none of them were the sort of emotions one could reveal to a man's mother, ranging as they did from lust to hate.

She began to stammer out an answer, but Lady Stonehaven merely smiled and went out the door.

12

While Julia was eating an excellent meal in her room at Stonehaven and going to bed at an unfashionably early hour, her sister-in-law was pacing the floors of their home in London. That afternoon Nunnelly had rushed into the house with the news that he had lost Julia.

"Lost her!" Phoebe had asked. "What do you mean?"

"I mean, my lady, that she is nowhere to be found. I've been ridin' all over the estate and onto Farrow land, as well. I've had the grooms out lookin'. It's crazy they're thinkin' me because no one knew she had come home." He set his jaw. "It's a judgment on me—I shouldn't have agreed to her crazy scheme."

"Oh, dear." Phoebe sank down into her chair. "But what about...?"

"His lordship? It's that that's got me right worried. He's clean gone."

"Oh, dear." Phoebe repeated, her face turning ashen.

Nunnelly nodded. "When I couldn't find her, I went straight to the hut. There wasn't a soul there. The door was standing wide-open, and inside I found a few scraps of rope and the chimney of the oil lamp, broken on the floor." He was wise enough not to mention the traces of blood he had seen on one of the shards of glass.

Phoebe's fears had been only partially calmed a few minutes later when a footman brought her a note from Julia, which he said had been delivered by a messenger to their door. Phoebe read it through twice, frowning, then conferred with Nunnelly, who understood as little as she.

"Why is she with Stonehaven?" Phoebe wailed. "What happened? I know she must be in some sort of trouble."

Nunnelly nodded lugubriously. "There's somethin' not right here, my lady. Why would his lordship be wantin' to marry Miss Julie? After she'd tied him up and all. It don't make sense."

"Oh, I knew I shouldn't have agreed to this mad scheme!" Phoebe wailed. "I can't think why Julia would have agreed to go with him. He must have forced her."

"Well, she says here she's looking for important information."

"Perhaps he forced her to write this note—to allay our fears, keep us from going to her aid. Or perhaps she's trying to trick him, pretending that she will marry him so that she can get inside the house and then look for evidence against him. If he figures out what she's doing, she could be in terrible danger."

"Maybe I ought to go up to this Stonehaven place and see what's afoot."

"You wouldn't get anywhere. Lord Stonehaven would close his gates against you. If anyone goes to ask questions…" Phoebe squared her shoulders "…it had better be I."

A look of amazement passed over the coachman's face, but he said only, "Yes, my lady."

After Nunnelly left, Phoebe paced the room in an agitated way for a few minutes, then sat down and jotted off a hasty note, entrusting it to one of the footmen. She resumed her anxious pacing, and every noise in the street sent her flying to the window to peer out. With each passing minute she grew more worried about Julia, and when at last she heard the sound of the front door knocker, it was all she could do not to run out into the hall to drag her guest inside.

As it was, when the footman announced the Honorable Geoffrey Pemberton, Phoebe jumped up from her chair and hurried forward, reaching out to take his hands. "Geoffrey! Thank heavens you came!"

"Dear girl! Whatever is wrong?" Geoffrey asked, his usually imperturbable face creasing a little with worry. "Your note sounded, well, almost desperate."

"It was! I am! Geoffrey, it's Julia."

"Of course it is." He led Phoebe over to the sofa. "Here, sit down and calm yourself. You know Julia never gets injured, she just gets everyone else in a pucker. The most tiring girl I ever met."

"But, Geoffrey, this is much worse than—oh, than anything she's ever done. She's gone to Buckinghamshire!"

"Has she?" Geoffrey looked faintly amazed. "Well, I daresay I wouldn't want to go there, but I don't suppose it's as bad as all that."

"No, no, you don't understand. That is where Lord Stonehaven lives."

"Stonehaven! Is she still on about that? I thought she had given that up."

"No. In fact, well, she abducted him."

Geoffrey's eyebrows flew up. "Well! Fancy that. And she's taking him home to Buckinghamshire?"

"No, no. Oh, I'm telling this all wrong. She took him to Greenwood, to a shepherd's hut there. She was going to make him tell her the truth." Phoebe let out a moan and sank her head in her hands. "Why did I let her do that? I must have been mad."

"Now, now." Geoffrey awkwardly patted her back. "One doesn't 'let' Julia do things. She simply does them. I am sure you could not have stopped her."

"But I did nothing!" Phoebe wailed and began to cry.

"Oh, dear. Now, don't do that." Geoffrey's usual sangfroid deserted him at the sight of Phoebe's tears. "Here. A spot of brandy. I'm sure that will fix you right up."

He hurriedly pulled the bell cord on the wall and, when a footman appeared, ordered brandy, adding, with a harried glance toward Phoebe, "In a hurry."

The footman brought the brandy without delay, and Geoffrey persuaded Phoebe to drink a sip. She gasped as the fiery liquid burned down her throat and blinked. "My goodness."

"There. You'll feel more the thing now. Brandy's the best medicine." In demonstration of this opinion, he proceeded to drink the rest of the snifter. "Now," he said, thinking that at least *he* felt more the thing, "if she has taken him off to Greenwood, what's all this about Buckinghamshire?"

"He escaped! At least, we assume that is what happened. Nunnelly came here this afternoon and told me that the shepherd's hut was empty, and neither Stonehaven nor Julia was anywhere to be found."

"Nunnelly?" Geoffrey asked, a little lost.

"The coachman. He helped Julia kidnap Lord Stone-haven."

"Odd sort of servants you have."

"He's terribly loyal to Julia. And to Selby."

"But if he didn't know what had happened to them, why do you think she's run off to Buckinghamshire?"

"I got a note from her. I was so confused. It came by messenger and was sent from here in London—yet I knew she was at Greenwood. And it is so odd. She assured me that she was safe. Then she said she was going to Buckinghamshire, and that Stonehaven wanted to marry her!"

"Marry her!" Geoffrey repeated. "Are you sure? You can't have got that right."

"I know. It sounds preposterous, but that is what she said—and right after that she said that she would not marry him. Here, see for yourself."

She handed him the note, much creased. "She wants me to send her a trunk of her clothes—to Stonehaven!" She turned the note over. "Look at what she wrote on the back—she wants her teak box. Now, isn't that peculiar?"

"Dash it! I should say so. What does a teak box have to do with anything?"

"I don't know. It seems very odd. She keeps mementos in it—a pressed corsage, some dance cards, mostly letters."

"Why would she be eager to have a few old keepsakes?" Geoffrey asked, perplexed, and Phoebe shrugged.

"The only thing I could think was that she was trying to send me some sort of message."

"Message?" Geoffrey looked blank. "Why didn't she just say so, then?"

"I thought maybe Lord Stonehaven was looking over her shoulder, so she could not be free in what she said. Perhaps she wanted me to know something, do something—only I am too stupid to figure it out!"

"No, no. Not a bit of it. I say, don't cry again."

Despite her perturbation, Phoebe had to smile at his horrified expression. "No. I shan't. But, Geoffrey, what do you think she was trying to tell me?"

Geoffrey looked back down at the note in his hand. After a moment he said, "Do you suppose she'd been hit on the head?"

"Geoffrey!" Phoebe cried.

"Well, it just doesn't make sense. If I had been kidnapped by some female and got loose, do you think I would turn around and ask her to marry me? And if I did ask her and she said no, would I drag her off to Buckinghamshire? I ask you."

"I know. But why would she write me such nonsense? He must have seized her and forced her to write it."

"Forced her to tell you she don't want to marry him? Or that she needs clothes and a box of letters? The truth is, Phoebe, she sounds to me as if she's foxed."

"Foxed! Are you saying she had been drinking?"

"It's the only explanation I can think of," Geoffrey admitted. "You didn't like the idea of her getting knocked in the head."

"But why would she be drinking? Julia's never drunk more than a glass of sherry in her life!"

"I daresay you're right," he conceded.

They were silent for a moment. "Perhaps it's all a hum," Geoffrey suggested after a moment.

"Julia would never play a joke like that on me," Phoebe protested.

At that moment the footman knocked on the door and

entered the room again. "The Honorable Varian St. Leger, my lady."

"Oh, dear."

"That Fitzmaurice ain't with him, is he?" Geoffrey asked suspiciously.

"No, sir. Merely Mr. St. Leger."

Phoebe cast a harried look at Geoffrey. The last thing she wanted at this moment was a social caller, but she could not escape the nagging hope that perhaps Varian would tell them something that would shine some light on their problem. "Yes, send him in."

A moment later Varian entered the room. "Ah, Phoebe, you are a picture, as always. And Pemberton. I say, you seem to be a fixture here."

"Well, family, you see," Geoffrey said by way of explanation.

"Of course."

"How are you, Varian?" Phoebe asked, putting on a smile. "Please, sit down."

"I am fine. But I heard some news this evening that I could hardly credit. I felt I had to ask you."

"Oh?" Phoebe's stomach clenched.

"Yes. I saw Fitz at my club just a few minutes ago. I was rather surprised. He had gone, you see, to escort Thomas and Pamela to Farrow, and I hadn't expected him back for a day or two. But he says Pamela was in such a snit that he decided to ride right back to town. You know how she can be. What had gotten her all discombobulated was hearing about Julia and Stonehaven."

"Oh?" Phoebe asked through stiff lips. "What about them?"

"They ran into the two of them at the inn in Whitley. Stonehaven told them they were married."

"Married," Geoffrey repeated blankly. "Already?"

"Then you knew about it?" Varian asked, surprised. "Were they planning to wed? I had never heard anything of it."

"No, we knew nothing, not until today," Phoebe said carefully, feeling as if she were navigating treacherous social waters. She did not want to create further scandal by denying that Julia and Stonehaven were married when he had already told people that they were. On the other hand, she did not want to pretend that they were married when Julia might return and say it was all untrue. "I received a note from Julia. It was as much a surprise to me as it was to you."

"Odd business, that. I would have sworn the two of them hardly knew each other," Varian mused. "Of course, Julia did say that she was trying to investigate Selby's—well, the embezzlement. Perhaps they were thrown together a lot."

"Perhaps."

"Still, hardly seems the sort of thing Dev would do. He's not usually impulsive. Very good fellow, of course—true blue, couldn't ask for a better friend in a fight—but not usually one to do anything rash."

"I am sure that we will hear the full story soon," Phoebe told him, smiling.

He stayed for a few more minutes, chatting, but neither Phoebe nor Geoffrey was terribly talkative, and before long he took his leave of them. As soon as the door had closed behind him, Phoebe whirled to look at Geoffrey.

"What do you make of that?"

"Very much what I make of the rest of it, which is nothing sensible. Julia says Stonehaven wants to get married, but she won't marry him. Stonehaven says they are already married—to Pamela St. Leger and Fitzmaurice, than whom there is no one more likely to spread word of it. Fitzmaurice is too big a chucklehead not to talk about it, and Mrs. St. Leger loves nothing more than gossip.'' He paused, then added judiciously, ''No, that's not true. She loves herself more than anything else, but gossip runs a close second.''

''Do you know Pamela well?'' Julia asked.

''Me? No.'' He shook his head. ''Pretty enough, but she's the sort that expects every man to dangle after her all the time. Tiring sort of thing to do, I think. 'Sides, she don't like Armigers, you know. Always going on and on about Selby—even now. Well, a fellow can't sit around and listen to someone denigrate his family, now can he? I mean, I'm not an Armiger, of course, but Selby was my cousin.''

''I know.'' Phoebe smiled at him. ''I think that's very good of you, Geoffrey.''

Geoffrey looked a trifle embarrassed. ''Now, now.'' He cleared his throat. ''About Julia...''

''Yes, of course. I'm sorry. Sometimes I am so scatterbrained. We must decide what to do about Julia.''

''I don't know that there is anything we *can* do.''

''I've been thinking and thinking about it, for hours. I can't help but think that Julia must be sending out a plea for my help.''

''Oh. Sending her the trunk, you mean? And that silly box?''

''No. I shall do that, of course. But I think what she wants is for me to go to her.''

''Eh? Now, dash it, I didn't see anything in that note about *that!*''

''I think it was a hidden message. She and I once read a book where the heroine sent a letter to her fiancé—

under duress, of course—saying that she had decided not to marry him. But she made reference in the letter to a certain statue of Ares, where she and he used to meet. Only he knew, you see, that they had never met at any statue, and he guessed from her using Ares that she was in need of a champion, his being the god of war and all.''

"Did he?" Geoffrey looked much struck by this idea. "I would never have figured that out from her talking about one of those plaguey Greek fellows. Never cared much for Greek studies, you see. They always seemed a dashed bunch of loose screws—always running about becoming swans or bulls or such, and turning girls into trees.''

Even in the midst of her turmoil, Phoebe could not help but giggle. "No. You are perfectly right. But the thing is, I think Julia was trying to send me that sort of message.''

"You think she's in need of a champion?" he asked doubtfully.

"I don't know. In need of help. I mean, there isn't any special meaning about that box that I can think of, except for its being so odd. I think she was hoping that I would realize that something was wrong. And indeed I do! I think something must be terribly wrong, and the only thing I can think of to do is to go to her. I will travel to Stonehaven. They can scarcely turn me away. After all, it would look quite odd not to let a future bride have the comfort and support of her relatives. Don't you think?''

"Yes. If they did turn you away, it would be obvious that they were holding Julia against her will. Do you think they are? I must say, it doesn't seem like something Stonehaven would do. Sounds more like one of those Greek chaps.''

''I'm not sure. But I do think that she needs me. So I must go to her.''

''But you can't go running up there by yourself,'' Geoffrey protested.

Phoebe turned limpid blue eyes upon him, and it was then that Geoffrey saw that he had been neatly caught. ''Oh. Yes, I see. You're asking me to escort you.''

''Would you, Geoffrey?'' Phoebe leaned closer, clasping her hands together eagerly. ''It would be so good of you. I know I really have no right to call on you, but I could think of no one else. All my family is in Northumberland, except for my brother Robert, but even he lives too far away. I would have to write him, and then he would have to come here and, knowing Robert, he would have to think about it, and well, it would take days. I need to go tomorrow.''

''Tomorrow!'' Geoffrey exclaimed. ''No, now, really, Phoebe, you can't have thought. You can't get packed and leave by tomorrow morning.''

''I can try. Maybe we can't be ready to leave in the morning, but surely by noon we could be gone. Buckinghamshire isn't far away. We could arrive by evening, don't you think?''

''I don't know. Never been there.'' Geoffrey was notorious for rarely leaving London. It was said that it took a death in the family to make him travel—and even then, that it had better be a close relative.

''I have been there a few times with Selby, and it was only a day's travel, and that was traveling from Greenwood.''

''Mmm. I daresay you're right. Still, I'm not sure that

from now until noon tomorrow is enough time to prepare oneself for the journey.''

"Certainly," Phoebe responded stoutly. "Your valet will pack all your things, won't he?"

"Of course." Geoffrey looked astounded that anyone could think otherwise. "Still, there are other things that need to be done. Must toddle to the bank to get some money, I should think. Can't go somewhere without a bit of ready, you know."

"Oh, Geoffrey!" Phoebe smiled at him, her face glowing. "Does that mean you'll escort me to Stonehaven?"

Geoffrey looked a trifle taken aback, then responded in a faintly surprised voice, "Yes, I guess it does."

"Thank you!" Phoebe reached out impulsively and took his hand. "You are so good. I knew I could count on you."

"Of course, of course. Your servant, you know that." He paused, then said a little reluctantly, "Well, I suppose I better go home and start getting things in order."

Phoebe almost had to laugh at his less-than-eager expression. She strongly suspected that Geoffrey's valet would be the one doing all the work, so she could not feel too sorry for Geoffrey. However, she did appreciate his escorting her to Buckinghamshire; she was not sure she would have been brave enough to go alone. So she walked him to the door, her hand linked through his arm, assuring him of how much she depended on him and how kind he was. By the time they reached the front door, he seemed to be in good spirits again and rather proud of himself for rescuing a damsel in distress.

He took his leave of her with his usual elegant bow, and Phoebe turned to the daunting task of getting herself, a child and his nurse packed and ready to go by the following morning.

Julia, worn out by the excitement of the last few days, slept late the following morning. She found the clothes she had worn the day before freshly cleaned and laid out for her. Even the little rip in the hem of her dress had been neatly mended. She took off the nightgown Lady Stonehaven had lent her—absurdly short on her, ending at midcalf—and put back on her clothes. Once she had her hair brushed and pinned up, she at least looked presentable, she thought, though she did spare a single wistful thought for the trunk of clothes she had written Phoebe to send.

She went downstairs, determined to look at the suicide note that Deverel claimed he had. That, she reminded herself sternly, was the only thing she was here for. She must forget all this nonsense about marrying that Stonehaven kept putting forth.

However, when she went into the dining room, she found only Stonehaven's mother sitting at the table. The older woman smiled happily when she saw her. "There you are, my dear. Do sit down. Would you like some eggs and ham? Tea?" She gestured toward the footman standing beside the sideboard. "Unfortunately, you have missed Deverel. He's gone to ride over the estate with the manager, since it's been over a month since he was here. He's very conscientious about such things. But I'm afraid it means that you are stuck with my company this morning."

"I couldn't think of better company," Julia replied. She did truly enjoy his mother; however, she felt deflated by the news that Deverel was not there. She was merely disappointed, she knew, that she would not get to look at the note immediately.

"How kind of you to say so—though I don't fool myself that spending the morning with an old lady is of more interest to you than being with a good-looking young man." She smiled. "Did you sleep well?"

"Oh, yes." Julia had eaten a hearty meal, then taken a long, soaking bath, and fallen into bed earlier than she could remember doing in years. It surprised her a little, now that she thought about it, that she had fallen asleep so easily in the heart of her enemy's territory. She supposed it was a testimony to how tired she had been. "Thank you for having my clothes cleaned while I was asleep."

"I only wish I could have lent you something to wear. But I knew that anything in my closet would be far too large and absurdly short. However, I have my dresser hunting through the wardrobe for a dress that has a long hem that she could lower. Then it would only require taking it in on the sides, and you would be able to wear it."

"You are too kind. I wrote to my sister-in-law, asking her to send some of my clothes." Color rose in her cheeks. "I am sure you must wonder how I could manage to arrive here in such a state—no clothes, no abigail, not even a nightgown."

"It is a trifle odd," Lady Stonehaven admitted. "And I would be less than human if I were not curious. However, I expect if you want me to know, you shall tell me, and if not—well, we are all entitled to our little secrets, aren't we? How awful it would be if we had to explain everything to everyone."

"But you must think me a—an abandoned creature."

"Don't be nonsensical. Deverel would never bring

home an abandoned creature as his future bride. Now…I thought I could show you around the house, if you'd like.''

"Certainly. That sounds very nice.''

And it was. Lady Stonehaven, who insisted that Julia call her Teresa, was a charming companion, and knowledgeable about both the house and the people who had lived there. She told amusing anecdotes about many of the rooms they went through, and the marks of her good taste were evident everywhere. Though none of the rooms were as cozy as her own sitting room, all of them were quite pleasant, some elegant and others more casual, some left in the furnishings of an earlier time period and others freshly up-to-date. They ended the tour in Lady Stonehaven's workroom.

The twining of leaves around the window in her bedroom had not prepared Julia for the scope and excellence of the older woman's art. She stood in awe for a few minutes, examining the detailed mural of an Athens scene that decorated one wall of the studio. This woman was no mere dabbler in painting, as many gentlewomen were; she was truly an artist.

"These are wonderful!'' she exclaimed, trailing slowly around the room and looking at the canvases propped up against the wall.

"Do you like them? Truly?'' Lady Stonehaven seemed as delighted as a child.

"Oh, yes.''

"Good. Sometimes I worry that people say so just to be polite. It is satisfying to sell them, of course, but since I do it through an agent, I don't get to hear what they say about the paintings. And friends, well, I know most of them would admire my work even if they looked like a child's scrawlings.''

"So you do sell your work?"

"Some of it. Whatever I can bear to give up. That's why I have such a store of pictures. There are more of them in the room next door, and we have them hanging about the house. I give some to friends, of course. It's much easier when one isn't obliged to have the money. Of course, I don't sell them as myself. I sell them under the name T. A. Emerson. Emerson was my maiden name, and no one realizes that T. A. stands for Teresa Anne."

They talked for some time about the paintings and her work, and Julia looked through all the canvases in her workroom and in the storage room next door. She did not even realize how much time had passed until Deverel's voice interrupted them. "I thought I would find you here."

Julia was shocked by the sudden and intense wave of desire that washed through her at the sound of his voice. She turned around shakily. Deverel was lounging in the open doorway of the storage room, still in his riding clothes. It galled her that she felt this uprush of pleasure at seeing him, that suddenly the room seemed brighter and warmer, the air sweeter. He grinned at her, and for an instant his expression was as welcoming, as warm and admiring, as it had been a few days ago, before he found out about her. Julia could not keep from grinning back. He took a step forward.

Then, abruptly, he stopped, and his face changed, the warmth receding, replaced by a cool, polite, faintly sardonic look, as if he had remembered who she was and what had happened. Julia's heart squeezed within her chest, and her throat was suddenly tight and constricted.

"Why, Deverel!" Lady Stonehaven greeted him. "How nice. I didn't expect you home so early."

"It's hardly early, Mother. It's almost noon. I have finished with Hammerton, at least for today."

"Wonderful. Then you will be able to join us for luncheon."

"Of course."

"De—Lord Stonehaven," Julia began, coming forward. "You had promised to show me that note."

He scowled. "Yes. I will show it to you. But first I must clean up. Why don't we do it after luncheon?"

Julia nodded, and he left them.

Later, during the meal, Stonehaven was remote and cool, leaving the conversation up to his mother and Julia. Julia made it a point to maintain a lively discussion without him. She suspected that he was regretting his promise to show her the suicide note. Cynically, she wondered if such a note even existed, or if he had only made it up in an effort to convince her of her brother's guilt.

After they ate, Stonehaven escorted her to his office, a large room lined with bookshelves and furnished in heavy mahogany. A huge desk dominated the room, and it was to this piece of furniture that Stonehaven went after closing the door behind them. He turned toward Julia.

"Are you sure you want to see this?" he asked abruptly. "I must have been mad to have said I would show you. It will only make you unhappy. That is why Varian and I decided to conceal it in the first place."

"I want to see it," Julia retorted flatly. "If, of course, you really have it. Or is it just something you made up?"

"Of course I have it," he snapped. "Unlike you, I am not in the habit of lying."

He took a small key from his pocket and unlocked one of the drawers of the desk. He rifled through it for a moment and came up with a piece of paper, which he held out to Julia expressionlessly.

Julia's stomach clenched, and her heart began to beat rapidly. She reached out with fingers that trembled slightly and took the paper. The familiar handwriting seemed to leap off the page, and she felt dizzy. She sat down abruptly in the nearest chair. It was her brother's handwriting, and she was suddenly frightened. It took all her courage to force herself to focus on the page.

To Whomever Finds This:

By the time you read this, I will be dead. I am sorry to add this latest sin to my list, but I cannot live with the burden of guilt any longer. I took the money from Thomas's trust. Thomas, I hope you will find it in your heart to forgive me. I knew it was wrong, but I had to come by the money without anyone knowing, and I could think of no other way. You see, there was a woman. (Isn't there always?) She lives in London, and I went there to see her as often as I could. I have no excuse other than that I was mad with love for her. I could not think straight; I lost all sense of honor. Nothing mattered except keeping her—and she was very expensive. She had to have a house, a carriage, jewelry, clothes. I could not afford to maintain two households, and it was too difficult trying to keep all my expenditures a secret. So I took the money from the trust. It was wrong and wicked of me; I see that now. But I could not stop myself.

In my madness, I ruined my life and those of everyone around me. I can no longer stand the shame. Please, forgive me, Phoebe, for all of it. Try to keep Gilbert from hating his father. I love both of you very much, and I cannot stand to stay here any longer and see the two of you hurt by my stupidity.

It was signed with Selby's bold, slashing signature.

The paper blurred before Julia's eyes. Her ears were filled with a roaring sound, and she thought she might be sick. "Oh, God!" she moaned, then clapped her hand to her mouth. But she could not stifle the sobs welling up in her throat. "Selby!"

She began to cry, harsh, racking sobs that shook her body. She raised her hands to cover her face. Dimly she was aware of Stonehaven letting out a curse, and in three strides he was around the desk and pulling her out of her chair. He cradled her against his chest, his arms encircling her.

"I'm sorry. Please forgive me. I shouldn't have let you see. I was a fool. If only I hadn't been so angry, I would have known better. Forgive me."

He murmured soft, meaningless words of comfort as he stroked her hair and back. Julia clung to him, crying her heart out, grateful for his strength and sympathy. She felt his lips press softly against her hair.

"Deverel," she breathed.

"Julia." He kissed the side of her face, her forehead. She tilted back her head, and suddenly they were kissing with all the hunger that had lain suppressed within them for two days.

Julia let out a little moan, and her hands went up behind his head, pulling him closer. The pain, the fear, all the tumultuous emotions of the past week, exploded and were burned up in the fire of passion. She was on fire for him, her body alive and aching. He kissed her as if he could never get enough of her, his mouth buried in hers. His hands slid down her back and over the curve of her hips, digging into her buttocks and lifting her up into him. She felt the hard length of his desire against her, heard the harsh rasp of his breath, and her own passion blossomed. There was a damp heat between her legs, and her loins felt as if they had turned to wax. His fingers began to knead the fleshy mounds of her buttocks, and she trembled.

He breathed her name again, and his lips left hers to travel across her cheek to her ear. "Thank God," he murmured as he began to kiss and nibble at her ear. "Now you understand. Now you know the truth."

Julia stiffened, alarms sounding in her head. She pulled back from him, looking up with sudden, sharp suspicion. "What did you say?"

"What?" Deverel looked bewildered. "Only that now you see that I am not what you think I am. That it was Selby who—"

"No!" Julia ripped herself out of his grasp, stumbling backward, suddenly filled with self-loathing. *How could she have forsaken Selby so quickly? How could she have believed the letter without question and then fallen into this man's arms?* "No, I don't—I can't—"

She bent quickly and retrieved the letter from the floor where it had fallen when Deverel had taken her into his arms. With a low cry, she turned and ran out of the room, the letter in her hand.

13

Julia ran to her room and locked the door, then threw herself onto the bed and indulged in another, shorter fit of tears. How could she have done what she just had? She felt as if she had betrayed her brother. She had vowed to clear his name, but she had crumpled at the first obstacle. She had looked at the suicide note and seen his handwriting, and she had, for a moment, believed that Selby had actually done it, just as everyone else had. Even worse, she had fallen into the arms of Selby's enemy, the man who had brought all this down onto Selby's head.

For a long time she lay on the bed, wrapped in misery and self-condemnation. She wished Phoebe were here, so that she could talk to her, but immediately on the heels of that thought came the realization that she could not show this letter to Phoebe. It would hurt her far too much. Irritation filled her as she realized that such a thought was exactly why Deverel said he and Varian had hidden the letter from them. She sat up, disgruntlement finally rousing her from her depression.

Getting up, she washed her face, picked up the letter from where she had thrown it on the bed and sat down in the chair to read through it again. She turned it over and looked at the back, running a thoughtful finger over the broken seal of wax. Turning it back over, she read it through a third time, then sat for some time, frowning in thought.

Finally she stood and marched downstairs, her back ramrod straight. She went to Deverel's office and knocked on the door. His voice answered, and she went inside, nerves dancing in her stomach. He looked up from the work on his desk and jumped to his feet when he saw her.

"Julia!" He came around from behind the massive desk. "Are you all right?"

Julia nodded, closing the door behind her. "Yes. I have been in my room thinking."

"I hope you will accept my apology. What I did was inexcusable and inappropriate, given your state of mind. I took advantage of your weakness."

Julia looked at his cool, carefully controlled face. He hardly seemed the same man as the one who had kissed her earlier with such heat and passion. "It doesn't matter. I came to talk to you about this letter."

"I see." If possible, it seemed as if his face shut down even more. "Of course."

"Selby did not write it."

Deverel sighed. "I might have known." He motioned to the chair in front of his desk. "Sit down and tell me."

Julia sat down while Deverel perched on the corner of his desk and folded his arms, looking at her with a determinedly patient expression. "You needn't look at me like that," she snapped. "I'm not a fool. I have perfectly good reasons for believing what I do."

"All right."

"For a moment I was fooled by the handwriting. If

those other letters look as much like Selby's hand as these, I can understand why everyone was taken in by them. But obviously, if they were forged, then there's no reason why this suicide note was not forged, as well.''

"Obviously."

"Do stop being so odiously superior and listen to what I have to say! I went over this note several times, and a few things became clear to me. The first is that I do not believe Selby committed suicide. He was a fighter. He would not have abandoned Phoebe and Gilbert and me to the world. That was the act of a coward, and you must agree that Selby was never a coward.''

"No. You are right about that. But even a strong man can break—and given the weight of the evidence, he must have known that he was caught. Pamela was pushing for a criminal investigation. He may have felt that he was saving his family from further scandal, stopping the investigation with his death. It would have been far worse for you if he had actually been tried and convicted and sent to prison as an embezzler.''

"If he wanted so much to save us from scandal, why would he have written a note confessing to the embezzlement and, more than that, admitting to having a mistress?'' As she said the words, a second question flickered through her mind: Why had Stonehaven not shown such a condemning note to the world? It would have put the final seal on Selby's guilt.

"Perhaps the weight of his crime was too much for his conscience. It happens. He was essentially a good man, and he went astray. His passion for a woman caused him to do things he would not normally do, and he was racked with guilt over what he had done. So he felt he had to confess, but he could not face the shame of it.''

"Oh, twaddle!" Julia snapped, letting go of the strange thought. "That is another thing that rings false. Selby loved Phoebe. He would not have been unfaithful to her. He would not have kept a mistress hidden away in London.''

"It is a common enough practice," Deverel remarked. "Even among men who love their wives.''

"Oh? Is that what you plan to do when you are married to m—'' She stopped, realizing what she was saying, and blushed to the roots of her hair. Suddenly the very air between them was alive with sensuality. "I—I didn't mean—''

"What I do or what you do is an entirely different case." Deverel's eyes shone with an odd light.

"Yes, of course," Julia replied caustically. "After all, Selby *cared* for Phoebe.''

"Perhaps that was because Lady Armiger never knocked her husband out and tied him up!''

Julia could not think of any reply, so she simply glared at him. They stood for a moment, scowling. Then Deverel got up and walked away, going to the window and looking out at the rose garden.

"I am sure," he said in a careful, even voice, "that Selby loved his wife and son. His having a mistress doesn't mean that he did not love them.''

Julia grimaced. "Don't condescend to me. I believe I knew my brother better than you. I know that he had mistresses before Phoebe, but he did not have one after he married her. Had you ever heard him speak of this woman? Had Varian? Or Fitz? Was there gossip about it in the clubs?''

"No, I heard no gossip. As for Fitz, or any of Selby's

other friends, I don't know what they knew. Varian seemed surprised, I think, when he read the note, but, then, we were both so shocked by his death that I'm not sure whether he knew about the woman or not. Selby certainly did not tell me, but I was not as close to him as either Walter or Varian. We had been better friends when we were younger, but over the years we had drifted apart. After Walter died, I frankly did not see him much.''

"Even so, don't you think it's strange that if Selby had a mistress no one had heard about it?''

"I don't know that *no one* had. Julia, you are building a case on thin air. You have no proof of anything, only unsupported beliefs and suppositions. Against that we have a letter in Selby's handwriting saying that he did it.''

"There are other things. One is that he hardly mentioned Phoebe and Gilbert, just a brief sentence to say that he loved them. Selby would have said far more than that. And I almost never heard him call her Phoebe. He always, always called her by a nickname, usually Fee. Sometimes Delight.''

"Really, Julia, I think you are reaching. This was his last statement to the world. It is likely to be more formal. He wouldn't use a pet name.''

"Selby would have. He always made up nicknames for people, and that is what he called them. He called me Jule or Julie. He called Gilbert Jin-Jin, because that was the closest Gil could come to saying his name when he was learning to talk.''

Deverel shrugged, obviously unconvinced.

"All right. No doubt you will discount this, too, but I find it significant. That note made no mention of me whatsoever.'' At Deverel's skeptical expression, she hurried on. "Yes, yes, I know. A man isn't going to remember all his relatives in his suicide note. But Selby and I were very close. I was his only near relative, except for Phoebe and Gilbert. Our parents are both dead. He wrote me a great deal when he went away to college, and when he was a young man and living in London, before he married and settled down. Even since his marriage, when he's been away, he has either written me or, in his letters to Phoebe, he has written a line or two to me, or asked her to tell me that he loved me. He would not have left me out when he was facing death. I know it."

"Julia…"

"If my knowledge of my brother is not enough, there's another, tangible proof. Look at the seal on this letter." She handed the letter to him, pointing to the pieces of red wax where the letter had been folded and sealed."

Deverel looked at the wax, then up at her. "Yes?"

"You see the imprint in that wax. That is Selby's signet ring. He used to use it to seal his letters. But at the time of this note, he did not have the ring." She paused to let the significance of this fact sink in. "He had lost it a month or two before. I know that because he had everybody turning the house upside down looking for it. It was very important to him."

"The ring was on his finger when we found him. He must have left it at his hunting lodge earlier, that's why he couldn't find it. Then, when he returned to the lodge, there it was."

"Oh!" Julia bounced up. "You are so maddening! You already have your mind made up! You won't listen to anything I say!"

He gave her a quizzical look, and Julia realized with

a start that she had been arguing with him over this letter, trying to convince him of its falsehood, as if he were an impartial observer. But that was ridiculous. Obviously, if he was the one who had done the embezzling, he already knew that the suicide note was false.

"Oh." She plopped back down in her chair, feeling very odd. "Of course. Why am I telling you all this?"

"Julia, have you thought about what you are saying? Do you realize that if this suicide note *is* a fake, if the same person forged it who wrote the other letters, then that person must have killed Selby? Why else would he have written a suicide note?"

Julia felt faintly sick at her stomach. Of course he was right, although she had not really thought about the implications of her argument. She had only been interested in clearing Selby of the suicide and of the things that were said in the letter. But now she saw that if the suicide note was false, then her brother had been murdered in cold blood by the person who had written it.

"Julia, I understand how little you want your brother to be guilty, how much you don't want to believe that he committed suicide. But you have advanced nothing but wild theories. You have no solid evidence to back up anything you've said."

"I know Selby."

"People change. They make mistakes. Sometimes, just for a moment, they act in ways that they would not normally." She regarded him with stony silence. He went on. "If you are right, that would mean that someone imitated your brother's handwriting so well that even he admitted that it looked like his. They wrote several letters in his handwriting getting the money, and they used 'Jack Fletcher,' all to make it look as if Selby was the embezzler. Then they stole Selby's signet ring a month or two before they killed him, forged the suicide note, and stamped the seal with his ring. Then they found out that he was staying at his hunting lodge instead of at home and went there, killed him, laid the false note on the desk and wrote another note in his hand to me to get me to come discover the body."

"When you put it that way, it does sound farfetched," Julia admitted.

"What other way is there to put it? That is how it would have had to happen for you to be right." He paused. "I have found over the years that the simplest and most obvious solution is generally the correct one."

"You *would* say that," Julia replied darkly and got to her feet. "I see now that it was useless trying to talk to you about it. You are determined not to believe it."

She turned and started toward the door. His voice stopped her. "Julia!"

Julia turned and looked back questioningly at him.

"Do you actually think that I did all this? That I embezzled that money and laid the blame on Selby? That I went to his hunting lodge and *killed* him?" His handsome face was bleak.

Julia wavered. Did she believe that Deverel had robbed the trust and killed Selby? Only minutes earlier she had caught herself trying to convince him that Selby had not written the note, which implied that he did not already know that. And there was that nagging question that had recently popped into her head: Why would the man who did those things then conceal the suicide note that would have made everyone believe that Selby had been guilty? Most of all, there was an odd feeling in her chest, a painful feeling, that cried out against the idea that Deverel was a murderer.

"*Someone* did it," she answered bitterly, and turned and walked out of the room.

Deverel watched her go. He supposed that her vague answer had been an improvement over her earlier accusations. Still, he found that his chest was filled once again with the same curiously cold and empty feeling, as if there were a hole there that could never be filled.

It seemed as if every succeeding thing that happened with Julia was worse than what had come before. First there had been her betrayal, the sickening realization that she had played him for a fool, lying to him with every kiss and caress. That had been followed by finding out that she was convinced he was an embezzler who had laid the blame on her innocent brother. Now the part she had assigned to him was that of a murderer.

His hands clenched unconsciously, and he was aware of an enormous desire to hit something. Why was she so bullheaded? So damnably devoted to Selby? Yet he knew he could hardly have wished her otherwise. Where she loved, she loved with all her heart and soul. It would be a sweet thing—if only one were the man she loved. He pulled his thoughts back from that dangerous territory. He did not want Julia Armiger's love. She was treacherous and deceitful.

Yet even as he thought the words, he knew that she had acted as she did only because of the strength of her convictions. She would not lie for her own gain or to hurt someone—unless, of course, they had hurt her or hers.

But it didn't matter, he reminded himself. He had less chance of receiving that love than any man he could think of. She hated him. She did not even want to marry him when circumstances dictated that it was the only thing she could do to save her good name. She had told him quite flatly that she would rather live and die in shame than be married to him. She could hardly have been plainer in her dislike.

He told himself that he was a fool to keep insisting that she marry him. Of course, after he had told that witch Pamela St. Leger that they were already married, he could hardly do anything else. He probably should have kept his mouth shut and let Julia stew in the mess she had made. It had been an idiotic notion on her part, anyway.

But as he thought about it, he could not suppress the faintly rueful smile that touched his lips. No other woman, he knew, would have dreamed up such a scheme, risking everything in a desperate attempt to salvage her brother's name. It had been foolhardy, of course, but, still, she was full of heart and courage. And the way she had kissed him…it was hard to believe that she was an inexperienced young woman of proper upbringing. Yet he had no doubt that she was; if there had ever been the slightest hint of scandal about Julia's virtue, Pamela St. Leger would have told everyone.

His thoughts strayed from memories of Julia's false kisses to thoughts of their marital bed, and his loins tightened. It annoyed him that he could still feel desire for her after the tricks she had played on him, knowing how she felt about him. Yet yesterday, stuck in the carriage with her all day, his thoughts had been consumed by her. He kept stealing glances at her breasts and thinking about how they had felt in his hands, full and soft, the nipples pebbling beneath his touch. Interspersed with such thoughts were memories of their kisses, of the softness of her long throat, of the little breathy sighs she had murmured as his lips explored her body. And this afternoon, when she had started to cry, at first he had just moved instinctively to comfort her, but it had taken only feeling her soft body pressed against him to turn him pulsing with desire, his mouth seeking hers. How galling that he could control himself no better than that!

It was even more galling to think that Julia must realize it, too. He had broken his constraints and kissed her twice since he had found out about her treacherous pretense of desire. How could she not realize the effect she had on him? Just as surely, of course, he had no effect on her. She had coolly, calmly manipulated him, after all, using her kisses, her body, her touch, to lure him into confessing. That was certainly not the mark of a woman who had any interest herself in their lovemaking. No, while he had panted with desire, she had been calculating how to bring him to his knees. Deverel's jaw tightened at the thought.

And yet…this afternoon she had responded to his kiss. Surely that had not been mere pretense. She had been weakened by her tears, rocked by reading her brother's suicide note; he could not believe that she had been capable at that moment of engaging in any manipulation. And did that not mean that gradually, as time wore on, he might be able to breach her defenses? That she might, with familiarity, come to feel something for him?

Deverel let out a low growl, disgusted with himself for the turn his thoughts were taking. That was not why he was marrying her, after all. He was marrying her because it was what duty and honor called for. It was what a gentleman would do. It had *nothing* to do with desire.

He returned to his seat behind the desk, and his eyes fell upon the suicide letter still lying there where Julia had placed it. He picked it up and perused it thoughtfully. All of Julia's points, he thought, strained credulity.

Only a loving sister could still maintain Selby's innocence in the face of this damning letter. To do so, she had had to paint Deverel black. If he were a kind person, he thought, he would let Julia continue to believe that Selby had not been guilty. But he knew he was not that good. He was growing exceedingly weary of seeing the suspicion and dislike in Julia's eyes when she looked at him. One way or another, he thought, he was going to prove to her that he was no criminal, even if it meant helping her conduct a full-blown investigation of the whole crime. Painful as it would be for her, he would make her see that her brother had indeed embezzled the money—and that she was wrong in her harsh judgment of himself.

Julia went down to dinner in the same dress, which she was growing thoroughly tired of. She thought that when she got her own clothes, she would throw this dress in the fire. Lady Stonehaven's dresser had come into her room late in the afternoon with one of her ladyship's dresses, which she had done her best to make over for Julia. But even after she had let out its hem full length, the dress was still short on Julia, ending comically above her ankles. Even her old dress was better than that.

She was grateful to see, when she went downstairs into the drawing room where they gathered before dinner, that Lady Stonehaven, with her usual kindness, had not dressed up for dinner, either, but was wearing a soft gray day dress. Lady Stonehaven, Julia thought, was quickly developing into one of her favorite people. She could not understand how such a woman could have turned out a son like Deverel.

They were just about to go in to dinner when there

was a loud knock on the front door. "How odd," Lady Stonehaven commented. "I wonder who that could be."

Stonehaven stepped out into the hallway, where he had a view of the front door as the footman went to answer it. "Good God!" he exclaimed. "Pemberton!"

"Who?" Lady Stonehaven asked, puzzled.

"What!" Julia shot up from her seat and ran into the hall to join Deverel.

Sure enough, there, standing just inside the front door, was Geoffrey Pemberton. "Cousin Geoffrey!"

He glanced down the hall and saw her. "Julia! You pesky child. I told Phoebe there would be nothing wrong with you, and, of course, here you are, looking healthy as a horse."

Julia started down the hall toward him, trailed by Deverel and his mother. "Whatever are you doing here?"

"What am I doing here? Chasing after you, my dear cousin. And damned uncomfortable it was, too, I might add. Had to go back and get something that silly nurse forgot, and then we found it after all in the bottom of a trunk. It was his favorite toy, too. I ask you, why would you bury that in a trunk when you knew he'd start howling for it right away?"

"Who?" Julia asked, staring at him blankly. "What nurse? Who was howling? What are you talking about?"

"Why, your nephew, that's who. I expect you may not realize it, but the lad's got a dreadful temper."

"Gilbert?"

"Yes, of course, Gilbert. Who else were we talking about? I say, Julia, are you feeling all right? First you write that dashed odd note to Phoebe and get her all in a pucker, and now you don't know who your nephew is."

"You mean, Gilbert came with you? Gilbert and Phoebe are with you?"

"Of course. Don't think I'd come up here on my own, do you?" Geoffrey looked shocked. "Phoebe took it into her head that you were in some sort of danger, and she talked me into going with her." He glanced toward Deverel and Lady Stonehaven, and looked abashed. "Silly, of course. I can see that now—you were just paying a visit, I daresay."

Julia ignored his speech, saying, "Where is she?"

"Out in the carriage. Thought I'd better knock first and see how the wind blew, you know."

"Oh, Geoffrey, that's wonderful!" Julia gave him an impulsive hug, startling him, then ran out the front door. "Phoebe!"

The carriage door opened, and Phoebe hopped out, her son right behind her. Julia ran down the steps toward them.

"I'm so glad you're here!" Julia enveloped Phoebe in a hug.

"I knew it!" Phoebe cried softly. "I knew you needed my help. What happened? Did he kidnap you? I was so worried when Nunnelly told me that you had vanished and Lord Stonehaven had escaped! And there was that strange note from you. Then Varian came to call and said that Fitz had told him you were already married to the man. Is that true?"

"No. Not at all. I have no intention of marrying him. But he didn't kidnap me—well, not exactly. I mean, he did at first, but then, when he found out who I was, well, I went with him in order to get away from Pamela—he probably would have forced me to go even if I hadn't wanted to. He is a very stubborn man. Then I thought I could learn more about the embezzlement if I came...."

She paused, remembering that she had decided not to tell Phoebe about the suicide note. After all, she was sure it was false, and showing it to Phoebe would only hurt her for no reason. However, she would have to tell her something, for she had written in her note to Phoebe that Stonehaven had "important information."

"But it turned out to be nothing," she went on slowly, her mind racing. "He, uh, he had a note that he had received from Selby, you see, asking Stonehaven to meet him at the hunting lodge. He thinks that proves that Selby committed suicide. But it proves nothing. It was forged, just like all the letters."

"Aunt Julie! Aunt Julie!" Gilbert, tired of being ignored, exclaimed, tugging at her skirts. "I lost a tooth. See?" He grinned widely to expose a gap in his front teeth.

"My goodness, so you did! When did that happen?"

"On the way here," Phoebe said, a giggle escaping her. "Poor Geoffrey—I thought he was going to be ill when Gil showed him the prize, still decorated in blood."

"Cousin Geoffrey said I was a damned rascal!" Gilbert added proudly.

"Did he now? Did you give your cousin a difficult time?"

"No!" Gilbert looked indignant. "I let him hold my soldier some of the time." The toy in question was still clenched in his fist, and he held it up to show it to his aunt. "And we played games. Didn't we, Mama?"

"Yes, dear. We counted cows and horses and sheep. It was most enlivening." Phoebe's eyes twinkled merrily.

"Oh, my." Julia looked at her sister-in-law as Gilbert skipped ahead of them to the steps. "I am trying to pic ture Cousin Geoffrey counting horses and cows and sheep.''

Phoebe laughed. ''Poor dear man. He was an angel, bless him. I was scared to come all by myself, and I am afraid I more or less trapped him into escorting me. I should have told him he might prefer to ride outside the carriage, but I forgot. Gilbert nearly plagued him to death with questions, and, poor little tyke, Gil got travel sick, as he so often does.''

''Oh, no.''

''Oh, yes. Four times.'' Phoebe held up her fingers to emphasize the point. ''We had to stop by the side of the road each time. Of course, Geoffrey had to ride facing backward, so that Gilbert could ride facing front, because it makes him less sick. But the crowning blow was when Gilbert put his fingers in his mouth and began to wiggle that tooth, as you know he does. When he pulled it out triumphantly, blood and all—well, I have never seen such horror on a man's face before.''

Julia laughed. ''I wish I had been there to see it! That would have been worth paying admission.'' She linked her arm through Phoebe's and followed Gilbert up the steps to the front door. ''Now, I want you to come in and meet Lady Stonehaven. She is almost enough to induce me to marry Deverel.''

Phoebe looked at Julia askance. Deverel? He was Deverel now, not the dreadful Lord Stonehaven? What was going on here?

14

Inside, they found Geoffrey talking to Lady Stonehaven and Deverel.

"Lady Stonehaven," Julia said, smiling and leading Phoebe forward. "Please allow me to introduce you to my very dear sister-in-law, Lady Armiger. Phoebe, this is Lady Stonehaven, who has been so kind to me. Lord Stonehaven, of course, you know."

"We have met," Deverel acknowledged, casting a sardonic look at Julia. "Of course, that was back when you wore spectacles, Julia."

His mother glanced at him oddly. "What—oh, I suppose that is one of your nonsensical jokes." She stepped forward to take Phoebe's hand. "Dear Lady Armiger, I am so glad that you are here."

Phoebe looked rather abashed and said, "I am sorry to drop in on you like this. It is just that when I got that note from Julia, it, uh, worried me."

"Don't give it another thought," Lady Stonehaven assured her breezily. "Of course you would want to be here to support Julia when she gets married, and I am sure that she wants you here. It is only natural to want one's family around. If anyone is to blame, it is Deverel, for giving us so little notice of the nuptials.''

"We will stay in the inn in the village, of course,'' Phoebe assured her, ignoring the subject of marriage.

"Nonsense. It is quite inadequate. I am sure you would not be comfortable. You must stay here. It's a big old house, and it will take only a few minutes to put rooms to right for you. It's so pleasant to have visitors.''

Phoebe looked doubtful, but she subsided with a grateful murmur. At that moment, Gilbert decided that it was time to make his presence known.

He had been staring up intently at Stonehaven from the moment they walked in the door, and now he piped up, "Are you a bad man?''

"I beg your pardon?'' Deverel looked down at the boy.

"Gilbert, no!'' Phoebe cautioned, blushing, and Geoffrey groaned, covering his eyes.

"My mother said we were going to take Aunt Julie away from a bad man. Is that you?''

"Gilbert!'' Phoebe clasped her hand over the boy's mouth, mortified. "I'm sorry, Lord Stonehaven, he—that is, I—''

"Yes?'' Deverel raised an eyebrow, listening politely.

"Deverel, do stop being annoying,'' Lady Stonehaven said crossly. "Our guests will think you are quite rag-mannered.''

"Yes, Mother.'' He turned back to Gilbert. "Actually, my boy, I think there are times when all of us tend to be bad men, so I have to admit that sometimes I am. Are you ever a bad boy?''

Gilbert nodded, not without pride. "Lots and lots of times. Yesterday Nurse said I was an imp of Satan.''

"Did she, now? You must have made her pretty angry."

"I took her ribbon, and she said I spoilt it." He added with a look of righteous indignation, "But I didn't lose it. It was right there round the kitty's neck. I needed a lead, you see."

"I am sure the ribbon made a lovely lead."

"It did!" Gilbert seemed impressed with Deverel's understanding. Apparently deciding that Stonehaven was worthy enough, he stuck his hand in his pocket and pulled out his tooth. He held it out to Stonehaven, saying, "I lost a tooth on the ride."

Behind him, Geoffrey made an inarticulate noise and turned away, but Deverel won Gilbert's respect by squatting down to his level to examine the boy's prize. "I must say, that's a fine-looking tooth. Was it very hard to get out?"

Gilbert shook his head. "I kept wiggling and wiggling, and all of sudden, pop! Out it came!" He grinned with delight at the memory.

"It sounds like an exciting trip."

"Yes, and I sicked up four times."

"Traveling by coach makes you sick? You must have been very brave to have come on the trip, then."

Gilbert considered the matter and nodded gravely. "I was."

"Sometime you must let me take you out in my curricle, for it hasn't a top, and I find that when the breeze is blowing in your face and you can see everything around, you don't feel nearly as sick."

"Really?"

"Yes, really."

"Lord Stonehaven, that is so kind of you," Phoebe

murmured, looking rather guilty. "Gilbert, you mustn't plague him."

"I wasn't plaguing him," the boy argued, with some justice. "The bad man wanted to talk to me. Didn't you?" He looked at Stonehaven for confirmation.

"Yes, I did. But perhaps you could call me Deverel instead of 'the bad man.'"

"All right."

"I say, the boy seems to like you," Geoffrey commented, a trifle awed.

"I like you, too," Gilbert assured Geoffrey.

"You do?" Geoffrey's eyes widened in such surprise that Julia had to smother a laugh.

"You let me play with your watch and fobs. And you didn't yell at me, even when I sicked up on your shoes."

"Oh. Well, poor little devil, I don't suppose you could help it," Geoffrey allowed, though he looked a trifle green at the memory.

"You know what, Gilbert? We shall have to go riding while you're here. Maybe fishing. We have a splendid pond." Deverel shot a twinkling look of mischief at Geoffrey. "Just us men—you and Cousin Geoffrey and I."

Gilbert jumped straight up with a screech and began to babble questions. Geoffrey began to try with almost equal energy to get out of the proposed expedition.

Lady Stonehaven interrupted both efforts, saying smoothly that dinner would be growing cold soon, and Cook would probably have all their heads if they ruined her lovely meal. The butler had already seen to it that two extra places were laid, and a maid whisked Gilbert and his nurse off up to the nursery, where, Lady Stonehaven assured Phoebe, it would be a delight to have a child again after so long.

"My only child, you see," she said with a mock disapproving glance at Stonehaven, "has been so very disobliging as to not yet provide me with an heir." She smiled fondly at Julia. "Of course, if I am very lucky, that will change."

After dinner the women retired to the drawing room for a cozy chat, while Deverel attempted to soothe Geoffrey's lacerated nerves with a brandy in his study. Then the men rejoined them for some more polite small talk. So it wasn't until the party broke up for bed that Phoebe was able to have a private talk with her sister-in-law and find out the answers to the questions that had been plaguing her.

Julia had suggested that Phoebe simply stay with her, so that the servants would not have to make up another room. As soon as the maid had helped them undress and left, Phoebe whirled on Julia.

"What happened?" she asked breathlessly. "What is all this about getting married? And why did you ask for your box of mementos?"

"You brought it, didn't you?" Julia asked a little anxiously.

"It's in the trunk with your clothes." Phoebe pointed toward the traveling trunk full of dresses.

"You are the best of friends, as well as the best of relatives!" Julia went over to the trunk and opened the lid, looking down at the dresses and undergarments folded as if the trunk contained the crown jewels. "Oh! I never thought I would be so grateful to see my clothes! You can't imagine what it's like to wear the same dress three days running, even if Teresa was kind enough to have it cleaned for me."

"Teresa?"

"Lady Stonehaven. Isn't she a jewel?"

"She's delightful," Phoebe agreed. "It's hard to imagine that Lord Stonehaven is her son."

"Isn't it?" Julia pulled out the teakwood box, caressing its smooth surface. She opened it. Inside lay packets of letters, bound with ribbons.

"I don't understand," Phoebe said. "Why did you want that box? Was it a secret message of some kind?"

"I wanted the letters. You see—" Julia stopped abruptly, suddenly realizing that she was about to let her wayward tongue run away with her. She could not tell Phoebe about the suicide note, at least, not until she had proved that Selby did not write it. "I, well, I was going to check them against the letters Selby supposedly wrote. To show that he didn't write them."

"Oh!" Phoebe began to laugh. "Wait until I tell Geoffrey. I was certain that you were trying to let me know that you needed to be rescued, the way that girl in the book did, you know...."

Julia began to laugh. "Oh, no! The one with the statue of Ares?"

"Exactly. But Geoffrey wasn't sure, because he never trusted those 'plaguey Greek fellows.'"

Julia laughed even harder. "I can just hear him. No doubt he thought them too tiring."

"Actually, he said that he thought they were a bunch of loose screws."

"And so they were." Julia wiped the tears of laughter from her eyes. "Dear Cousin Geoffrey."

"He was very kind, you know, to bring me here. I'm sure he didn't really want to, not a bit. But enough about that. Tell me what happened! Why are you at Stonehaven? And why did Lord Stonehaven tell Pamela that you were married?"

"Let's sit down, and I'll tell you." She climbed up

onto the high bed, patting a spot beside her, and Phoebe followed suit. "Nunnelly was right. Deverel escaped. But he didn't run away. He waited until I came back—strangely enough, I came back to let him go, because I could see that it wasn't going to work at all. He would never have told me anything. But he didn't realize who I was. He thought I was part of a gang that was trying to extort money from him. I certainly wasn't going to tell him any different. He carried me off to the inn in Whitley. Fortunately, the landlord didn't see my face. Deverel told him I was his wife, and he had me wrapped up in my cloak so that the man couldn't see that I was tied up."

"Tied up!" Phoebe's face paled. "Oh, Julia!"

Julia saw her gentle sister-in-law's expression and was instantly contrite. "I shouldn't have told you that. I'm sorry. It wasn't terrible. He didn't hurt me. He was just frightfully angry—which I can understand," she conceded. "He started trying to find out about this supposed gang, and finally I made something up, but he didn't believe me. Anyway, the long and short of it is—" she finished blithely, leaving out a great many of the details of that night "—that the next morning I tried to escape down the stairs, and he came after me and, well, he had his arms around me and we were struggling." There was no reason, she thought, to mention the kiss. "And who should walk in the door but Major Fitzmaurice and Pamela St. Leger? Even Thomas was there! Fitz was escorting them home, you see, and they had stopped for a late breakfast before they got to Farrow."

"Julia!" Horror was written on Phoebe's face. "Oh, no! This will be the ruin of you!"

Julia sighed. "That is what Deverel said. That's why he told them that it was all right, because he and I were married. I could have kicked him, of course, because that will make it look even worse if I don't—I mean, *when* I don't marry him.''

''Not marry him! But, Julia, love, how can you not?'' Phoebe protested. ''I mean, to be caught together at an inn in the morning.''

''Without our shoes on,'' Julia enlarged upon the scandalous elements of the scene. ''We had obviously just gotten up.''

Phoebe grew even whiter. ''This is horrible. Pamela will spread it everywhere! Why, Varian already knows about it. Fitz told him as soon as he got back. That man could never keep a secret.''

''I'm sorry, Fee....'' Tears welled in Julia's eyes, and she took Phoebe's hand. ''I know it will be a great scandal when I don't marry him, but—''

''Don't say that!'' Phoebe cried softly. ''Julia, you *have* to marry him.''

''No! Not you, too, Phoebe? How *could* I marry him? After everything he's done?''

''But...what if we were wrong?'' Phoebe asked worriedly. ''What if he isn't the person who took the money? I mean, we have no real proof that he did. He acted like a gentleman when he pretended that you and he were married, in order to save your reputation. He didn't have to, you know. He could have told them the whole story, and then you would have been in an even worse scandal.''

''He said...'' Julia continued in a small voice. ''He said it was his duty. He said he had compromised me by kidnapping me that night.''

''Does that sound like the sort of thing a man who embezzled money and put the crime off on another would do?'' Phoebe began to chew at her lower lip. ''He was so good with Gil tonight. He knew just what to say.''

''That doesn't mean he's not an embezzler. He probably felt guilty because Gil is Selby's son.''

''I don't know. What if we did those things to an innocent man?'' Phoebe looked in horror at her sister-in-law.

''We don't know that. None of those things prove that he didn't embezzle the money.'' Julia frowned, her own doubts welling up in her again. She tried to suppress them. She could not let herself think that way; it was too horrible to contemplate. It was as if a great pit yawned at her feet. *What if she had been wrong? What if she had set out to ruin an innocent man? What if she had permanently alienated herself from the one man whom—*

''No!'' Julia jumped off the bed and began to pace. ''How can I marry him after all this? What *I've* done? What *he's* done? There's no hope for us! He hates me. How could I live the rest of my life with a man who hates me? No. It's impossible.'' She turned, her eyes flashing. ''I have too much pride to accept his charity. He would be able to hold it up to me my whole life, how he saved my good name by marrying me.''

She made a disgusted face.

''All right,'' said Phoebe, who had been watching Julia's nervous movements with some anxiety. ''Of course you don't have to marry him if you're set against it. I just thought—but we won't talk about it any more tonight.''

''Thank you.'' Julia looked at her a little sheepishly. ''I'm sorry. I hate this feeling of being forced…and I have despised him for so long.'' Her voice dropped to a tormented whisper. ''What if he didn't do it? Who else could it be? It wasn't Selby. It could not have been Selby."

"No! No, of course it wasn't," Phoebe assured her. "You must not think that way. Come. Let's go to bed now."

Julia nodded, and climbed into the bed. They crawled under the cover in troubled silence and waited for sleep to come.

Julia awoke the next morning feeling hardly more rested than when she had gone to bed. She could not get the thought of marrying Stonehaven out of her mind, and it occurred to her that perhaps a walk after breakfast might help her to straighten out her thoughts.

She and Phoebe found Lady Stonehaven still at the table when they went into the breakfast room. The older woman greeted them with a smile.

"You've missed Deverel, I'm afraid. He left rather early this morning, with young Master Gilbert. I believe they were going to investigate possible fishing spots." She turned her twinkling gaze on Julia. "Deverel was certain that you would wish to be included on their expedition, Julia, dear, but I managed to persuade him that you needed your sleep."

Both Phoebe and Julia, who well knew Gilbert's lively nature early in the morning, laughed. "Thank you, ma'am," Julia said with real gratitude.

"Poor man," Phoebe added. "I wonder if he knows what he is in for."

"Dev seems to be rather good with children," his mother said with evident pride. "He got off to a bad start with poor Thomas, but I blame that largely on Thomas's mother. Pamela never liked him, you see, and when Thomas was young, she discouraged him being around Deverel.''

"That sounds like something Pamela would do," Julia agreed. "Why did she dislike him? I always thought Pamela had a decided partiality for handsome men.''

"He is handsome, isn't he?" Lady Stonehaven agreed fondly. "Actually, I think it was Pamela's partiality for men that made her dislike him. Walter was Dev's best friend, and Deverel would never have done anything to hurt Walter."

Phoebe's eyes widened. "You mean, you think Pamela made advances toward Lord Stonehaven?"

Teresa shrugged. "He never told me. But having seen the way Pamela acted around him, I have little doubt of what she wanted. She was hardly subtle in the way she flirted and hung on his arm at every opportunity. It was obvious to everyone except Walter, of course. I never could understand how such a nice man could be so smitten with her. Then she started acting very cold toward Deverel, and she obstructed his seeing Walter—coming down with an illness when Walter was about to come visit us, so that he couldn't leave Farrow, or deciding that they should go to Bath for a few weeks at a time when Dev was scheduled to go there. That sort of thing. It was obvious that something had made her furious at him. The only thing that I can think of is that she grew too bold and direct, and Dev turned her down.''

"Oh, my!" Phoebe looked shocked. "I can hardly believe it.''

Julia let out a snort of disgust. "I can. I can believe anything of that woman.''

"What woman?"

The three women turned toward the doorway to see Geoffrey standing there.

"Cousin Geoffrey!" Julia said, smiling. "I can scarcely believe my eyes. I thought you never rose before eleven."

He rewarded her with a pained expression as he came forward into the room and sat down in the chair Lady Stonehaven indicated. "Normally that is the case." He shook his head and sighed. "I had forgotten how noisy it is in the country."

"Noisy?" Julia asked, her eyes brimming with laughter.

"Yes. All sort of rustlings and howls and things. Some bird hooting all night. As if that weren't enough, at the crack of dawn, a bunch of silly birds started twittering. Now, I ask you..."

Julia began to giggle, but Phoebe patted Geoffrey's hand and said commiseratingly, "You poor thing. Why don't I pour you a cup of coffee? Or would you prefer tea?"

"Coffee sounds like just the thing," Geoffrey allowed, brightening a little. "It's no wonder people keep such dreadful hours in the country."

"Yes, I know," Lady Stonehaven said. "It seems to go against nature, doesn't it, getting up when the sun starts shining?"

"My point exactly." Geoffrey beamed at her understanding and shot his giggling cousin a dark look. "No doubt you do not understand that, Julia, having always been far too lively. You probably love arising early."

"Indeed, yes," Julia agreed pertly. "It gives me so much more time to get into mischief."

"Minx," he replied without heat and set about assuaging his battered nerves by tucking into a hearty breakfast.

"Geoffrey, did you know that Lady Stonehaven is an

artist?'' Julia asked. She added, to Teresa, ''Cousin Geoffrey is a collector of artworks.''

''Really? How delightful.''

Geoffrey smiled deprecatingly and said in explanation of this odd habit, ''It's a restful sort of hobby.''

''I quite agree. So much more enjoyable than riding to the hounds, say.''

''Exactly.'' Geoffrey gave a visible shudder.

''Lady Stonehaven does wonderful work,'' Julia added. ''You'll have to get her to show you around her studio later.''

''Really, my dear, you shall put me to the blush,'' Lady Stonehaven protested.

''It's true. I have seen your paintings, remember, so you can't pretend that you are a mere dabbler.''

''No, I shan't do that. I am afraid I have far too much of the sin of pride. I shall be happy to show Mr. Pemberton my workroom, if he wishes to see it—and Lady Armiger, too.''

Both Phoebe and Geoffrey asserted that they were eager to see her work, and it was arranged that she would take them on a tour as soon as they finished eating. Julia bowed out of the expedition, since she had already seen the workroom, and said that she thought she would like a walk instead.

''That sounds delightful,'' Lady Stonehaven told her. ''Just follow the path through the garden, and it goes eventually into the trees. There's a pleasant grove or two, and a lovely brook running through them.''

Shortly after breakfast, Julia donned a chip straw hat and a light shawl, which Lady Stonehaven had recommended to combat the slight chill that sometimes prevailed in the wooded areas, and set off through the garden. She stopped to admire the roses and smell their sweet scent, then struck off along the path that led through the lower garden and into the grove of trees beyond.

It was not a heavily wooded area, for shafts of sunlight cut down through the trees, and, as Lady Stonehaven had said, there was a very pleasant grove. As a tree had fallen there in such as way as to provide a perfect seat, Julia sat down for a few minutes to lazily contemplate the dance of dust motes in the stream of sunlight slanting down through the trees. She had intended to think through her problems, but she found it difficult to concentrate. The air was too peaceful, even somnolent, and she found herself nodding off.

A loud crack brought Julia wide-awake, and she whirled around, looking for the cause. She expected to see some animal, or even a person who had stepped on a branch and broken it, but to her surprise there was nothing. She stood up, and as she did, there was another crack, and immediately after it, something thumped into the log where she had been sitting. Julia looked down at the log, amazed to see that a chunk of wood had been gouged out of it. At one end of the strip of freshly debarked wood, she saw a small metal ball lodged in the wood.

Someone had shot at her!

She stood for an instant, frozen, staring at the ball. Then she whirled and took off through the trees, screaming.

15

Julia ran like a deer, dodging around trees and leaping over rocks and fallen tree limbs. She half expected to hear someone crashing through the trees after her, but she heard nothing, even when she tripped and fell, knocking what little remaining breath she had out of her. She lay on the mossy ground, struggling to breathe, straining her ears to hear the sounds of pursuit. There were none.

Cautiously she sat up and looked around. The woods were still, except for the sounds of a few birds tweeting in the trees. A squirrel scampered across a tree limb and gazed down at her with bright eyes, its tail twitching. She told herself that this was far too normal a scene for anyone to be chasing through the woods after her with a gun.

No, two guns, she reminded herself. There had been two shots in succession, too quickly for someone to have reloaded. Surely he would not have had more pistols than that, and he would have had to stop to reload. With her taking off at top speed, perhaps he had not even bothered to follow her, knowing that his guns were empty. On the other hand, she thought, it could be that he had taken off after her immediately and was even now hiding out there somewhere, reloading his pistols and waiting for her to stand up again.

Instantly, she flopped back down. She wanted to curl up into a ball. But she knew she could not do that; it would only make her easier prey. She had to get away from here, had to return to the house.

Just as she sat up again, preparing to rise, she heard noises—the crunch of twigs and leaves beneath feet, a few low words. Julia panicked, looking around for someplace to hide.

"Hello!" came a male voice in the distance.

Julia turned in the direction from which she thought it had come, searching frantically. *Was her attacker trying to lure her out of hiding?*

"Is anyone there? We heard screams. Is someone hurt?"

She froze. Was it someone who had heard her screams when she started running and had come to her rescue— or was it the person who had fired upon her? Moving as softly as she could, she stepped over a fallen tree branch and made her way to a large bush, wincing every time leaves crackled under her feet. She crept around to the other side of the bush and huddled down behind it, peering through its thick branches. She was, however, able to see almost nothing. Her back prickled as she thought of someone sneaking up behind her, and she turned her back to the thick bush, keeping a watch on the woods behind her.

"Hello!" came another drawn-out call.

"Hello!" piped up another voice, this one that of a young boy.

Gilbert! Julia shot to her feet.

"Can you hear me?" Was that Deverel's voice?

"Can you hear me?" came the child's voice again in laughing imitation of his elder.

"Gilbert!" Julia cried, starting in the direction of the voices. "Gilbert, is that you? Deverel?"

"Who's there? Julia?"

There were more noises in the distance, the heavy sound of running. Then, somewhat off to the right of where she had thought they were, she caught sight of a man leading a horse. Beside him was a pony with a small boy perched on top.

The boy cupped his hands around his mouth and yelled, "Aunt Julia!"

"Here!" Julia waved her arms over her head and began to hurry toward them. She didn't know when she had ever been so glad to see anyone.

"Julia!" Deverel saw her now and broke into a trot, his horse shambling along behind him.

In her relief, Julia ran straight to Deverel and leaped at him. He caught her, his arms wrapping tightly around her, and she clung to his neck. "I am so glad to see you! I was so scared!"

Deverel squeezed her against him, burying his face in the crook of her neck. "Julia. Julia." His lips touched her skin, then her hair, then her cheek. Behind them, Gilbert was chanting her name in a happy singsong.

Finally Julia recalled that she was acting shamelessly in front of her nephew—not to mention hugging a man whom she despised—and she dropped her arms from around his neck.

"I'm sorry."

He hesitated a moment before he released her, letting her slide back down to the ground. "What happened? We heard strange noises as we were riding back to the house, so we went looking for the source. Did something scare you? Were you lost?''

"I am…now," Julia admitted. "I have no idea where I am. I just started running. Someone shot at me.''

"Shot *at* you!" Deverel looked thunderstruck. "Are you sure he was aiming at you?''

"Of course I'm sure," Julia snapped, irritated. "The ball hit the log where I'd been sitting.''

"Bang! Bang!!" Gilbert decided to make his contribution to the conversation from atop his pony. Pointing his finger like a pistol, he pretended to aim and fire all around him.

Deverel's brows drew together in a black scowl. "It's those damned poachers! They'll fire at anything that moves. I'll have their hides for this!''

Poachers! Julia nearly sagged with relief. Of course, that was it. It had been an accident, a mistake. Why had she assumed that they had been trying to kill her? "Do you really think so?''

"Of course. What else could it have been?'' He looked puzzled; then his face cleared. "Don't tell me you think someone was shooting at you *on purpose.*''

It sounded exceedingly foolish when he said it, and Julia blushed. "I—I don't know what I thought. It just scared me, and I ran.''

"Well, of course it did. I would say you'd be justified in being terrified by someone shooting at you, whether it was accidental or purposeful. I certainly would be.'' He took her hand and picked up the reins he had dropped when she ran full tilt at him. "Come on, let's get back to the house. No doubt you could use a rest. I'll get my gameskeeper right on it. Where were you when they shot at you?''

"I don't know," Julia admitted. "I'm not sure I could

find it again. It was a clearing, the first one I came to after I started into the trees.''

They made their way out of the woods, and when they got beyond the trees, Deverel helped Julia mount his horse. They continued at a slow pace toward the house, and gradually Julia's nerves calmed. Looking back on it, she saw that Deverel must be right. The person who fired on her had surely done it by accident. It was absurd to think that anyone would try to kill her. No one had any real grudge against her—except Deverel, of course, but since he could easily have gotten rid of her by sending her home and was instead insisting that she marry him, it seemed unlikely that he would try to kill her. Besides, he had been out with her nephew this morning—and anyone who knew anything about youngsters would never attempt something secretive with a six-year-old around.

Julia was not sure why she had jumped to the conclusion that someone had been trying to kill her, instead of assuming that it was an accident. She supposed it was because there had been two shots. One might be an accident, but it seemed unlikely that someone would fire a second shot so close to her. Whoever it was must have been aiming at her. Of course, she had been low to the ground, sitting on the log, perhaps partially hidden by bushes, and she had been wearing a hat and brown shawl. It was possible, she guessed, that from a distance someone might have mistaken her for an animal, unflattering though the idea might be.

The more time that passed, the stranger and more unreal the incident seemed. By the time they reached the house and Gilbert began excitedly to tell the story of finding Aunt Julia, she had dismissed the oddities of the occurrence and agreed with Deverel that in all likelihood it had been the mistake of a poacher.

"And a very grave mistake he shall find it, too," Deverel promised grimly. "He might have harmed you!"

From the look on his face, Julia thought that she would hate to be the poacher if he was able to discover the man's identity. Stonehaven obviously took his territorial rights very seriously.

"This is awful!" Lady Stonehaven exclaimed.

"Julia! How terrible it must have been," Phoebe commiserated. "You must come upstairs and rest. Let me put some lavender on your temples."

"I'm all right, Fee," Julia assured her, smiling. "I really didn't come to any harm, except for getting dust on my dress."

"Damned peculiar place, the country," Geoffrey opined. "I must say, Phoebe, I think we ought to go back to London."

"Yes, Geoffrey, of course. We will soon."

Julia allowed Phoebe to take her upstairs, where she undressed and bathed away the dirt of her experience. She got into bed and submitted to the handkerchief dipped in warm water and lavender drops with which Phoebe insisted on bathing her forehead and temples. Rather tired after her experience, she soon dropped into a restful sleep.

When she awoke, she found that a servant had brought a cold luncheon up to her on a tray. Also on the tray was a note from Deverel, requesting her to come to his study. Julia grimaced, thinking that a request from Deverel was more like an order, but since she had intended to ask him if he would give her Selby's suicide note, she decided that she might as well comply with his wishes and meet him.

She got up carefully, wincing at the soreness in her muscles that was a reminder of the morning's ordeal. She discovered that she was famished, and she dug into the food with zeal, then dressed and went downstairs to Deverel's study.

"Julia." Deverel stood up from his desk when she entered. "How are you feeling?"

"Fine. Rest works wonders."

"Here. Sit down." He guided her toward a chair.

"I'm not an invalid," she told him tartly.

"Of course." He stiffened, and his hand fell away from her arm. "I realize that you, of course, do not need my help."

Julia felt a trifle guilty. She would not have snapped at anyone else for doing what he did. It seemed as though, around him, she was always on her worst behavior.

"I talked with my gamesman," Deverel continued. "He was much shocked by what happened to you this morning. He said he had not heard any rumors of poachers on the land lately."

Deverel did not add that the gameskeeper had found it highly unlikely that anyone would be idiotic enough to poach that close to the house, anyway. The man's opinion had increased Deverel's uneasiness about the incident, but he was not about to worry Julia with the vague fears it had aroused in him.

"He has gone out to investigate the clearing, and he's going to hire some more men, so that we can keep the grounds better patrolled."

"There is no need to turn the place into an armed camp," Julia protested. "I am sure that whoever did it won't return. He is bound to realize his mistake, and he would be foolish, indeed, to come back." Julia stifled her own doubts about the shooter being a poacher. After all, who else could he have been?

"No doubt. However, you must allow me to take every precaution for the safety of my guests."

"Of course. It's your decision." Julia shrugged, dismissing the subject. "I wanted to ask you if I could borrow Selby's note."

"The suicide note? Julia—do you really think it's wise to dwell on it?"

"The *supposed* suicide note. And I am not dwelling on it, as you say."

"You don't propose to show it to Lady Armiger, do you?"

"No. I'm not as insensitive as that. Until I can prove that Selby didn't write it, it would only cause Phoebe pain." She paused, then added reluctantly, "I understand why you did not give it to her."

"Why, thank you." He gave her a mocking half bow. "I thought never to hear such words from your lips."

"Don't be snide. May I have the letter?"

"Of course." He reached into a drawer of his desk and withdrew it. "Here." As Julia took the letter and started to rise, he went on. "No, wait. There is another matter we must discuss."

He picked up an official-looking piece of paper, adorned with a seal, from his desk. "I received our special license this afternoon."

Julia froze, staring at him.

"We can be married now. The sooner, the better, I would say, since we've told Pamela St. Leger that we are already married."

"*You* told her, you mean," Julia pointed out acidly. "I had nothing to do with it."

He shrugged. "That scarcely matters now. The point

is, we need to be married right away. I suggest this evening. The rector will come round and do it right here in the house. Or we can go to the church, if that is your preference. You have Lady Armiger and Mr. Pemberton to act as witnesses.''

''Wait. I never agreed to marry you.''

Deverel grimaced. ''Are you still going on about that? I thought you had realized that you have no other choice.''

''One *always* has a choice,'' Julia argued. ''I do not want to marry you.''

''I am well aware of your feelings toward me,'' Deverel said stiffly. ''I do not presume to think that we would have any sort of real marriage, or that you would feel toward me as a wife usually feels toward her husband. It would be a marriage entirely of duty.''

''Duty,'' Julia repeated, aware of a heavy sickness in the region of her stomach. ''Then there would be no—'' Her throat stuck on the word *love*.

''We would have separate bedrooms, if that is what you are asking,'' Deverel replied, his eyes glittering with a fierce, cold light. ''I have no evil designs on your virginal body. Nor do I delude myself that your past pretense of desire was anything but that—a pretense.''

Julia was not sure why his words filled her with such cold. ''Then you are speaking of a marriage in appearance only?''

''Certainly. What else would be possible between us?''

''Nothing, of course,'' she answered through numb lips. ''Is that what you want—to tie yourself to a loveless marriage?''

''It is not a question of what I want. Or of what you

want. It is a question of what we have to do. Or do you
not believe that you have a certain duty to your family?''

"Of course I believe I have a duty to them.''

Julia thought of Phoebe's horror-stricken face last
night, as Julia had recounted the story of their meeting
Pamela St. Leger. It had been obvious that Phoebe believed Julia's reputation to be ruined. Julia thought that
she was willing to live ostracized by Society, even
though she knew that it would be worse than the way
she and Phoebe had been cut after Selby's scandal. This
time, even good people such as the vicar's wife would
avoid her. Still, even that seemed better than a cold and
loveless marriage with a man who hated her and whom
she suspected of having ruined her brother. But the burden that would fall on Phoebe and Gilbert, through no
fault of their own, was too awful. They would be tainted
by her scandal, just as they had been by Selby's, except
worse. Two successive scandals would ruin them.

She was miserably aware that her own headstrong behavior had led to the scandal that would swamp the Armiger family. She had thought up the plan to trick Deverel, and Phoebe had never even known the full extent
of it. It seemed horribly unfair that Phoebe and Gilbert
should have to pay for her stubborn insistence on doing
something dangerous.

Julia looked over at Deverel. She had sworn she could
not marry the man who had ruined her brother, but had
he really been responsible for that? Her faith in Stonehaven's guilt had been shaken the past few days. Deverel
obviously did not need the money. He had not shown
that damning suicide note to anyone—and while perhaps
it might have been Varian who decided they shouldn't
show it, Julia was certain that if Deverel wanted it
known, it would not have been hard to let the news leak

out. And, most of all, having been around him for some time now, Julia was finding it harder and harder to believe that he was capable of theft or of setting out to ruin Selby—and once she had realized that whoever had stolen the money must have actually murdered Selby, her doubts had mushroomed. Much as she wanted to, she could not believe that Deverel could cold-bloodedly murder anyone.

She was beginning to be afraid that the awful truth was that she had foolishly, pigheadedly ruined both their lives. She knew that the ultimate responsibility for everything that had happened was hers. She had been headstrong and rash, and the result had been disastrous. How could she balk at doing the one thing that would save her family from being ruined by her actions? Deverel obviously hated her, but he was willing to make the sacrifice for his family's name. How could she refuse to do the same?

Everything inside her quailed at the idea of facing a lifetime of a loveless, even antagonistic, marriage. Yet she knew that to refuse to do it would be the act of a coward.

Julia straightened her shoulders and looked Deverel squarely in the eyes. "All right," she said. "I will marry you."

The rector married them that evening in the privacy of the small drawing room, with only Lady Stonehaven, Phoebe and Geoffrey in attendance. Deverel was stony-faced throughout the proceeding, and Julia grew colder and colder with each passing moment. Lady Stonehaven and Phoebe did their best to put a cheerful face on it, but Julia could tell that the rector found them a decidedly odd bride and groom. Lady Stonehaven had refreshments laid out afterward, but they made a very subdued little party. More than once, Julia saw Phoebe cast a concerned look at her.

After the rector left, the others tactfully disappeared, leaving Julia and Deverel alone together. The situation did not improve.

"Well, it's done," Deverel said grimly, and Julia nodded her head.

He looked at her for a long moment, then went on in a brusque voice. "It would be customary for you to move into the room adjoining mine, now that you are Lady Stonehaven."

The title sounded foreign to her. Julia wanted to protest that she was not Lady Stonehaven, not at all. But she said only, "I see. Then I, uh, suppose that I should do that."

"I will tell the servants to move your things." He paused, then added, "It does not mean anything more, of course. I won't touch you."

His words inexplicably added to the heavy weight growing in the region of Julia's heart. She looked away. "Of course."

"Fine." He hesitated, then turned and left the room.

Julia sank down into the nearest chair, tears filling her eyes. She should be relieved, she knew, that Deverel did not intend to demand his marital rights. It was bad enough that her husband despised her, that her impulsive actions had forced him to marry her. It would be even worse if she had to face the idea of going to bed with him. But somehow his words had only lowered her already gloomy spirits. She put her head in her hands and gave way to a bout of tears.

It was some time later that she went upstairs to bed. No one else seemed to be around, and she wondered if they had all retired early in an effort to give the newlyweds some privacy. *That showed how little they knew about the marriage.* She felt odd, climbing the stairs and walking down the hall by herself. This was her home now, but she still felt like a guest. The enormity of what she had done struck her, and she wanted to cry all over again, but she refused to give in to the weakness.

The door to the room beside Deverel's stood open, and she went to it and looked in. It was clear that this was her new room. Her box of mementos lay on the mahogany dresser, along with her silver brush and mirror. She opened one of the drawers to find her underclothes and nightgowns carefully folded inside. The wardrobe held the dresses that Phoebe had brought to her.

She turned and surveyed the room. It was a larger one than the guest chamber where she had been put before, and the furnishings were perhaps a trifle more elegant. However, she did not like it as well. It was too dark, she thought, and gloomy. The very richness of it weighed down her spirits.

The maid came in to help Julia undress and put on her nightgown. The girl pulled Julia's nicest nightgown from the dresser, presuming that Julia would wish to look her best on her wedding night. Then she brushed Julia's hair to a burnished gleam and left it hanging down her back. Julia closed the door into the hall and went to bed.

It occurred to her at that moment that she was not the slightest bit sleepy.

She looked over at the door connecting with Deverel's room. She wondered if she ought to lock it, but she rejected the idea. He had, after all, made it clear that he would not seek her out. She wondered if he was in his bedchamber. She had heard nothing from that room since she came in, and she did not know whether he had already gone to bed or was not there at all. Telling herself that it didn't matter where Deverel was or what he was doing, she turned over on her side, facing away from the door, and closed her eyes.

She realized after a moment that she was lying stiffly, her whole body tense, listening for a sound from the room next door. With an exasperated sigh, she pushed off her bedcovers and got up and lit a candle. If she could not go to sleep, she thought, she would read. However, a quick search of the room established that there were no books here. She thought of the large selection of books in Deverel's study. Surely he would not mind if she chose a book to read. After all, she reminded herself, she was his wife now, and this was her house, too, however much she might feel like a stranger.

Opening the door softly, she slipped out into the hall and down the stairs, her candle casting a small, wavering light in the dark hallway. She had some qualms, thinking that Deverel might be in the study himself, but she saw with relief that the door was open and the room dark. She lit an oil lamp to relieve the darkness of the room and set about searching for a book. Nothing caught her interest, but finally she pulled out a slender tome that was a history of Stonehaven and its family.

Julia curled up in a chair and began to peruse the book. It was there that Deverel found her an hour later, sound asleep, clad only in her nightgown, her flaming hair tumbling down, and the wide scoop neck of the gown slipped down on one side to reveal a rounded white shoulder.

16

Deverel, too, had been unable to sleep. He had retired to his study shortly after the brief ceremony, leaving his mother to deal with the rector, who, no doubt, had found it the most curious wedding he had ever performed.

He had sat there for an hour or more, unable to read or work or do much of anything except think about Julia. He had gotten what he wanted, but never had a victory been so hollow. Julia hated him. She thought him responsible for her brother's disgrace and death. She had married him only to save her family from disgrace, and no doubt she despised Deverel for bullying her into doing it, too.

Deverel had thought of spending the rest of his life with Julia, unable to touch her or kiss her, barred eternally from her bed. It was not a pleasant picture. He had promised her a marriage in name only because he had been certain that she would not marry him any other way, but he was honest enough to know that such a marriage was not what *he* wanted. He had told himself, as well as her, that he did not want her, but Deverel knew it wasn't true. Not a day had gone by since he met Julia that he had not thought about making love to her.

It wasn't that he loved her, of course. She was a scheming, heartless hussy—when she wasn't being amusing or witty or fired with righteous indignation. It was just that she was the most beautiful woman he had ever met, and his body longed for her with a mindless intensity.

His thoughts had driven him to a restless pacing, and finally he had gone upstairs to his bedroom. It had been even worse there, for he had heard the maid in the room next door, arranging Julia's things, and he could not keep his mind off the fact that he would be sleeping next door to Julia every night...having sworn not to touch her.

He had left his bedroom, cursing, and gone for a long walk. On his return to the house, he saw the light in his study, so he went to investigate.

There was Julia, sound asleep in one of the chairs, her legs curled up under her like a little girl, a book open on her lap. He approached her softly and stood for a moment looking down on her. Her nightdress was white and tied enticingly beneath her breasts. The dark circles of her nipples were visible through the light material. The bodice of the nightgown closed with three pearl buttons down the front, and the wide scoop neck revealed a great deal of her white chest. In her sleep, the gown had slipped off one shoulder, revealing even more.

The room was suddenly hot.

Deverel reached down and eased the book from Julia's lap. His eyebrows rose in amusement as he saw that she had been reading his grandfather's history of the Grey family and Stonehaven estate. *No wonder she had fallen asleep!* He closed the book and set it aside on his desk, then bent down and slid his arms beneath Julia's legs and back. He picked her up carefully, and she did not awaken. Instead, with a sigh, she snuggled against his chest, and heat flooded him.

He bent to blow out the lamp and her candle, then made his way through the dim hall and up the stairs with the surefootedness of one who had lived there all his life, aided only by the pale light of the moon streaming in through the windows. Julia was soft and warm in his arms. Just the feel of her set up a throbbing in his loins. Deverel wondered whether any of the passion she had shown when he kissed her had been real. How could she have imitated it so well? He would have laid odds that she had never known a man, had probably never even kissed another man passionately, for her responses had seemed untutored, even naive at times. But if that were true, how had she known how to pretend desire so well...unless it was not pretense, and she had actually felt it?

His heart was pounding in his chest, and he knew it was not just from exertion. It had been a grave mistake, he told himself, to have picked her up and carried her to bed. He should have awakened her and let her walk. He had not, he knew, precisely because he had wanted to feel her in his arms again. The thought irritated him immensely. He was used to having better control over himself than this.

He let out an exasperated noise, and Julia's eyes opened. She blinked, looking up at him sleepily, and smiled. It was a warm, welcoming smile that made his heart turn in his chest, but in the next instant, she recalled who and where she was, and she scowled.

"What are you doing?" she snapped. "You swore that you would not—"

"Believe me, my lady, I have no evil intentions toward you," he retorted. He had reached her room by now, and he crossed it in a few quick strides. "I found you asleep in my study, so in an attempt to be thoughtful, I carried you up here." He reached her bed and let her drop down upon it with rather more carelessness than he would normally have used. "Obviously a mistake on my part."

Julia bounced a little as she hit the soft mattress. Sputtering with outrage, she put her hands down on the bed and pushed herself up into a sitting position. She caught her gown beneath her hand, however, and the force of her surge upward caused the top two buttons of the gown to pop. The nightdress sagged on one side, exposing a round, creamy breast.

They both froze, Deverel's gaze riveted to her naked breast and her eyes on his face. Without thinking, Deverel reached out toward the soft, pale orb. Julia gasped and flinched away, flooded with embarrassment. Deverel snatched his hand back as if it had been burned. With a curse, he turned and strode rapidly out of the room.

Julia sat for a long moment, staring at the closed door through which he had gone. The moment had passed so quickly that she had scarcely realized what had happened until it was over. When Deverel had stared at her in that hot, hungry way, her loins had melted. She had ached for him to touch her, and she had jerked away out of embarrassment and intense self-loathing. How could she be so filled with desire for him? He hated her!

Deverel had told her that he had no desire for a real marriage. In fact, he had said flatly both today and at the inn that he felt no passion for her after the trick she had played on him. If he had touched her, she knew, it would have been only because he had been seized with a brief, impersonal lust. She did not want him that way.

The thought surprised her. She did not want him in *any* way, did she?

Julia pulled her nightgown around her and slid under the covers. She wished she could hide under them forever and never have to see Deverel again. She wanted to lose herself in a storm of tears, but this time they would not come.

The next morning, after breakfast, Julia sat down to study Selby's suicide note. She opened the box of mementos which Phoebe had brought and took out one of Selby's letters. Laying the two letters down beside each other, she went through them word by word. Gradually she began to see a pattern. Just to make sure, she took out another letter he had written to her from London several years ago and compared it to the note.

With a smile of triumph, she jumped up and ran lightly down the stairs, the three letters clutched in her hand. Earlier she had wondered how she would face Deverel again after the embarrassing episode last night, but her discovery had chased away all such thoughts, and she headed straight for his study.

"Deverel!" she said breathlessly, rushing inside right after she knocked on the door, not waiting to be told to enter.

"What is it?" He stood up and came toward her, his expression softening at the obvious excitement on her face.

"I have found something!" In her eagerness, Julia reached out and took his hand to pull him over to his desk, and for an instant everything seemed perfectly natural and right between them.

She laid the three letters down on the desk, the "suicide note" in the middle. Deverel saw what the pages were, and his pleasant expression changed to a frown. He should have known, he thought, that she was not hurrying in to see him, but to argue a point about Selby.

"Julia..." he began wearily.

"Wait. Don't reject this before you see it. I have been going over this note, and I am certain that it isn't really Selby's writing. Look." She pointed to a letter *y* in the suicide note. "Do you see how this loop on the end of the *y* comes up into the line above? Here is a letter Selby wrote to me when he was at the university. Do you see the *y?* It stops right at the bottom of the other letters."

"It is a little different," Deverel admitted.

"There's more. This note is too regular."

"What do you mean?"

"Do you see how, when Selby writes, his capital letters are usually large, just as they are in the note. But some of them are a little larger, some smaller. The ones in the suicide note are uniform. They are all exactly the same size. You see how in Selby's letter to me he leaves more space between some sentences than he does between others? In the suicide note, the spaces are almost exactly the same."

"True. But these are very slight differences. Look at the whole letters." He pointed from one page to the next. "Don't you see how similar they are?"

"Of course. It is an excellent forgery. But it's not real. Don't you see? There are other things. The way he connects *d*s to the other letters, for instance. And the dots of the small *i*s are all right over the letter. Half of Selby's are off to the side."

Deverel looked at each example she showed him, his frown deepening. He felt a twinge of unease. "But those letters of Selby's were written a long time ago," he argued. "His writing probably changed over the years."

"A little, perhaps."

"You have to remember that a suicide note would have been written under great stress. No doubt his thoughts were all a jumble. He was probably writing quickly, under the force of great emotion."

"Yes, but don't you see?" Julia smiled up at him victoriously, and the glow on her face was enough to take his breath away. "The writing in the suicide note is not at all agitated! It is the one that is so uniform, so regular—all the spaces the same, the letters the same. Look at it. Does it make any sense that a suicide note would be so neat and precise? The writing so perfect?"

"No...I suppose it doesn't."

Seeing that she was making headway, Julia pressed her point. "The other letters he wrote flowed from his thoughts. He didn't think about his handwriting or worry about whether the letters looked right. But in this suicide note, when he should have been in great agitation, he was very careful to get each letter exactly the same size and the spaces perfectly uniform. Why would he do that? I'll tell you why," she went on without giving him a chance to answer. "He did it because he wasn't distressed. He wasn't even Selby. He was not writing from the heart but carefully copying something. His main concern was to make the writing look exactly right."

Julia gazed at him expectantly. Deverel sighed.

"It is a little odd," he admitted.

"A little! I should say it is very odd indeed."

"But these are such small things," he protested. "It hardly seems enough to prove that Selby—"

"Oh!" Julia cried out in frustration. "You are determined that it should be Selby! You will not consider anything else. Whatever I say, you have some sort of argument against it. You even discount what is right before your eyes.''

"I have no desire for Selby to have committed suicide,'' Deverel replied stiffly. "It seems to me that it is you who is determined to make me the villain of this piece. I never wished Selby any harm. God help me, I didn't *want* to believe that he was guilty. He was my friend. I tried my damnedest to find some way to prove that he did not do anything wrong.'' He broke off and turned away. He stood still for a long moment, then sighed and turned back to her. "Look. I promised you that we would investigate the embezzlement all over again, and we will. The letters that were written about the money are in London, at the office of the fund's agent. I suggest that we go there and look at them. You can compare them to these letters of yours. We can talk to Varian and Fitz again. We'll see if there is anyone who knew Selby's mysterious mistress.''

"There won't be, because she didn't exist,'' Julia said firmly. Her eyes were shining again with eagerness. "Oh, Deverel! I know we'll find out the truth. You will see that Selby didn't do it.''

"I thought you were firmly convinced that I already knew Selby didn't do it—because I was the one who did.'' He looked at her a little quizzically.

"Oh.'' Julia felt herself blushing. She could not meet his eyes. "I—I am not so sure anymore.''

"I am very glad to hear that.'' Deverel's first instinct was to reach out and pull her into his arms, but he resisted the impulse. Just because Julia was beginning to have doubts about his guilt did not mean that she wanted him to touch her.

They stood for a moment awkwardly. Then Julia

turned and gathered up her letters, starting toward the door. She stopped and looked back at him.

"Thank you," she said softly.

Deverel raised his brows. "For what?"

"For helping me. For going to London and making the agent let me look at the letters. I have tried, you see, and he would not allow me."

There was a glow of gratitude in her eyes that Deverel found did odd things to his chest. "You're welcome. I am not truly an ogre."

She started once again to leave, but turned back. Not looking at him, she said in a rush, "I hope, too, that someday you will forgive me—for what I did to you. It was my fault that you had to marry me. I shall regret it every day of my life."

Deverel stiffened, the warmth that had been ignited by her earlier words suddenly dying. "Pray, do not dwell on it."

His voice was as icy as a mountain spring, and Julia was miserably aware that he had not said that he forgave her. He would, she thought, probably hate her forever. She nodded, unable to look at him, and left the room.

Two days later, they left for London with Phoebe and Geoffrey. Julia rode in the carriage with Phoebe and Geoffrey, and Deverel accompanied them on horseback, pleasing Gilbert and saving the rest of them much grief by taking the boy up on his horse in front of him, where he suffered no travel sickness.

When they reached London, it was an odd experience for Julia when Phoebe's carriage left her and Deverel at his house, then trundled on to the Armiger home without her. She was all alone with him now, she realized as they walked through the front door. Before there had

been Lady Stonehaven and the others with them, and it
had seemed more as if she were visiting than married.
There was no getting around it here, however. The butler
who hurried to greet Stonehaven had obviously been told
that Deverel was bringing home his bride, for he bowed
and welcomed Julia as Lady Stonehaven. The other servants lined up, as well, to be introduced to her, and Julia
greeted each of them with a smile, hoping that she would
remember as least some of their names.

Afterward, the butler escorted them upstairs into the
master bedroom, where a beautiful crystal vase filled
with flowers greeted them. It was a lovely room, spacious and well-furnished. Julia assured the waiting butler
that everything was lovely, indeed, but all the while the
pit of her stomach had turned to ice. Obviously Deverel
had not informed them that they should prepare two bedchambers.

When the butler had bowed out, closing the door and
leaving them alone, Julia turned toward Deverel. Her
fingers were clasped tightly together. She wasn't sure
exactly what feeling gripped her: anger, fear, excitement.... No, surely it was not that. It was distress that
she felt; it had to be.

"I am sorry," Deverel said stiffly, interpreting her
look as alarm. "I forgot to tell them to prepare an extra
bedroom. It—I—there is no connecting chamber with
this one. They would not have thought..."

His voice trailed off, and Julia realized with astonishment that he was embarrassed. He did not want the servants to know that though he had taken a bride, he was
sleeping alone. In the country house, with their connected bedrooms, it had not seemed so strange.

"I see."

"It will have to do for tonight," he said. "I shall sleep on the couch. You needn't worry."

Julia was not about to tell him that the emotion she had felt had not been worry.

Accustomed to country hours, they had an early supper, and afterward they sat together in the informal sitting room. Julia had thought that the evening would be unbearably stiff and awkward, the two of them trapped alone together. However, Deverel began to talk about Gilbert and his progress on his pony, and they soon had a lively conversation going about their own early experiences riding. As both of them had enjoyed riding all their lives, they found it easy to talk and even laugh. It didn't become awkward until late in the evening, when Julia stifled a yawn and Deverel said casually that it must be time for bed.

Suddenly the air was charged with meaning. Julia felt heat rising up her throat, and Deverel glanced away from her. "I—uh, that is, if you are ready to retire, I believe that I shall go to my study and, um, have a brandy."

"That sounds fine. I find I am somewhat sleepy." Julia could not keep her voice from sounding stilted.

Deverel nodded, rising as she stood up and left the room. She went upstairs and dressed for bed, a shy upstairs maid helping her with her dress and hair.

"'Cor, you have beautiful hair, my lady," she sighed, taking up the brush and beginning to run it through Julia's hair. "Like fire, it is, and so soft."

Julia remembered when she had taken her hair down in the carriage that night when they were driving to Kent...how Deverel had thrust his fingers into the heavy mass, murmuring at its lush softness.

"Thank you," she said abruptly, taking the brush. It was dangerous to think of such things.

The maid curtsied and left, and Julia brushed her hair briskly, pacing as she did so. She reminded herself that it did not matter how much Deverel had once wanted her. The fact of the matter was that now he had no passion for her. He had told her that he would not sleep with her. And, of course, that was what she wanted, too.

Impatient with her own thoughts, Julia put down her brush and climbed into bed. However, she found it difficult to sleep, and she was still awake when the door opened quietly and Deverel entered the room. His movements were soft, but she could not help but be aware of them. She listened as he took off his clothes, her mind full of vivid, disturbing images. She tried not to think about Deverel removing his shirt, or what his chest and arms looked like bare, or how he had felt lying against her that night at the inn. However, it seemed as if the harder she tried, the more she thought about him, and her mind kept her awake until long after he had lain down on the sofa. She waited, listening to his breathing as it slipped into the regular rhythm of sleep. It was vastly irritating that he could go to sleep so calmly and quickly, while she was still tossing and turning.

She did at last fall asleep, but almost as soon as she did so, she began to dream. Her dreams were dark and sensual.

She was walking through a meadow, and every sense was unusually alive. The grass was soft and springy beneath her feet, the breeze warm on her skin. She could smell the scent of flowers on the air. It was evening, and there was only a faint glow of sun left on the horizon. Her loins were heavy and warm. She realized without much surprise that she wore no clothing. She could feel the night air over every inch of skin. But she was not embarrassed. It seemed natural, just as it was perfectly normal a moment later when Deverel was suddenly beside her in her dream.

She stopped walking, and Deverel began to caress her skin. He kissed her cheeks and eyes and neck and ears, his mouth traveling over her languidly. Her whole body surged with desire, and she arched up against him, aching for his touch. Then his hands began to move on her, and she was lost in a swirl of pleasure.

Deverel came awake abruptly. He sat up, looking around him, puzzled. Then the noise came, a low, muffled sound from the bed, and he knew that must have been what had awakened him. He lay still, listening. He heard Julia moving in the bed, tossing and turning; then a groan came from her.

He thought she must be sick or having a nightmare, so he got up and walked across the floor to the side of her bed, lighting a candle to help him see. He stood for a moment, looking down at her.

Julia had thrown off all her covers in the course of her tossing and turning, and her nightgown had ridden up to her thighs, exposing the white expanse of her long legs. She twitched, and her breasts bobbed beneath her white gown, the darker nipples visible through the thin cloth. The buds were hard and small, thrusting against the material. His gaze moved upward.

She turned her head, and her tongue stole out to lick her lips. Her mouth was full and moist, slightly pouting, and there was a certain slackness to her features. She moaned again, one hand going to her stomach and moving over her own body in a caressing way.

Deverel's throat went dry. She was not having a nightmare. She was obviously in the grip of a passionate dream. He watched as expressions of desire flitted across her features. She moved and twitched, and her hand caressed first her breast, then her stomach, a faint frown of frustration forming on her face.

Deverel watched, his own passion welling up inside him, as her breath came faster, her breasts rising and falling. A faint sheen of sweat formed on her skin, giving her flesh a golden glow in the candlelight. She writhed, her hips churning, and let out a breathy noise that was part gasp, part groan. Deverel felt as if he were on fire, watching. He ached to touch her, but some remnant of good sense kept him from doing so.

She murmured a word. He thought it was his name, but he could not be sure if she had said "Dev" or if it was merely wishful thinking. He swallowed, his hands curling into fists, as if to keep himself from caressing her. She gave a little gasp, then another, and her body tightened all over. She let out a long, low groan and gradually relaxed.

He knew that Julia had reached a peak of pleasure. He sank his teeth into his lower lip to stifle his own groan. Never in his life had he wanted anyone as he wanted her now. Yet he knew that to take her here, vulnerable in her sleep, after he had sworn to her that she was safe from his advances, would be the act of a scoundrel. She would hate him, he thought, if she was brought out of sleep by his falling on her like a ravenous animal.

He stood for another long moment, fighting for control, then turned and walked slowly back to his sleepless couch.

Julia awoke feeling languid and warm. There was an odd, melting feeling between her legs, not quite an ache, yet something that was not entirely satisfied, either. Her nerves seemed unusually sensitive all over her body, as if she could feel the very air moving across her skin. She got out of bed and rang for a maid to help her dress. She noticed that Deverel had gone, and with him all indications that anyone had spent the night on the couch instead of in bed.

When she was dressed, she wandered downstairs to the breakfast room, where she found Deverel sitting, reading the newspaper over a cup of coffee. He looked up and saw her, and for an instant, a hot flame glowed in his eyes. "Julia."

A shiver ran through Julia, and suddenly she remembered her dream of the night before. Deverel had been caressing her, and she had been completely awash in pleasure. She remembered, too, that final jolt of intense feeling. The soft, warm, yearning feeling between her legs increased.

"Deverel." She was sure that she was blushing. What would he think if he knew what she had dreamed?

He stood up and pulled out a chair for her, and Julia forced herself to walk across the room and sit down. As she sat down, she thought she felt his fingertips slide up her bare arm in a soft caress, but when she glanced up quickly, his face was blank, giving nothing away.

"Coffee?" he asked.

She nodded mutely, and he poured her a cup.

"Would you like some breakfast?" he asked, reaching for the bell cord.

"Just toast." She knew there was no way she could force down a whole breakfast, not with the sudden turmoil in her stomach. She took a piece from the serving rack and began to spread it with marmalade.

"Did you sleep well last night?" Deverel asked, and Julia's head snapped up.

He couldn't know, she reminded herself. He was merely being polite. "Yes. I—it was fine."

"Good. I am glad that you found the bed... agreeable."

"Very." The toast tasted dry as dust, and Julia had trouble swallowing. The warmth between her legs was growing, beginning to throb. She shifted restlessly on her chair, trying to ease the sensation.

She realized what she was doing, and she stopped. She glanced at him surreptitiously and saw that he was watching her, a faint smile upon his lips. *He knew!* She could not imagine how, but somehow he knew what she had dreamed!

"Uh..." Heat spread up her throat and into her face. Julia shoved back her chair abruptly and jumped up. "I—I—excuse me."

She turned and started toward the door, but Deverel was after her in an instant. He reached the door just before she did and closed it, holding his arm across it like a bar.

"No, wait. Don't go." His voice was low and almost breathless. His eyes bored into hers. "I am a fool to tease you. I'm..." He looked away, as if searching for a word, and finally said, "Jealous. I awoke last night. I heard you."

Julia made a choked noise of embarrassment and pressed her palms to her hot cheeks. She looked down.

"No. Don't look away from me." Deverel put his forefinger under her chin and tilted it up until she was forced to look at him. Julia trembled at the heat in his eyes, almost a physical caress. "I was envious—of nothing. Of a dream!"

He opened his hand beneath her chin and slid it gently down her throat. "I wanted to have, even for a moment," he said huskily, "what you gave to someone in your sleep." He cupped the back of her neck with his hand, his thumb gently stroking the side of her throat.

Shivers streaked through her at his light touch, shooting from where his thumb slid over her skin all through her body and finally gathering, hotly, in her loins. "Deverel…"

"I thought I heard you say my name last night. Did you?" His hand moved up, caressing the side of her face. His thumb traced the line of her lips. "Was I the man who—"

"No! Please don't ask me this. I can't—" The caress of his fingers was distracting her so that Julia could hardly think. She was aware of an almost overpowering impulse to open her lips and take his thumb between them.

He must have seen something of the thought in her eyes, for his skin suddenly flushed with heat, and his eyes darkened. "I want you, Julia," he said baldly. "Are we to spend the rest of our lives without pleasure?"

"You swore you would not—"

"I said I would not demand my rights as your husband," he countered. "I did not promise that I wouldn't ask."

He bent and brushed his lips across hers. The touch was light and velvety and made Julia tremble. She remembered the taste of his mouth on hers, the pressure, the texture, and she ached to feel them again.

"Well, Julia?" he breathed. "What is it to be?" His fingers trailed down onto her throat, then still lower, until they reached the neckline of her dress. "I have discovered that pride makes a lonely bedfellow."

He bent and kissed the side of her neck softly. Julia

could not hold back a soft moan. She could feel her nipples hardening, yearning for his touch.

"But you hate me," she murmured.

"I want you."

"Oh..." She brought her hands up to her temples. "I'm so confused."

"Let me help you clear your mind," he offered, and his lips fastened on hers.

17

He kissed her gently, almost teasingly, at first. His tongue slid along the crack between her lips, parting them and slipping inside. He explored her mouth tenderly, caressing, advancing, retreating. Julia sagged against him, lost in the pleasure of his kiss. One of his arms went around her back, holding her up. The other hand slid up between them, cupping her breast through her dress. Her breasts were full and aching, her nipples pointing.

His fingers fumbled at the buttons of her dress, ripping one or two off in his haste. The line of buttons seemed interminable, and when finally he reached the end of them, he let out a growl and yanked down the bodice of her dress. Julia gasped at the ferociousness of the movement, but her body flooded with heat, too. He jerked the ribbon tied in a neat bow at the top of her chemise, and the garment sagged open. He picked her up, his arms going under her buttocks and lifting her high, and nuzzled her breasts, shoving the top of the chemise down and exposing her breasts to his predatory mouth.

He fastened on one plump orb, suckling and teasing the nipple with his tongue until it hardened into a tight bud. Julia could not hold back the noises of pleasure that rose in her throat, and they spurred Deverel's passion. He carried her to the table and laid her down upon its polished length, shoving their dishes aside.

"Deverel!" Julia cried out softly, a trifle shocked. "On the table?"

He bent over her, his dark eyes glittering fiercely. "I intend to feast on you," he told her, and bent once again to his task.

He took her nipple in his mouth, stroking, licking, sucking, until Julia was writhing with pleasure, unable to hold back her moans. Deverel was wild with desire, barely holding on to a single thread of control. He shoved up her skirts and caressed her legs, his hand coming to rest at last upon the hot, damp center of her desire. Julia gasped and jerked when he touched her there, both startled and thoroughly aroused.

He rubbed his fingers against her through the material of her undergarments, and she flooded with moisture at his touch. The pent-up desire of the past few weeks was now surging through him, wild and almost out of control. He pulled down her stockings and pantalets, and his fingers touched her wet, bare flesh. A shudder shook him. For a moment he stood still, fighting for control. Then he began to explore her, his fingers sliding over the slick folds of flesh. Julia whimpered under his ministrations, her hips moving instinctively.

Deverel groaned. He unbuttoned his trousers, tearing at them, and his swollen member sprang forth, engorged and throbbing. He put his hands beneath Julia's hips, pulling her to the edge of the table and lifting her. Slowly, as gently as he was capable of in his raw desire, he began to ease himself inside her. Julia stiffened at the strange sensation, but he caressed her, murmuring reassuringly, and she relaxed. He met with the resistance of her virginity and pushed carefully on until, with a surge, he was inside her. She was gloriously tight, encasing his stiff manhood completely. He moved slowly in and out, luxuriating in the pleasure he had hungered for for so long. Julia clutched at him, saying his name with urgency, and suddenly she shuddered, clamping around him, the pleasure rippling in waves through her. He cried out hoarsely then, unable to hold back any longer, and toppled headlong into the dark vortex of passion.

Slowly Deverel emerged from the red haze of lust. He felt Julia's soft body beneath his, heard her quiet breathing, felt the warmth of her skin. An utter peace filled him, the surcease of hunger and something more, a fulfillment that he had never quite experienced before. Then it sank in on him what he had done. He stiffened in horror, replaying the scene in his mind.

In his mad desire for Julia, he had taken her like an animal, throwing her down right here on the table and having his way with her. She was a virginal, inexperienced girl, and he had treated her like a doxy. He had not moved slowly and gently, had not introduced her to the act of sex gradually and with loving care. No, he had taken her fast and hard, driven by his lust.

Julia had not protested or fought him, but he could hardly count that as willing participation. The fact was, he knew, that he had been so on fire for her that he had broken his promise. From the moment he kissed her, he had been ruled by his loins. It should have come as no surprise; it had been that way with Julia from the first.

Shame swept through Deverel. He was not sure how he could face her. Julia must hate him now. She must think him a callous, rutting cad. After his assurances that he would not demand his marital rights, he had done so in the most basic, peremptory way. He had been swept away by his hunger—and he knew that Julia would not trust him again.

He rose from her, unable to bring himself to look her in the eye. "I am sorry," he said stiffly, fumbling at his clothes. "Eternally sorry. I pray you will accept my apologies. This was a mistake—I never meant for it to happen. It will not happen again, I promise you."

Julia stared up at him, not quite able to take in his words. A few minutes earlier Deverel had filled her with a joy so intense she had scarcely been able to breathe. She had never felt anything like it, and she had known in that instant what she had been trying to deny for days: she loved him. No matter what had happened between them before, despite all her protestations to the contrary, she had fallen in love with Deverel. She had lain there in bliss—until he stood up and spoke, his voice clipped, hard and full of regret.

Unlike her, there had been no joy for Deverel in their lovemaking, she realized. Apparently he had made love to her almost against his will, driven by a passion that had overwhelmed his good reason. He had not really wanted to make love to her, to be her husband in every sense. It was just that his lust had taken over.

"I will tell the servants to make up another bedroom for you," he continued, still half-turned from her.

Julia sat up, choking back tears, unable to speak. She was embarrassed now at her nakedness, and she swiftly began to adjust her clothing, not looking toward Deverel. How could something that had been so wonderful for her only have made Deverel angry and guilty? Did he despise her that much?

He turned and left the room.

Deverel was true to his word. The servants made up one of the other bedchambers for Julia and moved her clothes into it. Deverel left the house and stayed away most of the day, not coming home until late in the evening.

Julia spent a lonely, miserable day, drifting from one room to another, trying to read, then to sew, and finally returning to her letters from Selby and going over all the differences between the handwriting in them and in the suicide note. She ate dinner alone at the massive table, uncomfortably aware of what the servants must be thinking—a bride left alone only a few days after the wedding, her things ordered out of the master bedroom and into a separate chamber. It was obvious to everyone, she was sure, how little her husband favored her.

The next morning Julia had breakfast brought to her on a tray, not feeling capable of facing Deverel at the breakfast table again. It would, she thought, put a cap on her misery. However, one of the servants brought a note to her with the tray. It was from Deverel, and it asked her if she wished to go to the offices of the trust's agent this morning. Julia gulped down her breakfast and hurried to get ready, giving herself a stern lecture on what they had come to London to accomplish. Taking Selby's old letters and the suicide note in hand, she went downstairs to join Deverel.

He greeted her with a formal politeness, but Julia was painfully aware of the way he avoided looking at her or touching her. He was as courteous and as cold as if they were strangers. They went out to the carriage and rode to the agent's office, neither of them speaking, as far apart on their facing seats as if they had been in different counties.

When the carriage came to a stop, Deverel got out,

reaching up to help Julia down. Julia placed her hand in his, and even through her gloves, she felt a tingle of awareness. She glanced at him and saw for just a fraction of a second a glimmer of the same awareness in his eyes.

As soon as they stepped into Henry Carter's outer office, the agent came bustling out of his inner office, beaming. "Ah, Lord Stonehaven! What a pleasant surprise! We had not expected to see you." He cast a curious glance at Julia.

"No. We came on the spur of the moment. Allow me to introduce my wife to you, Mr. Carter. My dear, this is Henry Carter, who has looked after the interests of Thomas's trust all these years. Mr. Carter, Lady Stonehaven."

"Lady Stonehaven! What an honor! What a privilege!" He went on at some length, exclaiming over Deverel's marriage and assuring them that he was delighted to have them in his office. It was some time before Deverel could draw him away from the subject to the one that interested them.

Finally, breaking into one of the agent's lengthy compliments, he said, "Mr. Carter, we came to look at the letters from Sir Selby Armiger."

The agent's face hardened. "The embezzlement letters, my lord?"

"Exactly."

"But, my lord, I—need we bring up that painful episode again?"

Deverel raised one lazy eyebrow. "Are you saying that you don't wish to show me the letters?"

"No, my lord. Of course not," the man began to babble. "I mean, after all, you have a perfect right to see them, needless to say." He turned and snapped his fingers at one of the young men who was seated at the two

desks in the outer room. "You, there. Teasely. Get out
the St. Leger trust letters, the…embezzlement ones." He
swallowed, as if the very words choked him.

The young man whom he had addressed rose and went
to one of the cabinets against the wall.

"Mr. Teasely can handle all your questions about the
trust, get you whatever you need," Carter told them, his
smile stiff. "And, of course, if you have any further
questions, I shall be in my office."

He bowed to them and retired to his office. Julia
glanced up at Deverel, and he bent to whisper, "Mr.
Carter takes the embezzlement very personally. He is
afraid that we will decide he mismanaged the trust, that
he shouldn't have sent the money, despite the instructions in the letters."

"Would you like to look at these at a table?" Teasely
approached them, several sheets of paper in his hand.
He was tall and spare, with a permanently hunched-over
stance from sitting reading papers for long periods at a
time.

"That would be very nice, thank you."

Teasely escorted them into another room, smaller than
the outer room and containing a single long table with
some rather uncomfortable-looking chairs. Teasely laid
the letters down on the table.

"Is there anything else I can get you?" he asked politely.

"Not at the moment. By the way, are you the one
who dealt with these letters?"

The man stiffened. "I opened the letters and read
them, of course. As it was a request for money, naturally
I showed them to Mr. Carter for his approval."

"Of course." Deverel smiled at him. "I am sure that
you did nothing wrong. I was merely curious as to the

actual handling of the money—how it was sent to this 'Jack Fletcher,' for example.''

Teasely's brow cleared. "Oh. I see. There was an address in the first letter." He pointed to the page on the top. "We sent it there."

"Did you personally carry it there?"

"No. I sent it by a messenger. That is our custom."

"I see. And who received it? Are there any written records?"

He looked blank. "I, uh, I can check, my lord."

"Thank you. I would appreciate it."

As soon as he bowed out of the room, closing the door after him, Julia turned to Deverel eagerly. "How clever of you! If we can find the person who actually took possession of the money—"

Deverel frowned. "I should have checked this before. I don't know why I didn't think of it. We had ample proof, but it is a loose end I should have tied up."

"We will now." Julia sat down at the table and began to read the letters.

She could not read them without her heart sinking. The writing was so much like Selby's, and that name, Jack Fletcher... By the time she finished reading them, she felt quite dispirited. However, she refused to let herself get discouraged, and she took out the letters she had brought and placed them side by side with the agent's letters. She and Deverel studied them carefully.

He was leaning over her shoulder, so close that he almost touched her, and Julia was unbearably aware of him. She could not keep from thinking of their love-making the morning before, of the warmth and smell and taste of him, and it made her tremble. She forced herself to concentrate on the pages before her.

"Look. There is that loop on the *y*." She pointed to

the first request for money. "It's here, in every one, just like the suicide note. And there is the same regularity in spacing and capitals." She turned her head to find Deverel's face only inches from hers.

Deverel straightened and stepped back, clearing his throat. "That's hardly odd. They were written by the same person."

"But not the same person who wrote these letters." Julia held up the two old letters Selby had sent to her. "They all differ in the same way from Selby's hand."

Deverel frowned. "The differences are so slight… Julia, I do not see how you can realistically say that this is proof that Selby did not write them."

Teasely returned, carrying four pieces of paper. "Here are the receipts, my lord, which the messenger brought back to us."

Deverel took the papers from him, and he and Julia bent over them. The top one was signed "Jack Fletcher."

"Look!" Julia pointed at the signature, her finger trembling a little with excitement. "That is not Selby's writing. It doesn't look at all like these others."

"No. You're right." Deverel's frown deepened. He turned to the next receipt, the signature of which was exactly the same. The next two, however, were in a different, feminine, hand and read "Mrs. Jack Fletcher."

"Mrs.!" Julia exclaimed. She felt confused and a little sick.

Deverel glanced at her, and she knew that his thoughts had flown immediately to the mistress mentioned in Selby's "suicide" note.

"No," she said firmly. "No."

"Thank you," Deverel told the clerk. "Let me write down this address, and you may have them back."

He quickly did as he said and handed all the papers back to Teasely. As soon as Teasely left the room, he turned to Julia.

"Selby did not have a mistress!" Julia said hotly.

"Obviously a woman signed for some of the money."

"Well, it was not Selby's mistress. Selby didn't steal the money."

"You know, I think it's time we looked into this business of the mistress. Let's call on Fitzmaurice and Varian, find out if they knew about the woman. If there was such a woman, and we can find out her name, we might be able learn the truth."

They went first to the major's apartments. Fitzmaurice jumped up when the butler showed them in, looking rather surprised.

"Deverel! And Julia—Lady Stonehaven, I should say."

"No, please, I am still Julia."

"Sit down. 'Fraid the place isn't too neat." He took a look around the room as if seeing it for the first time. "Not used to receiving ladies, you know."

"Don't worry. It's perfectly all right."

The three of them sat down and looked at each other. Finally Fitzmaurice said, "Well. I must say, I didn't expect to see you any time soon. Going to Buckinghamshire, weren't you?"

"We had to tell Mother the news, of course," Deverel said smoothly. "But we had no intention of making it a long visit. Had to return to London, of course."

"Of course." Fitzmaurice did not understand the reasoning, but he was quite used to not understanding things, so he accepted it without question.

"Fitz," Julia began, leaning forward a little. "We came to ask you about Selby."

"Selby?" He looked startled. "What about Selby? You mean about those letters I signed? I don't remember doing it, you know. But that don't mean much. Selby often gave me a letter to co-sign, and I always signed them. He knew much more about the trust and Thomas than I did." He shrugged. "I never read any of the letters he gave me to sign. Don't understand most of those things, anyway, you know."

Julia nodded. "Yes, but that isn't really what we wanted to ask you. We wanted to know if Selby had a mistress."

Fitzmaurice looked so shocked that Deverel had to stifle a laugh. "Julia, must you be so blunt?" he murmured.

"I don't know any polite way to say it," she retorted.

"I suppose you are right." Deverel looked at the other man. "Well, Fitz? Did you know Selby to keep a mistress? I mean, in later years."

The major's face flushed. "Dev, old boy...hardly the thing to discuss in front of the man's sister."

"No doubt," Julia interjected crisply. "But it is the sister who wants to know. Please, Fitz, forget about propriety and tell us the truth. It is desperately important to me. I don't want any lies to soothe me."

"I...ah—" Fitzmaurice cast a last beseeching glance at Stonehaven, but received no support there. Finally he said, "Well, yes, I had heard rumors about it."

"What sort of rumors?"

"Only that he was, um, keeping a light-o'-love in a house in town, and that he used to come to visit her regularly."

"Did you ever see him with her?"

"No." He looked vaguely indignant, as if she had accused him of doing something improper. "Never."

"Did he ever say anything to you about her?" Deverel asked.

"No. I'm not the man you'd tell something like that if you wanted it kept secret. Never have been good at that sort of thing."

Julia knew that that was certainly true.

Deverel asked, "Do you remember when you heard the rumors? Was it while Selby was still alive?"

Fitzmaurice looked surprised. "Why, I don't know. I never thought about it." He wrinkled his brow, concentrating. "I'm not sure. I think—you know, I believe it was after he died, because I remember thinking that we shouldn't be speaking ill of the dead."

"We?" Julia perked up. "Do you remember who you were talking to?"

"Mmm. No. I can't remember the exact time I first heard it. Maybe it was at my club."

It was pointless trying to get any more details from him. The major had stretched his intellectual limits to the maximum. So they turned to Varian, whose family's town house was only a few blocks away from Fitzmaurice's quarters. They walked along, talking about their conversation with Fitzmaurice, the constraints they had felt earlier largely gone. As they stepped onto a cobblestoned street, Julia's ankle twisted, and she lurched to one side. Deverel grabbed her arm. Suddenly both of them were very aware of the physical touch. Deverel stiffened, his hand falling away. The moment of comfortable companionability was gone. All Julia could think of was his hands on her body, the hard table beneath her, the way it had felt when he came inside her, filling her completely.

She bit her lower lip and looked anywhere but at him. They were silent the rest of the way to Varian's.

Varian seemed equally puzzled to see them in London again, but he was too polite to quiz them about it. Nor could he remember signing the letter that had borne his signature.

"Which is odd," he added, "because generally I did read the letters. I'd ask Selby about it if it was something I wasn't sure of." He looked at Deverel. "Didn't you?"

"Yes, that was customarily what I did. I think he usually discussed them with you, but the ones that he sent to me, I read before I signed."

"I would have remembered a letter like that," Varian added. "Because of the Jack Fletcher thing in it, you know. I never understood why he used that name. It made it so obvious, don't you think?"

"That is because he didn't write the letters," Julia was quick to respond. "I have been trying to tell everybody. Selby wasn't stupid. He would not have used that silly name if he had actually stolen the money."

"The other thing we were wondering about," Deverel continued, ignoring Julia's interjection, "was the matter of Selby's mistress."

"Dev!" Varian cut a sideways look at Julia.

"Don't go all prudish on me, Varian. I read the suicide note."

Varian's brows went up. "You let her read that?" he said in an accusing way to Deverel.

"I insisted," Julia stated. "And I'm very glad I did, because I could tell that the handwriting wasn't precisely the same as Selby's."

Varian's jaw dropped. "No! You're bamming me."

"Not a bit."

"There are slight differences," Deverel said temperately.

"I say." Varian looked thunderstruck.

"So I read about the mistress. But I don't believe it. That's why I wanted to know if you had ever heard of this mistress before you read the suicide note? Did you ever see her, or did Selby talk about her?"

"No. Selby never talked about other women. He was head over heels crazy for Phoebe, had been since the first time he saw her. That's why I was astonished when he confessed that he had been keeping a mistress. In that letter, I mean."

"So the note was the first time you'd heard of this mistress?"

He nodded. "I did hear rumors later, though. I heard she was a stunner—blond, a ballet dancer, I believe. I may even have heard her name, but I can't remember it."

"Who told you those things?"

"Who?" He shifted in his chair. "Let's see. I...um..." He made a vague gesture with his hand. "I don't remember exactly where I heard any one particular thing, or who told me. It was just...around."

Later, when they had finished talking with Varian and were strolling back to their house, Julia said, "Did it seem to you that Varian was telling the truth about who told him the rumor?"

Deverel glanced down at her. "So he looked suspicious to you, too?"

"You mean you thought that he was not quite telling the truth?" Julia felt unaccountably pleased that he agreed with her.

Deverel nodded. "He looked uncomfortable when he answered that question. The rest of the time he seemed quite open."

"I wonder why?"

"I don't know. Perhaps he heard it someplace that he would be embarrassed to mention in front of a lady."

"Like in a brothel."

He let out a bark of laughter. "Really, Julia, you say the most outrageous things."

"I know. Phoebe thinks it's because I never had a coming out." They continued walking for a few more minutes. "Or perhaps it's because of *who* told him."

"What? Oh. Varian. Yes, I suppose that might be it."

They rounded the corner and started up the street on which Deverel's house lay. They had almost reached the house when a carriage came rolling around the corner at a fast clip. They glanced toward it. The driver, in a cape and with a hat pulled low on his head, lashed the horses, and the team broke into a hard run, hurtling down the street straight toward Julia and Deverel.

18

Julia froze. Deverel grabbed her arm and jerked her to the side, and they fell in a tumble at the foot of the steps to the Stonehaven house. The carriage whipped past them so closely that Julia could feel the breeze of its passing on her skin. It rattled off down the street, turned the corner and was gone.

"Are you all right?" Deverel asked anxiously, sitting up and bending over her.

"Yes. I—I think so." Julia sat up carefully. She felt as if the entire right side of her body was numb from hitting the hard stones. "That driver must have been mad!"

"Or drunk."

Both of them turned to look in the direction in which the carriage had gone, but it was out of sight. Deverel stood up, picking Julia up with him. She shook out her skirts and adjusted her hat. There was a streak of dirt down one side of her dress, and she began to brush at it. Deverel brushed the dirt from her sleeve, and his hand grazed her bare arm. He pulled his hand away immediately and stepped back.

"Well," he said stiffly. "Thank God we weren't hurt."

Julia nodded, distracted by his touch. They went inside. Deverel was frowning.

"You know," he said slowly. "That almost seemed purposeful, didn't it?"

Julia turned to look at him. "What do you mean?"

"The way he ran those horses straight at us."

Alarm rose in Julia's chest. "You think he meant to hit us?"

"I don't know. It seems absurd. But this is the second time that you have almost been killed."

"The third, actually," Julia murmured, her throat tightening.

"What? What are you talking about?"

"This probably has nothing to do with it, but earlier, after Phoebe and I had come to London, someone broke into my room. It woke me up, and I fought him and screamed, and Phoebe and everyone came running. We assumed it was a burglar, of course. But it *was* odd that he climbed a tree to enter through my window when there was much easier access downstairs. Not to mention the fact that the safe and the silver and most of the expensive things were on the ground floor."

Deverel stared at her for a long moment, then turned away, shaking his head. "This is madness. Why would anyone try to harm you?"

"Because I am trying to find out who really embezzled the money?" Julia suggested.

He turned back to her, and Julia could see that he was shaken. "Selby embezzled it. Nothing we have found has proven anything else."

"Maybe someone isn't as sure of Selby's guilt as

you," Julia suggested. "Someone who has good cause to know that Selby did *not* do it."

She could see that her remark had hit home. They did not discuss the matter any longer, but all through dinner, Deverel was distracted. When they were finished with the meal, he stood up abruptly.

"I'm going to the club," he announced almost grimly.

"All right." Julia did not look forward to an evening by herself, but she was not about to ask him to stay with her. It had been obvious for two days now that the last thing Deverel wanted was her company.

"I want to ask around, see if anyone else knows anything about this woman." He turned and fixed her with a stern gaze. "I don't want you going anywhere."

Julia stared at him. "Whatever are you talking about? Where would I go?"

"I don't know. But I want you to stay inside the house tonight. I—I'm not sure what to think, but too many strange things have been happening."

Julia nodded, warmed by his words. He might not want to make love to her, or even be around her, but at least he was worried about her.

Deverel hesitated. He had never felt so confused in his life. He ached to pull Julia into his arms and squeeze her to him. The last thing he wanted to do right now was leave the house. He wanted to stay here and make sure that nothing happened to her. But he also knew where it would lead if he were to spend the evening in the same room with her. Before long, he would be pawing her, despite all his good intentions, despite his promises, just as he had yesterday morning. And he could not allow that to happen a second time.

The past two days had been hellish. He had avoided Julia assiduously all the day before, not just from embarrassment at his low behavior, but also because all his thoughts centered around making love to her again. Their lovemaking had not assuaged his lust. Indeed, it had seemed only to increase it. He had had to be around her today, for he could not go on ignoring what they had come to London for, but every moment with her had been pure torture. All through their time together, he had been aware of a low, thrumming pulse in his body, a supreme sensitivity all over his skin, so that the slightest touch made his nerves leap with sizzling anticipation.

He was determined that he would not allow his body to overcome his reason again. The only way he could do that, it seemed, was to avoid Julia. He wondered how he was going to manage that feat for the rest of their lives.

"You will be quite safe here," he told her, reassuring himself more than her. There was no real reason for him to stay here instead of going out. It was simple weakness on his part.

"I know."

Deverel heard the colorless tone of her voice, and he felt sure that Julia would be glad to be rid of him. It could not be comfortable, he reminded himself, to be sitting there waiting, wondering if he was going to lose control of himself again. With a stiff bow, he took his leave.

Julia sat up in bed. She had retired some time ago, but she had not been able to go to sleep. Instead, she had lain in bed, listening for the sound of Deverel's return. She had spent the evening reading, but, unable to concentrate, her thoughts had strayed first to the accident—*was it possible that someone could actually be trying to hurt her?*—then to Deverel.

She must be, she supposed, a thoroughly wanton woman. All day, throughout the investigations they had conducted, she had been distracted by Deverel's physical presence. Every sense had been attuned to him. She had not looked at him without feeling a rush of desire; the sound of his voice sent tingles through her. Even now, she felt jangly, unable to sleep or think of anything but his kisses and caresses, a low-level heat running through her body. There was a tender ache between her legs, and she could not keep from remembering the supremely satisfying way in which Deverel had filled it.

Did every woman feel this way about her husband…even when he didn't want her? But, no, it wasn't that he did not want her. Inexperienced as she was, Julia was certain that Deverel had been desirous of her the morning before. The problem was that he disliked her and disliked his hunger for her. He apparently felt as if he had betrayed himself by giving in to that lust.

She heard the sound of footsteps in the hall and waited, tensing. Deverel must be home from his club. Would he come to her and tell her what he had found out? He walked past her door, and it seemed to her that the steps hesitated for just a moment as he went by. Then there was the sound of his door opening and closing behind him. Julia flopped back in her bed. He wasn't coming, even to tell her what he had learned.

She lay there for a moment, listening to the faint sounds Deverel made in his room next door. She pictured him walking about, taking off his cuff links and shirt studs, beginning to undress. Julia bit her lip and rolled over, burying her face in her pillow. It was foolish to think this way. It was only stirring her up more!

But she could not stop. She kept imagining Deverel's shirt falling open, exposing a wide swath of chest. She thought of sliding that shirt off his body, revealing his bare arms, swelling with muscle, his flat stomach.... Julia groaned and threw aside her covers. She hopped out of bed and began to pace. She found herself inexorably drawn to her door, and after a moment's hesitation, she opened it and peered out. Light still shone beneath Deverel's door. He was up. If she went to him...

No. She couldn't do that. It would be too immodest, too bold. But then, she reminded herself, there had been a time when Deverel had not minded her bold behavior. If she enticed him enough, might he not give in to his lust again? She smiled secretively, unconsciously running a hand down her front. If he could be brought to her bed time and again, didn't it follow that his dislike for her would gradually wear away? Surely, she thought, she could bring him to feel, if not love, at least *something* for her.

Quickly she moved down the hall to his door. There she hesitated, not sure she had the nerve. It occurred to her that she had no reason for seeking him out, but then she recalled his purpose in going out this evening. She would ask him about that, as if her curiosity had not let her sleep.

She tapped at the door and opened it immediately afterward, not waiting for an answer. Deverel was standing in front of his dresser, laying the last of his shirt studs upon it, and he turned at her entrance. He had removed his coat and ascot, and his shirt hung open down the front, just as she had imagined it. She could see a wide swath of his chest, smooth and muscled, lightly sprinkled with hair, and her mouth was suddenly dry. The words she had prepared flew straight out of her head.

Deverel started toward her, then stopped.

"I—um, I came to see what you had found out to-night," Julia said.

"Found out?" His eyes ran down her figure, clad in only the white nightgown. With some difficulty, he pulled his gaze back to her face. "Oh. Yes, of course. Not much, I'm afraid. A few men I spoke with had heard the rumors. One thought he had heard she was a ballet dancer. Another thought the name was Bessie or Betsy something. They had heard it at parties, or they couldn't remember where. Everyone was quite vague."

Julia couldn't keep from looking at his chest. She wanted to open up the shirt. She wanted to run her hands all over him. Her heart was racing. "It—it sounds as if none them had actually heard anything directly from Selby."

"No. I think it was all rumors."

Julia nodded. She had no excuse to stay any longer. She cast her mind about for something to keep her there. "Shall I help you with your boots?"

Deverel looked at her blankly. "What?"

Julia pointed to his glossy, tight-fitting boots. "Your valet's not here. I could help you take off your boots."

"All right." His voice sounded a trifle odd, and the skin on his face looked tightly stretched across his bones.

Julia moved closer. "You'll have to sit down."

He sat down on the bed, the nearest place, and Julia bent over, putting her hands on his heel. She began to tug on the boot, working it down. Her breasts bobbed with her efforts. Bending over as she was, Deverel could see straight down the neck of her gown to the lush blue-veined orbs. He dug his hands into the bedspread.

Julia looked up. "What? Did you say something?"

He shook his head, his lips pressed tightly together. There was a fine sheen of perspiration across his upper

lip. She knew with satisfaction that he was not immune
to her. She returned to working on the boot. When it
finally came off, she set it aside and turned to the other
one. This time she turned her back to him and straddled
his leg, bending down to grasp the boot and pull.

"Julia..." She felt his hand caress her buttocks.

She pulled off the boot and put it down, turning to
face him. Deverel's face was taut with passion, and his
eyes blazed into hers. He reached out and put his hands
on the outsides of her thighs, sliding them up, then
down. With a groan, he wrenched his hands away, ball-
ing them into fists and clamping them against his legs.

"Dammit, Julia, this isn't fair. I told you I
wouldn't—"

"I know," Julia said quickly, "but I have been thinking. About children. I don't want never to have children.
Do you? Wouldn't you like to have an heir?"

He stared at her, swallowing hard. "Are you saying
that you want—that it's all right with you if we...make
love?"

Julia nodded, throwing caution to the winds. "Yes, if
you are willing."

If he rejected her, she would simply have to live with
the humiliation, she told herself. But she had to try her
utmost. She could not let this man slip away from her
into a distant, celibate marriage.

Slowly Deverel stood up, his eyes never leaving Julia's face. "If I am *willing?*" He let out a brief, breathy
laugh.

He started to reach for her, but Julia smiled sensually
and said, "No, this time you aren't going to have all the
fun. I want to touch you." She put her hands on his
chest, between the edges of his shirt.

She felt a tremor run through him. "All right," he breathed. "Anything you want."

Julia smoothed her hands over his skin, exploring the curves of his musculature, following the lines of his ribs, running her fingers down the narrowing trail of hair over his stomach to the top of his trousers. His chest rose and fell rapidly as she covered every inch of his exposed skin. Then she slid his shirt off over his arms and tossed it onto the bed. Her hands went to his arms, exploring them in the same way, and finally she walked around him to caress his back. His skin trembled beneath her touch, and she heard him draw in a sharp breath now and then, but he made no move to stop her, simply stood and let her do what she willed.

She leaned forward and placed her lips against his back, tasting the salt of his skin, feeling the firm pad of muscle beneath it. He let out a low groan. She drew back, but he shook his head.

"No, don't stop. Please...don't stop."

She began to kiss her way down his spine, starting on tiptoe and moving ever lower. Sliding her hands around his waist, she caressed his stomach and chest as she used her mouth on his back. She nipped the flesh with her teeth and soothed it with her lips, tracing lazy patterns on his skin with her tongue, and as she did so, her fingertips found his flat, masculine nipples and began to play with them. She could feel his skin flush with heat, and a soft moan escaped him.

"Do you like this?" she asked, and he let out a breathy chuckle.

"Yes. Oh, yes, I like it."

"Good," Julia said a little smugly. "I like it, too."

She moved back around to his front and began to do the same things to his chest. When her lips closed around one of his nipples, he jerked a little, and his hands dug into her hair. Julia imitated the movement of his own lips yesterday on her nipples, and his breath caught in excitement. She could feel the hard line of his masculinity throbbing and pressing against her, making his arousal clear. It responded wildly to each new thing she did. Julia realized that she wanted to see him, to touch him there, as well.

She pulled back a little, and her hands went to the waistband of his trousers, unbuttoning them. He helped her with great alacrity, shoving the pantaloons down and stepping out of them, and peeling off his socks. He was now naked, and Julia looked him over without shyness, fascinated by the strength and beauty of his body. The sight of him stirred her. Her eyes went to the swollen member that thrust from his body, proof of his desire for her. She had felt its power the other morning, but she had not really seen it. Now she looked at it with a kind of awe, thinking that this had been inside her, filling and satisfying her. Tentatively she reached out and touched the engorged staff, then stroked both her hands along it.

It was obvious from Deverel's reaction that she could not have done anything to arouse him more. He bit his lip, his face tight with concentration, his eyes closed. She caressed him, her hands moving down to his legs and back to his buttocks, stroking and squeezing.

Deverel could hold back no longer. He bent and pulled up her nightgown, lifting it off over her head and revealing her nakedness to his eyes. He caressed her as she did him. His hand slid down her abdomen and between her legs, and he began to move it in a gentle, rhythmical pattern. Julia sighed, her eyes fluttering closed in pleasure. Watching her, desire slammed through Deverel like a fist. He bent and kissed her mouth.

They kissed for what seemed like forever. Heat built up in Julia's loins, fierce and explosive. He picked her up and laid her in his bed. Julia opened her arms, welcoming him as he moved between her legs and came inside her. Inch by delightful inch, he sank deeply into her, until Julia was almost sobbing with desire. She wrapped her arms and legs around him. He bent and kissed her as he began to move within her, with aching slowness at first, stoking the fires of her passion until Julia was writhing beneath him, urging him on. He thrust faster and faster, driving them both into a higher realm where nothing existed except the joining of their bodies. Julia dug her fingers into his back, crying out in longing, and her passion exploded within her. She went taut as the waves of pleasure rippled through her, and Deverel bucked, calling her name hoarsely.

He collapsed upon her, and they lay, still joined, floating together in the blissful afterglow of love.

The world looked much sunnier the next morning, Julia found. She awoke to find Deverel standing before his shaving stand, clad in a dark brocade dressing gown, humming as he slid the razor across his face. The drapes on one window stood open, letting a stream of golden light into the room. Julia stretched like a cat, luxuriating in delicious languor.

As if sensing that she was awake, Deverel turned and smiled. Julia thought she might melt at that smile. "Good morning."

She returned the greeting, a little shy before him, remembering the wild and wanton way she had behaved the night before. She hoped he would not bring it up. To her relief, he did not.

He said only, "I thought that after breakfast this morning we would go to the address where they sent the money."

"Oh, yes," Julia agreed, sitting up in her excitement, remembering to clutch the sheet to her only at the last moment before it slid down her body, revealing her nakedness. She had no idea how appealing she looked, her bright hair tumbling wildly around her shoulders, her shoulders bare above the sheet, and her face still stamped with the relaxed satisfaction of lovemaking.

Deverel could barely restrain himself from going across the room and kissing her. But while Julia's uninhibited and very voluntary lovemaking the night before had convinced him that she was not an unwilling or even passive participant, he was not sure how to act with her. He doubted somehow that she would welcome any demonstration of affection from him.

Julia put on her nightgown, with only a slight embarrassment at being naked before Deverel in broad daylight. She returned to her own room and bathed and dressed, singing as she got ready.

They set out in Stonehaven's carriage soon after they ate breakfast. The address they had been given lay in the East End, in a less-than-savory area, and it took even the experienced coachman, a lifelong resident of London, some time and several stops for directions to finally find it.

The place they sought was a tall, narrow house that advertised Rooms To Let on a sign above its door. Stonehaven got out and extended a hand to Julia, glancing around him carefully. This looked to him to be the sort of place where one was likely to be lightened of one's purse. He knocked peremptorily on the door, and some time later, after he had repeated his knock twice, the door swung open to reveal a slatternly, middle-aged woman.

"Orright, orright, 'old yer 'orses, would ya?" she whined. Her eyes widened when she saw Deverel and Julia, quickly taking in their expensive clothes and the carriage waiting for them at the end of the narrow street. A speculative look came over her face. "Now what would you fine folks be wantin' with Jenny Cooper?"

"Are you the landlady of this establishment?" Deverel inquired.

"I might be," she allowed cautiously.

"We are inquiring after a certain man who rented a room here about three years ago. Were you the landlady then, also?"

She nodded emphatically. "I was. But I won't be re-memberin' someone from that long ago. I get a lot o' customers, I do, and I can't be expected to remember 'em all."

"Of course not. But perhaps you will remember this one. He had four parcels delivered to this address. It's not every day you get messengers with packets for one of your tenants, is it?"

"Can't say it is," the woman said, her face turning crafty. "I might be able to remember 'im, if I thought about it. Course, I ain't got much time for sittin' around, thinkin' about things like that. I got me work to do."

"I am sure. However, I am willing to pay you for your efforts." He held up a gold piece, and the woman's eyes grew almost as big as the coin.

She reached for it, but Deverel palmed it quickly and held it behind him. "First, I want the information. Then we'll see if it's worth the money."

"Orrr, you wouldn't 'old out on a 'ardworking woman, now, would ya?"

"Not if you don't try to cheat me. Tell me about the man who rented room 14."

"It was a gentleman, I remember that. I probably wouldn't remember 'im, 'cept 'e didn't belong 'ere. Dressed real nice, and talked good, too."

"Did he live here?"

"Oh, no. He just come 'ere a few times—to meet his fancy piece or to get one o' them packages you was talkin' about."

"His fancy piece?" Julia asked faintly, her stomach plummeting, thinking of the rumors of Selby's mistress.

"Yes, ma'am, she come 'ere several times."

"What about the man?" Deverel asked. "What was his name?"

The woman screwed up her face. "Cor, guvnor, after three years, you think I remember 'is name? I'm doing well to remember 'im at all."

"Then tell me about him. You said he spoke and dressed well. What did he look like?"

"Well, now, he weren't the sort you'd remember. Sort of…ordinary. Brown 'air, brown eyes, medium tall." She shrugged.

Julia straightened. "Brown hair?" she repeated, struggling to keep the excitement out of her voice. "Are you sure it wasn't red?"

"Red? Like yours, you mean?"

"Yes, very like."

"Oh, no." The woman shook her head decisively. "I would remember that. 'Is 'air was brown."

Relief poured through Julia, and she felt suddenly weak. She turned to Deverel and saw the astonishment in his eyes.

"My God," he breathed.

"It wasn't Selby!" Julia cried, tears suddenly gathering in her eyes. "It couldn't have been Selby. His hair was bright red!"

19

⚜

"I know," Deverel said, looking stunned. He handed the landlady the gold coin he had been holding and said, a little blankly, "Thank you. You have been a great help."

They turned and started toward their carriage. Julia linked her arm through Deverel's. She felt as if the sun had suddenly broken through the clouds.

"It could have been that he hired someone to come pick up the money. We don't know that the man who let the room was the embezzler," Deverel stated.

Julia looked at him skeptically. "Would you steal that much money and then entrust it to someone you hired to run an errand for you?"

"No. You're right."

They climbed into the carriage, and it started toward home. Deverel stared sightlessly out the window.

Grimly he said, "I accused the wrong man." He leaned his head back against the seat cushions and closed his eyes. "I was so sure that I was right. I hounded an innocent man to his death."

His face looked ravaged, and Julia was filled with pity for him. She reached out and put her hand on his arm.

"No. You didn't hound him to his death. I am certain that Selby did not kill himself. Remember, the suicide note is in exactly the same handwriting as the embezzlement letters. The embezzler wrote that note, I'm positive. *He* killed Selby."

"Still, I knew Selby, and I didn't believe him. I had known him for years, but when I saw those letters, I was so convinced he had done it that I didn't even consider any other possibility."

"The evidence against him was very strong," Julia reminded him. "Even I was shaken when I read those letters. The handwriting looked so much like his."

"But you believed in Selby, not the evidence."

"You didn't know Selby the way that Phoebe and I knew him. You could hardly be expected to believe in him the same way."

He glanced at her oddly. "You would not have said so a few weeks ago."

"That was before I knew you." Julia colored faintly. "I did not know what kind of man you are, how honorable you are, how much you believe in doing one's duty. You are the kind of man who would shackle himself for life to a woman he disliked just because he saw it as his duty." Deverel started to speak, but Julia hurried on. "I began to understand how a man such as yourself could hate the crime so much that he would pursue the embezzler diligently. I saw that you could not have let it go. You would have felt it was a betrayal of your friend Walter."

"Yes. I did," he agreed. "It was probably the most painful thing I have ever done, to reveal a friend's treachery. But I should have listened to Selby more. I didn't give him a chance to prove that he had been wronged. I should have talked to that landlady back then.

The address was there. I was just so convinced by the letters that I didn't bother.''

He turned and gripped her hands, gazing intently into Julia's eyes. ''I swear to you, I did not embezzle that money. That is not why I pursued Selby.''

Julia smiled. ''I know. I came to that realization long ago. I would not have married you otherwise. I could not have shared your bed.''

He pulled her into his arms, holding her tightly against him, and he rested his cheek on the top of her head. ''You are the best of women.''

Julia felt tears threatening. To keep them at bay, she said saucily, ''Besides, after talking to the landlady, it was clear that it could not have been you. There are many things one might say about you, but no woman would ever term you 'ordinary looking.'''

He chuckled and kissed the top of her head. ''Ah, Julia…thank God you came up with that absurd scheme to kidnap me. Otherwise, I would have gone on convinced that Selby had done it.''

They reached their house and went inside, going to the small, less formal sitting room on the second floor. Deverel rang for tea, then began to pace thoughtfully back and forth across the room.

''We have to clear Selby's name,'' he said, frowning. ''The question is, how? I don't think the landlady's statement that he wasn't her lodger will be enough to convince everyone, not with those damning letters.''

''No,'' Julia agreed. It was so warm and satisfying having Deverel join her in her quest. ''We have to find the real embezzler.''

''And killer,'' Deverel added grimly. ''I am convinced that he killed Selby and wrote that suicide note. It pretty effectively proved Selby's guilt. I certainly

never wondered about it again…until you came along."
He frowned. "And those 'accidents' you've had—I am
more and more convinced that they were his work, too.
Now that I know Selby was murdered, it makes sense
that he would have been so desperate that he tried to kill
you." He paused. "Who knew you were looking for the
real embezzler?"

Julia shrugged. "Any number of people, I suppose.
Phoebe and Thomas, of course. We were the ones who
came up with the idea. Nunnelly and some other servants. Cousin Geoffrey. And I told Varian and Fitz one
afternoon when they came to call…" Her voice trailed
off, and she looked at him.

He sighed. "Yes. We have to face it. Varian and Fitz
are the most likely candidates."

"It is so hard to believe it is either one of them,"
Julia opined. "They were both good friends to Selby,
and—" She broke off.

"The same logic that you used to decide it was me
convicts them," Deverel observed. "The trustees are the
most likely candidates. It had to be someone who knew
the workings of the trust and who knew about the name
Jack Fletcher. Since we are working on the knowledge
that neither Selby nor I did it, that leaves only Varian
and Fitz."

"I know, but—well, frankly, I don't think Fitz could
bring off something like this. Do you?"

"No. You're right. He wouldn't have the wit. The
physical description could be either one of them, of
course, but the most likely person seems to be Varian."

"I cannot conceive of it being Varian!" Julia cried.
"He was one of the few people who wasn't convinced
it was Selby. I've heard him say several times that he
couldn't believe Selby had done it."

"Easy enough to do, I suppose, when you know that you have arranged everything so that the evidence points right at the man. It would tend to cool anyone's suspicion that you had been the one who did it."

"I suppose you're right." She shook her head. "Still, it's hard to believe that Varian is that duplicitous."

"Who else, then? Your cousin? He would have known about 'Jack Fletcher,' and Selby might have told him how the trust worked."

"Geoffrey?" Julia laughed. "Now that truly is absurd. Geoffrey would never devote that much energy to anything. Besides, he has scads of money. He was the only heir of his mother's father."

"Phoebe? She would have known it all."

That remark merited only a roll of Julia's eyes. He might as well accuse her of doing it as Phoebe. "All right. You made your point. Varian is the only real candidate we have."

"Now that I look back on it, it was rather fortuitous that he was there when I got that message from Selby. He could have gone to the hunting lodge, killed Selby and left the suicide note, sent me that message begging me to come see Selby, and then ridden over to Stonehaven. That way he would have been certain of my finding Selby and the note. If I decided to ignore Selby's plea to come see him, Varian could talk me into it."

Julia nodded sadly. "Yes, and he, of all the people involved in this, had the most need of money. His side of the family is financially strapped."

"So I've heard. I suppose, growing up, knowing that he would have the title but that Walter would have much more money, might have worked on him forcibly. He could have come to feel that it should have been he who was wealthy, not Walter or Thomas."

"Perhaps." They were both silent for a moment. Then Julia said, "How can we know for certain, though? We have to prove it, not just speculate."

"There's always the possibility of kidnapping him and forcing him to confess," Deverel suggested with a twinkle in his eyes.

"Hush," Julia admonished. "Be serious, now."

"It *is* a possibility," Deverel mused. "I think Varian would be more likely to confess than I would. However, the problem with forcing a confession is that then you are never sure if it is true. And what sort of thing are we willing to do to him to make him confess? I have never much pictured myself as a torturer—and I know that you were willing to set me free after a couple of hours, even though you hated me. And," he added sternly, "I will not allow you to seduce him into talking."

"Don't be absurd," Julia said loftily. "I realize that my plan was a mistake from start to finish. But we have to find some way to prove it. Perhaps if we could get a drawing of Varian and show it to the landlady...ask her if he was her lodger."

"Good idea. Can you or Phoebe draw a reasonable likeness?"

She shook her head. "I'm all thumbs. Phoebe is more accomplished in such ladylike pursuits, but I don't think she could do it unless Varian posed for her, and what reason could we give for that?"

Deverel frowned, thinking. "Perhaps I should pay Varian a visit. There might be a miniature of him lying about the St. Leger house. Mothers always have portraits of their children, don't they? I could look for one and, shall we say, borrow it for a day or two."

"Deverel! You are becoming positively larcenous."

"You're a bad influence on me."

"I shall go with you," Julia said. "Two sets of eyes are better than one."

He shook his head. "No. You are staying here. It's too dangerous."

"Really, Deverel! What can be dangerous about visiting Varian?"

"You can ask that after three attempts on your life?"

"But you could as easily have been killed the last time! You are in as much danger as I."

"I can look after myself." He could see Julia was about to fire up, so he reached down and pulled her up, stifling her words with a kiss. "However, if I have to watch and worry over you, it will be much harder to take care of either one of us."

"But, Deverel..."

"Please, Julia. I am asking you as a favor to me. Let me handle this visit by myself."

"Oh, all right," Julia said grudgingly. "But it's hardly fair of you."

"I will tell you all about it."

She grimaced. "It's not the same."

Deverel left for Varian's after they ate their luncheon. Julia soon grew bored, and it was a great relief to her a few minutes later when the butler announced that her cousin had come calling.

"Geoffrey!" she cried, leaping to her feet and going to him, holding out her hands. "It's so good to see you. I was just sitting here feeling miserably bored."

"Oh, no." Geoffrey hesitated at the threshold of the door. "You aren't going to ask me to take you somewhere, are you?"

"No. I wish I knew of someplace to go, but I don't. Come in, sit down. Tell me all the gossip."

"Most of it is about you," Geoffrey replied, sauntering into the room and sitting down. He was, as always, the picture of elegance, from his gleaming black boots to the gold-handled cane he carried as an accessory. "Everyone is agog about your and Stonehaven's sudden marriage."

"I am sure they are shocked because Deverel married someone with such a scandalous background."

"Mmm, that and because no one knew anything about it beforehand. Old Mumford said something to me about its being sudden, so I told him that of course the families had known about it for some time."

Julia grinned. "But Dev told Fitz and Pamela that we were going to Buckinghamshire to tell his mother the news."

Geoffrey fluttered his hand. "Details. Can't let yourself be swamped in them. With enough stories circulating, no one will know what to believe. Anyway, no doubt they'll have a new story to chatter about in a week or two."

"I hope they will have the news that Selby was wrongly accused," Julia said earnestly. "We found out something." She went on to tell him of their encounter with the landlady.

"I say, that seems very encouraging."

"It is. It was enough to convince Deverel, thank goodness, but I am sure it will take more than that for the general public. And Pamela—she loves having the Armigers as villains."

"Demmed unfriendly female," Geoffrey agreed. He sat in thought for a moment. "So you don't suspect Stonehaven anymore?"

"No. I soon realized that it could not have been him."

"Didn't think it was," Geoffrey reminded her sagely. "But then, who was it?"

"We're not sure. The thing is, there was this rumor about Selby, that he had a mistress."

"What? Old Selby? Nonsense. Adored Phoebe."

"I know. But you see, I had not told you before, because I haven't really talked to you alone. I didn't want Phoebe to know." She poured out the story of the suicide note and the rumors of the mistress and their inability to locate who had been spreading them. "If we could pinpoint the person who started the rumor, I think we would find that it is the same person who—who wrote the suicide note."

Geoffrey stared at her, goggling at all the new information she had thrust upon him. "You are saying that—that someone *murdered* Selby?"

"He must have. I don't see how it could have happened any other way."

"But who could it have been?"

"I don't even like to speculate on it," Julia said sadly. "It was much easier when I thought Stonehaven was the villain. I didn't like him. It has to have been someone close to Selby—someone who knew about the trust and Jack Fletcher. How could anyone close to him have killed him?"

Geoffrey shook his head, bewildered.

"The worst of it is, I don't know how to find out who started the rumor. I'm not received in Society, and—"

"That will be different now that you are married to Stonehaven. All the old biddies will be agog to meet you. I shouldn't be surprised if you receive a flurry of invitations to parties now. 'Course, it would be a bit awkward asking everyone about whether your brother had a mistress."

"I don't care for that. I'll ask anyway."

"I daresay." He paused, thinking. "You know, I'll ask my man Bouldin. One's valet is always the best source of gossip. Oh! That puts me in mind—why don't you ask Selby's old valet about the mistress? If anyone would know whether she existed, it would be his valet."

"Osgood! Of course! Why didn't I think of him earlier? I would love to see him again. You're right, he would be the one to know, oh, everything about Selby." The man had left their employ right after the funeral, his services no longer needed. Julia had been too distraught at the time to talk to him, but she could see now that he might have invaluable information.

"Owns a haberdashery now, you know. Quite a good one, too. I've bought several things there myself. Got a fine-looking shirt there not long ago."

"Where is it?"

"The shirt? At home, of course, where else—"

"No, no, his shop! I must go see him."

"You can't—not by yourself!" Geoffrey exclaimed, looking shocked. "That wouldn't be the thing at all. Women don't go along Bond Street unaccompanied, you know. All men's stores and such."

"Then you must take me," Julia replied decisively. "That will make it all right with Deverel, too, I expect. He wouldn't want me going out without an escort." She blithely ignored the fact that Deverel had in fact not wanted her to go out at all.

"I might have known you would wind up finding someplace for me to take you," Geoffrey said with some bitterness. "All right. Let us go." His expression brightened a little. "I've been needing some new gloves anyway."

* * *

Osgood recognized Julia the moment she entered the store on Geoffrey's arm, and he hurried forward to greet her, his thin, almost funereal face lighting up. "Miss Armiger! I cannot tell you how delighted I am to see you. I have thought about you so many times these past years and wondered how you and Lady Armiger were."

"We are fine, Osgood, and Gilbert, too."

"But you must not stand out here in the shop," Osgood said, always as expert in the proprieties of a situation as he was in the cut of a suit. "Please, come back to my office."

Julia left Geoffrey happily discussing the merits of a pair of gloves with a clerk and followed her brother's former valet to the rear of the store. Osgood fussed about, making sure that the chair in front of his desk was just right for her, then offering biscuits and tea. Julia smilingly declined.

"You have a beautiful shop, Osgood."

"Thank you, miss—that is to say, Lady Stonehaven."

"Ah, so you know my news. I should have expected that."

"When I first saw you out there, it slipped my mind, but, yes, I had heard of your wedding to Lord Stonehaven. I wish you very happy, my lady."

"Thank you."

"The shop is Sir Selby's doing, of course. As you know, he left me a legacy in his will, enough to set this up." He sighed. "I'd happily give it back, though, if we could have the master with us again."

"I know. I am sure you miss him very much."

"Yes. I was with him from the moment he came to London, just a green lad." He smiled reminiscently. "It must have been ten years that I served him."

"Osgood, I came here to ask you something. Will you answer me honestly?"

"Of course, my lady!"

"Even if you think it's improper or…not something Selby's sister should hear? This is very important. It's about Selby's innocence, you see."

He gazed at her for a long moment, then nodded his head. "Yes, my lady, I will answer you, no matter what you ask—anything if it will help to prove that Sir Selby did not take that money."

"Did my brother keep a mistress in London?"

The man's jaw dropped open. "My lady!"

"I told you it might be improper."

"Your brother was always the most faithful of husbands," Osgood replied firmly. "He was most in love with Lady Armiger, and she with him. Theirs was a very happy marriage."

"Yes, I know. But there have been rumors that Selby kept a mistress in London, that—that he stole the money so he could support her in secret."

"I have heard those rumors," Osgood admitted with an expression of distaste. "But I give no credence to them. It is merely the work of petty minds."

"I think it might be more than that."

"I am sure that Sir Selby kept no mistress, my lady—although I did wonder about it when he said he was going to London right before his death."

Julia frowned, confused. "London? Selby didn't go to London right before he died."

"Yes, miss, he did," Osgood assured her. "That is where he was going when he left the house, three days before he died."

"He went to his hunting lodge. Don't you remember?"

"That is what he told everyone. But he told me that he was actually going to London. I had wanted to go with him as I always did, but he told me that I could not. He said that he was not going to his hunting lodge, at least, not at first. He was going to London beforehand. He said he would stay at an inn, since the house would be closed up, and that one of the servants at the inn would valet for him." Osgood gave an expressive shudder at the thought of a mere inn servant being able to do for Selby what Osgood did.

Julia stared at him. "I don't understand. Why would he have told us he was going to the hunting lodge if he was really going to London?"

"I don't know, miss, but he was quite definite about it. I did wonder, then, if perhaps he might be slipping off to see a woman of a certain sort. I remember he said, 'The ladies don't know about it, Osgood, so you must keep your mouth clamped shut.' As if I would have told anyone! And he gave me a wink. With any other man, I would have been certain he was going to see another woman, but I could scarcely believe that of the master. Of course, when I heard that he had gone to the hunting lodge, after all, I realized that he had told me that story about London just to keep me from accompanying him. He must already have been planning to do away with himself, and he knew that I would have stopped him."

"I am certain that he was not planning to kill himself," Julia told the man firmly. "Osgood, Selby did not commit suicide. I am sure of it." She explained to him about the note that had been left, confessing Selby's guilt and an affair, and about the way the handwriting matched the embezzlement letters but not Selby's old letters. By the time she had finished, Osgood looked at her as though his head was reeling.

"But why... Do you suppose he really went to London? Did he go there first and then on to the lodge?" the valet asked, confused.

"I don't know. He traveled by post chaise, you remember, so he didn't take Nunnelly, either. Looking back on it, I see that he was being very secretive. That would have fit, perhaps, with his committing suicide, but I am certain that he did not. He did not write that note!"

"I never dreamed that day or any other that he might kill himself," Osgood told her sadly. "He would not have left Lady Armiger like that. And I would have sworn that Sir Selby's mood the day he left was not that of a man facing death. He was so cheerful, smiling and—oh, he was in a better mood than I had seen him in in months, since the scandal first began."

"But why would Selby have gone to London? And why keep it a secret from everyone?"

"I'm not sure. He said something like he 'didn't want to get Lady Armiger's hopes up.'"

Julia stared. "Get her hopes up! About what?"

"He didn't say, my lady. He just looked at me so— oh, full of mischief. It reminded me most forcibly of the old days, when he was a young man and about to get into some scrape or another. You could have blown me away with a feather when I heard that the master had killed himself. But then I decided he must have been putting on a grand performance, to lull me into thinking that everything was all right. I wish he had let me go along! It wouldn't have happened if only he had had me with him."

"You must not blame yourself, Osgood." Julia leaned forward and patted the older man's hand. "You know what Selby was like when he got the bit between his teeth. He would not have let you go if he didn't want you to. And even if you had been there, you wouldn't have been with him twenty-four hours a day. Whoever killed him could have slipped in and done it without your knowing."

"It would have been much harder." He sighed. "However, you're right. I could not have talked him into doing anything else, once he had his mind set on it."

"I wonder…" Julia nibbled thoughtfully at her lower lip. "Look, I am convinced that Selby was murdered by the same man who embezzled the money. Therefore, it follows that the story he told you was not to throw you off the scent, but the actual truth. He really *was* going to London, and the reason for his trip was something that excited him, but which he wanted to keep secret from Phoebe for fear it might get her hopes up. What else could it be except that he expected to find out something in London that would clear his name?"

"My lady! Do you really think so?"

"Yes. I do. Why else would Selby have been excited? Why else would he talk about not getting Phoebe's hopes up? Oh!" Julia jumped to her feet. "I must go home. I have to tell Stonehaven about this. Thank you, Osgood, thank you. You have helped me so much. I think this is exactly the information we needed."

"I am happy to help, my lady, in any way I can." Osgood looked at her with a slightly bewildered but hopeful expression.

"You have. I promise you, you have."

Julia hurried back into the outer room of the store, Osgood following her. There she found Cousin Geoffrey involved in a deep study of two silk handkerchiefs. "Ah, Julia, there you are," he said somewhat distractedly. "I say, which of these do you prefer? Do you think the peacock blue is a trifle… I don't know, loud?"

"It's fine," Julia said, scarcely glancing at the two elegant pieces of cloth. "Geoffrey, we need to leave."

"Yes, yes, we will, shortly. Just let me get my purchases wrapped up. I found just the right pair of gloves. I shall have to come back here more often. Kid leather, and as supple as a second skin." He turned his attention back to the squares of silk. "But I can't decide which of these would look best for the pocket of my new dove-gray jacket."

"It doesn't matter, Geoffrey, just choose. I have to leave." She glanced outside impatiently. "You know, I believe that I shall just walk back by myself. It isn't far, and I must—"

On those words, she was gone, heading for the door determinedly. It took an instant for her cousin to realize what she had said, and when he did, he whirled in horror. "Julia! No! You can't walk down Bond Street by yourself. It isn't the thing at all!"

But Julia, of course, was ignoring him, already opening the door and stepping out. Hurriedly, Geoffrey thrust both handkerchiefs at the clerk and grabbed up his cane and hat. "Here. I'll take them both. Wrap them up, and I'll send a servant for them later."

He hustled toward the door after Julia.

Julia started down the sidewalk, not about to let a little thing like her cousin's notions of propriety stop her. The only thought on her mind was to get home and tell Deverel about her discovery and the new theories that were tumbling about in her head. She paid scant attention to the carriage that sat in the street outside the door, slightly ahead of her. Nor did she glance that way when the door of it swung open and a man stepped out. It was only when he reached out and clamped a hand around her arm that she turned, with an outraged gasp at his temerity, and saw, to her amazement, that his face was a blank, black mask. She opened her mouth to scream, but he clamped his other hand over her mouth and, with a steely grip, began to drag her toward the waiting carriage.

20

Julia jerked her elbow back as hard as she could, slamming it into her attacker's ribs. He let out a surprised grunt of pain. Julia stomped down hard on his foot.

"You hellcat!" The man wrapped both his arms tightly around her, lifting her from her feet, and carried her to the carriage.

This action freed Julia's mouth, and she screamed with all her might, flailing her arms and legs. At that moment Geoffrey came hurrying out the door, intent on saving Julia from the solecism of walking down the street unattended. What he saw made his eyes bug out.

"I say!" He crossed to the carriage, where the man in the mask was now trying to shove Julia through the door. "Let go of her! What the devil do you think you're doing?"

Geoffrey raised his elegant cane and brought it down hard across the attacker's back. The man cried out in pain, reflexively letting go of Julia. She fell to the pavement, knocking the breath from her.

The man in the mask staggered and spun around to face Geoffrey, who lifted the cane again and started forward when, much to his amazement, the masked man reached inside his coat, pulled out a pocket pistol and fired.

Geoffrey reeled back, clutching his shoulder. The attacker jumped into the carriage, and it took off, the door open and swinging wildly.

Julia pushed herself up to her knees and looked around dazedly. She saw Geoffrey lying on the ground a few feet away from her, a spot of red on his coat near his shoulder. It took a moment for what had happened to register with her.

"Geoffrey!" She crawled across the sidewalk to her cousin.

By this time a crowd of people had gathered around them, and an excited babble rose in the air. Osgood came hurrying out of his shop. "My lady! What happened? Oh, my Lord! Mr. Armiger!"

"He shot him!" Julia cried. "Geoffrey!" She bent over him, tears spilling from her eyes.

"I say," Geoffrey said faintly, "don't get tears all over my cravat."

"Oh, Geoffrey! I'm so sorry." She looked up at Osgood. "We must get him a doctor at once."

"Right away." He turned and gestured to one of his clerks, standing gape-mouthed in the doorway of the store. "Here, Tim!"

"Send him to Phoebe's house," Julia instructed. "I'll take Geoffrey there."

"Phoebe's?" Geoffrey asked. "Oh, no. Mustn't put Phoebe out. My man Bouldin can take care of me."

"That may be, and we shall send for him, of course, to help Phoebe. But there is nothing Phoebe loves as much as taking care of someone. I couldn't deprive her of the pleasure."

Swiftly Osgood arranged the proceedings. He sent one

clerk for the doctor and another one to inform Lord Stonehaven of what had happened and where Julia was going. In the meantime, someone had hailed a hackney, and several of the men picked up Geoffrey and put him into the vehicle. Julia climbed in after him, and they set off at a slow pace for the Armiger house. Julia sat beside Geoffrey, pressing her handkerchief to the wound on his shoulder, dismayed by the rapidity with which the fabric was turning red. Geoffrey, on the other hand, was just as quickly losing color. By the time they reached Phoebe's house, Julia had had to rip off a large piece of her petticoat to staunch the wound, and Geoffrey had slipped into unconsciousness.

Julia ran to the door and pounded on it. Within moments she had the footmen and butler out to carry Geoffrey inside. Phoebe came running down the stairs from the upper floor.

"Julia! What happened?" Her face turned pale. "Geoffrey! Oh, my God!"

"It's all right, Phoebe," Julia said, hurrying to her side and taking her arm. "He's alive. He was shot. He was protecting me."

"You dear, brave man!" Phoebe said, her eyes filling with tears.

These words were apparently enough to rouse Geoffrey, for he opened his eyes and said, "Hallo, Phoebe. Sorry to barge in on you."

Phoebe had to chuckle through her tears. She gestured to the servants. "Take him upstairs and put him in the green room. Don't just stand there!"

The servants carried him up the stairs, Phoebe following them with exhortations to take care. The doctor arrived within minutes, and Julia led him up to the green room. The bedchamber was by this time crowded with servants, agog at what was happening, and Julia herded them out the door, closing it firmly behind them, leaving the butler, Phoebe and the doctor to deal with the situation.

At that moment the front door crashed open, and Stonehaven's voice shouted, "Julia!"

"Deverel!" Julia let out a choked cry, joy and relief swelling her chest. She ran down the hall and started down the stairs. Deverel looked up and saw her, and he ran to her, taking the stairs two at a time.

"Julia!" They met on the stairs, and Deverel swept Julia up into his arms. He squeezed her tightly to him, saying, "My love. Thank God! My sweet, sweet love."

He continued to crush her to his chest, murmuring endearments and raining kisses over her hair. Julia cuddled close, floating in the bliss his words and actions raised in her. *He had called her his love!* She wanted to ask him if he had meant it, if he truly did love her, but she didn't have the nerve. The moment was too special to spoil.

At last he paused and pulled back slightly from her. His eyes swept her from head to toe. "Are you all right? They said that there'd been a shooting. I thought—" He stopped abruptly, staring at a stain on her dress. "Julia! That's blood! Were you injured?"

"No. It's not mine. It's Geoffrey's blood."

"Geoffrey! He's not—"

"No. The attacker caught him in the shoulder, and the doctor is up there working on him right now."

"What happened?" Deverel put his arm around Julia and took her down the stairs, moving as if she were a piece of glass that might break. Normally Julia would have scoffed at such behavior, but at the moment it felt very nice indeed.

"A man tried to pull me into a carriage. He wore a black mask, so I couldn't see his face. Geoffrey came out of the shop and attacked him with his cane."

"Did he?" Deverel smiled. "I should have liked to have seen that."

"I am sure it was a sight. I didn't really see any of it, as the man was holding me from behind. When Geoffrey hit him, he let me go, and I fell so hard it took me a moment to recover. He shot Geoffrey, and by the time I got up, the carriage was gone, and Geoffrey was lying there bleeding."

Tears sprang into Julia's eyes. "It is all my fault! I should have stayed home, as you said. I just got so excited when Geoffrey suggested I talk to Osgood that I couldn't wait. Since Geoffrey was going to be with me, I told myself I would be amply protected. And I was, of course. But at what an expense! What if something happens to Geoffrey? What if he doesn't pull through?"

Deverel gave her shoulders a squeeze. "I am sure he will be fine. You mustn't worry about it."

"I can't help it. It was all my fault. It's a wonder you haven't rung a peal over my head."

"I may yet," he promised, looking amused. He took her into the drawing room. "Here. Sit down. First, I want to find out what you're talking about. Why were you out? Why was Geoffrey with you? Who is this Osgood fellow?"

"Selby's valet. You see, Geoffrey came to call, and as we were talking, he said that the person I should see was Selby's former valet. I realized, of course, that he was right. Who knows more about their masters than a personal servant? Or hears more gossip, either? I hadn't even thought about Osgood. Right after Selby died, Osgood left our employ. Selby had given him a small legacy in his will, and Osgood used it to set up a haber-dashery in London. I haven't seen him the past three years. When Geoffrey mentioned him, I had to go talk to him. I was sure that he would have the answers.''

''And did he?''

Julia shook her head ruefully. ''I am afraid he only added to the questions. Osgood said that Selby went to London, not the hunting lodge.''

''What? You've lost me. Are you talking about the days before his death? He was in London?''

Julia nodded. ''Selby told us that he was going to the hunting lodge, but Osgood said he told *him* that he was actually traveling to London.'' She repeated the gist of the conversation with Osgood.

Deverel gazed at her blankly. ''This grows more mad by the moment. Why would Selby have gone to London? And why would he have lied about it to you and Phoebe? It makes no sense. Besides, he obviously did go to the lodge. That is where we discovered him.''

''Yes, but I think he must have spent most of the time he was gone in London. It would be quite easy. I mean, one passes through London, anyway, going from Green-wood to Buckinghamshire. He could easily have stopped here for a time, then driven on to the hunting lodge. The whole thing makes more sense that way. I had wondered how the killer knew that Selby would be at his hunting lodge then. He couldn't have been skulking around Greenwood for days or weeks, waiting to follow him. Selby's leaving was a spur of the moment thing. We were all quite surprised when he announced that he had decided to visit his hunting box. But if he was in London for a while, the fellow could easily have followed him from there.''

''That's true.'' Deverel frowned. ''But what was

Selby doing in London? And why did he tell you he was going somewhere else?''

"I don't know. But I wanted to rush home and tell you about it. Geoffrey was being maddeningly slow, trying on gloves and looking at handkerchiefs and such. So I decided to walk home by myself.''

"Naturally," Deverel said dryly.

"I didn't know the man was lurking out there!''

Deverel sighed. "I think we can hardly fool ourselves anymore that these attempts are mere accidents.''

"No. Someone is trying to stop our investigation. That is why we need to press ahead quickly.''

Deverel gave her a look, but he had to smile. "Some might say that the intelligent thing would be to quit.''

"Nonsense. He won't stop unless we find out who he is.''

"I am afraid that you are right.''

They both turned at the sound of footsteps in the hall. It was the doctor. His face was serious, and Julia's stomach turned to ice. But then he spoke, relieving her fears. "I removed a ball from Mr. Pemberton's shoulder, and he is doing fine.''

"Thank God.''

Deverel shook his hand. "Thank you for coming, Doctor.''

The man nodded. "I am happy to say that Mr. Pemberton did not lose a great deal of blood. I expect he will do quite well under Lady Armiger's care. His valet is with him, too, and he seems most competent.''

Julia had to go upstairs to look in on Geoffrey in order to satisfy herself that he was alive and doing all right. Geoffrey was sound asleep, his face almost as pale as the white sheets on which he lay. His valet, Bouldin, was bustling about, cleaning up the mess left by the doctor's visit, and Phoebe was sitting in a chair beside the bed. She got up when she saw Julia, and they went out into the hall.

"I think he will be fine," Phoebe assured Julia, closing the door to Geoffrey's room behind them.

"Really?"

"Yes. I don't think Geoffrey would dare die with that valet there."

Julia smiled. "Geoffrey says the man's a tyrant. I can spell you, watching him. I am sure that Deverel would not mind."

"I'm not so sure about that, but, really, dear, it's not necessary. I think I will be lucky if Bouldin allows me to tend to Geoffrey at all."

Julia was reluctant to leave, feeling guiltily that she ought to do something, but finally Phoebe convinced her to return home, assuring her that she would send a message to Julia if she needed help.

During the walk home with Deverel, Julia was quiet, sunk in thought.

When they entered the house, she turned to her husband, saying, "Do you still have the note you got from Selby? Not the suicide note, but the message asking you to meet him at the lodge?"

Deverel looked surprised, but said only, "Yes. It's in the box with the suicide note."

"You mean it's here? In this house?"

Deverel nodded. "Do you want to see it?"

"Yes," Julia said eagerly. "I have an idea."

They went into Deverel's study, and he pulled out a slim box from a cabinet. Inside were several pieces of paper, including the suicide note and the two of Julia's old letters from Selby that they had used to compare to the letters at the agent's office. Deverel removed them from the box, setting them on the desk, and pulled out a small, folded sheet of paper beneath.

He handed the note to Julia, and she opened it and read it. The letter was obviously written in a hurry, the writing larger and more scrawled than usual. Tears sprang into Julia's eyes, and she had to sit down in the chair behind the desk, her knees suddenly weak.

"Selby wrote this."

"What?" Deverel looked at her, puzzled.

"That's really Selby's hand. Look." She placed the note between one of Selby's actual letters and the false suicide note. "See the *y?* The capitals, the spacing? They're all like the old letters from Selby, but not like the forgeries."

"So Selby actually did write to me, wanting me to come see him? Is that what you hoped to find?"

Julia nodded. "Selby told his valet that he didn't want to tell Phoebe, because he didn't want to get her hopes up. What could he have been talking about except the scandal? I think he must have had an idea, some clue that would prove he did not do it. Maybe he even thought he knew who did. I don't know what, but something set him off, and he decided to go to London—maybe to look for another clue. Perhaps he even came here to confront the real embezzler. After he did whatever he came here for, he wrote that note to you and took off for Buckinghamshire."

"He was going to tell me his suspicions, convince me that I had gotten the wrong man," Deverel said, following her reasoning.

"I think so."

"But why did he decide to go that particular day? Something must have happened to make him suspect someone. What?"

"I don't know." Julia looked at Deverel with barely repressed excitement. "If we can figure that out, maybe we'll have the answer."

The next morning Julia and Deverel paid a call on Phoebe. They had spent the rest of the evening—except for the very pleasant hours Deverel took to demonstrate to Julia just how glad he was that she was alive—discussing what Selby could have learned that sent him hastening off to London. They could come up with no ideas, and they could think of nothing to do except query Phoebe about her husband's actions and conversation the day before he left.

The butler, Sidle, showed them into the drawing room, and a few minutes later Phoebe came in, smiling.

"How is Geoffrey?" Julia asked anxiously.

"Very well. He had a fever during the night, but it's gone down. He's asleep now."

"Thank heavens." Julia hugged her sister-in-law. "I knew this was the best place to take him."

Phoebe demurred, but Julia could see from the heightened color in Phoebe's cheeks that she was pleased by the compliment. Julia hesitated. She hated to spoil Phoebe's happy mood by bringing up the subject of Selby's death. However, she could see no way around it.

"Phoebe...I need to talk to you about Selby."

"All right, dear." Phoebe looked at her inquiringly, and it occurred to Julia that for the first time she could remember, Phoebe's eyes did not darken with sadness at the mention of her dead husband.

"Do you remember Selby saying anything the day he left? Anything about the embezzlement or the trust?"

Phoebe raised her eyebrows. "My goodness, that was

so long ago. I—I don't remember everything exactly. Why? What does it matter?''

"We think that maybe Selby discovered something about the embezzlement." She explained what Osgood had told her the day before, and Phoebe's eyes grew bigger and bigger.

"Oh, my," Phoebe said inadequately when Julia finished. "I—well, let me think. He came into the sitting room where I was that morning, and he told me that he was going to the hunting lodge. You know..." She paused thoughtfully. "I do remember that he seemed excited, but I didn't think anything about it. I thought he was just happy to be going to the hunting box. You know how he liked it there. But he didn't say anything special, just that he had decided to go hunting. He said, 'Maybe I'll come back with a prize catch this time, Fee,' and his eyes twinkled—oh, my.'' Realization hit her, and she turned pale. "Maybe he wasn't talking about hunting animals. Maybe he meant—"

"He was going to catch the embezzler," Julia concluded with satisfaction.

"This makes me feel so odd." Phoebe pressed her hand against her stomach. "To think that all this time we didn't know. We should have done something earlier, Julia!"

"If we had known what Selby was doing, we would have. Oh, why couldn't he have told someone what he was up to?"

"Lady Armiger." Deverel leaned forward. "Do you remember Sir Selby's mood earlier that morning? When he got up, say?"

"He seemed as usual, I would say."

"Not excited?"

"No. It was only later, when he came into the sitting room, that he was excited."

"So whatever happened did so between breakfast and when he came into the sitting room."

"Yes, I suppose so. But what could it have been? We didn't have any visitors. Julia, do you remember anything?"

"No." Julia shook her head. "I was hoping that you would. I can't recall anything about that morning."

"Perhaps Sidle can," Phoebe suggested, brightening.

"Who?" Deverel asked.

"The butler," Julia explained. "Of course. That's a good idea. He was at Greenwood then. He would have noticed anything unusual."

However, the butler, when they called him in, looked blank. "The day he left, ma'am?" Sidle turned his face up toward the ceiling, as if he might find an answer there. "I don't recall anything happening."

"Did anyone come to call?"

"No. It was an ordinary morning. We got the mail, and I took it into Sir Selby's study. Then, as I recall, there was some sort of contretemps in the kitchen, which I went to resolve. The next time I saw the master was when he came out of his study, calling for a footman to take a message down to the stables. He wanted his curricle brought round."

Deverel came to his feet. "The mail. That's it. He got a letter!"

"Of course!" Julia breathed, her eyes shining. "Sidle, who were the letters from?"

The usually imperturbable butler appeared daunted by this request. "Oh, miss—I mean, my lady—I don't recall. I don't know that I even looked at them. I just took the mail in to Sir Selby."

Deverel sighed and dismissed the butler. He turned to Julia. She felt ready to cry with frustration.

"How can we have come so close and still not know?" she wailed.

"I know what he got," Phoebe said quietly.

It took a moment for her words to sink in. Julia whirled to stare at her. "What did you say?"

"I said, I know what was in Selby's mail." Her face was soft and sad with remembered sorrow. "After...after his death, I went into his study. I sat behind his desk, and I cried for a while. I looked at everything on it, thinking that maybe somehow I would find a clue to why he'd done it. But there was nothing there. Only a letter, open, as if he had read it and left it there. I read it over and over—you know how it is sometimes. Your mind won't stop. It was stupid. The letter had nothing to do with his death, but I kept reading it. I practically memorized it."

"What was it?"

"I don't think it's much help. It was merely a letter from the man who runs the mine in Cornwall that Selby's father bought. You remember. His name is Jordan. It was a very ordinary letter. I remember thinking that the last thing Selby received should have been more special, but it was about a problem there and whether they should get new equipment. Mr. Jordan said he was going to send a letter to a Mr. Underhill—I don't know who that was—and that he would take the liberty of putting Selby's signature on the letter, as he had done before. Then he said he hoped that all—"

"Good Lord!" Deverel exclaimed, looking thunderstruck. "Why didn't I think of it before?"

"What?" Julia turned to him, her heart beginning to race with hope. "What is it?"

"A person who sounds and looks like a gentleman, as the landlady said, who's very familiar with the trust, who knows Selby's handwriting—the trust's agent!"

21

There was a moment of stunned silence. Finally Julia repeated, "The agent? For Thomas's trust?"

"Yes. Mr. Carter. I don't know why we never considered it before. He would know the trust as well as anyone. Think of the examples of Selby's handwriting he had the opportunity to look at—and copy."

"But what about Jack Fletcher? How would he have known about the name?"

"I daresay Selby might have mentioned it to him sometime—or Walter. Carter was Walter's agent for years before he died. Why, any of us might have said something in his hearing, I suppose. He had samples of all our handwriting. He could have copied Fitz's and Varian's signatures, too."

"But—couldn't he have taken the money, anyway?" Phoebe asked.

"That's true," Julia agreed. "He was handling the funds. Why go to all that trouble?"

"Ah, but then it would have been obvious that he had taken it. Using the letters, there was always the hope that the trustees would not even question it. If we did, the letters ensured that he had a handy scapegoat."

"What an evil man!" Phoebe exclaimed. "Why did he blame it on Selby? Why did he hate him so?"

"He probably didn't," Julia reasoned. "It was probably just circumstances. It was Selby who made most of the requests, so his letters would seem the least suspicious."

"*If* it was Carter," Deverel cautioned. "This is merely speculation, after all."

"True. But I think that this must have been what occurred to Selby. When he read that letter—a trusted manager who could imitate his signature—his mind must have leaped to Carter, and that is why he went off to London."

"The thing to do, then, is to question Carter. I would be very interested in finding out whether Selby came in to see him right before his death."

"I would, too," Julia agreed decisively, rising to her feet. "Let's go."

"*I* will go," Deverel countered. "You are not confronting a possible killer. Especially not after what happened yesterday."

"Perhaps he's right, Julia," Phoebe agreed. "You could have been killed."

Julia made a face. "I wasn't, though."

"No, but Geoffrey was shot trying to protect you," Deverel stated bluntly.

Guilt pierced Julia. "I know, and I am very sorry. I should not have embroiled Cousin Geoffrey in it. But the fact that there is danger makes it all the more imperative that neither one of us should go there alone. Do you think that I want *you* facing a killer alone?"

"I am prepared for him," Deverel said grimly. "I will be able to handle him."

"You won't be any less able to handle him because I am there. If anything, I can help you."

"Julia...I explained to you yesterday that I can't be distracted by worrying over what's going to happen to you."

"There's no need for you to be. Besides, there is very little likelihood of anything happening to either one of us. Yesterday he came after me. He was prepared. But today we will be mounting a surprise attack on him. He won't be expecting it. I doubt he brings his pistol to the office, don't you agree?"

"I have no idea. I would not have taken him for the type of man who would do any of this. He always seemed very mild-mannered, obsequious, even." He paused, then went on, "Can I not persuade you to stay here?"

"No." Julia shook her head. "I can't force you to take me with you, but I shall go in a separate carriage if you refuse."

Deverel sighed. "I am sure you will. I must have been mad to agree to marry you. I can see now that you will never give me a day's peace."

"Agree to marry me!" Julia exclaimed indignantly. "Why, you did everything but *force* me to marry you! But you are right. I probably shan't give you any peace." She grinned. "However, marriage with me won't be dull."

"I'm certain of that. All right. Let us go."

They took their leave of an anxious Phoebe and went to the agent's office in a hackney. They walked up the stairs and into the outer office. Mr. Teasely, who had helped them a few days ago, and the other clerk looked up, surprise touching their faces when they saw who it was.

"Lord Stonehaven?" Teasely asked, rising. "I shall tell Mr. Carter you're here."

But that was unnecessary. The agent was already bustling out of his office, saying unctuously, "Lord Stonehaven! What an unexpected pleasure—twice in one week! To what do we owe this honor?"

"I recalled that I had forgotten to ask you something when we were here the other day."

"Of course. Ask away. I shall be happy to help if I can."

"I am sure you remember the tragic death of Lady Stonehaven's brother, Sir Selby Armiger, a few years ago."

"Oh. Yes. Yes, indeed." Carter glanced nervously toward Julia.

"It was in March, I believe, a little more than three years ago." The other man nodded. "I was wondering why he visited you shortly before he, er, passed away."

Mr. Carter looked at him blankly. "But Sir Selby did not visit us three years ago. Not around the time of his death. A few months before that, when, uh, the, um, irregularities first came to light, he did come here, but not after that."

"Are you sure?" Stonehaven asked, his eyes narrowing dangerously.

The agent looked uncomfortable and cast his eyes toward his employees. "He was not here, was he?"

"I don't recall it, sir, no," Teasely said politely.

The second clerk spoke up, "I remember it. He was here."

Everyone's gaze turned toward him. He was a short fellow, with thinning hair and a mousy face, and he gazed at them solemnly from behind thick glasses. "You weren't here, Mr. Carter. That was the time when you had that terrible fever and missed almost two weeks.''

Carter's face cleared. ''Ah, yes, that *was* three years ago, wasn't it? My, how time flies.''

''You did not speak to him?'' Deverel's gaze never wavered from the agent's face.

''Why, no, not if he came during that time. I could barely speak to anyone. Worst fever I ever had.''

Deverel turned to Teasely. ''You don't remember him being here at that time?''

''I'm not sure of the dates. I, uh, he did come here once or twice, but I don't remember the exact times.''

''Oh, you must remember, Teasely,'' the other clerk declared. ''He came in, and we said Mr. Carter wasn't in, and he said that he hadn't come to see Mr. Carter. Then you and he went into Mr. Carter's office and closed the door. There was a terrible shouting match, and Sir Selby left in a huff. Don't you remember?''

Julia felt Deverel tense beside her. She knew what he was thinking, for she was thinking the same thing: all the explanations for the agent being the embezzler would apply to the agent's clerk, as well. She turned to look at Teasely, as did everyone else.

Teasely forced a chuckle. Julia thought she could see a touch of panic in his eyes. ''Oh, yes, I do remember that conversation. I didn't recall what particular day it took place. You are probably right, Foster. It must have indeed been when Mr. Carter was ill, or he would have talked to Mr. Carter.''

''What did you discuss?'' Deverel asked, his voice flinty.

''Well,'' Teasely began, shifting nervously, ''we talked about the, uh, letters Sir Selby wrote to the trust, you know, requesting that the money be sent to Jack

Fletcher. He wanted to see them, but I did not think that I should allow him to, since he was no longer a trustee. Since Mr. Carter was not here, I couldn't refer the matter to him. So I, uh, stood firm on it. I told Sir Selby that he would have to wait until Mr. Carter returned, that I did not have the authority to allow him to see the letters. It made him quite angry. He shouted a good deal. Then he stormed out of the office.''

''I see.'' Deverel paused. ''Odd that you wouldn't remember something like that immediately.''

''Well, of course I remembered it.'' Again Teasely let out a false-sounding laugh. ''I just didn't remember that it occurred at the time you were talking about.''

''Even though you had to deal with Selby because Mr. Carter was out sick?'' Deverel queried. ''I would have thought the date would have been quite memorable.''

''I knew it was when Mr. Carter was ill, my lord,'' Teasely explained, his fingers moving nervously over his watch chain. ''I, uh, simply did not recall the dates.''

The man was growing more and more uneasy under Deverel's basilisk gaze. Deverel stared at him without speaking for a moment, and Teasely shifted his feet and cleared his throat.

''I don't think you discussed whether or not Selby could look at the letters,'' Deverel told him, iron in his voice. ''I think he came here to confront you. He figured out that it was you who had forged his handwriting, and he accused you of it. Isn't that what you were arguing about?''

The other clerk's mouth dropped open. Mr. Clark looked bewildered. Only Teasely did not seem surprised.

''No. No,'' he protested agitatedly. ''That wasn't it at all.''

''No?'' Deverel raised his eyebrows, a sardonic smile

touching his mouth. "I think you are going to have to be more truthful than that. You see," he bluffed calmly, "we found the notes Sir Selby wrote concerning his suspicions of you."

Teasely glanced around wildly. "J-just because he saw me signing those letters for Mr. Carter a couple of years ago and I—I showed off a little about my—my skill, it doesn't mean that I forged his hand! I did not take that money!"

"I think you did," Deverel said coldly. "And when Selby figured out that you had done it, he went to Buckinghamshire to tell me his suspicions. So you followed him to his house, didn't you? You killed him so that he couldn't reveal the truth!"

"No!" Teasely cried. "I didn't! You can't prove *anything!*"

"I will get the proof," Deverel growled, and started toward him.

"I didn't kill him!" Teasely shouted hysterically.

Reaching behind him, he grabbed a ledger book from his desk and flung it at Deverel. Then he turned and vaulted over the railing separating the clerks' area from the rest of the office and ran out the door. The book hit Deverel on the shoulder and bounced off, but it slowed him down for a precious moment. He took off after the tall clerk, jumping the railing as Teasely had done. Julia and the others followed at a slower pace, taking the more usual way around the railing.

They raced down the stairs and burst out the front door. Julia stopped, looking around the busy street, to see where they had gone. Carter and the other clerk skidded to a halt beside her. From the vantage point of the top of the steps, Julia soon spotted Deverel's familiar figure. He was halfway down the block, running out into the street. Teasely was a few yards ahead of him, dodging around a carriage. He cast a panicked look behind him as he ran.

Julia gasped, seeing the heavy wagon rumbling down the street toward Teasely, only a few feet away. Deverel shouted a warning, pointing, but Teasely, panicked, ran on, not looking up until it was too late. He darted directly into the path of the huge draft horses. The left front horse crashed into him, knocking him down, and he disappeared under the animals' feet.

22

"Such a horrible way to die," Phoebe said with a shudder. "Even though he killed Selby, I would not wish such a death on him."

"It was awful," Julia agreed.

It had been a week since Teasely had run out in front of the wagon and been trampled beneath the horses' feet, but Julia still could not quite get the scene out of her mind. The first two nights she had had nightmares about it, but the memory was beginning to fade gradually.

"I say, when is Stonehaven going to get here?" Geoffrey asked. "If I've got to be hauled off to the country, I'd as lief get started on it."

He was half reclining on a couch in Julia's drawing room, as befitted his invalid status, a thin blanket across his legs. He had recovered almost entirely from his bullet wound over the past few days, but he was still a trifle pale, and his face was a good deal thinner. Phoebe had decided that what he needed to get well was a few weeks spent in the healthful air of the country. To Julia's amazement, Geoffrey had agreed to this scheme, and they were waiting now for Deverel's return, so that they could set off for Greenwood.

"I am sure he will be here soon," Phoebe assured Geoffrey, smiling at him, and went over to tuck the blanket more securely about his legs.

Stonehaven had gone to a meeting with the Bow-street runner whom he had engaged to investigate Edmund Teasely and his embezzlement of three years ago. Deverel and Julia were driving down to Greenwood, as well, so that Julia could pack up her clothes and other possessions to ship to Stonehaven, where they were planning to go to spend a few quiet weeks by themselves while Deverel's mother was visiting friends in Brighton. They were travelling in caravan, with Geoffrey and Phoebe riding in Phoebe's carriage, and Deverel and Julia taking Gilbert along with them in the open-air curricle, to alleviate his travel sickness. Geoffrey, Julia thought, had met this news with great relief. Gilbert's nurse, the butler and much of their baggage had already gone ahead in a slower wagon.

There was the sound of footsteps in the hall, and all three of the occupants of the room turned toward the doorway as Deverel strode in.

"Good morning," he greeted them all, but his eyes went to Julia, and he smiled in a way that was almost a caress.

"How did it go?" Julia ask.

"Yes, what did you find out?" Geoffrey asked.

"Teasely was the embezzler. There's no question about it. Fitz and Varian were with me at the meeting with the runner, as well as the agent. They'll make sure that everyone learns of it. Varian said he would drive down to Farrell to tell Pamela and Thomas himself."

"Thank goodness!" Phoebe exclaimed.

"Yes, except now you will be forced to meet Pamela socially again," Julia pointed out dryly.

"The runner searched his rooms. He found a pocket pistol and a black face mask, such as the man who attacked you and Geoffrey wore. He also discovered several possessions that are far too expensive for a man on a clerk's salary to afford. That watch and chain he wore, for instance. Well-tailored clothes, expensive furniture. In his desk, at the bottom of one drawer, he found several sheets of paper on which Teasely had practiced copying Selby's handwriting. Most damning of all, there was a miniature portrait of Teasely in the rooms, and he took it over to the landlady. She firmly identified Teasely as being the 'gentleman' who rented the room from her as Jack Fletcher."

"It seems odd that he knew about that name," Geoffrey mused.

"Yes. But I suppose Selby must have mentioned it sometime in his hearing."

Julia sighed. "I wish—I thought that when we found out who the real embezzler was, I would feel more... satisfied, somehow. I mean, I'm very glad that now people will know it wasn't Selby who did it, and Gilbert won't have that scandal hanging over him. But I thought it would seem more final, like the end of something. I thought it would make me happier."

"Perhaps it was seeing him die in that awful way," Phoebe said.

"It was terrible," Julia admitted. "But I think I feel empty because he didn't confess. I wanted to know exactly what happened, and for everyone else to know it, too. This way, there is still some doubt. I am afraid that there will be those who will continue to wonder whether it was him or Selby. Or maybe it's that I realize now that finding Selby's killer will never make up for losing him."

Deverel reached over and took her hand, and Julia cast a glowing look up at him. Phoebe, watching them, smiled to herself.

"Come, Geoffrey," Phoebe said, standing up. "It's time to get you into the carriage."

"Mmm. Likely to take a while." Geoffrey took off the blanket and swung his legs onto the floor, levering himself to his feet with his cane. "Gad, now I know what it will feel like when I'm eighty."

He left the room, leaning on his cane and with Phoebe solicitously supporting his other arm. "I shall send up for the maid to bring Gilbert down as soon as I get Geoffrey into the carriage," Phoebe told them over her shoulder as they shuffled out the door.

Julia had seen Phoebe glance at them and smile, and she suspected that her sister-in-law had purposely given them this time alone together. Julia was glad that she had.

"Deverel…"

"Yes?"

"This is very hard for me, but I have been thinking about this for days. I have to say it. I—I must apologize for what I did to you. For thinking that you could have been the one who embezzled the money. And for doing those awful things to you."

A lazy smile quirked his mouth. "You mustn't be sorry. I'm glad they happened. Otherwise I wouldn't have met you."

"But at least you wouldn't have been forced into marrying me."

Deverel smiled enigmatically. "I think you will find that I am rarely forced into anything."

Julia looked at him. *Was he saying that he had married her because he wanted to, not because of propriety?*

She laced her fingers together and gazed down at them. "The other day, did you mean what you said?"

"When? What did I say?"

"When you thought that I had been shot, and you came running in. You—you called me your love, and I—wondered if you meant that."

"Yes."

Julia's head snapped up. "Really?"

He chuckled. "Yes, really. Why are you so surprised?"

"Because—well, because of everything. The way I tricked you, the things I did to you, what I thought about you. At the time you married me, you despised me, and I was afraid that you would never feel anything for me except that."

Deverel took her hand and looked into her eyes. "I love you. God knows, I tried not to, and when I couldn't keep from it, still I tried to hide it from you. But I think I've loved you from the first moment I saw you. When I found out that you had only pretended passion for me, I was hurt. I was furious with you, but I don't think I would have been so angry if I hadn't felt so much for you."

"I didn't pretend it," Julia told him candidly. "I planned to worm a confession out of you, but when you began to kiss me, I—well, the desire was all real, not feigned. I couldn't think. I had no control over myself, let alone you. That's why I decided to kidnap you. I realized that if I continued doing what I had been doing, I would wind up sleeping with you and still learning nothing."

He smiled faintly and raised her hand to his lips. "You have done much to soothe my wounded ego."

Julia made an exasperated noise. "As if you did not

know that! I think I have amply demonstrated my desire for you.'' She turned her face away, embarrassed by her own blunt words.

''I have hoped so.'' He reached out and took her chin, gently pushing her face back to face him. ''But women are more easily able to feign such feelings than men.''

''I have not feigned it. Why else do you think I came so boldly into your bedroom that night? I threw myself at you.''

''You wanted children.''

''I wanted *you*.''

''Julia...'' He gazed at her wonderingly, reaching out to touch her cheek with his fingertips.

''I suppose I want children, but they were not what was uppermost in my mind. It was the only decent excuse I could think of. After you made love to me that morning, then set me aside and said it wouldn't happen again, I didn't know what to do. I wanted so much for you to make love to me again, but you didn't want me. I tried to seduce you, coming into your room that evening, but still you put me away. So I said the only thing I could think of.''

''Didn't want you! My God, Julia, I wanted you more than anything in the world. Why do you think I stayed away so assiduously? I was afraid that if I was around you, I wouldn't be able to control myself and I would take you again, even though I had promised not to. I thought you must hate me, the way I took you after all my vows not to—and so crudely, too, throwing you down on the table because I couldn't wait to go upstairs to bed. Your first time should have been tender and gentle, and instead I—''

Julia smiled up at him. ''I didn't want to wait, either.

I—I found it very exciting. That morning was when I knew that I loved you.''

Deverel sucked in a surprised breath. "Julia..." He started to speak, then pulled her into his arms, burying his mouth in hers.

They were interrupted by the entrance of a small whirlwind in the shape of a six-year-old boy. "Uncle Dev! Aunt Julie! Look, I'm all clean. Mama says I can ride in your curcal.''

With a reluctant sigh, Deverel released Julia and turned to the boy. "Curricle. Yes, you may, and I think you will probably feel much better than riding in the carriage.''

"Yippee!'' Gilbert demonstrated his elation by jumping straight up several times. When he stopped, he tucked his hand in Deverel's and confided, "I'm glad you're my new uncle.''

Deverel smiled and looked at Julia. "You know, my boy, so am I.''

23

J ulia sat on the terrace, gazing out across the peaceful gardens of Greenwood. The past two days had been blissful—primarily, Julia knew, because she had spent them with Deverel. She loved Greenwood, but she knew that she would be just as happy when they went on to Stonehaven. The one thing she needed to be happy anywhere was Deverel.

She turned at the sound of footsteps on the flagstones behind her. Geoffrey was walking toward her, and Phoebe was beside him, her hand tucked into his. Geoffrey looked much better than he had two days ago, and Julia thought that the country air must indeed be good for one's health. She noticed that Phoebe seemed radiant, as well.

"Hello," she said, curious. "What are you two up to?"

"Is it that obvious?" Phoebe asked, and her smile broadened even more.

"I'm not sure. I don't know what 'it' is, but you both look...so happy. As if you knew a wonderful secret."

Phoebe chuckled. "We do. We came out here to tell you."

"What?" Julia leaned forward, intrigued by Phoebe's words.

But Phoebe did not respond immediately. Instead, she waited while Geoffrey sat down. Then she had to fuss over him for a few minutes to make sure that he was comfortable and warm, but without the sun shining in his eyes.

"Phoebe…" Julia said warningly. "Will you please tell me what you're talking about?"

Phoebe grinned as she sat down beside Geoffrey. She glanced at him, and it was he who spoke. "Phoebe has done me the great honor of consenting to become my wife."

Julia gaped at them. "What?"

"Geoffrey and I are getting married!" Phoebe cried. "It's still a secret, for we haven't told Gilbert yet, but I—"

"Phoebe!" Julia interrupted her, jumping up from her chair and running to hug her friend. "Geoffrey! Congratulations! I never dreamed—" She began to laugh. "I must have been blind. I had no idea." She bent down to hug Geoffrey, as well, though carefully.

"Not one to wear my heart on my sleeve," Geoffrey explained. "Always admired Phoebe, though."

"I never thought you would expend the energy to get married," Julia teased.

"My God, Julia, I've visited the country twice in the past month," Geoffrey drawled. "What more could a man do for a woman?"

Julia laughed merrily. "I hadn't thought about that. You're right, of course. But, tell me, are you planning to turn Phoebe into a city girl?"

"We've agreed to divide our time between the two places," Phoebe answered for him. "I will be quite happy in the city, but Gilbert must spend a good portion of the year here, on the property that will be his. Geoffrey says that's very important.''

Julia was reminded of the way Phoebe had always peppered her conversation with the words ''Selby says.'' It made tears threaten, although Julia wasn't entirely sure whether they were tears of happiness or sorrow.

''I am sure he's right,'' Julia agreed. ''But, tell me, when is the wedding to be? And where?''

Geoffrey, foreseeing a long session of thoroughly female talk threatening, rose to his feet. ''Believe it's time for that nap.''

''Coward,'' Julia gibed at him.

''Nonsense. But a fellow has to get his sleep—demmed difficult to do at night out here. Did you know—'' he continued indignantly, ''that there's a wretched bird *here* that hoots all night, too?''

''Owls do that,'' Julia said, struggling to keep a straight face.

''Imagine that. I had thought it was something peculiar to Buckinghamshire.'' With those words, he hobbled away.

Julia turned back to Phoebe, reaching out to squeeze her hand. ''Oh, Fee, I'm so happy for you.''

''Are you really? I'm glad. I was afraid you might feel that I was—betraying Selby's memory.''

''No. Of course not. It's been three years. It's time for you to stop grieving over Selby and begin your life again. You are too young and far too wonderful to immure yourself in widowhood.'' She paused, then grinned. ''Though I must confess, I am somewhat surprised that it was Geoffrey.''

''I know. When I began to realize that I had tender feelings toward him, I told myself I must not, for Geoffrey was not the sort of man to marry. Imagine my surprise when he asked for my hand. You could have knocked me over with a feather.''

"No, I did not mean I was surprised that Geoffrey wanted to marry you. He was a confirmed bachelor, of course, but someone like you could change any man's mind. I am surprised that *you* agreed. He is, well, so unlike Selby.''

"I know. Isn't it odd? But I think that is one reason that I was able to fall in love with him. I wasn't always comparing him to Selby. He was so different that I never even thought of it. I fell in love with his own qualities. It's not the same as it was with Selby, of course. Everything with Selby was so grand and romantic and exciting. But, you know, I don't think I want excitement anymore. I feel comfortable with Geoffrey, warm and good. I think he is the sort of man with whom I could happily grow old.''

"I'm so glad.''

"Which way is it with you and Deverel?'' Phoebe asked.

Julia paused, thinking. "I guess it's a little of both. I was beginning to think that I would not ever find a man I wanted to marry. Isn't it odd that that man should turn out to be Lord Stonehaven?''

They settled down after that to the happy discussion of wedding plans, and almost an hour sped by before one of the footmen came out onto the terrace.

"My lady, the Honorable Varian St. Leger, Mrs. St. Leger and Master Thomas are here.''

"Oh, dear.'' Phoebe's face fell. "That is, I mean, show them into the drawing room. We shall be right there.''

The footman bowed and withdrew. Phoebe looked at Julia and sighed.

"We are bound to have to see her sometime," Julia said.

"Yes, I know. It's just...why did she have to spoil today?"

"Look at it this way, at least I am still here to share the burden."

"There is that." Phoebe brightened a little.

They strolled into the house, going to the drawing room, where their three visitors awaited them.

"Julia! Phoebe!" Thomas cried. "Isn't it the most wonderful news? I *knew* it wasn't Selby. But imagine it being that Teasely fellow. I was sure it was Stonehaven. Of course," he added naively, "it's quite good that it turned out that it wasn't, since you married the fellow."

"Yes, it was fortuitous," Julia agreed. "Hello, Thomas." She went to give him a kiss on the cheek and a hug, then turned to the others. "Varian, it's good to see you again. And Pamela—so *good* of you to call." She gave the words an ironic inflection.

"Julia." Pamela flashed a painful smile. "Phoebe. When Varian told us what had transpired, I felt we had to come. Isn't that right, Varian?"

"Of course. I was terribly happy to find out it wasn't Selby. Always had trouble believing that he could have done such a thing. Didn't I say so at the time?"

"Yes, you did, and you were absolutely right," Julia agreed, feeling a stab of guilt as she remembered the way she and Deverel had suspected Varian of engineering the plot against Selby. "You were one of the few who doubted the lies." Julia cast a glance at Pamela, which Pamela returned with venom.

They sat down in a stiff group and looked at one another. Finally Pamela said, "I am having a party in honor of Varian's visit. Just a small thing, of course, nothing grand. Dinner and perhaps a little dancing, if everyone is inclined. I hope I may count on the two of you."

"I am afraid that Stonehaven and I will have gone home by then," Julia said.

"But I did not tell you when it was."

"Nevertheless," Julia replied pointedly.

Pamela raised her eyebrows at the implied insult. "Really, Julia, you must learn to mind that tongue of yours if you hope to move in the sort of company Lord Stonehaven keeps."

"Deverel admires my wit."

"Indeed. How odd. But then, Stonehaven was always different."

A silence fell after that. Gamely Varian started up the conversation again with a few commonplaces about the weather, and Phoebe fell in with it. Julia said little, but Pamela soon recovered her tongue and embarked upon her favorite subject: herself. She discussed her visit to London, the new dresses she had bought and the redecoration that she planned for the music room at Farrow. Julia watched her, somewhat amazed that even Pamela could come to call after three years of cutting her and Phoebe socially and act as if nothing had happened.

Finally Thomas broke into his mother's monologue as she paused to catch a breath. "How did you figure out that it was Teasely?" he asked. "I want to hear the whole thing. Varian didn't know the details."

Julia obligingly began to tell him about it, noting with amusement that Pamela was growing more and more impatient at the talk about something other than herself.

With a tinkling laugh that grated on Julia's nerves,

she said, "Well, I for one never liked that Teasely fellow. I am not at all surprised it turned out that he did it."

"That's odd," Julia commented acidly. "Given how often you trumpeted it about that Selby was the thief."

Pamela put on a wounded expression. "How can you say such a thing? I was always very fond of dear Selby. He was so kind to Thomas, always coming to see him or going riding with him and whatnot—when it must have been tiresome, you know, being with a child so much."

Anger flared up inside Julia at the uncertainty that touched Thomas's face at his mother's words. "Selby was very fond of Thomas," she said bitingly. "I am sure that he never thought of it as being 'kind.' He enjoyed Thomas's company."

"Why, of course." Pamela forced a smile. "That is exactly the sort of man Selby was. It was difficult for me to believe that he had stolen anything from Thomas."

"I noticed that you overcame the difficulty quite well."

"I thought he must have done it—like everyone else who heard the evidence. It was so clear, so obvious, that I did not trust my instincts. Why, I don't think I would ever have accepted it if Selby had not committed suicide and left that note. It is hard to deny it when a man admits his own guilt."

Julia went still. She could feel the hair on the back of her neck start to rise.

"What note?" Phoebe asked in confusion.

"Yes, Pamela, what note are you talking about?" Julia asked in a hard voice. "Do you mean the one Stonehaven never made public? The one no one knew the contents of besides Deverel and Varian?''

Pamela went pale. She stared at Julia, not saying a word.

''What are you talking about?'' Phoebe said, bewildered. ''There was no suicide note. Was there?''

''We didn't know about it, Phoebe,'' Julia answered her, but she never took her eyes off Pamela. ''Stonehaven and Varian kept it a secret, because it contained things they thought too painful for you to know. Lies, of course, lies that the embezzler wanted us to believe. Tell me, Pamela, how did you know the contents of the note?''

''I—why, I'm not sure. There was gossip everywhere.''

''Not about that note. No one knew about it.''

''Doubtless Varian told me.''

Varian turned a blank expression on her. ''No. I never told you. Dev and I agreed that no one should know about it.''

''It was you, wasn't it?'' Julia surged to her feet, her fists clenching by her sides. ''You were in on it!''

Varian's jaw dropped. ''Pamela?''

''Don't be absurd!'' Pamela, too, stood up, and began to move nervously away from Julia. ''It was my own son's trust.''

''That is what makes you even more despicable. I should have guessed you were in on it. You were always complaining about how small your widow's mite was. I remember you standing right here and talking about how unfair it was that Walter had left his entire estate to Thomas, leaving you a mere pittance.''

''A mere pittance!'' Varian exclaimed. ''Damme, I'd like to have such a pittance to live on. How could you have said that, Pamela? Walter was most generous with you.''

"No doubt she did not reveal that side of herself to you, Varian. It was Selby she was always pressing to authorize the trust to give her more money.''

"I was his mother! I was raising him. Surely I was entitled to enough money for his upkeep!''

"New draperies for your bedchamber—and that only six months after you had entirely redecorated it. New clothes, a new barouche because you had decided that your carriage was too 'dowdy.' You call that Thomas's upkeep? Oh, no, Pamela, that game won't work with me. Phoebe and I know how you badgered Selby for money time and time again. Everyone in the whole house could hear your arguments.''

"So what?'' Pamela tossed her head. "That doesn't mean anything!''

"There is the landlady. She said that the only times Teasely came to his rooms were when he received a packet and when he came with his 'fancy piece.' That was you, wasn't it? You carried on an affair with Edmund Teasely. You conspired with him to steal money from your own son's trust. No, wait! Now that I think about it, it was probably *your* idea. You doubtless seduced the poor man into doing it!''

"You've gone mad.''

"Have I? You know, that landlady had a good eye—and a good memory. She identified Teasely immediately. I wonder what she'll say when we show her a drawing of you?''

"She couldn't! I always wore—'' Pamela stopped abruptly, realizing how she had just indicted herself.

She whirled and started to run from the room, but Julia threw herself on the other woman, and they fell to the ground. They rolled across the floor, kicking and hitting, while the other occupants in the room looked on in horror. Finally Varian pulled himself out of his daze and ran over to the two women. Putting an arm around Julia, he lifted her up and set her on her feet. She tore away from him and started after Pamela again, but Pamela had used the momentary reprieve to grab her reticule and stick her hand into it. She pulled out a small pistol and aimed it at Julia's heart.

"Ha! That stopped you, didn't it?" She stood up, never taking the gun off Julia. "Miss High-and-Mighty. You always know everything, don't you? You're always right. Easy for you to say that I had ample money. Selby was exactly the same. 'Oh, no, that doesn't justify the trust's expending money on it,'" she mimicked, her face drawn into bitter lines. "You would have thought the money was his, not Thomas's, the way he acted."

"You—you killed Selby?" Phoebe asked shakily.

"It was his fault!" Pamela screeched. "All of it was. I wouldn't have had to do any of it, if only Selby had cooperated. But no, Saint Selby was too good, too pure." Her voice had slipped into caustic mimicry again. "He couldn't even be unfaithful to his wife. Precious little Phoebe!" Pamela shook the gun wildly at Julia. "Do you think I wanted to do it? Do you think I *wanted* to sleep with that fool Teasely?"

"I am sure not, Pamela," Varian said soothingly. "We understand. You didn't want to do any of it. Why don't you put the gun down? Then we can talk."

"Do you think I'm a fool?" Pamela's lips curled with scorn.

"No. I think you're a black-hearted villain," Julia replied, facing her with cold defiance.

"At least you're honest."

"You put Teasely up to it, didn't you?" Julia asked. "Somehow you learned that he had a skill for copying other people's writing, and you seduced him into writing those letters. No doubt you were the one who knew about Jack Fletcher and added that little twist."

"Of course I did. Walter was forever laughing about Selby's idiotic made-up name, as if it were a grand joke. Schoolboy pranks! I thought it was a grand joke to use the name on him."

"Naturally. It was a wonderful way to get revenge on the man who had spurned you, wasn't it? To make it appear that he had been the one who embezzled the money."

"Yes, it was." A malicious sparkle appeared in Pamela's eyes. "It was wonderful, watching him topple— seeing all the Armigers brought low."

"What did it matter if you had to give yourself to a nonentity, a clerk, in order to accomplish that?"

"Nothing! It mattered nothing at all!" Pamela's eyes glittered, and bright spots of color stained her cheeks.

"Tell me," Julia continued in the same hard voice, "what did you have to do to get him to kill Selby?"

"Kill Selby! That coward? He hadn't the nerve for it. Why, he couldn't even get rid of you. He bungled it every time. How could he have gone up against a man like Selby? All he could manage was to write that paltry note. *I* had to go up there and do it!"

"Mama!" Thomas cried out. His face was ashen, and his eyes huge and staring. "Mama, how could you?"

Pamela turned toward him, and for an instant even she looked abashed. Then her face closed down, and she snarled, "Don't look at me like that! You don't know what it was like! None of you! I couldn't stand having to take handouts from the trust, having to beg and crawl for every bit of money...."

She backed up as she spoke, as if she had to move away from her son's appalled expression. She reached the open doorway of the room.

Suddenly an arm lashed out from the other side of the door, slamming down hard on Pamela's gun arm. The pistol dropped harmlessly to the floor and skidded away. In the same smooth motion, Stonehaven stepped from his hiding spot beside the door, both his arms going around Pamela tightly and lifting her up off her feet. She began to shriek and kick back at him, her face contorted with fury.

"Damn you! Damn you! Let me go!" Her voice dissolved into unintelligible gabblings and high-pitched screeches.

Geoffrey appeared in the hallway beside Stonehaven, and behind him came two footmen. Geoffrey stepped around Deverel and his wriggling, screaming burden and rushed into the room.

"Phoebe! Love, are you all right?"

"Geoffrey!" Julia ran to him. "It was horrible! Thank God you're here."

"Of course, dear. Where else should I be?" Geoffrey set himself to the task of soothing her.

Stonehaven turned over the raving Pamela to the footmen. One of them took her legs and the other her torso, and they carried her out of sight. Stonehaven hurried into the drawing room and drew Julia into his arms. Julia, who had been standing rigid throughout the whole scene, surprised them all by collapsing into tears against him.

"It's all right. It's over," Deverel murmured, stroking her hair and back.

"I'm sorry," Julia sniffled, trying to control her wayward tears. "I—I don't know what came over me. I'm not usually like that."

"I know." Deverel smiled. "But I don't mind. Actually, it's rather nice to find that you are not always made of iron."

Julia smiled weakly. Their arms loosened around each other, but she continued to lean against him. "I think it was the shock. All this time, I never even considered Pamela. No matter how much I disliked her, I would never have dreamed that she was capable of murder!"

"I know. I've had some experience with her when she didn't get her way, and I knew she could be vindictive and even cruel, but I didn't suspect her of this."

"Poor Thomas," Julia sighed, looking over at the boy. He sat slumped in a chair, his head in his hands. "He knew she had many faults, but still, she was his mother. He must be in agony."

"I know. We'll help him all we can."

"What will become of him?"

"He can come and live with us. We'll have to be his family now."

Julia looked up at Deverel with glowing eyes. "You are so kind."

He smiled. "Nonsense. Merely practical. I can scarcely have my wife running down to Kent every week or two to see how Thomas is doing, now can I?"

"Say whatever you like. You can't fool me." She laid her hand against his cheek. "You are the finest man I know."

"Only a man who is very much in love with his wife." He took her hand and pressed his lips into her palm.

"That's enough for me." Julia smiled and stood on tiptoe to kiss him.

Epilogue

Julia linked hands with her husband as they strolled across the ballroom toward Phoebe and Geoffrey. "Wasn't it a lovely wedding? Didn't Phoebe look beautiful?"

"Radiant," Deverel agreed, smiling down at her. He bent and placed a quick kiss on her forehead. "But not as beautiful as you."

"Oh, you." Julia smoothed a hand down the front of her dress. "I feel as big as a house."

"Nonsense. You hardly show yet. And even when you do, you will still be the most beautiful woman in the room."

"How fortunate that I am married to a man with vision problems," Julia joked, but his words warmed her.

They reached the other couple, and Julia stretched out her hands to take Phoebe's. "Phoebe. Cousin Geoffrey. It was the most wonderful wedding."

"I thought it came off rather well," Geoffrey said. "Had a bad patch there when I ruined three cravats in a row. I was afraid the whole day would go the same way, but then the next one turned out perfectly. It just goes to show."

"Doesn't it?" Deverel agreed solemnly.

"Auntie Julia! Uncle Dev!" They were interrupted by
Gilbert, who had spotted his aunt and uncle and raced
through the crowd to them, followed as usual by his
harried nursemaid. He flung himself against Julia, wrapping his arms around her legs, and looked up at her.

"Gilbert, my little love." Julia bent to kiss him and
ruffle his hair.

"Have you seen my new pony?" he asked, shrugging
aside the kiss and going straight to more important matters.

"No, I haven't. What's he like?"

"He's a real 'goer,'" Gilbert announced proudly.
"Cousin Geoffrey got him for me."

"Did he really? Then I am sure he *is* 'a real goer.'"

"I can keep him in London and ride him in the park."

"That will be fun."

Gilbert nodded. "Then it won't be so boring there."
He grinned and cast a mischievous look up at Deverel.
"But not as much fun as Stonehaven."

"Good gracious, no," Stonehaven responded, grinning.

"'Cause we're going fishing."

"Absolutely."

"And riding."

"Of course."

"And 'sploring in the woods."

"You may count on it."

Phoebe laughed. "I can see how much he is going to
miss me." She stooped to plant a kiss on her son's head.
"Now go on with Nurse, you scamp. I'll be up to see
you in a few minutes."

As the nursemaid led her charge off, Phoebe turned

to Deverel and Julia. "Thank you for taking Gilbert with you while Geoffrey and I are on our honeymoon."

"It's no trouble," Julia assured her.

"Speak for yourself," Deverel laughed. "That rascal will run me ragged."

Julia chuckled. "And you will love every minute of it. Besides, it will be good practice for you."

"You're right." He turned to Phoebe. "I am only joking, of course. We love the boy and are happy to have him."

"Thank you. I did so hate to leave him with just Nurse and the staff. And he would be unhappy at my sister's house. But I could not imagine hauling him all around Europe on our honeymoon."

"Good God, no," Geoffrey agreed, paling at the thought. "It's bad enough traipsing to all those places with just the two of us. Had the devil of a time packing, you know—not sure what one wears in Venice. Actually, I'm not sure what one *does* in Venice, either."

"Soak up the atmosphere, I believe," Deverel told him.

"Do you? By Jove! Sounds like a rum sort of place." Geoffrey looked thoughtful.

Quickly Phoebe changed the subject. "Where is Thomas? I haven't seen him today."

"Across the room." Julia gestured toward the opposite corner, where Thomas was in an animated conversation with another young man. "He's enjoyed being back at Farrow this last week and has been getting reacquainted with his friends."

"He looks well. I mean, he seems happier and more relaxed than I would have dreamed."

"Being away from Pamela has probably been soothing to his nerves," Deverel said dryly. "I think it's been good for him to be at Stonehaven since the scandal broke. The gossip about his mother hasn't been as bad there as it would be here in Whitley."

"No one there would dare offend Stonehaven," Julia said impishly.

Deverel let out a chuckle. "I had heard it was more fear of the new *Lady* Stonehaven, who is as fierce as a lioness protecting her cub."

"I see you two still can't agree," Geoffrey commented. He cocked a brow at Stonehaven. "You'll never win, you know. Known Julia all my life, and I can tell you, it's easier to give in from the start. Saves a lot of time and trouble."

Deverel's eyes twinkled. "Ah, but I would not have married Julia Armiger if I wanted life easy." He raised Julia's hand to his lips in a graceful gesture and kissed it. "Isn't that true, my love?"

Julia smiled back. "But of course."

Phoebe took Julia's hand and pulled her aside. "You truly are happy?" she asked in a soft voice.

"Of course!" Julia responded, surprised. "Can't you see it in my face?"

"Yes." Phoebe smiled. "I just wanted to be sure. The way you were married...the way you used to feel about Stonehaven...well, I wanted to know for certain. You are still my sister-in-law in my heart, you know."

"You're terribly sweet." Julia hugged the other woman. "But you needn't worry." She turned her glowing gaze on her husband. "I am very happy. Deverel and I have the most fun—whether we're fighting or making up or just laughing ourselves silly over something or other. I always dreamed of it, but I was never sure that I could find a husband whom I could love so much.

But I find that every day I love Dev more and more.''
She blushed. "Do I sound like an utter fool?''

"No. Like a very happy woman. And I am so pleased.''

"It's exactly what I wish for you, Phoebe.''

"Oh, that is what I have,'' Phoebe assured her calmly. "Geoffrey would not do for one such as you, but for me he's perfect.''

"The orchestra's started, my dear,'' Geoffrey said, turning toward them. "I believe that we are supposed to lead the dancing.''

"Yes.'' Phoebe smiled as he led her onto the dance floor.

Deverel turned and cast an inquiring look at his wife, his hand extended toward her. Julia paused, savoring the sweetness of the moment, then smiled and went to him.

"Penny for your thoughts,'' he murmured, brushing his lips against her hair.

"Oh, no. They're worth much, much more than that.''

"That good, eh?''

"Good enough for a lifetime.'' Julia smiled and leaned against him as his arm went around her tightly.